Everlasting Love

Everlasting Love

Jayne Ann Krentz

Linda Lael Miller

Linda Howard

Kasey Michaels

Carla Neggers

POCKET BOOKS

New York London Toronto Sydney Tokyo Singapore

An *Original* Publication of POCKET BOOKS

POCKET BOOKS, a division of Simon & Schuster Inc.
1230 Avenue of the Americas, New York, NY 10020

ISBN: 0-671-52150-0

First Pocket Books printing May 1995

10 9 8 7 6 5 4 3 2

POCKET and colophon are registered trademarks of Simon & Schuster Inc.

Printed in the U.S.A.

Contents

JAYNE ANN KRENTZ

Connecting Rooms

1

No one ever said that the devil couldn't have a rose garden, Amy Comfort thought. It just seemed a trifle out of character. On the other hand, the rose garden of the old Draycott place was no ordinary one. And Owen Sweet, Amy had decided, was no ordinary gardener.

"Are you, or are you not, a private investigator?" Amy demanded.

"Depends," Owen Sweet answered. With the lethal precision of a fencer, he used a pair of garden shears on a clotted mass of evil-looking vines.

"What does it depend on?"

"On whether or not I feel like working at it." Owen took hold of the severed vines with heavily gloved hands. He ripped the old vegetation away from the window with a single, powerful motion. "I'm a little busy at the moment."

"Yes, I can see that."

Owen took no notice of her sarcasm. He seized another tangle of vines and dispatched them with ease.

Amy watched, morosely fascinated. She couldn't help it. She liked watching Owen Sweet.

The vegetation he was attacking with such diligence had grown so thickly over the windows of the old house that it had effectively blocked all sunlight from reaching some of the rooms.

Not that sunlight was a common commodity here on Misplaced Island, Amy thought. The forgotten little patch of land located off the coast of Washington sat squarely in the middle of a rain shadow. A perpetual mist shrouded the island on good days. Dense rain poured down the rest of the time.

The local joke was that the island had earned its name when its original discoverer had temporarily misplaced it in the fog. Whatever the truth of that story, there was no doubt but that one had to be determined to find Misplaced Island.

And, Amy thought, one had to have either a powerful motivation or an extremely odd sense of whimsy to make one's home here. She wondered which of those two possibilities applied to Owen Sweet.

"Owen, this garden went wild years ago, just like the house." Amy was growing increasingly exasperated. Time was running out, and she needed Owen Sweet. "It can wait a few more days before you tame it."

Owen paused briefly to look at her. His sea-green eyes gleamed in the misty gray light. "I'm in the mood to do it now."

Sweet was definitely a misnomer, Amy reflected, not for the first time. As far as she had been able to discern, Owen was anything but sweet, in either nature or temperament. She suspected he was yet another result of a baby having been switched at birth. Happened all the time, they said. Amy wondered what Sweet's parents had thought when they discovered that they had been given a little green-eyed, black-haired demon to raise.

He was proving to be stubborn and thoroughly irritating, but there was something about the man that fascinated Amy. She did not know him very well, even though she had sold him the Draycott place. No one on the island really knew Owen Sweet.

CONNECTING ROOMS

He had moved to Misplaced Island two months ago. Amy
had met him when he walked into the real estate office she
operated out of the parlor of her cliffside cottage. She had
been stunned by her reaction to him. Hunger and longing
and a singing sense of joyous discovery barely began to
describe it.

She had tried to squelch the feelings. True, she was a
struggling romance novelist on the side, but Amy was far too
pragmatic to believe in love at first sight. On the other hand,
she trusted her own instincts when it came to people. They
had stood her in good stead in the real estate business, and
she saw no reason to discount them when dealing with
members of the opposite sex. One thing was for certain.
Those instincts had never reacted with such overwhelming
intensity to any of the handful of men she had dated.

Owen had appeared oblivious of her carefully concealed
response to him. He had announced without preamble that
he'd already toured the island on his own and had checked
out the available properties. He had decided to buy the
Draycott place.

Amy had been horrified. Everyone on the island knew
that the old Draycott house, a Victorian monstrosity, was a
disaster from foundation to roof. She had dutifully done her
best to steer Owen toward other real estate opportunities,
but he had refused to listen to her advice. In the end a sale
was a sale. Amy had reluctantly written up the deal.

The only good part about the transaction, she had told
herself, was that Misplaced Island was a very small community. She would see Owen Sweet again. She could only hope
it wouldn't be in the course of a lawsuit over the Draycott
sale. Some buyers tended to blame the real estate agent
when they discovered they had made a bad bargain.

But Owen had appeared to be content with his new home
when, to her secret delight, Amy had begun to encounter
him with increasing regularity at the post office, in the
checkout line at the island's only grocery store, and at the
tiny bookshop. One of the few facts that she had gleaned
concerning him was that he was a voracious reader. At the

rate he ordered books from Mrs. Akers, the owner of the bookshop, he would single-handedly keep her small store in the black during the coming winter.

But last week had been the real turning point. After running into her at the post office, Owen had invited Amy to join him in a cup of coffee at the town's one and only cafe. The conversation had concerned such riveting matters as the weather, the latest novels they had each read, and the limited ferry schedule. Amy had walked on air all the way back to her cottage. Hope had bloomed within her.

She stifled a small, wistful sigh as she watched Owen free another window from its shroud of clinging vines. There was a lean, supple strength about him that captivated her senses. While it was true that, objectively speaking, Owen's grim features could have been created by someone who would have been equally adept at designing junkyard dogs, Amy found him strangely compelling. Which probably said far too much about the limited social life on Misplaced Island, she told herself.

Then again, she had not even been aware of a lack of a social life until Owen had arrived.

She watched him now with brooding determination. This was the first time she had paid a call on Owen Sweet since he had moved into his crumbling abode. She had come on business, not for social reasons. She needed this man. She needed him badly.

It wasn't as if she had a lot of choice. The small sign on the front door of the old Victorian ruin Owen called home said it all. It read SWEET INVESTIGATIONS.

Owen Sweet was the only private investigator on Misplaced Island. There was not a lot of call for his type of work in the small community. Amy was quite certain that since his arrival he had yet to get a single case. She had naively believed that he would be thrilled to have work. Obviously, she had been mistaken.

Amy braced one hand against the garden's stone wall and drummed her fingers with simmering impatience. Unaware or uncaring of her irritation, Owen Sweet went about his work among the grotesquely tangled rosebushes which clogged the garden.

The roses had been abandoned along with the crumbling ruin of a house years ago. Instead of dying off in a bittersweet, genteel manner, they had gone wild, with a vengeance. They climbed the garden walls as though bent on escaping a prison. They formed impenetrable thickets across the cracked paths, choked the empty fishpond, and had apparently been intent on marching up the steps and into the sunporch. Owen Sweet had arrived in the nick of time.

"Can I take it from your attitude that you are not interested in working for me?" Amy asked bluntly.

"Yeah." Sleek muscles moved easily beneath Owen's black T-shirt as he shifted an armload of defeated vines to a growing pile in the center of the garden. "You can draw that conclusion."

"Very well then, you leave me no choice." Amy removed her hand from the stone wall and straightened in resignation. "I shall have to find someone else."

Owen's mouth curved slightly. "Good luck. The last time I looked in the phone book, I was the only PI on the island."

Amy brushed her hands together and started toward the sagging gate. "I had hoped to give my business to someone local because I believe in supporting the local economy. But since you're not interested, I'm sure I can find someone in Seattle who will be happy to take my money."

"Seattle?"

Amy was aware that Owen had gone very still behind her. She did not turn around. "If I hurry, I can catch the afternoon ferry."

"Damn. Hold on just a minute."

Satisfaction surged through Amy. She had been in real estate long enough to sense when a buyer had undergone a quick change of heart. She paused at the gate to smile at Owen with polite inquiry.

7

"Was there something you wanted, Owen?"

He scowled ferociously, an expression which did nothing to soften his harsh face. "Yeah. Some answers."

"Sorry, I don't have time to chat. The ferry leaves in a couple of hours and I haven't finished packing."

"Let's get real here." Owen stripped off his gloves as he strode toward her along the garden walk. "What does a woman like you need with a private investigator?"

"'A woman like me'?"

"No offense, Amy, but you're hardly the type to have the sort of problems that require the services of someone in my line of work."

"What would you know about my problems?"

Owen came to a halt in front of her and planted his fists on his hips. "You're not exactly a mystery woman. You've been living on Misplaced Island for nearly a year. During that time you've opened a real estate agency and published a romance novel. Before you came here, you worked the condominium market in Seattle. You aren't exactly rich, but you did all right in your own real estate investments."

Amy was taken back. "Good grief. How did you—"

"Everyone on the island seems very fond of you," Owen continued ruthlessly. "I seriously doubt that you have any enemies around these parts. You are thirty years old and have never been married. You do not flirt with married men, so the local women have no reason to dislike you. You are not dating anyone at present, so you have no reason to employ an investigator to tail an errant boyfriend."

Amy gazed at him with mingled anger and amazement. "Are you quite finished?"

"No, not quite. You appear to live like a cloistered nun, Ms. Comfort. Therefore, I find it difficult to believe that you have got yourself into a situation which requires an investigator."

"You seem to have done a fairly thorough job investigating me. May I ask why?"

Owen wiped his sweat-dampened forehead with the back of one muscular bare arm. "That should be sort of obvious."

"Well, it's not obvious to me."

He gripped the top of the drooping gate and contemplated her with narrowed eyes. "No, I can see that."

"I don't know what this is all about, nor do I have the time to find out. If you're not going to accept my case, I've got to find someone else. Please excuse me."

Amy tried to open the gate. Owen took no notice of her effort. Instead, he leaned heavily back against it and folded his arms across his chest. He looked annoyed but resigned.

"Okay, tell me about it," he said.

"Tell you about what?"

"This problem of yours. The one that requires an investigator."

Amy fixed him with a frosty glare. "It's a confidential matter. I see no reason to discuss it with someone who is not going to be working for me."

"Hell, I'll take the case. Now tell me what's got you in such an uproar."

"I don't think that I care for your unprofessional manner."

"Sorry, it's the only manner I've got." He considered her thoughtfully for a few seconds. Then he came away from the gate and took her arm. "Come on, let's go inside. I'll make you a cup of coffee and you can tell me all your problems."

"I'm no longer sure that I want you handling my case."

"Don't be silly. A few minutes ago you were practically begging me to take your precious case."

"I was not begging you. And furthermore, I've changed my mind."

"So have I."

Amy thought about digging in her heels, but her options were extremely limited. It would take time to hunt up an investigator in Seattle. And money. She did not possess unlimited quantities of either. She allowed Owen to lead her up the steps.

The interior of the house was as run-down and abandoned-looking as the garden, but at least nothing appeared to be actually growing on the walls or springing up through the floorboards.

Threadbare velvet curtains that had faded to a peculiar shade of maroon flanked the grimy windows. An atmosphere of gloom and decay hovered over the front parlor. Several pieces of heavy, claw-footed furniture clustered near the black-marble fireplace. There was very little paint left on the walls and the wooden floors were raw and scarred.

A pang of guilt went through Amy, temporarily erasing her irritation. "I did try to warn you that this was a fixer-upper."

"A fixer-upper?" Owen gave her a derisive look. "It's a life sentence. Wiring's shot. Plumbing's rusted out. Roof needs repair. I'll have to replace the furnace before winter sets in, along with all the appliances."

"Don't you dare blame me. I made you read every single word on the seller's disclosure statement. You knew what you were getting into when you bought this place."

"Did I? That's debatable." But Owen appeared perversely satisfied with his purchase. "Have a seat." Not ungently, he pushed her toward a high-backed, velvet-covered sofa. "I'll get the coffee."

Amy sat down gingerly and surveyed the shabby interior of the parlor. She shook her head in amazement. It was true that she had sold him the house, but she had no idea what he was doing here in it. Why had he come here to Misplaced Island, she wondered.

Owen reappeared a few minutes later carrying a tray laden with a French press coffeepot and two cups. He set his burden down on the battered old coffee table.

"All right, tell me what this is all about." He sank into the depths of one of the massive wingback chairs.

"It's a very straightforward case," Amy said crisply. "My aunt, Bernice Comfort, has recently announced her engagement. I want you to investigate her fiancé, Arthur Crabshaw."

Owen looked up as he poured coffee. "Why?"

"Because there's something about Crabshaw that I don't quite trust. I met him a couple of weeks ago, and I have the distinct feeling that he's hiding something. He appeared out of nowhere a few months after her husband, Uncle Morty, died, and immediately swept Aunt Bernice off her feet."

"You write romance novels, don't you? I would have thought you'd have approved of Crabshaw's technique."

"If you're not going to take this case seriously, please tell me now so that I can find another investigator."

"I'm serious. You have no idea just how serious."

She glowered at him. "What's that supposed to mean?"

"Forget it. Why are you suspicious of Crabshaw?"

"My aunt was left quite comfortably well off after Uncle Morty died two years ago," Amy said carefully. "She lives in a small town on the coast. Villantry, Washington. Know it?"

"I've heard of it."

"It's the sort of town where everyone knows everyone else. Crabshaw lived there himself at one time, but he left the place some thirty years ago. Now he's back."

"And you think he returned because he heard that your wealthy aunt is available?"

"Let's just say that there's something about Crabshaw's appearance on the scene which smacks of opportunism," Amy said.

"What exactly is it about Crabshaw that worries you?"

"It's hard to explain." Amy frowned. "He seems nice enough, and Aunt Bernice is obviously mad about him. But I sensed something a bit shifty beneath the surface."

"Shifty."

"Yes."

"Shifty is a rather vague term, Amy."

"I can't be any more specific. I just know that there's something not quite right about that man. I have very good people instincts, you know."

"Is that a fact?"

"Yes, it is," Amy retorted. "Look, I'm going to drive to Villantry this afternoon. Just a social visit, as far as Aunt

Bernice is concerned. I'll be staying at the Villantry Inn for a couple of days, because my aunt is having her house remodeled. I want you to come with me."

Owen looked baffled. "What the hell do you expect me to do?"

"Check out Arthur Crabshaw, of course. Surely you don't need me to tell you how to conduct a simple investigation."

"You'd be amazed at what I need."

Amy scowled. "I want you to rummage around in Crabshaw's background. Find out if he's on the level. But I don't want my aunt to realize what you're doing. If he's legit, I'd rather she didn't know that I hired you. It would be embarrassing and awkward."

"Embarrassing and awkward." Owen nodded sagely. "That's me."

Amy blushed. "I didn't mean that as a personal remark."

"Right." Owen leaned back in his chair and stuck out his legs. He crossed his booted feet and regarded Amy with a truculent expression. "I'm supposed to go to Villantry with you, but no one is supposed to know who I am or what I'm doing there, is that it?"

Amy gave him an approving look. "Precisely."

"Villantry is a very small town. I'm not going to be able to hide very easily."

"I don't intend to keep you hidden."

"Just how do you plan to explain my presence?"

Amy smiled a trifle smugly. "Don't worry, I've got it all worked out. I'll pass you off as my fiancé."

2

*T*HAT EVENING OWEN SAT NEXT TO AMY IN THE RESTAURANT OF the Villantry Inn and wondered what the hell had come over him. But the question was strictly rhetorical. He knew the answer. Amy Comfort had come over him. Or, to be more precise, he sincerely hoped that their acquaintance would develop to the point where that eventuality became a distinct possibility.

He'd wanted Amy Comfort from the first moment he'd seen her. He would never forget that shattering instant of acute knowledge. He had walked into her parlor office, intent on purchasing the old Draycott place. The moldering pile of timber and stone had appealed to him on sight. He had determined to possess it, regardless of the price.

He'd felt the same way about Amy, although there was nothing moldering about her. Just the opposite. She was fresh and vital and alive. Her chin-length hair was the color of honey and her intelligent eyes were a mesmerizing shade of ultramarine blue.

She was not beautiful in the classic sense, but there was an appealing quality in her firm chin, high cheekbones, and straight little nose. There was something else there, too, an indefinable essence that he suspected an older generation would have labeled strength of character.

She reminded Owen of the wild roses in his garden. She would not fade when the going got tough, the way his first wife had. Amy would endure and flourish, just as the flowers in the Draycott garden had endured and flourished. Owen was not sure how he knew that, but he was very certain of it.

The extent of his desire for Amy had astounded him, because he'd assumed that he was well past the point when passion and desire could dazzle his senses and shake up his world. He was within spitting distance of forty, after all, and he had not got this far the easy way. One broken marriage and a checkered career that included a stint in the military and later as a private investigator had taught him that the world was painted in shades of gray.

But the day he had met Amy, Owen had started viewing life in living color again for the first time in years.

He had decided upon his goal in a heartbeat, but years of training had taken over at that juncture. He was, by nature, a careful, methodical man. He had told himself that he had to approach Amy in a subtle manner. Misplaced Island was a very small community. If he moved too quickly, there would be gossip. Amy might be embarrassed. The last thing he wanted to do was scare her off.

It was clear to Owen that she led a busy, but largely solitary life. He had established immediately that she had not dated anyone since her arrival on the island. That meant the path was clear for him.

He was no ladies' man, but he had determined to woo her with all the finesse at his command. Carefully planned trips to the post office, the grocery store, and the bookshop had netted him a series of seemingly casual encounters. He had told himself that she was getting used to him. She certainly seemed happy enough to run into him several times a week.

He had been encouraged with the results of his invitation to coffee last week. He had been consumed with plotting a dinner invitation when she'd blindsided him with the offer of a job this afternoon.

He had been dumbfounded when she had strolled into his wild garden and offered him a case. He had also been chagrined to learn that weeks of cautious maneuvering had been for naught. After all his painstaking efforts, she apparently viewed him only as a man who happened to have a useful expertise. She wanted to do business with him, not go to bed with him.

Owen stifled a silent groan. His only hope now lay in the fact that he had managed to get connecting rooms here at the Villantry Inn. There was something about adjoining rooms which created a sense of intimacy, he told himself.

To hell with delicacy and masculine finesse. It was obvious to Owen that the time had come to take a more aggressive approach to the business of courting Amy Comfort. Subtlety was lost on the woman.

"I do wish you two could have stayed with me," Bernice said for the fourth time. "But what with the remodeling and all, there's just no place to put you. The house is a mess, isn't it, Arthur?"

"Afraid so." Arthur Crabshaw, a sturdy man with gray hair and friendly eyes, smiled at Amy. "You know how things are during a remodel. Chaos and destruction. And I don't have room at my place."

"The Inn is perfect for us," Amy said quickly. "Isn't that right, Owen?"

"Yeah. Fine." Owen was vividly conscious of the fact that the curve of Amy's thigh, demurely draped in a flowing hunter-green silk skirt, was less than six inches from his leg. Wistfully, he considered the connecting rooms one flight above. "Perfect."

Arthur Crabshaw forked up a fried oyster with gusto. "The Inn's got the best food in town." He winked fondly at Bernice. "With the exception of Bernice's cooking, that is. Nothing compares to that."

Bernice, a robust, athletic-looking woman in her mid-

15

fifties with lively eyes and short, upswept hair that had been dyed a pale gold, blushed. Her eyes sparkled as she smiled at Owen.

"Amy's quite a gourmet cook herself," Bernice confided to Owen. "But I'm sure you've already discovered that."

Owen felt Amy stiffen next to him. He slid her a sidelong glance and was amused to see the barely veiled panic in her gaze. She was apparently not accustomed to subterfuge. She was on the verge of coming unglued at the first mild probe into their relationship. Gallantly, he stepped in to fill the breach.

"So far I've done all the cooking," he said, thinking of the pot of coffee he'd made that afternoon.

"Oh, then you must be a vegetarian also," Bernice said brightly.

Owen heard Amy's fork clatter loudly on the wooden table. He glanced down at the chunk of halibut which sat squarely in the middle of his plate. "I make an exception for fish. Health reasons."

"Well, Amy eats fish on occasion, too." Bernice waved that aside, as if it were common knowledge. "Now, then, the two of you must tell us everything. How did you meet? I swear, Amy, when you told me that you were going to move to that little dinky island, I was extremely worried about your social life."

"I know you were, Aunt Bernice," Amy said.

"I realized you were burned out after that dreadful incident last year," Bernice continued. "And I knew you wanted peace and quiet so that you could devote more time to your writing. But I never thought you'd be happy for long in such a small, isolated community."

Amy shot Owen a quick, unreadable glance. "Misplaced Island suits me. I've been very happy there."

"So I see." Bernice bubbled with enthusiasm. "Imagine, after all these years, you've finally discovered the man of your dreams on Misplaced Island."

Amy turned pink. "Uh, yes, well, you know what they say. Love is where you find it."

"The name of the island says it all," Owen said dryly. "I guess Amy and I weren't fated to find each other until we both got ourselves misplaced in the same place."

"I'm not so sure it's any harder to find love in a small town than it is in a big city." Crabshaw chuckled. "Just look at Bernice and me. If I hadn't come back to Villantry after all these years, I never would have found her."

"What made you return to Villantry, Arthur?" Amy asked boldly.

Owen winced at her less than casual tone. But Crabshaw did not seem to mind the pointed question.

"I got tired of the desert," Arthur said. "After thirty years of Arizona sunshine, I realized I missed the rainy Northwest. The only thing I miss about Phoenix is the year-round golf."

"Arthur loves golf," Bernice explained. "He plays every chance he gets, don't you, dear?"

Arthur smiled. "I do, indeed. Got a game scheduled for tomorrow morning, in fact. The Villantry Golf Course is not exactly world-class and the rain has a way of canceling out a lot of games, but I figure that's a small price to pay to live here."

"Life is so unpredictable," Bernice said. "What a coincidence, eh, Amy? You and I both finding true love where we least expected it."

Amy began to look anxious again. "Right. Hey, what's all the excitement about here in Villantry? We saw banners hanging over the main street. Something about fireworks in the park on Saturday evening."

"Didn't you know?" Arthur popped another oyster into his mouth. "The town is going to dedicate the new wing of the Raymond C. Villantry Memorial Public Library on Saturday. Big event. Madeline Villantry and her son, Raymond Junior, are pulling out all the stops."

"The new library wing is really a very generous gift to the community," Bernice said politely.

Amy raised her brows. "Do I detect a note of dutiful peasant gratitude?"

Bernice made a face. "Sorry about that. The Villantrys are nice enough in their own way, and Lord knows they've done a lot for this town. But they never forget for one minute that they are the leading family in Villantry. Very conscious of their position, if you know what I mean. Madeline is quite good in the role of Lady Bountiful."

Owen grinned briefly. "But the noblesse oblige stuff from the lady of the manor gets to be a bit thick at times, I take it?"

Bernice rolled her eyes. "I'm afraid so. Then, too, even though we're all adults now, I suppose a part of me can't quite forget that when we were in high school together, Madeline was the acknowledged beauty of the town. She got every boyfriend she wanted, including one or two of mine."

Arthur shifted uneasily in his chair and cleared his throat. "Villantry Fishing built this town. Most of the jobs here are connected to the company. I worked for Villantry myself years ago, before I went off to Arizona."

"What did you do in Arizona?" Owen asked easily. He pretended not to notice Amy's sharp glance.

"Started a construction company. Got lucky. Hit the building boom in Phoenix. Always thought I'd retire there, but after my wife died I felt restless. Did some traveling and then, on a whim, I decided to see what had happened to my hometown."

"We met in the library," Bernice said with a rueful laugh. "So I suppose one could say that we owe the Villantrys."

Arthur paused with the fork halfway to his mouth. "Speaking of Villantrys," he murmured, "here comes the lady of the manor herself, and Junior. He runs the business now, you know. Took over when his old man died three years ago."

Owen glanced up to see a handsome woman in her fifties moving regally down the aisle between a row of tables. She was followed by a man in his early thirties who looked as if he was on the wrong coast. He wore a pale yellow sweater tied around his neck and a bored look that spoke of having grown up with a sense of entitlement.

The dining room hostess trotted deferentially ahead of the pair, as though to make certain no rude serfs lumbered into their path. Madeline paused briefly at various tables to greet people with heavy-handed graciousness. Raymond Junior paused with her. He was not so gracious, however. He appeared impatient.

A moment later the entourage halted beside the table where Owen and the others sat. Owen and Arthur got to their feet. Madeline acknowledged their chivalry with an aloof inclination of her head. The nod said more plainly than words could have that such good manners were only expected.

"Do sit down, both of you." Madeline's smile was polite, but her voice was laced with a certain pinched quality. Her gaze touched Arthur briefly before sliding away. "Bernice, Arthur, I'm so glad we ran into each other here tonight. I heard about your engagement, and I want to congratulate both of you."

"Thank you, Madeline." Bernice gestured toward Owen and Amy. "I'd like you to meet my niece, Amy Comfort, and her fiancé, Owen Sweet. They're visiting."

"How do you do," Madeline said. "This is my son, Raymond."

Raymond gave Owen a curt nod. "Our table's ready, Mother."

A fleeting frown of disapproval flickered across Madeline's noble features, and then it was gone. "Yes, of course. You will excuse us?"

"Enjoy your dinner," Bernice said cheerfully.

"Thank you." Madeline glanced once more at Arthur and then she was gone.

Something in Arthur Crabshaw's gaze caught Owen's attention. In spite of his opinion of the crazy case and the fact that he had more important things on his mind at that moment than solving it, his instincts went on yellow alert.

Not red alert, Owen noticed, just yellow. But a warning light had definitely flashed. He felt Amy go very still beside him. He wondered if she had sensed the same thing he had.

No doubt about it: Arthur Crabshaw and Madeline Villantry had a history.

Two hours later Owen sat in a chair near the window of his darkened room and contemplated the closed door that stood between him and Amy.

He had been studying the door for nearly twenty minutes, ever since he and Amy had returned from dinner and coffee in the lounge.

After due consideration, Owen had finally concluded that the logical approach was the obvious one. He would simply knock on the connecting door. When Amy opened it from her side, he would tell her that he wanted to discuss the case. It was as clever an excuse as any.

Having considered and determined upon a course of action, he gripped the padded arms of the chair and started to get to his feet. An authoritative knock from Amy's side of the door stopped him in midrise.

"Owen? Are you in there?" Her voice was muffled, but the excited urgency in it was unmistakable. She knocked again, this time with a bit more insistence.

Owen told himself not to get his hopes up. The odds were against the likelihood that Amy had fallen for him sometime during dinner and now wanted to share a passionate good-night embrace.

Nevertheless, he walked across the room with enthusiasm and opened the door with anticipation.

Amy stood there, her hand raised for another peremptory knock. Her honey-colored hair was pinned in a frothy knot on top of her head. She was wearing a heavy, quilted bathrobe that rendered the average nun's habit scandalous in comparison. Owen smiled at the sight of her. She looked freshly scrubbed, and he was willing to bet that she had already brushed her teeth.

"I thought you might want to discuss the case," she said eagerly.

Owen's enthusiasm and anticipation vanished in a puff of

smoke. So much for his fond dream of having Amy fall into his arms. Back to Plan A. "I was afraid of that."

Her brows snapped together. "What?"

"Never mind." Owen stepped aside and swept his hand out to invite her into his room. "Come on in and have a seat. I'm at your service. Hell, I'm even willing to unlock the little refrigerator over there and open one of those itsy-bitsy bottles of wine."

Amy scowled. "Those tiny bottles are horribly overpriced for what you get."

"No problem. I'll just put it on my expense account."

Amy halted midway into the room. Alarm flared in her eyes. "Expense account?"

"Sure. That's how this PI business works, you know." He closed the connecting door and strolled to the small refrigerator. He used the small key to open the door. "I bill you by the hour and then tack on all the little extras. Adds up nicely."

"Good heavens. I hadn't realized. That could get rather pricey."

"Yes, indeed." Owen removed a minuscule bottle of brandy and paused to examine the label. "Name of the game, I'm afraid."

"Maybe we should have discussed your fees in more detail."

"Too late." Owen splashed the brandy into two glasses. "I'm already on the job. And once I start something, I always finish it."

Her expression relaxed. "You're teasing me."

"Am I?"

"Yes." She took one of the glasses from his hand. "You know, you've been acting a little weird since you agreed to take this case."

"Maybe that's because the case is a little weird." He took a sip from his glass. "First time I ever went undercover as a client's fake fiancé. By the way, you want some advice?"

She looked immediately wary. "What advice?"

"Try not to get that deer-caught-in-the-headlights expression in your eyes whenever someone makes a reference to our engagement. Sooner or later you'll blow our cover."

Her mouth fell open in shock. "Good grief. I'm that bad?"

He stared at her full, parted lips. "Maybe you just need to loosen up a bit."

"Loosen up?"

"Mellow out. Get into the role." He closed the distance between them with long, slow strides. "Try to become more comfortable with the idea of having a relationship with me."

She nibbled on her lower lip. "Relationship?"

"It should feel natural." He stopped in front of her. "Otherwise you're going to panic whenever someone says the magic word, *engagement.*"

"Don't be ridiculous. I'm not going to panic."

"No?" He put his hands on her shoulders. "How will you react if, for the sake of maintaining the deception, I do something like this?"

He bent his head and covered her mouth with his own.

3

*A*MY FROZE BENEATH THE IMPACT OF OWEN'S KISS. *JUST LIKE A deer caught in a car's headlights,* she thought. Owen had been right. The concept of an intimate relationship with him did strange things to her nerves.

But the rest of her body seemed to have no problem with the idea. Owen was kissing her. After all these weeks of her wondering and fantasizing, he was actually kissing her.

Hot excitement flashed through Amy, erasing the momentary paralysis. With an awkward, slightly jerky movement, she wrapped her arms around Owen's neck and kissed him back with all the bottled-up passion she had been concealing for nearly two months.

Her response appeared to take Owen by surprise. He staggered a little under the gentle assault. But he did not release her. He recovered his balance immediately and began to rain kisses on her throat.

"Amy?"

"Oh, my God, this is amazing."

"You can say that again." Owen scooped her up in his

arms and carried her across the room to the bed. "When I think of all the time we've wasted."

"Yes, yes, I know what you mean."

He set her down on the bed and fell on top of her. Her bathrobe had been a faithful friend for years, but it had not been designed to defend its wearer from such treatment. It promptly separated. One of Owen's jeaned legs found its way between Amy's thighs.

"Owen."

"Damn," he whispered. "This is incredible. You're incredible."

Amy was dazed by the waves of passion that were coursing through her. She felt deliciously crushed beneath Owen's not inconsiderable weight. The heat of his body triggered a series of lightning strikes within her. She could feel the fires they ignited. The flames burned most intensely in her lower body, liquefying all that they touched.

Owen found the pins in her hair and tore them free. "Like honey in my hands." He seized a fistful of the stuff and buried his nose in it. "You smell so good."

"So do you." The realization astonished her. She had never before noticed a man's smell unless she happened to be standing downwind of one who had failed to use deodorant.

But this unique scent that belonged to Owen was different. Enticing. Enthralling. It did crazy things to her senses. She wanted more of it. More of him.

"Hang on, let me get you out of this thing." Owen levered himself up on one elbow and tugged at the sash of her robe.

Amy gazed at him, fascinated by the passion that blazed in his eyes. Wonderingly, she touched his hard jaw. "I can't believe this is happening."

"The delay was my fault. I was going for the subtle approach." He put a heavy, warm hand on the bodice of the soft cotton gown. His fingers closed gently around one breast. "Don't ask me why."

"You feel so good." She flattened her palm against his chest, delighting in the strength of him.

"So do you." He bent his head to kiss a nipple. His mouth dampened the fabric of her gown. She gave a small, muffled cry and clutched at his shoulders.

Owen began to tug the nightgown downward. "Amy, you don't know what you're doing to me."

Realization burst through Amy's dazzled senses. "Oh, my God, you're right. This is all my fault."

"Huh?"

"It's the case." She clutched wildly at her sliding nightgown and struggled to sit up. "Don't you see? It's the situation we're in that's causing you to act like this."

"What the hell?" Owen fell to the side as Amy squirmed out from underneath him.

"I thought this was all very sudden." Amy tugged the lapels of her robe together and grabbed for the sash. Her hands were shaking.

"Sudden?"

"Well, it's not as though you've shown any great interest in me until tonight."

"Amy, for God's sake, listen to me. You've got this all wrong."

"I don't think so." She glowered at him as she scooted to the edge of the bed. "We've known each other for several weeks and you've never once indicated that you felt anything other than sort of friendly toward me."

"Sort of friendly?" Owen was beginning to look mildly dangerous.

Amy was mortified. "It's worse than I thought. You weren't even feeling particularly friendly, were you? That was just my imagination."

"Amy, I think we have a small problem here," he began in an ominous tone.

"Please, it's all right. I understand exactly what's happening."

"I'm glad one of us does."

"Well, they do say that women are more inclined to analyze situations."

"Hell."

"I've read about this sort of thing," she said defensively. "But I should have thought that since you're the expert in these matters, you'd have been alert for just this type of unprofessional occurrence."

"Unprofessional?"

She was suddenly outraged by his obstinacy. "Don't look at me as if you don't know what I'm talking about. I'm sure that as a private investigator, you've faced this sort of situation hundreds of times."

Owen reached out to clamp a hand around her wrist. "For the benefit of this nonanalytical, slow-witted investigator, would you kindly explain what the hell you're talking about?"

Amy flushed. "You know what I mean. A situation like this, where two people are thrown together in close confines. A situation in which they face a threat of danger. Why, it's bound to generate a heightened sense of intimacy. Intimacy often breeds passion. Especially when the two people involved are single and of the opposite sex."

"Hold it." Owen put his fingers against her lips to silence her. "Stop right there. Let's take this from the top. First, I have been an investigator for over ten years, and I can assure you that I have never, ever made love to a client. Until now, that is."

Amy stared at him. "I see."

"Furthermore, although I will admit that the situation in which we find ourselves has a built-in degree of intimacy, thanks to the cover story you invented for us, I see absolutely no danger here. Therefore, I think we can discount its impact on our sex lives."

Amy frowned. "I'm not so sure about that. We really don't know what we're facing yet. There could definitely be some risk involved."

"No," Owen said authoritatively. "There is no threat involved in this damn-fool situation. A certain amount of idiocy on the part of the PI, perhaps. An amazing imagination on the part of the client, definitely. But no threat. Unless you count the threat to my sanity."

"Owen, we don't know that for certain." Amy got up quickly and tied the sash of her robe. "You haven't even begun to investigate Arthur Crabshaw. The possibility of danger must be present somewhere in the back of your mind. You're a trained investigator, after all."

Owen flopped back against the pillows and threw one arm over his eyes. "You'd never know it."

Amy bit her lip. "Please, I didn't mean to upset you like this. I should never have knocked on your door tonight. If I'd had any sense, I would have recognized the volatile nature of the situation and waited until morning to discuss the case."

"Yeah, right."

Amy edged back toward the connecting door. "I'm sorry."

"Uh-huh."

"It's the adrenaline and hormones and things like that at work. Not genuine emotion."

"Uh-huh."

"But you're right about my imagination," she added sadly.

He removed his arm from his eyes and stared at her with sudden intensity. "What?"

"I do have an overactive imagination. I suppose it's an occupational hazard for a writer."

Owen sat up slowly. "So you admit there's no real danger involved in this loony case?"

She shook her head decisively. "No, I still think we mustn't discount the very real possibility that Arthur Crabshaw is not what he seems. Did you see the way he reacted to Madeline Villantry tonight?"

Owen hesitated. "Okay, I'll admit that there may be some kind of connection between them."

Amy brightened. "I got the exact same impression. This is amazing, Owen. We're on the same wavelength here."

"That's a matter of opinion." Owen sat up on the edge of the bed. A thoughtful expression began to replace the combination of irritation and passion that had burned in his gaze a moment earlier. "Don't get carried away with your brilliant deduction, Amy. It makes sense that Madeline and Arthur knew each other at some point in the past. It's a small town, after all, and Crabshaw told us that he worked for Villantry before he went off to Arizona to make his fortune."

"The thing is, Madeline Villantry and Arthur Crabshaw would have been worlds apart socially in those days. After all, she was married to the town's leading citizen. Arthur worked for her husband. But tonight I got the feeling that there was something more intimate between them."

"Maybe there was." Owen stood and began to pace the room. "But whatever happened occurred over thirty years ago. It doesn't mean anything now."

"Then why did Crabshaw get that funny look in his eyes when Madeline stopped by our table tonight?"

Owen came to a halt and swung around to face her. "I don't know."

Amy was momentarily sidetracked by the sight of him. His dark hair was tousled. His denim shirt had come free of his jeans. All in all, there was a tantalizing, seductive look about him that made her pulse begin to pound once more.

"Something wrong?" Owen asked.

"Uh, no. I was just trying to think this thing through."

"If you can think clearly at the moment, you're way ahead of me." Owen ran his fingers through his hair. "Look, it's late. Go to bed. In the morning I'll call some people I know. Have them check into Crabshaw's Arizona background. I can at least make sure that he doesn't have a criminal record and that he's financially solvent."

"That sounds like a good start."

"Thanks. I do try to give satisfaction."

Aware that he was in a strange mood, Amy backed meekly toward the door. She was almost through it when Owen stopped her with another question.

"Amy, what did you mean a few minutes ago when you said you had an overactive imagination?"

She paused in the doorway, clutched the lapels of her robe very tightly, and gave him her best real estate saleswoman smile. "Nothing. Nothing at all."

"Have I told you that you're a very bad liar?"

"Don't ask me any questions if you don't like my answers," she flared.

Owen raised his eyes briefly to the ceiling in a beseeching expression. Then he fixed her with a look of dogged patience. "Amy, the relationship between a private investigator and his client is founded on mutual trust and confidentiality. If I don't feel that I can rely upon your answers, I won't be able to work for you."

"Oh." She frowned.

He took a deliberate step toward her. "I think we need to get this relationship back on track. The fastest way to do that is to be completely honest with each other."

"What do you want from me?" she asked.

He spread his hands. "I'll get right to the bottom line. Did you really kiss me a few minutes ago because you were driven into a paroxysm of violent passion by the close confines and threat of incredible danger that we face together?"

"Well, no. At least, I don't think so."

"So why did you kiss me?"

She gripped the edge of the door and lifted her chin proudly. "If you must know, I kissed you because I've been wanting to kiss you ever since I sold you that Victorian horror of a house. There. Are you satisfied?"

He stared at her as if he'd just walked into a brick wall. *"Amy."*

"Good night, Owen. I'll meet you downstairs for breakfast. I shall want a complete status report on this case and a detailed outline of your plans for the remainder of this investigation by eight o'clock tomorrow morning. We have no time to waste."

Amy slammed the connecting door behind her and hurried into her room. She took a deep breath. After a few seconds she opened the door again. Owen was still standing in the middle of the room, staring at the door. "Why did you kiss me?" she asked.

His mouth quirked and a sexy gleam appeared in his eyes. "Same reason. Been wanting to do it since I bought the house."

Amy felt her insides turn to jelly. "Oh."

"See you in the morning."

"Right." Amy closed the door again, this time very quietly. Then she snapped off the light, removed her robe, and threw herself down onto the bed.

She contemplated the shadowed ceiling for a very long while before she finally went to sleep.

4

OWEN USED A COPY OF THE *VILLANTRY GAZETTE* TO SHIELD his gaze as he watched Amy walk toward him. The no-nonsense impact of her determined stride across the Inn's coffee shop was severely undercut by the pink in her cheeks and the shyness in her eyes.

It took a lot to make a real estate agent turn shy, Owen reflected with some satisfaction. Last night's events had obviously had an unsettling effect on Amy. He took that as a good sign and set about composing his strategy for the day.

She was self-conscious about what had happened between them, preferring to blame it on adrenaline and hormones. He would act as if nothing at all out of the ordinary had occurred. He would be businesslike and professional. That might help her relax.

The important thing was that now, after weeks of shilly-shallying around with the subtle approach, he finally knew for certain that she was anything but indifferent to him. She might have concocted a ludicrous reason to explain away the white-hot desire that had flashed between them, but she was definitely not indifferent.

"Good morning." He put down the paper and lazily got to his feet as Amy reached the table.

"Hi." She gave him a practiced real estate agent's smile as he pulled out her chair, but her eyes reflected far less certainty. "How are things going?"

Owen blanked at the question. He seriously doubted that she was inquiring about how he had survived a night complicated by an erection the likes of which he had not endured since his late teens.

"What things?" Owen asked cautiously.

"The investigation, of course. You said you were going to make some calls this morning."

"Oh, yeah, right. The investigation." Owen tried a businesslike smile of his own as he resumed his seat. "It's going just fine. I made my calls before I came downstairs. Should know something by this afternoon."

"Great." Amy opened her menu with a snap. "What about the next step?"

Owen cleared his throat. He did not delude himself into thinking that she was referring to the next step in their relationship. "We'll have to see what sort of information comes in from my contacts before we can make concrete plans."

"In that case, why don't we go to the library later this morning."

He shrugged. "Why not? There's not much else to do until I get some response to my calls. We can take a look at this fancy new wing the town plans to dedicate on Friday."

Amy looked up from the menu with a small frown. She glanced hurriedly around the room and then leaned forward and lowered her voice. "I meant that we should go to the library to do some research, not to kill time."

"Research on what?"

"On Arthur Crabshaw."

"In the *library?*"

"For Pete's sake, you're supposed to be the trained investigator here. Why am I having to do all the work?"

"Because you have a natural aptitude for it?" he suggested with bland innocence.

"Stop teasing me. You know perfectly well why I suggested the library."

"I do?"

"Of course. We might be able to learn something about Crabshaw if we look through old newspapers from the time when he worked for Villantry."

"You know something, Amy? You have a one-track mind. I suppose you need it in the real estate business, though, don't you? What do you do? Sink your teeth into a client and refuse to let go until he signs on the dotted line?"

She gave him a puzzled look. "I'm just trying to keep you focused on the job at hand. Are you always this vague about your work? Does the pressure get to you or something? Is that what went wrong in Portland?"

Owen drummed his fingers on the table. "Amy, you are not going to find anything of interest on Crabshaw in thirty-year-old editions of the *Villantry Gazette.*"

"What makes you so sure of that?"

Owen swore under his breath. "Think about it. If Crabshaw had been involved in an old scandal or if he had left town under a cloud, do you honestly believe that Madeline Villantry would have been so polite and gracious to him last night?"

"Hmm. I hadn't thought about that."

"She went out of her way to congratulate him and your aunt on their engagement. This is a small town, and the Villantrys have obviously ruled it for years. If Crabshaw had done anything thirty years ago that was considered the least bit unsavory, Madam Villantry would not have stopped at our table."

"I suppose you have a point."

"Thank you. I like to think that I'm not completely unsuited to my work."

"Still, it won't hurt to look in the old papers, will it?" Amy continued brightly. "As you said, it's not as if we have anything better to do this morning."

Owen narrowed his eyes. "Is this why you had to quit your high-powered real estate career in Seattle? In your zeal to close a big deal did you finally manage to push one of your clients a little too far?"

To his amazement, Amy paled. "That question does not deserve an answer." She took a deep breath and returned her full attention to the menu.

An hour later Owen found himself reluctantly ensconced in front of a microfilm reader. He was supposed to be perusing the headlines of the old issues of the *Villantry Gazette* that were rolling slowly past his gaze, but his real attention was on Amy. She sat at the machine next to him, her attention on another reel of the *Gazette*.

Owen was still berating himself for the unwitting crack about her real estate tactics. He had obviously stumbled into awkward territory. It didn't take Sherlock Holmes to deduce that something bad had happened in Seattle. He recalled a remark Bernice had made at dinner. Something about Amy being burned out after "that dreadful incident last year."

At the time, Owen had concluded that Bernice had been referring to an affair that had gone sour. He hadn't paid much attention to the comment because whatever it was, it was in the past. He was only concerned with Amy's future.

"Find anything interesting?" Amy asked in a muted tone.

"Interesting?" Owen paused to read the headlines that were moving slowly across the screen. "Let's see. 'Villantry Eagles Break Six-Game Losing Streak.' How does that sound?"

"About as exciting as 'Raymond C. Villantry Dedicates New Library.'"

Owen glanced around. "I guess that would be the old library now. The one we're in."

The Raymond C. Villantry Memorial Public Library, a sturdy structure in the tradition of old-fashioned municipal buildings, was surprisingly busy for a small library on a

Friday morning, Owen thought. As a book lover himself, he took a certain pleasure from that fact.

In one corner a gaggle of pre-school-age children had assembled to listen to fairy tales read by a librarian. Their shouts of glee and shrieks of horror drifted across the cavernous main room. The children's mothers, no doubt grateful for the respite in parental duties, perused the display of new books.

The janitor, a balding, middle-aged man in coveralls, set up a sign in front of the women's room and disappeared inside with his wheeled bucket and well-used mop.

Three elderly men sat at tables in the newspaper section poring over copies of the *Wall Street Journal.* Two librarians and a small group of what appeared to be concerned citizens hovered near the entrance to the new wing. They were apparently making final arrangements for Saturday's dedication ceremony. As Owen watched, they were joined by Raymond Villantry Jr., who strode through the door wearing a business suit. When he appeared, there was a chorus of respectful greetings. Then the entire group disappeared into a conference room and closed the door.

"Look, here's a picture of Madeline Villantry standing next to her husband." Amy leaned closer to the screen. "I'll bet she was prom queen, homecoming queen, and head cheerleader."

"You can tell all that from a photo?"

"See for yourself."

More than willing to take advantage of the offer to move closer to Amy, Owen shifted position to get a better view of her screen. "Right. Definitely prom queen."

The old black-and-white photo was grainy and blurred, but there was no hiding the fact that Madeline Villantry had been a beautiful woman in her younger days. She stood beside her husband, the late Raymond C. Villantry Sr., who was holding forth from a lectern in front of the library.

Amy wrinkled her nose. "He looks like a politician."

"Yeah. Junior is a dead ringer for his old man, isn't he?"

"Yes." Amy frowned at the photo. "I'll bet that was not a happy marriage."

Owen glanced at her in surprise. "What makes you say that?"

"I'm not sure. Something about the expression on Madeline Villantry's face. Poised. Gracious. Aloof. Dutiful. Anything but happy."

"I think you're trying to read a little too much into a thirty-year-old photo."

"Maybe." Amy shrugged. "Not that it matters to us. Aunt Bernice said that Raymond C. Villantry Sr. died three years ago."

"And young Raymond Junior took over the company. Wonder how he likes being called Junior."

"Between you and me, he doesn't look any nicer than his father."

"I don't think that being nice is a job requirement for running a company the size of Villantry." Owen took advantage of the situation to lean in just a little closer.

He caught a whiff of the flowery fragrance of Amy's hair and inhaled deeply. Along with it came a more intriguing scent. Warm, female, and deliciously spicy. He did not think he would ever be able to get enough of it. Of her.

"Owen," Amy hissed.

"Sorry, I was just trying to get a better look at the picture."

"Never mind that. Look."

"At what?"

"Arthur Crabshaw. He just walked into the library. See? Over there by the magazine rack."

Owen straightened reluctantly and turned to look at the racks. Sure enough, Crabshaw was leafing through a new copy of *Newsweek.* "So what?"

"What's he doing here?"

"Reading a magazine?"

"That isn't funny. Owen, he told us that he was going to play golf this morning." Amy scowled impatiently. "It's not raining, so why did he cancel his game?"

"Why don't we ask him?"

"Don't be silly. He's up to something. I know it. I told you there was something shifty about that man."

"Amy, the first rule in the investigation business is not to jump to conclusions. Crabshaw simply dropped into the library to scan a few magazines. Don't make a federal case out of it."

"He's leaving the magazine rack. Don't let him see you."

"Why not?"

"Because we want to keep an eye on him. We need to find out where he's going."

"I think he's headed for the men's room," Owen said.

"Oh."

Owen rested one arm over the back of the hard wooden library chair and watched Arthur Crabshaw disappear into the men's rest room. Amy looked severely disappointed.

"Cheer up," Owen said. "Maybe he'll do something really suspicious when he comes out of the john."

"You think this is amusing, don't you."

"I think you're overreacting," he said gently. "Why are you so determined to prove that Arthur Crabshaw is up to no good?"

"I told you, I don't want him to take advantage of Aunt Bernice."

"Just because he happened to return to Villantry a few months after your uncle died doesn't mean he's out to marry Bernice for her money."

"I still say the timing is very suspect. Be careful, he's coming out."

Owen dutifully retreated a little farther behind the shelter of the microfilm reader. Arthur Crabshaw emerged from the men's room and headed swiftly toward the front door of the library.

"He seems to be in a big hurry all of a sudden," Amy observed.

Owen chewed on that for a while. He hated to admit it, but there was something about Crabshaw's behavior this morning that was at odds with the genial man who had entertained them at dinner last night. Whatever it was, it reminded Owen of the look that had been in Crabshaw's eyes last night when he had chatted with Madeline Villantry.

Owen reached a decision.

"Wait here, I'll be right back."

He got to his feet and walked casually toward the men's room. He passed the three elderly men bent over their financial papers. None of them bothered to look up from the stock market listings. The janitor, whose name tag read E. TREDGETT, had finished mopping the women's room. He started off toward the new wing with his clanking wheeled bucket.

Raymond suddenly emerged from the conference room, apparently intent on heading toward the rest room. He walked out just as the janitor went past the door. The toe of Villantry's Italian leather shoe struck the bucket. Sudsy water sloshed over the edge.

"Damn it, Eugene, watch where you're going."

"Sorry, sir." Eugene Tredgett seemed to fold in on himself. He hurriedly used his mop to clean up the spill.

Raymond appeared to realize that Owen was watching the small incident. He scowled and then apparently changed his mind about his destination. With a disgusted shrug, he turned back into the conference room and closed the door.

Owen gave the janitor a sympathetic smile. Tredgett acknowledged it with a wan nod and trundled off with his bucket and mop.

Owen went through the swinging door of the men's room.

The gleaming, white-tiled facility was empty. Owen dismissed the two urinals with a glance and then considered the two stalls. Amy would never forgive him if he didn't make a thorough search of the premises.

He walked into the first cubicle and lifted the tank lid. There was nothing inside the tank except water and the usual float-ball assembly.

He went into the second stall and tried again.

A sealed envelope was taped beneath the lid.

5

"TAKE IT EASY, AMY," OWEN SAID. "CALM DOWN. THIS MAY have nothing to do with Crabshaw. I need time to think. I've got to get more information before I can decide what to do next."

Amy scowled at him across the picnic table. It wasn't easy. Every time she looked at Owen a flood of memories washed over her. She could still feel the heat of his mouth on hers. She was certain that his arms had left permanent impressions on her body. But his stubbornly slow, methodical approach to his work was going to drive her crazy.

"Are you nuts?" she demanded. "It's got everything to do with Crabshaw. There's a thousand dollars inside that envelope and Crabshaw was the last man to go into that rest room before you. He must have been the one who left the money under the tank lid."

"It could have been left by someone earlier this morning."

"Hah. What are the odds?"

"Okay," he muttered, "I'll grant you that a coincidence like this is something of a long shot."

39

"That's putting it mildly." Amy threw up her hands, exasperated. "Who else would have left that money inside a toilet tank? I think it's safe to say that there aren't that many people here in Villantry who could come up with that kind of cash."

"Amy, that envelope could have been taped inside the lid at any time during the past week, or even the past month. Hell, it could have been left there sometime during the past year, for all we know. No one checks the inside of a toilet tank unless the toilet acts up."

"You're going to be difficult about this, aren't you."

"I'm going to be careful. Methodical. I'm going to take it one step at a time. That's the way I do things, Amy."

"Hmm." Amy folded her arms on the picnic table and glumly surveyed Villantry Park. She and Owen had come here to discuss their next move, but so far all they had done was argue about it.

They were seated at a table located near a magnificent mass of rhododendron bushes. The stately Raymond C. Villantry Memorial Public Library was at the far end of the park. The Villantry Inn was on the opposite side. There was a bandstand in the center.

A pond, complete with ducks and a couple of geese, added eye appeal to the attractive setting. Banners announcing fireworks hung over the entrance of the park.

Amy was frustrated by Owen's approach to this startling new development in the case. On the other hand, she had to admit that he was the expert.

"All right. Hypothetically speaking," she said, making an effort to sound reasonable, "what sort of scenario do we construct to explain that envelope you found?"

Owen raised one black brow. "Hypothetically speaking, I'd say that it looks as if Arthur Crabshaw is being blackmailed."

"*Blackmail.*" Amy tasted the word with a sense of dreadful wonder. "Holy cow."

Owen fingered the envelope in his hand. "It's conceivable

that he's been told to leave the money in the men's room of the library. Think about it. Anyone can go into a public library at any time when it's open. A person can hang around for hours, a whole day even, without anyone taking much notice. The victim can leave the money at any time. The blackmailer can pick up the payoff whenever he feels like it."

Amy peered at him as she digested that. "You do realize what this means."

"Why do I have the impression that you're about to enlighten me?"

She ignored that. "It means Crabshaw really does have some deep, dark secret. Something he's hiding from my aunt. Something that is worth paying blackmail to conceal."

"Maybe."

"What do you mean, maybe?"

"It's a possibility," Owen conceded. "That's all I'm willing to admit at this point. I will, however, add the simple observation that the blackmailer is probably male. Which does eliminate approximately half the people in town."

"Male? Oh, yes, of course. The payoffs are being left in the men's rest room. So whoever goes in to retrieve them is probably of the masculine persuasion. Right. Good thinking."

"I try," Owen said.

"All right, Mr. Hotshot PI, what do we do next?"

"We follow Plan A."

"Which is?"

"We wait for some of my morning phone calls to be returned. I want a little more information in hand before I confront Crabshaw."

Amy's mouth went dry. "You're going to confront him?"

"Sometimes a surprise frontal assault is the quickest way to get an answer. I'll pin him down this afternoon."

Amy hesitated. "Shouldn't we go to the cops or something?"

"With what? A handful of money that we happened to

find in the men's room? There's no way in hell to prove that it's a blackmail payoff. They'd probably put an ad in the *Villantry Gazette* inviting someone to claim it."

"I see what you mean," Amy said. "But confronting Crabshaw could be dangerous. If he's so desperate to protect his secret that he's willing to pay blackmail, he won't take kindly to your questions. He might become violent."

Owen smiled slightly. "I don't believe this. Are you actually worried about me?"

"Yes, of course I am. I've hired you to solve this case. I would feel terrible if something happened to you."

Owen's green eyes darkened with irritation. "Have a little faith, Ms. Comfort. I realize that I no doubt appear to be downwardly mobile, professionally speaking, but I think I'm still capable of dealing with the likes of Arthur Crabshaw."

Amy flushed. "I didn't mean to insult you. And I don't think you're downwardly mobile just because you gave up your business in Portland and moved to Misplaced Island. Heck, I did the same thing."

"True."

Silence fell on the picnic table. Amy was suddenly acutely conscious of the chattering of a pair of ravens, the distant shouts of youngsters playing on the swings, and a large, furry dog that was pointing one of the ducks on the pond.

"So why did you move to Misplaced Island?" she finally asked very softly.

Owen shrugged. "Got burned out, I guess. After I got out of the military, I got my PI ticket."

"Somehow I don't see you in the military. I'll bet you don't take orders well."

Owen smiled wryly. "You're right. It wasn't a good career path for me. But I had married young. No education to speak of. I needed a job, and the military provided a way to support a wife. She left me after I got out of the service. Said she couldn't take the unstable income. She fell for someone else while I was working to get my business up and running.

After the divorce I worked harder. Spent the last ten years doing other people's dirty work."

"Dirty work?"

"Staking out people who try to defraud insurance companies. Trapping embezzlers. Finding missing persons. That kind of thing."

"And you got tired of it?"

"Let's just say I woke up one morning and realized I didn't like my clients any more than the people they paid me to catch. The insurance company executives spent their time trying to avoid paying legitimate claims. The corporate executives were more cold-blooded than the embezzlers who stole from them, and the missing persons usually had very good reasons for not wanting to be found."

Amy smiled sympathetically. "Nothing was black-and-white, huh?"

"Just shades of gray. A lot of gray. I had made some money on the side by buying fixer-uppers, doing the repairs myself in my spare time and reselling the houses at a nice profit. I decided to invest some of the money and use the rest of it to fix up my own life."

"On Misplaced Island."

"That's it." Owen looked at her. "What about you?"

"Me?"

"What made you decide to move to Misplaced Island?"

"Seattle real estate is hard on a body. I worked the downtown condo market. There was a lot of pressure. I guess I burned out, too. Also, I wanted more time to write. And then something happened last year."

"Your aunt called it a 'dreadful incident.'"

Amy grimaced. "I still get occasional nightmares."

"What happened?"

"Most people don't realize it, but real estate agents tend to lead adventurous lives. They never know what they're going to find when they open the door of what is supposed to be an empty house or condo. I've had a variety of surprises."

"Somehow, knowing you, that does not amaze me."

She smiled wryly. "I once showed a condo to a staid, elderly couple. I'd finished the tour of the front room, kitchen, and bedrooms. We walked into the master bath and found two people making love in the jetted tub. They were so involved in what they were doing that they never even heard us."

Owen grinned briefly. "Make the sale?"

"Yes, I did, as a matter of fact. It was the jetted tub that clinched the deal. The elderly couple couldn't wait to try it out themselves."

"I take it that was not the 'dreadful incident' that made you decide you'd shown one condo too many."

"No." Amy propped her elbows on the table and rested her chin on her hands. "Walking in on a murder in progress did that."

"Murder."

"Uh-huh. I came through the front door just after a respected businessman named Bernard Gordon had shot his partner. A little dispute over investment capital, apparently. Gordon was on his way out of the condo just as I arrived. We collided in the front hall."

Owen's gloriously unhandsome features shaped themselves into an ominous mask. "You could have been killed."

"Gordon tried to do just that. He knew I could identify him. Fortunately, he was already rattled because of the first killing. His shot went wild. I had a chance to hurl my cellular phone at him. He instinctively ducked. I ran back the way I had come and headed for the emergency stairwell. I didn't dare wait for the elevators."

Owen closed his eyes briefly. "My God."

"Gordon tried to chase me down the stairwell. But he stumbled on one of the steps." Amy shuddered. "He fell to the bottom. Broke his neck."

Owen exhaled heavily. "Damn." He reached across the table and took one of her hands in his. He crushed her fingers gently in his own.

Silence descended once more. Amy and Owen watched the ducks on the pond for a long while.

"Nothing. Nada. Zilch." Owen glanced at the notes he had made during his last phone call. He flipped the small notebook shut and tossed it onto the bedside table. He looked at Amy, who was lounging, arms folded beneath her breasts, in the connecting doorway. "Arthur Crabshaw is as clean as you can expect a fifty-five-year-old businessman to be."

"No scandals while down in Arizona?"

"No. At least not that my sources could determine in such a limited period of time. I suppose it's possible that Crabshaw left a few bodies buried under one of his strip malls, but I don't think it's very likely."

Amy tapped her toe, thinking. "The blackmail arrangement we witnessed this morning seemed fairly amateurish, didn't it?"

"Yes." Owen walked to the window and looked out at the park. "A toilet tank lid in a library rest room. Definitely the work of an amateur. And a local amateur, at that."

"Local?"

"Crabshaw was told to leave the money in the public library. The implication is that he's being blackmailed by someone here in Villantry."

"Okay, that makes sense. But he's been gone for thirty years."

"And that means that his deep, dark secret, whatever it is, probably dates back thirty years," Owen said softly.

"To the time when he worked for Raymond C. Villantry?"

"Yes." Owen turned away from the window. "I think it's time I paid a call on Arthur Crabshaw."

"I'll get my purse."

"You will stay right here in this room," Owen said.

"I'm paying your tab, remember? That means I can make executive decisions."

"When I'm on a case, I give the orders."

"You need me to help analyze his reactions," Amy said

persuasively. "I'm very good at that kind of thing. It's my real estate sales experience, you see. I'm what you might call an amateur practicing psychologist."

"Forget it, Amy. I'm handling this alone."

Arthur Crabshaw looked momentarily nonplussed to see Amy and Owen on his doorstep. Amy was sure she saw evidence of tension around his eyes. But he recovered with alacrity. He smiled genially and ushered them into his front room.

"Well, well, well." He closed the door. "This is a surprise. What can I do for you two?"

"How was the golf game this morning?" Owen asked softly.

Arthur's smile slipped for only an instant. He quickly got it back in place. "Fine. Just fine. Shot a three over par. Although I have to admit that on the Villantry Golf Course that's not saying a great deal."

"Must have been a fast round," Owen said.

Arthur's gaze turned wary. "Why do you say that?"

Amy held her breath as Owen removed the incriminating envelope from his pocket.

"Because you finished in time to visit the library, didn't you?" Owen said.

Arthur stared at the envelope. Then he raised his eyes to meet Owen's unrelenting gaze. His expression crumbled into weary despair. "How did you find out?"

"Amy and I were in the library at the time. We saw you go into the rest room. I went in after you and found this." Owen glanced at the envelope. "I thought maybe you'd like to talk about it."

"There's not much to say now, is there?" Arthur sank down heavily into an armchair. "If you've got the money, that means the blackmailer didn't get his payoff. He'll reveal the truth, just as he threatened to do in his first note."

Owen went to stand in front of Arthur. "What happens if he does reveal the truth, Crabshaw?"

"Madeline Villantry will be humiliated in front of her

family and the entire town." Arthur sighed. "And I seriously doubt that Bernice will marry me when she discovers that Madeline and I once had an affair. Bernice is such a sensitive woman. Bad enough that Madeline used to steal her boyfriends back in high school. How will she feel if she finds out that I was once Madeline's lover?"

6

I THINK YOU'D BETTER START FROM THE BEGINNING," OWEN said.

"I worked for Madeline's husband, Raymond C. Villantry." Arthur massaged his temples. "Just like almost everyone else did at the time. I was young. Couldn't afford college. But I was determined to make something of myself."

"At Villantry?" Amy asked.

"No, I had my sites set a lot higher. But Villantry was a start, and a good one. I knew who Madeline was, of course. Everyone in Villantry did. Her family was as rich as the Villantrys. I didn't move in Madeline's circles in those days, though." Arthur grimaced. "Only the Villantrys did."

"Go on," Owen said.

"Madeline married Raymond Villantry right out of college. Everyone said it was a perfect match. I honestly believe that she was wildly in love with him in the beginning. But Villantry just took her for granted. He was accustomed to getting whatever he wanted. Then, after he got it, he lost interest. The only exception was the company. He was passionate about it."

"What happened?" Amy asked gently.

"I was doing well at Villantry." Arthur leaned his head back against the chair. "Had a flair for business. Madeline and I were thrown together on a number of occasions because she was on the planning commission for the original library building. Civic duty and all that."

"Why did that bring the two of you together?" Amy asked.

"Villantry's firm had expanded beyond fishing by then. It was into construction. It was going to build the library. I was assigned to act as a liaison between the planning commission and the company. Raymond Villantry had better things to do with his time than fuss with the library that was to be named in his honor."

"Such as?" Owen asked. He was aware that Amy's gaze was softening rapidly. He was not surprised. He recalled their conversation regarding his move to Misplaced Island. He'd suspected all along that she had a soft heart.

Arthur's mouth twisted. "Such as making a number of trips to Seattle. Villantry was having an affair in the city. A lot of people were aware of it, but of course no one actually said anything to Madeline. No one thought she knew. I came across her one day after a committee meeting. She was sitting all alone in a conference room, crying her heart out."

Amy looked at him with sympathetic eyes. "And you comforted her?"

Arthur nodded. "One thing led to another. She wasn't in love with me, nor I with her. But she needed someone, and she was a lovely woman. And so very brave." He moved his hands in a vague gesture. "What can I say? We had an affair."

"What ended it?" Owen demanded. "Did her husband discover what was going on?"

"Oh, no." Arthur frowned. "No one ever discovered us. At least, I thought no one knew. We were very, very careful. Madeline had her reputation and her family to consider.

49

She was so terrified of being caught that she ended the affair after a couple of months."

Amy frowned. "Why?"

"She said she had to consider the future of her two young children. She didn't want to jeopardize their inheritance by risking a divorce. And she had her parents to think of, too. She was their only child. She was afraid that they would be humiliated if we were found out."

"Hmm," Amy said.

Owen glanced at her. He was starting to recognize that tone in her voice. "Yes? Did you have something you wanted to share with the rest of the class?"

Amy shrugged. "Not really. It just occurred to me that Madeline made a very financially astute decision."

"It was a very brave decision," Arthur corrected gallantly. "For which she paid a great price. She endured an unhappy marriage for years in order to salvage her children's inheritance and to protect her family from humiliation."

"There is that," Amy agreed.

It occurred to Owen that Amy had already deduced the truth about Madeline Villantry's marriage from the photo she had seen in the old edition of the *Villantry Gazette*. He turned to Crabshaw. "How many blackmail payments have you made?"

"Two. Or, rather, one. I got the first note a few weeks ago, right after Bernice and I announced our engagement." Arthur nodded glumly at the envelope Owen had placed on the table. "The thousand in there was supposed to be the second payment."

"So the blackmail is recent?" Owen asked sharply. "You weren't bothered by any demands until a few weeks ago?"

"No." Arthur dropped his head into his hands. "I thought there would only be the one payment. Then, two days ago, there was a second demand."

"There always is," Owen said.

"But it hasn't been made, because you took the envelope," Arthur whispered hoarsely. "Now it will all come out into the open. Madeline's reputation will be ruined. Bernice will be crushed. And all because of me."

"No." Amy stepped forward quickly and patted him on the shoulder. "Don't worry, Arthur. Owen will take care of everything. He'll find out who the blackmailer is and stop him before anything else happens."

Owen stared at her. "I will?"

She gave him a bracing smile. "Of course you will."

Owen narrowed his eyes. She had apparently forgotten that she had hired him to discover Arthur Crabshaw's secrets. He had done precisely that. Nothing had been said about saving Crabshaw's rear. "Uh, Amy, maybe we'd better discuss this out on the porch."

"Later, Owen. Right now we need to figure out how to keep the blackmailer silent."

"The quickest way to pull the blackmailer's teeth is to call his bluff," Owen said.

"I can't risk it," Arthur whispered.

"Of course not," Amy murmured. "Owen will handle this."

Arthur sighed heavily. "What can Sweet do? It's too late to replace the money. I left that envelope in the rest room shortly after ten this morning. It's nearly five. By now the blackmailer will have checked the toilet tank lid and realized that I didn't follow his instructions. He'll be furious."

"Don't fret about it, Crabshaw," Owen said. "There will definitely be a second chance. And a third and fourth chance, as well. If we allow this thing to go on that long."

"Which we won't," Amy said confidently.

Owen raised his brows but offered no comment. He didn't need a weather report to tell him that Amy had recently undergone a sea change.

Arthur lifted his head and gave Owen a quizzical look. "What do you mean there will be a second chance? The blackmailer said in his note that he would reveal everything if I didn't make the payments."

Owen smiled grimly. "You're a businessman, Crabshaw.

Look at this from the blackmailer's point of view. If he reveals the truth, it's all over for him. He can't expect his victim to make any more payments once the secrets are out in the open."

The anguish and frustration faded in Arthur's eyes. Intelligent perception replaced it. "Good point. I hadn't thought of that."

"The only way the blackmailer can make money is to keep quiet and apply more pressure on you," Owen said.

Amy searched his face. "That makes sense. He's got nothing to gain by revealing the truth, and everything to lose. I'd say he definitely has a strong incentive to try to persuade Arthur to continue with the payments. And when he does, we'll be ready for him, won't we."

"It's beginning to look that way."

Arthur stared at Owen with dawning hope. "You're going to help me?"

Owen looked at Amy, who gave him a glowing smile. He was briefly dazzled by it. He wondered if it was her sign-here-and-you've-got-yourself-a-house smile. He'd never actually seen that smile because when he'd bought the Draycott place from her, he'd almost had to type up the papers himself. She had tried to talk him out of the deal right up until the ink was dry. He had to admit the smile was very effective.

"Something tells me I don't have a lot of choice," Owen said.

Owen waited until he heard the shower stop in Amy's room. He killed a few more minutes pacing his room and then strode to the connecting door. He knocked peremptorily.

"Come in, I'm decent," Amy called.

That was unfortunate, Owen thought wistfully. He yanked open the door. "I want to talk to you."

"Yes?" Amy met his gaze in the mirror. She was dressed in a pair of blue silk trousers and a matching silk tunic that turned her eyes into jewels.

For a few seconds Owen just stood there, transfixed by the sight of her putting a gold earring on one delicate ear. Desire swept through him, hot, unexpected, and laced with longing. Damn. This was getting bad, he thought. Very, very bad.

"Is something wrong?" Amy prompted.

Owen took refuge in righteous irritation. He braced one hand against the doorframe. "Mind telling me what happened in Crabshaw's living room this afternoon?"

"What do you mean?" She finished attaching the earring and turned to face him. "We're going to help Arthur. What's so complicated about that?"

"Amy, you told me you wanted to prove he was concealing something. Okay, I proved it. Case closed."

Her eyes widened. "For heaven's sake, Owen, we can't stop there. Bernice loves him, and this afternoon I finally concluded that he loves her. We have to help him."

"I had a feeling you were going to say that. What the hell made you decide that Arthur is a good guy after all?"

"Intuition. And the fact that he's trying to play the gentleman for Madeline's and Bernice's sake."

"The gentleman?"

"A man who cares about a lady's reputation and who doesn't want to see anyone hurt, even thirty years after the affair, must have a strong sense of honor. A man like that will do right by my aunt."

"Sometimes I forget that you write romance novels in addition to selling real estate," Owen muttered.

She smiled. "Ready to go down to dinner?"

Two hours later Owen stood with Amy on the veranda that ran the length of the Villantry Inn and contemplated night-shrouded Villantry Park. The summer evening was cool but not cold. The tang of the sea was in the air. Bernice and Arthur had left the Inn after dinner. Owen finally had Amy to himself.

Amy and her case, he amended silently.

"Want to take a walk?" he asked.

Amy nodded. "Sounds lovely."

He took her arm, and together they went down the steps and strolled into the park. The globes of the tall, old-fashioned lamps that lit the paths cast a warm glow. The Friday night band concert had just concluded its performance. People streamed out of the park.

By the time Owen had got Amy as far as the pond, the crowd had dwindled to a handful. Owen studied the library through the trees and rhododendron bushes. It was closed for the day, but the lights were on inside.

Everything about this case seemed to center on the library.

"Looks like someone's working late tonight," he said, indicating the building on the far side of the park.

"Maybe some of the people in charge of the dedication ceremonies are holding a last-minute meeting."

"Let's see what's going on." Drawn by the force of his curiosity, Owen steered Amy along the path that meandered toward the library.

Amy glanced at him speculatively. "Are we going to look for clues?"

"Have I ever told you that you have an overactive imagination?"

"I believe you've mentioned it once or twice. So, what are we going to do?"

"I'm not sure. I just want to have a look around. It occurs to me that even though the public library rest room is not a bad choice on the part of the blackmailer, it is a little unusual. Whoever he is, he must feel quite comfortable there."

"A librarian?"

"Maybe."

The path that led to the library was deserted. The trees and shrubs that grew in this portion of the grounds were among the oldest in Villantry Park. They blocked the light from the tall lamps and deepened the already thick shadows on the graveled walk.

Owen and Amy had almost reached the library when the front door opened. Voices floated out into the night. Several people appeared in the entrance. Owen brought Amy to a halt in the shadows.

"You were right," he said softly. "Looks like a committee meeting breaking up."

They watched the small group cluster for a few minutes on the broad steps in front of the building, exchanging pleasantries. Madeline Villantry appeared in the doorway. Raymond Junior was with her. Raymond appeared terminally bored, as usual.

"Is everything taken care of inside, Betty?" Madeline asked.

"Yes, I think so, Madeline." A silver-haired matron paused on the steps. "Eugene will turn off the lights and lock up."

"I'll see you all tomorrow evening at the ceremony, then," Madeline said. "Good night, everyone. And thank you once again for your time and effort."

The committee members moved off in various directions. Most headed toward the small parking lot on the far side of the park.

Madeline and Raymond started along the path that would take them past Owen and Amy.

Owen automatically started to pull Amy into the bushes, then realized belatedly that the rhodies were impenetrable and opted for another means of concealment.

He drew Amy into a passionate embrace in the shadows.

"What are you doing?" Amy hissed, startled.

"Don't want 'em to see us," Owen muttered. "Kiss me. Make it look good."

She hesitated only briefly, more out of surprise than anything else, Owen realized. And then she was kissing him back. Her arms locked around his neck. Her mouth opened for him.

Owen's priorities shifted in a heartbeat. The problem of Madeline and Raymond suddenly dwindled dramatically in importance. All that mattered was the taste and feel of Amy.

He folded her close, hungry for the essence of her, frustrated by clothing, location, and a possible audience.

Amy's mouth was warm and moist and inviting. The gentle curves of her breasts were crushed against his chest. Her soft, muffled whimper of excitement threatened to make him lose control.

The scrape of shoes on gravel, a mildly disapproving murmur, and a soft masculine chuckle brought Owen back to reality. Madeline and Raymond were passing directly behind him now. They had obviously seen the couple in the shadows. Owen hoped that the darkness and the manner in which he was enveloping Amy combined to provide effective concealment.

"Some people have no sense of propriety," Madeline said coolly.

"Some people have all the luck," Raymond drawled.

The sound of footsteps on gravel receded into the distance. Owen waited until he was sure Madeline and Raymond were gone and then raised his head. He looked down at Amy, aware that his pulse was still beating heavily and his insides were clenched.

Amy regarded him with eyes that were pools of unfathomable promise. Her lips were still slightly parted.

Owen thought optimistically of the connecting rooms that awaited them back at the Inn. He took a deep breath and released Amy. "We'll get back to this a little later."

"We will?" She sounded pleased.

"First things first," he said manfully. "I want to check out the library's back door."

He took her hand and started around the building. There were no tall lamps in the drive behind the library. The only light was from the moon and a weak yellow bulb set above the library's service entrance. A row of city utility trucks was lined up on the far side of the drive. The graveled area apparently served as a parking lot for Villantry's service vehicles.

"Why are we going to look at the back door of the library?" Amy asked.

"Because I like to know all the entrances and exits in a situation such as this. I wouldn't be surprised if the next blackmail note Crabshaw gets instructs him to make the payment tomorrow night."

"During the dedication festivities?" Amy glanced at him in surprise as she hurried to keep pace with him. "Why then?"

"Think about it. The library will be swarming with people. That means there will be a steady stream of traffic in and out of the rest rooms. Perfect cover for the blackmailer."

"I get it," Amy said enthusiastically. "You're going to stake out the men's room, right?"

"Right. I'll bet you can see now why I became a big-time private eye."

"Because of the thrilling excitement?"

"Just think about it. Staking out a men's room. Got to be the fulfillment of every young man's dreams of swashbuckling adventure."

"Yes, of course. I envy you."

"From what you've told me, real estate has its moments, too."

"Don't remind me." Amy smiled briefly. Then she frowned in the shadows. "But, Owen, I don't see how you can be so certain that the note—" She broke off suddenly as one of the city trucks roared to life. "What in the world?"

Across the drive, a set of headlights flashed on at full beam, blinding Owen. He realized that he and Amy were pinned in the glare. And to think he had accused Amy of looking like a deer caught in headlights. This was the real thing, Owen thought. He couldn't see what was happening. But he could hear all too well.

Tires screeched as the big vehicle shot forward. The truck bore down on Owen and Amy with deadly intent.

7

AMY HAD BARELY REGISTERED THE BLINDING LIGHT WHEN SHE heard Owen suck in his breath.

"Damn," he whispered.

In the next instant she felt his arm wrap around her waist with the force of a steel band. He lifted her off her feet and hauled her up the three steps that led to the library's back entrance.

The truck engine thundered.

"Owen."

"In here. Move. He may have a gun."

Owen half-pulled, half-carried her into the shadows of the small alcove that concealed the doorway. Then he shoved her hard against the stone wall and held her there. She gasped for breath, dimly aware that he was shielding her with his body.

The city truck came so close to the steps that Amy was almost convinced it would plow straight through the back door of the library.

But at the last possible instant, it veered aside. With an

angry howl it lumbered off into the night, a ravenous beast deprived of its prey.

Owen did not move as the sound of the truck engine receded into the darkness. Amy was pressed so tightly against the cold stone she could feel the grit on her cheek.

"You okay?" Owen finally asked. His voice was curiously flat.

"Yes. I think so."

He slowly stepped back, releasing her. "Son of a bitch." There was no emotion in the phrase. "He was aiming for us. You could have been hurt. Killed."

Amy hugged herself. The unnaturally even tone in Owen's voice was somehow more frightening than the near miss. This was a whole new side to the man. A dangerous side.

"An accident," she said, grasping for a more reasonable explanation than the one Owen had concocted. "Some kid taking a joyride in a city truck."

"Maybe, but I doubt it. I have a hunch that it was attempted murder."

Amy was dazed. "You think that the blackmailer was behind the wheel?"

"I think there's a very high probability of that, yes."

"But how could he know that you're a threat to him? As far as everyone in town is concerned, you're just my fiancé."

"My guess is that he doesn't know I'm out to trap him," Owen said quietly. "It's more likely that he's figured out that I took Crabshaw's money before he could get to it. I told you that I thought he was in the library yesterday, watching the payoff. He saw me go into the rest room after Crabshaw left. And when he went to make the pickup there was no envelope."

"So he leaped to the conclusion that you had gotten to it ahead of him. But following that logic, how does he think you learned of the payoffs and where they were made?"

Owen frowned. "Maybe he figures that I accidentally discovered the envelope. Or he may think that Crabshaw confided in me. Who knows? He probably believes that you and I are in this together."

"Perhaps he was simply trying to frighten us away from Villantry," Amy suggested slowly.

"It's possible that was his goal." Owen took her hand.

"Where are we going?"

"To wake the local chief of police."

Amy instantly dug in her heels. "But, Owen, if you tell him about this, you'll have to tell him everything. I don't want to betray Arthur's confidence unless we must."

"Don't worry. I'm a professional, remember? I know how to talk to a cop."

Amy looked at him. "What does that mean?"

"Don't ask. It's a trade secret."

"Some joyridin' kid, no doubt." George P. Hawkins, chief of police of Villantry, poured himself a cup of coffee.

Amy smiled weakly. "That's what I said."

"Or a drunken transient." Hawkins carried the cup back to his desk and lowered his considerable bulk into the chair. "Happens once in a while. Come mornin' we'll find the truck abandoned outside of town or in a ditch. You'll see."

Owen lounged against the wall near the office window and studied Hawkins with brooding speculation. "Whoever was behind the wheel aimed directly for us. If we hadn't made it up the steps and into the alcove, we wouldn't be here talking to you now."

Hawkins squinted at Owen. "Which brings up an interestin' point. Mind tellin' me just what you two were doin' out there behind the library at this hour of the night?"

Amy caught Owen's eye and held her breath. She could hardly blame him if he told Hawkins the whole story, but a part of her still wanted to protect Arthur Crabshaw.

Owen shrugged. "Amy and I took a walk in the park after the band concert."

"The park I can understand," Hawkins said. "But what the hell were you doin' behind the library buildin'?"

"Looking for privacy," Owen said smoothly. "We got there just as some meeting was ending. We went around the corner to avoid the crowd."

Hawkins gave him a man-to-man look. "You two want privacy, you better leave Villantry. This is a small town. Everyone knows everyone else's business here."

"Is that a fact?" Owen asked politely.

"It's a fact, all right."

Owen straightened away from the wall. "Then it shouldn't take too long to find out who was behind the wheel of that city truck, should it? If and when you do find out who nearly ran us down tonight you can reach us at the Villantry Inn."

Hawkins glowered at him. "I know where you're stayin'."

Owen smiled coldly. "Right. This is a small town. You know everything."

"Yep. I also know you two got connectin' rooms at the Villantry Inn. Try usin' them next time, instead of takin' a walk in the park."

"What a rude man," Amy said as they walked into the Inn lobby a short while later.

"Hawkins is a cop," Owen said with a surprisingly philosophical air. "Rudeness is a job requirement."

"I fail to see why."

"You wouldn't if you ever took a job as a cop."

The front desk clerk, a thin young man with thick glasses, smiled tentatively at Owen. "Mr. Sweet, there's a message for you. From Arthur Crabshaw. He wants you to call him."

"Thanks." Owen paused at the front desk to collect the slip of paper.

Amy was aware of the tension in his hand as he guided her toward the stairs. She said nothing as they walked up the one flight to their rooms. When they started down the hall, she slanted a questioning glance at Owen's set face.

"What is it?"

"I won't know for sure until I return Crabshaw's call. But I can make a guess."

"Oh, my God, you don't think—"

"Shush." Owen opened the door of her room and ushered her inside.

Amy turned, expecting him to go next door to his own

61

room. Instead, he stepped through her door and closed it behind him. She raised her brows.

Owen smiled faintly as he switched on a light. "No point being coy, is there? We're supposed to be engaged. Hell, even the local chief of police knows we've got connecting rooms."

Amy flushed. "Yes, I know, but—"

"When you go undercover, you've got to make it look real or it won't work."

"I keep forgetting you're the professional here," Amy muttered.

"I've noticed." He went to the table, picked up the phone, and dialed the number on the slip of paper.

"Arthur? This is Owen Sweet. Yeah, I got your message. What's up?" Owen fell silent, listening for a moment. "I hear you. Calm down."

Amy watched anxiously.

"Right. Tomorrow night," Owen said. "Just as I thought. Follow instructions exactly. We're going to nail the bastard this time. I'm not in the mood to give him any more rope. He just tried to run us down. No, I'm not joking. Amy could have been killed." Owen paused. "Yes, I'm sure it was him. A kid? That's what Amy thinks, too, but I'm not a great believer in coincidences."

Amy waited until he had hung up the phone. "Another blackmail note?"

Owen nodded. "Arthur says it arrived earlier this evening. He's to leave the money in the library rest room tomorrow night."

"Just as you suspected." Amy was impressed. "But why would the blackmailer use the same location over and over again?"

"He probably can't think of a safer place. The rest room is still the one spot where any man in town can be seen with no questions asked. And as I told you, it will be busier than usual tomorrow night because of the crowd."

Amy nibbled thoughtfully on her lower lip. "If the blackmailer suspects that you know about the payoffs, he'll be nervous when he sees you at the dedication ceremonies tomorrow evening."

"Not necessarily. He realizes that although he knows who I am, I don't know who he is. He can go in and out of the men's room just as freely as I or any other man in the crowd can. But he won't take any chances this time. He'll make it a point to get in there right after Crabshaw. He won't know that I know about the drop-off. He'll think it's safe to go in as soon as he can."

"Before you have a chance to grab the money?"

"Right."

Amy listened to the silence from the adjoining room for a long time before she couldn't stand it any longer. She could almost hear Owen's brain grinding away in solitude.

It struck her that he had probably spent a lot of his life alone. The very nature of his chosen profession indicated that he was accustomed to relying solely on himself. There was a core of strength in Owen Sweet that rarely developed in those who relied on other people.

He possessed an old-fashioned, Wild West sort of character, she thought. He was the kind of man who, a century earlier, would have ridden into town alone, cleaned out the bad guys, and then left without a backward glance.

She pushed aside the covers, got out of bed, and padded to the closed door that linked the two rooms. She put her ear against the wooden panel and listened. Still no sound. But she was certain that he was not asleep.

She knocked once, very softly. Owen opened the door immediately.

Almost as if he had been waiting for her.

She smiled tremulously up at him. "You're not in bed."

"I'm thinking."

"I know." She shivered. "I can't sleep, either. I keep seeing those headlights coming straight toward us."

"Amy." He drew her into his arms. "I'm sorry."

Amy felt something inside her begin to relax. She rested her head on his shoulder. "It's all my fault. I'm the one who should be sorry."

"For what?"

"For getting you into this mess. I swear, I never had any idea that this would get so complicated."

He framed her face in his powerful hands. His eyes gleamed in the shadows. "You don't have a clue just how complicated things have gotten, do you?"

Before she could answer, his mouth was on hers.

His kiss was different this time. Instead of reckless eagerness and hot passion, there was gentleness and a tender warmth. Amy gave herself up to the sweet persuasion without a single qualm.

"Amy?" His voice was ragged but under control.

"Yes," she whispered. "Yes, yes, yes."

"Thank God," Owen whispered against her throat. "I thought I was going to go crazy."

He picked her up and carried her through the doorway into his room, then set her down amid the turned-back sheets of his bed. She looked up at him with dawning wonder as he stripped off his shirt and jeans.

She loved him.

The realization came with quiet certainty, not as a bolt out of the blue. Amy knew that she had recognized the truth deep inside weeks ago. She reached up to take him into her arms.

Owen came to her then.

His body was heavy with desire. Amy felt him shudder at her touch. His hands trembled slightly as he eased aside her quilted robe.

"I've never wanted anything so much in my life," he said against her mouth.

He kissed her throat as he undressed her. And then he lowered his mouth to her breasts. Heat flooded Amy's body. Owen's hand slid upward along her leg, squeezing gently. His fingers moved to the inside of her thigh. Amy gasped.

Owen covered her mouth once more, drinking in the small sound she made. He cupped her softness and then probed, opening her to his intimate touch. She gave another muffled cry and clutched at his shoulders. A frantic sense of urgency stormed through her.

Owen continued the tender torment, stoking the flames within Amy until she could not stand it any longer. She twisted on the sheets.

"Owen, please." She parted her legs and fought to pull him to her. "Please."

"I think I've been waiting for this forever." Owen leaned across Amy to open a drawer in the bedside table.

The movement brought his broad, strong chest directly over Amy's face. She kissed one flat, male nipple and ran her fingers through the curling hair that surrounded it. Then she reached down between their damp bodies to stroke him. It was like touching warm steel. Owen was utterly rigid with his need. Hard and hot and throbbing. When her fingertips moved on him he shuddered. Amy's body responded with another tidal wave of heat.

A moment later Owen was ready. He moved between her thighs, braced himself on his elbows, and looked down at her with burning eyes. He held her gaze as he pushed slowly, carefully, deliberately into her. Amy drew in a sharp breath as her small muscles stretched to accommodate him.

And then he was inside, filling her completely.

"*Amy.*" There was a world of wonder and need in the single word.

Owen began to move. Amy took flight. Mindlessly, she gave herself up to the delicious, spiraling tension. It was unlike anything she had ever experienced. She heard her own voice calling Owen's name over and over again.

And then, without warning, her climax exploded in a series of rippling vibrations that sent pleasure to every nerve in her body. Amy was breathless. All she could do was cling to Owen as the world whirled around her.

She was vaguely aware of his fierce, hoarse shout of

masculine satisfaction. He surged into her one last time. She felt every muscle in him tighten.

After a long, long moment, Owen shuddered and collapsed along the length of her. Together they drifted in the darkness, locked in each other's arms.

A long while later, she stirred beside Owen. She stretched languidly, aware of a sense of joyous satisfaction. Before she could even begin to savor her newfound love, a thought struck her. She sat bolt upright in bed.

"Good grief, Owen."

"What's the matter?" Owen sounded like a sleepy lion that had recently been very well fed.

"I just thought of something." She turned to look down at him. "If you're right in thinking that it was the blackmailer who tried to run us down tonight, then that means that it was a . . . what do you call it?"

"A crime of opportunity?"

"Right, exactly. A crime of opportunity. After all, he couldn't have known we'd be walking behind the library at that hour. He must have followed us."

"Maybe." Owen sounded unconvinced.

"You think there's another possibility?"

"Amy, there are lots of possibilities. It could have been one of the people who attended that meeting in the library tonight or someone who was wandering around in the park after the band concert. Whoever it was, he saw us and recognized us, in spite of the fact that we were wrapped up in each other's arms."

"No great trick, I suppose, when you think about it. This is a town in which everyone knows everyone else. We must stand out like sore thumbs, even in the dark."

"Yeah."

Amy had a sudden vision of Madeline Villantry's son. She recalled his comment as he had walked past Amy and Owen. "You don't think Raymond Junior is behind this, do you? I think he might have recognized us tonight."

"We'll find out tomorrow night." Owen tugged her down

on top of him. "In the meantime, I've got better things to do."

She smiled demurely. "I suppose you want to get some sleep."

"Hell, no. Us private eyes can go for days without a good night's sleep. It's in the genes."

8

... AND SO I AM PROUD TO DEDICATE THE NEW WING OF THE
Raymond C. Villantry Memorial Public Library." Madeline
Villantry's cultured tones rang out from the speaker's
podium that had been set up in the center of the library.
"We should all be proud of our community's commitment
to literacy. A free nation cannot exist without such a
commitment. I thank you, friends and neighbors. I salute all
of you who helped make our fine library what it is today."

Enthusiastic applause broke out from the large crowd
gathered in the library. Madeline Villantry smiled gracious-
ly from the lectern.

Owen leaned toward Amy, who was standing next to him
in the throng. "You get the feeling she really means all that
talk about progress and literacy?"

"Yes, I do," Amy said resolutely. "I know she looks like
she's trying out for the role of Queen of Villantry, but Aunt
Bernice and Arthur believe that Madeline is honestly com-
mitted to this town's welfare. I think they're right."

"Maybe. But I'm not so sure about Raymond Junior over
there. I have a hunch he's not the altruistic sort."

"I won't argue that point." Amy scrutinized Raymond, who was following his mother down from the small speaker's stand. "But who knows? Maybe he'll learn."

"I won't hold my breath." Owen stopped clapping. He kept his eyes on the door of the men's room as the crowd broke up and began to mill around.

Amy stood on tiptoe in an effort to see over the heads of the people swarming in front of her. "What's happening?"

"Crabshaw went inside the men's room a few minutes ago. He just came back out. Now he's headed outside to join your aunt at the punch table."

"Darn, I can't see a thing."

"I can," Owen assured her.

There had been a light but steady stream of males coming and going through the swinging men's room door during the past hour. Tredgett, the janitor, had been busy as he made a heroic effort to keep up with the demands that had been placed upon the facilities. As Owen watched, Tredgett emerged from the women's room, removed the small sign he had temporarily placed in the doorway, and wheeled his bucket and mop next door to the men's room.

Raymond Junior followed the janitor inside.

Amy peered at Owen. "So? What do you see?"

"Someone who's bent on cleaning up," Owen said softly.

"What the heck does that mean?"

"It means that this case is almost concluded." He gave her a repressive look, aware that he had to be forceful and authoritative if he wanted Amy to follow orders. She didn't seem to take them any better than he did. "Wait right here. I'll be back in a few minutes."

Amy's eyes widened. "Where are you going? Did you spot the blackmailer?"

"Yeah."

"I'll come with you."

"No, you will not. You will do as you're told. I'm not taking any more chances with your neck."

"But, Owen, what can possibly happen here?"

"That's what I said to myself last night when we made

that little detour behind the library," he muttered. "Stay put."

Without glancing over his shoulder to see if Amy had obeyed him, Owen slipped away from her side and began to ease through the crowd. The conversations ebbed and flowed around him.

In a few minutes it would all be over, Owen thought as he made his way toward the men's room. The identity of the blackmailer was obvious. It should have been from the beginning, but Owen admitted to himself that he'd been distracted by more personal considerations.

It was time to confront the culprit, wrap up the case, and get back to worrying about the more important dilemma he faced. Nabbing a blackmailer was simple compared with the problem of trying to figure out if Amy loved him.

He'd been sweating that out since he had awakened to an empty bed this morning. His initial response to the discovery that Amy was not lying beside him had been a surge of emotion that he knew came very close to something that could be labeled fear. For a terrible instant his sleep-fogged brain had registered an anguished sense of loss. Amy was gone.

Reality had returned with the sound of the shower in her room. She had not left him in the middle of the night. She had merely risen to take her morning bath.

Owen had taken a deep breath and regained his usually unshakable sense of control. But he had not been able to shake the memory of the unnerving sensation he had experienced when he had found himself alone in the bed.

The door of the men's room swung open. Raymond Junior strolled out. He paused for a moment to search the crowd. His gaze fell on Owen. He nodded sternly and then turned to walk toward the knot of people gathered around his mother.

Owen propped one shoulder against the wall and watched the swinging door. He did not have to wait long. It soon opened again.

Tredgett, the janitor, emerged, dragging his bucket behind

him. Without looking at anyone, he trundled off toward a door at the far side of the central gallery.

Owen followed at a leisurely pace. When he reached the door, he went through it quietly. He found himself in a dimly lit storage room. Stacks of aging magazines and newspapers lined one wall. The shelves on the opposite wall were filled with dusty books that looked as if they were awaiting repair.

There was no sign of the janitor, but a sliver of light gleamed beneath a closed closet door. Owen smiled humorlessly. He went toward the closet and opened the door. He found himself gazing into a small space filled with mops, sponges, and other assorted janitorial equipment.

Tredgett was inside the closet. He was busy counting the bills he had just removed from a plain white envelope. He jumped at the sight of Owen.

"Busy day," Owen observed.

Panic and rage lit Tredgett's eyes. He clutched the money in one fist. "Damn you," he whispered. "Who the hell are you, anyway? Why have you been nosing around in my business?"

"I'm the naturally curious type."

Tredgett's face worked furiously. "Bastard. I warned you last night. If you and your lady friend think I'm going to share this money with you, you're crazy."

"The janitor," Amy murmured from the shadows behind Owen. "Of course. The one man who is always going in and out of rest rooms."

Owen groaned. "Amy, I told you to wait outside."

"I couldn't let you finish this alone."

Tredgett's desperate gaze shifted wildly from Owen to Amy and back again. "Leave me alone or I'll tell all." He picked up a jar of cleaning solvent and hurled it at Owen.

Owen easily sidestepped the jar. Unfortunately, in the process, he collided with Amy, who had come up behind him. She yelped as she fetched up against a row of metal bookshelves. The shelves shuddered beneath the impact. Several tattered volumes cascaded down from the top shelf.

Owen whirled around at the sound of the toppling books. "Amy, look out."

She reacted instantly, leaping aside. Two heavy volumes struck the floor at her feet, barely missing her head.

Tredgett seized the opportunity. He burst out of the janitorial closet and made for the back door.

"You okay?" Owen asked Amy.

"I'm okay. Owen, be careful."

He whirled around and sprinted after Tredgett, who was already at the back door.

It wasn't much of a contest. Tredgett was twenty years older and thirty pounds overweight. Owen caught him just outside the door. He pinned the janitor to the wall of the alcove.

"I'll tell everyone about the affair between Crabshaw and Mrs. Villantry," Tredgett blustered. "I swear I will."

"And go to jail for blackmail?" Owen asked pleasantly. "Now, why would you want to do that?"

"Crabshaw will never press charges. He'll never admit that he's been paying blackmail. You can't prove a damn thing."

"I wouldn't be too certain of that." Madeline Villantry emerged from the storage room. She was followed by Arthur and Bernice and Raymond Junior. "Arthur finally told me what was going on this morning. I informed him that if his private investigator discovered the identity of the blackmailer, I would insist that he press charges. One simply cannot tolerate this sort of thing."

"Now, Mother," Raymond began. "I think we should talk about this before we make any decisions."

"There is nothing to discuss," Madeline assured him.

Tredgett jerked furiously in Owen's grasp. "Private investigator?" He stared at Owen and then looked helplessly at Arthur Crabshaw. "You hired this damned PI?"

"I hired the damned PI," Amy said briskly. "And he's solved the case brilliantly."

"Thank you," Owen said.

"He certainly has." Bernice smiled warmly at Owen.

"Arthur also told me everything. It was very gallant of him to try to protect Madeline and me, but entirely unnecessary. Arthur's relationship with Madeline is thirty years in the past. Who cares about it now?"

"Precisely," Madeline murmured. "My parents are dead and my children are adults. There is no one left to protect."

Arthur looked at Owen. "You were right. The best way to pull the blackmailer's teeth was to tell everyone involved what was going on."

"It's usually the easiest way to put a stop to this kind of thing," Owen said.

Raymond Junior scowled in confusion. "For God's sake, Mother, are you telling me that you and Arthur Crabshaw had an affair thirty years ago? And that the janitor knew about it?"

"Eugene Tredgett used to work for Villantry," Madeline explained. She gave Tredgett a disgusted look. "Apparently he saw something that was none of his business."

"No one ever notices the janitor," Tredgett muttered.

"Good God." Raymond looked scandalized. "I can't believe this."

"Don't worry about it, Raymond." Madeline turned to go back into the library. "It's none of your business, either. These things sometimes happen, even in the best of families. Now, stop blathering on about it. We have our civic duty to perform this evening."

"But, Mother . . ." Raymond hurried after Madeline. The pair vanished into the shadows.

Arthur took Bernice's hand. He looked at Owen. "I owe you."

"No you don't," Owen said. "Amy is the one who hired me. She's already taken care of the bill."

Shock and pain replaced the admiration that had lit Amy's eyes a moment earlier. Too late, Owen realized that she had misinterpreted his words. She thought he meant that he had taken last night's lovemaking as payment for services rendered.

Police Chief Hawkins lumbered out of the storage room

gloom. "What the hell's going on? Mrs. Villantry said I was needed out here." He paused when he caught sight of Owen. "Damn. Shoulda guessed that this would involve you, Sweet. You know something? We've had more trouble in the forty-eight hours you've been in town than we've had in a year."

"Just doing my civic duty, Chief."

"Sure." Hawkins squinted at the defeated Tredgett. "Any chance you'll do it somewhere else in the future?"

"Count on it," Owen said.

Owen stood on his side of the doorway that linked the two Inn rooms and watched Amy as she packed her suitcase. This was the first opportunity he'd had to speak to her in private since Eugene Tredgett had been taken into custody earlier in the evening. He'd been waiting for this moment for hours. Now that it was here, he couldn't seem to find the right words.

Amy had been determinedly cheerful and aggressively polite while they had been in the company of others. It seemed to Owen that she had chattered on about everything under the sun except their relationship. She had finally fallen silent when they had climbed the stairs to the connecting rooms.

"Amy . . ."

"I'm almost packed," she assured him as she stuffed a pair of jeans into the suitcase. "I know you want to be on the road first thing in the morning. We'll be able to leave right after breakfast."

"Forget it. I'm not worried about leaving on time." Owen shoved his hands into his back pockets. "Amy, I want to talk to you."

"I'm listening." She disappeared into the bathroom to check for any items she might have left on the sink.

Irritation replaced some of Owen's uneasiness. "I'm trying to have a relationship discussion out here," he called.

She emerged from the bathroom with her quilted robe

over her arm. "Good thing I checked the hook on the door. I almost forgot my robe."

Owen gazed at the robe with a shattering sense of longing. "Amy, I think you misunderstood something I said tonight. When I told Crabshaw that you had paid for my services, I didn't mean it the way I think you think I meant it."

"Really?" She came to a halt in the middle of the room. "How did you mean it?"

"I just meant that you and I had a separate understanding."

She stood very still, clutching her robe. "Do we?"

"I thought so."

"What sort of 'understanding' do we have, Owen?"

Owen began to feel desperate. He was no good at this kind of thing. "For God's sake, didn't last night mean anything to you?"

"Everything."

"I realize we haven't known each other very long." Owen shoved a hand through his hair. "I had planned to take it slow. I wanted you to get to know me. I wanted you to—" He broke off abruptly. "What did you say?"

"I said that last night meant everything to me." Amy's eyes were brilliant. "What about you?"

A joyous hope welled up inside him. He was dazzled by the brilliant colors that suddenly lit his world. "It meant everything to me, too. Amy, I love you."

"I love you, Owen." Amy dropped the robe and opened her arms.

Owen gathered her close and kissed her for a very long time. "Something tells me we're not going to get much sleep tonight," he said eventually. "Maybe we'd better not try to get that early-morning start after all."

"If we don't check out before noon, they'll charge us for an extra night," Amy warned him.

"Don't worry about it." Owen picked her up and carried her through the connecting door into his room. "I'll just put the extra night on my expense account."

JAYNE ANN KRENTZ, who also writes under the pen name Amanda Quick, is the author of sixteen consecutive *New York Times* bestsellers, and has more than twenty million copies of her books in print.

In addition to writing fiction, she is the editor of and a contributor to *Dangerous Men and Adventurous Women: Romance Writers on the Appeal of the Romance,* a collection of essays published by the University of Pennsylvania Press.

Jayne has believed in the importance of romance fiction since the beginning of her publishing career. With each passing year she grows more convinced of its significance and its contributions to the lives of women everywhere.

She is married and lives in the Pacific Northwest.

LINDA LAEL MILLER

Resurrection

1

NOBODY IN PLENTIFUL WOULD HAVE BLAMED MISS EMMELINE if she'd put a bullet right between Gil Hartwell's eyes, showing up out of nowhere the way he did, and after all that time had gone by. It only made matters worse that she'd defended him every day of those seven years, swearing up and down that Gil was dead, for he'd surely have come back to her otherwise. Most everybody else figured Gil had taken up with another woman, or gotten himself thrown into jail, though the compassionate ones kept their opinions to themselves.

Emmeline was teetering on top of a stool in the fragrant garden just off the screened veranda that fateful afternoon of his return, hanging the last of several dozen brightly colored paper lanterns from one of the lines she'd strung between the house and the sturdy oaks her grandmother had planted as a bride.

"Miss Emmeline?"

She froze at the sound of that dear and well-remembered voice, and the stool, precariously positioned in the soft, sweet grass, swayed wildly. She flung her arms out wide in a desperate bid for balance, and would have hurtled to the ground if two strong hands hadn't closed around her waist just in the nick of time. Even that simple touch sent unseemly sensations ricocheting through Emmeline, and she put a trembling hand to her heart as she turned to face the man who had broken her heart.

Emmeline was not given to swooning. Though slender, she was tall for a woman, and strong, and she generally took a pragmatic view of things. For all of that, her head felt light enough to float away, like a soap bubble, and her heart was pounding so that she could barely catch her breath.

"Gil," she whispered, amazed, stricken. He was solid and real, though thinner than she remembered. His dark hair was in want of barbering, and the fiercely blue eyes held a mixture of tenderness, humor, and some hard-won wisdom. He was wearing the plain, sensible suit he'd worn to their wedding.

"Sit down," Gil said hoarsely, and took her elbow.

Emmeline allowed him to lead her to the wooden bench next to the rose arbor and seat her there. "Where have you been?" she asked, at last, in a raw whisper. Along with joyous disbelief, she was beginning to feel a cold, quiet fury.

Gil took a seat at the end of the bench, holding his battered hat by the brim, letting it dangle between his knees. He took in the carefully decorated garden with a sweep of his eyes and smiled, showing the fine white teeth she had always admired. "I didn't stay away by choice, Emmeline," he said quietly. "I want to tell you everything, and I plan to, if you're inclined to listen, but it's not a simple story, nor a short one. It needs telling in private, and from the looks of things, you're planning some kind of celebration."

Emmeline swallowed hard and willed herself not to break down and sob. She'd loved this man with the whole of her being, and gone to his home and his bed in innocence, as a trusting and pliant bride. Gently and with infinite patience, he had taught her the intimate rites of marriage, and she had responded to his attentions with such primitive abandon that she blushed to recall it, even now.

80

Still, seven precious years had gone by, years during which Emmeline might have borne children and made a fine home. She had mourned Gil Hartwell without reservation, but she'd finally managed to set aside her grief and get on with her life.

Tears blurred her vision as she gazed at him. A shameless desire possessed her; she wanted to take him by the hand, lead him up the rear stairs to her bedroom, and close the door against the world while she lost herself in his caresses.

"This is my wedding day, Gil," she said instead.

He stood up suddenly, but instead of looming over her, he turned, so that his back was to her. She watched as he set his shoulders, and pressed her hand to her bosom when he faced her again.

"You already have a husband," Gil pointed out, in a quiet voice.

Emmeline dashed at her tears with the back of one hand. "Yes," she said, reeling with joy and heartbreak, wild anger and the tenderest of affections, "it appears that I do. Not that I'd have known it by your behavior, Mr. Hartwell."

Gil drew near and dropped to one knee before her, looking up into her wet eyes. "Do you love this other man?" he asked gruffly. "If you do, if you want him—"

She couldn't help herself; she reached out then, and touched the beloved face, ever so lightly, with her fingertips, half expecting Gil to dissolve, like the visions she'd conjured so many times. "There won't be a wedding today," she said. "But that doesn't mean you're forgiven, Gil Hartwell." She withdrew her hand. "How do I know, for one thing, that you don't already have a wife waiting somewhere else, with a whole houseful of children?"

"You'll have to trust me, I reckon," he answered, with a sad smile. Gil raised himself from his knee and took a seat on the bench again, but this time he didn't keep his distance. He sat disturbingly close, and Emmeline was aware of him in every nerve ending. "Is that what the good people of Plentiful believed, Emmeline? That I left you for some other woman?"

"Yes," she said, and she had to push the word out of her mouth, it was so hard to say. She had suffered greatly from the gossip that surrounded Gil's disappearance, and she dreaded the idea of going through the singular agonies of it all over again.

"And what did you believe?"

"That you were dead," Emmeline replied, as fury swelled within her again, fresh and bitter. "I even erected a fancy monument to your memory, over in the churchyard. Would you like to see it?"

Gil flinched slightly, in mock horror, and though there was humor in his eyes, it was tempered, as before, with some deep and very private pain. Before he could reply, a third voice spoke from behind them.

"I was told," said Neal Montgomery, as both Gil and Emmeline turned to watch him descend the veranda steps, "that it was bad luck for the groom to see the bride the day of the wedding. I should have heeded the warning."

Emmeline had no opportunity to offer a reply, for by the time she'd recovered, Gil was on his feet, facing his old antagonist. Gil's small but well-chosen homestead, abandoned all this while, bordered Neal's much larger ranch, and there had been bad blood between them from the first. Neal had never made a secret of the fact that he wanted to annex Gil's hundred and sixty acres to his own one thousand.

"I might have known it would be you," Gil said. "How long was I gone, Montgomery, before you started courting my wife?"

Emmeline touched Gil's arm in a feeble effort to silence him, but her gaze was fixed on Neal. Tall and broad-shouldered, with fair hair and golden-amber eyes, he was a handsome man, much sought after even in Plentiful, where women, respectable or otherwise, were scarce. She sighed.

"I am sorry, Neal," she said, and if her voice was a bit tremulous, it still carried. "I certainly didn't expect this to happen."

Neal was not looking at her, but at Gil. Something intangible but innately violent passed between the two men,

82

and even though the weather had been fair for a week, a chilly breeze came up all of a sudden, causing the Chinese lanterns to rustle and flutter overhead, like dry leaves. "No," Mr. Montgomery replied. "Nor did I, my dear."

"I'll just bet you didn't," Gil answered. His eyes were slightly narrowed as he assessed Neal. "Tell me, Montgomery—did you sweet-talk Emmeline into selling you my land, or were you marrying her to get it?"

Emmeline stiffened in indignation, realized that Gil had taken a light grasp on her arm, and wrenched free of him. Since anything she'd have tried to say would have come out as an insensible sputter, she held her tongue.

Neal crossed the grass to stand a few feet away, and his fancy spurs, fashioned of pure Mexican silver, like the wide band gleaming on his hat, made faint, jingling music as he moved. His dark suit was expensive and flawlessly tailored, like his white linen shirt, and even though this was his wedding day, he wore a Colt .45 strapped low on one hip. His gaze was locked with Gil's, and a tiny muscle leaped in his jaw before he deigned to answer the other man's inflammatory question.

"I was marrying Miss Emmeline because I love her, and my plans haven't changed. Your presence is irksome, Hartwell, but probably temporary, and therefore of no real concern to me."

Gil's smile was anything but genial. He slid one arm around Emmeline's waist, and this time she didn't—couldn't—pull away. "We've got things to settle between us, Emmeline and I, and maybe when all the dust settles, she'll choose you for a husband. In the meantime, the lady is still my wife, and I'll thank you to keep a proper distance."

"A divorce should be a simple matter," Neal observed easily, even cheerfully, as he tugged at one glove and flexed his fingers under leather so thin and pliant that it fitted like a layer of skin. "God knows you've given the woman ample grounds."

Emmeline flushed. "I would like to participate in this discussion, if neither of you mind," she announced, gathering the skirts of her practical serge dress and starting toward the veranda. "It will be continued inside, in the parlor."

The two men followed her into the house in the end, but Emmeline had a few bad moments in the interim, wondering if they would engage in fisticuffs right there in the garden.

"Izannah!" she called, as soon as she'd crossed the threshold into the spacious room that had been her grandfather's study until his death eighteen months before.

Her young cousin, resplendent in her pink organza dress, glided down the main staircase as Emmeline entered the foyer. The poor girl was going to be disappointed that the wedding was being called off; social events were thin on the ground in Plentiful.

Izannah, a pretty child with brown hair and eyes, blushed fetchingly at the sight of Neal, for she found him charming. Her mouth formed a perfect O when her gaze drifted past Mr. Montgomery to rest upon Gil.

"Great Zeus," she murmured.

Gil bowed, his eyes dancing. "I am gratified, Miss Izannah," he said, "that you remember me."

"Of course I remember you," Izannah said, and though she'd come to a stop in the middle of the stairway earlier, she now descended with theatrical grace. "You were Emmeline's husband." Her complexion paled slightly as she realized the implications of this fact, and she sat heavily on the bottom step. "Good heavens," she said.

"Collect yourself," Emmeline said firmly. "You must find Ezra and ask him to spread the word around town that there isn't going to be a wedding today."

"This is quite scandalous," Izannah commented, rising from the pool of organza like Venus coming out of the sea. "Can you imagine what people will say?"

"Only too well," Emmeline muttered, swishing forward into the parlor with a grandeur that was wholly feigned. The situation might have been worse, she thought, rather frantically, as she waited for Neal and Gil to enter the inner sanctum, then calmly closed the sliding doors. It hardly bore considering, what would have happened if Gil had arrived even a day later. "Sit down, gentlemen," she said.

That room, in the heart of the house, was Emmeline's domain, and she usually felt strong there, and very much in charge of things. It would be within those walls, she decided, that she would hear Gil's mysterious tale.

Neither man honored her request to take a chair, as it turned out. Neal took up a post at the window, and Gil stood beside the cold fireplace, one hand resting on the ornately carved mantelpiece.

Emmeline began to feel dizzy again—it was so completely unlike her—and put one hand to her throat. Her pulse raced beneath her fingertips.

"Neal," she began, and because the name came out sounding like the squeak of a rusted hinge, she had to pause and clear her throat. "Mr. Montgomery," she said. "I do apologize for the shock and inconvenience this development has undoubtedly caused you." She caught a glimpse of herself in the mirror over the fireplace, being very careful to avoid meeting Gil's gaze, and saw that her dark red hair was tumbling messily from its pins. "You may be sure that I will offer you a full explanation, once I have received one myself." She cleared her throat again. "If you would be so kind as to leave Mr. Hartwell and me alone to talk—"

Neal turned from the window and crossed the room with startling speed to stand before Emmeline, glowering down into her face. Out of the corner of her eye, she saw that Gil was watchful and his arms were folded. Although he seemed poised to spring, his body was still.

"Leave you alone?" Neal demanded, a slow flush climbing his neck to pulse in his aristocratic face. "With this . . . this drifter? Emmeline, must I remind you of the scandalous fashion in which he abandoned you?"

Emmeline's throat constricted for a moment, aching, and she subdued a fresh flood of tears by sheer effort of will. In Plentiful, folks had raised personal censure to the level of an art form.

"No, Neal," she said softly. "No one needs to remind me

of that. Every pitying look I received, every whisper of gossip, has been pressed into my heart like flowers between the pages of a remembrance book. But Gil Hartwell was—is —my husband, and I will hear him out, for my own sake, if not for his."

Neal brought his emotions under control with visible effort, cast one killing glance at Gil, and laid his hands gently on Emmeline's shoulders. "If you need me . . ."

Emmeline swallowed hard. "I'll send for you," she promised.

He studied her face for a long moment, then released his hold and strode to the doors of the parlor. He lingered briefly, without speaking or turning around, before going out.

Emmeline turned slowly to her husband, who still stood next to the fireplace. He was examining a small likeness of Izannah, housed in an oval frame, a thoughtful expression on his face, and she realized that he had focused on the tintype in an effort to afford Emmeline a modicum of privacy. She could not bring herself to thank him.

"You didn't answer my question," he said, setting the frame back in its place on the mantel. "The one I asked earlier, in the garden."

Emmeline's skirts made a swishing sound as she turned away from him and with one hand gripped the back of the leather chair her grandfather had always favored. "You wanted to know if I love Neal Montgomery," she recalled.

"Yes."

She bit her lip, feeling Gil's gaze on her nape like a caress, then made herself face him. "I haven't the faintest idea," she said, in a rush of soft, defiant words. "I was bitterly lonely after you went away, and Mr. Montgomery is a fine-looking and genial man."

"With money."

Emmeline's right hand tensed; for the first time since she'd known him, she wanted to slap Gil Hartwell—slap him so hard that he'd reel from the blow. "The judge left this house to Izannah and me in his will," she said reasonably. "We had planned to turn it into a hotel, or take in boarders."

Gil raised one dark eyebrow. "But you were saved from that fate by a proposal from Mr. Montgomery," he speculated.

"It wasn't like that," Emmeline said. Her chin was trembling, and she hoped Gil couldn't see. "You know better than that. I wouldn't have married *you* if I'd wanted money, now would I?"

He smiled, then crossed the room to stand before her. "I'm sorry, Emmeline," he said. "I have no right to question any decision you might have made during these past seven years."

Tacitly, they agreed to sit down, and took seats on the horsehair settee facing the fireplace. Gil brushed the back of Emmeline's hand with his fingertips, and then enclosed it in a tentative grasp.

A silence settled between them, and they simply sat together for a little while. Emmeline spent those moments trying to moderate her heartbeat and her breathing, and to get used to the fact that the man she'd long believed to be dead was very much alive.

Finally, Gil thrust one hand through his unruly hair—in a gesture so dearly familiar that Emmeline felt a tug in her soul at the sight of it—and began to talk. To his credit, he met her gaze and did not look away.

"I guess you didn't get any of my letters," he said.

Emmeline bristled. For the first year after Gil's disappearance, hoping for word from her missing husband, she'd met every stagecoach and waited in the general store while old Mr. Dillard sorted through the mail. "I told you," she said stiffly, "I thought you were dead."

Gil sighed heavily. "Yes," he said, and sighed again. "Well, there were times when I wished I was, but it isn't my intention to burden you with my personal trials and tribulations." He raised her hand, seemingly unaware of the motion, and brushed his lips lightly across her knuckles. "I went to San Francisco to meet with a banker about a loan to buy more cattle, just like you and I agreed," he began. "Everything went well, and I was ready to catch a stage-coach back here, but the next one wasn't leaving for two days, so I decided to explore the city a little. I met up with some friends and told them all about you, and the ranch, and the steers we were about to add to the herd. We went to a saloon, the night before I was going to leave, for a farewell drink."

Emmeline straightened her shoulders and lifted her chin slightly, but offered no comment. Gil had been a reasonably temperate man during their marriage, but he had taken a drink now and again, and she had no call to think he was putting a varnish on the truth. Yet.

Gil sat back on the settee, still holding Emmeline's hand, but instead of looking into her eyes, like before, he stared off into the middle distance, as though watching a scene unfold in the ether. "I've wished I'd stayed in my room a thousand times since then," he continued presently, his voice low and rough as gravel. "But there's no sense in wanting to change the past, of course. I'd bought a brooch that day, to bring home to you, and my spirits were so high I just had to celebrate. I recall that I threw back a couple of shots of whiskey and watched the dancing girls for a while." He paused again, and lowered his head. A tremor went through him, barely perceptible, and then he faced Emmeline again. "My friends wanted to stay, so I left the saloon by myself and started back to the rooming house, by way of an alley. The last thing I recall is something striking the base of my skull. When I woke up, I was in the hold of a ship out in the harbor."

Emmeline's mouth fell open. Gil's story seemed a bit overdramatic, and she wasn't at all sure she believed it. "You were shanghaied?" she breathed. She'd thought of a thousand and one yarns he might tell just since he'd appeared in the side garden like some latter-day Lazarus, but this particular scenario hadn't occurred to her.

Gil used his free hand to rub the back of his neck, as though some shadow of pain still lingered in the bones and muscles there, and sighed again. "I spent the next six and a half years hauling lines and raising and lowering sails. Every time we made port, I tried to escape, but I never even got to the end of the wharf before I was caught and brought back."

"But finally, somehow, you got away," Emmeline whispered, marveling. She was caught up in the story, whether it was true or not.

Gil nodded, but there was no triumph in his face, only a grim, haunted expression. "We were at anchor in Sydney Harbor one quiet night, scheduled to set sail with the morning tide. The water was smooth as glass, and so clear that the moonlight reached right to the bottom."

"What happened?" Emmeline dared to inquire, barely breathing by that point.

For a moment, she thought he would fling her hand away and bolt from the room, there was such tension in him, coiled tight and ready to spring. But then Gil relaxed—by conscious choice, she could tell—and even managed a faltering smile.

"Perhaps one day I'll tell you the details, my love. For the moment, it's enough I was lucky, and got safely to shore."

Emmeline's stout heart was fluttering again, and the images were vivid in her mind. If Gil was lying, she said to herself, he'd missed his calling, choosing to scratch out a living on a small ranch; he could have made a fortune writing dime novels. "My word," she remarked, too shaken, for the moment, to say more.

Gil reached into the inside pocket of his frayed and musty coat, and when he opened his hand, a small porcelain brooch rested on his calloused palm. "This belongs to you," he said.

Nearly overcome, Emmeline gnawed at her lower lip and concentrated all her considerable energies on maintaining her composure. Then, with unsteady fingers, utterly unable to resist, she reached out and claimed the trinket. It was not an expensive piece, just a simple porcelain oval with a sheaf of golden wheat painted on in the most fragile of brush-strokes.

The thought of Gil carrying the small treasure with him, through all sorts of privations and ordeals, touched her heart in a way the prettiest and most poetic words in the language could not have done.

Her eyes were awash with fresh tears when she looked at him, holding the brooch in a tight fist and pressing that fist to her bosom. "So help me, Gil Hartwell, if I ever find out you made that up, that you bought this from some peddler in Missoula or Butte, I'll never forgive you."

"I'm telling the truth, Miss Emmeline," he said. He hesitated, obviously weighing his next words. "You've got to get used to the idea of my being back in Plentiful, I know, and that's sure to take a little time. I'll stay clear of you if that's what you want—God knows, there's plenty to do at the ranch while you're thinking things through. But when I was working on those ships, darlin', there was only one thing that kept me going, and that was the belief that I could find my way back to you some fine day."

A tear spilled down Emmeline's cheek, and she made no move to wipe it away. She just sat there, listening, waiting, wondering if all the love in the world was enough to mend the damage that had been done by an unkind fate.

"I often imagined kissing you, Emmeline, the way I used to do. That's all that kept me from throwing myself overboard and breathing water until I went under. And that's all I'm asking of you now. One kiss."

Emmeline didn't speak. She just nodded, and leaned forward slightly, closing her eyes.

He curved a finger under her chin, like in the old days, and tilted her head back. She felt him close to her, and his breath on her mouth set her flesh to tingling, first just on her lips, then all over her body. She let out a soft moan of relief and regret when he claimed her, tenderly at first, tentatively, and then with a slow-building power, fueled by passion.

Emmeline was lost; Gil's touch had always affected her that way. She would have given herself to him, right there in the broad light of day, on her grandmother's horsehair settee, if he'd chosen to take her.

But he didn't. He drew back, one corner of his mouth kicking up in a semblance of a grin as she opened her eyes, lashes fluttering, to gaze at him in consternation.

"I do apologize, Miss Emmeline," Gil said, "for any inconvenience or embarrassment I might have caused you by coming back when I did." He touched her lips, still swollen and sensitive from the most thorough and compelling of kisses, with the tip of an index finger. "Mind, I didn't say I was sorry for spoiling your wedding."

Emmeline blinked, still too confused to speak. She loved Gil Hartwell as much as she ever had, but she was going to let him walk away, let him return to his homestead without her, because he was right about one thing: She needed time to ponder, to work out whether she believed him or not.

If Gil was lying to her, she'd know it, somehow, and no amount of love would make her set up housekeeping with a man who had betrayed her. Emmeline was a proud woman, and she'd been taught to put a high value on herself. She could not reconcile her hopes to anything less than complete loyalty.

Gil stood, his hand cupped beneath her chin, and their fingers, interlocked until then, loosened, separated, fell away.

"I love you, Emmeline," he said. And with that he turned and walked out of the parlor without looking back.

Emmeline sat rigid until she heard the front door close smartly, then covered her face with both hands and let out a wail fit to break a banshee's heart.

Izannah, who had been hovering outside the parlor for some time, burst into the room and hurried over to sit beside Emmeline and put an arm around her. Mrs. Dunlap, their nearest neighbor, was close on Izannah's heels, clucking and wringing her hands and muttering "Lord have mercy" over and over again.

"What did that rascal say to you?" Izannah demanded.

Emmeline snuffled inelegantly. "He said he loved me," she confessed, and promptly began to sob again. Even now, after all the humiliation she'd suffered, all the tears she'd shed and all the prayers she'd prayed, she wanted to chase after Gil Hartwell and ask him to take her home with him.

"The brute," Izannah said, furiously sympathetic.

"Lord have mercy," said Mrs. Dunlap.

Emmeline drew a great, shuddering breath. "Did you—send Ezra—around town with the news?" she managed between watery gasps. "About the wedding being called off, I mean?" She couldn't have borne it if guests had begun to arrive, full of merriment and the expectation of a ceremony.

Izannah was patting her hand—the same hand that bore an invisible tattoo of Gil's. "Yes, dear, of course I did. Don't worry. By now, everyone in town knows that Gil Hartwell has come back. It's very romantic, don't you think? Even though he should be shot—Gil, I mean."

"Do stop prattling," Emmeline pleaded. She'd developed a headache, and her wretched sobs had turned to hiccups. "Brandy," she cried. "Get me some of Grandfather's brandy, please, and quickly!"

Izannah hastened to comply, for she was fond of drama, being young and quite sheltered, and probably reasoned that brandy could only make the situation more interesting.

Mrs. Dunlap offered a few lame protests, and actually winced when Emmeline downed one dose of liquor in a decidedly unladylike gulp, then held out the snifter for another.

Gil had arrived in Plentiful aboard the afternoon stagecoach and gone straight to Emmeline's grandfather's house, having learned from one of his fellow passengers that she'd taken up residence there several years before. Now, with the first confrontation behind him, he bought a horse at the livery stable and rode right through the center of town. His aim was to let folks know he was back, and that he wouldn't be taking to the back roads, like a man with some cause for shame.

His cabin and the hundred and sixty acres he'd proved up on before marrying Emmeline lay two miles south of town, and it took him half an hour to make the ride. If his wife were there, waiting for him, the way he'd dreamed she would be, he'd have had good reason to hurry. As it was, he could take his time

Gil's heart, already bruised, sank to his boots when he saw the state his property had fallen into while he was gone. The roof of the cabin had caved in, probably under heavy winter snows, and part of the corral fence was down. The doors of the barn gaped open, and the hay inside had long since rotted. His horses and cattle had been sold, driven off, or stolen, and the outbuildings he'd sweated to put up—the well house and the privy, the chicken coop and the storage sheds—were nothing but piles of fallen timber, dappled with bird scat.

None of which would have mattered, Gil thought, swinging down from his horse, if Emmeline had been beside him.

He swept off his hat and ran his forearm across his eyes. At least he'd gotten back to Plentiful before she'd married Montgomery. Christ in heaven, he thought, he'd stood a lot in his time, but he wasn't sure he could have borne that. Just the idea of Emmeline sharing that sidewinder's bed was enough to make a man's belly clench.

Gil slapped his hat against his thigh, startling the skittish livery-stable horse, threw back his head, and let out a yell. He was home, by God, and Emmeline was well, and still his wife. For the time being, it was enough.

He calmed the gelding, whistling softly through his teeth, and then led it to the stream and the mantle of deep, sweet grass that grew beside the water. After removing the saddle and bridle, Gil tethered the animal to a birch tree by a long rope and left it to its supper.

There was fishing line inside the cabin, along with a few hooks, and it wasn't long until Gil had caught a meal of his own farther down the creek bank. He had a feast of trout sizzling in a pan, over an open fire, when Montgomery rode in.

Gil had been expecting the visit, and though he didn't hold with gunplay, he had laid down his hunting rifle within reach, against the trunk of the apple tree Emmeline had planted to shade the house. It was tall now, that tree, and weighted with hard green fruit.

"I see you've changed out of your wedding clothes," Gil said as Montgomery leaned forward in the saddle, his face shadowed by the brim of his hat. His mount was a big sorrel, deep-chested with sturdy legs. "I guess the least I can do is offer you dinner."

Neal swung one leg over the pommel of his saddle and slid deftly off the horse. "I ought to shoot you right here and now," he said, and though Gil could see that the other man was smiling, there wasn't so much as a hint of humor in his voice.

"That might be a hard thing to explain, even for you. How I managed to get myself shot on the very day I came back and ruined your plans to marry my wife, I mean." Gil's stance was easy and loose-limbed, and his hands rested on his hips, but he could see that hunting rifle out of the corner of his eye, and reach it in a blink. He sighed and shook his head. "No, sir, no jury in the world would see that as a coincidence. I guess you'd better just leave me be, and go find yourself another woman."

Montgomery took off his hat, and his fair hair glinted in the last blinding dazzle of a summer sun. "I've found the woman I want," he replied, "and I'll have her."

Gil dropped to his haunches beside the fire and turned the trout in the pan. He remembered the way Emmeline had responded to his kiss, there on that fussy settee in her parlor, and smiled to himself.

He was home. Emmeline still cared for him, whatever her misgivings, and Neal Montgomery hated him as much as ever.

Life was good.

2

EMMELINE PINNED GIL'S BROOCH TO THE BODICE OF HER NIGHT-
gown just before she went to bed, and lay down telling
herself she mustn't be foolish about things. True, the man
told a good story, and he could make her dizzy with a look,
but there were certainly other factors to consider. He'd been
gone seven years, she reminded herself, with not a word
from him in all that time, and she'd spent perfectly good
money putting up a suitable monument in the churchyard.

Lying in the darkness, Emmeline blushed to think of the
scandals Gil had spawned with his unconventional doings.
First he'd gone off and left her, and she'd made an idiot of
herself, going around in widow's weeds long past the customary mourning period, proclaiming his good character to
all and sundry. And now he'd returned, on the very day she
was to marry Neal Montgomery. By now, everybody in
Plentiful and half the tribes in the Indian nation were surely
talking about how close Miss Emmeline had come to taking
on one too many husbands.

She closed her eyes, willing herself to go to sleep and thus escape her contradictory feelings, but even after all the brandy she'd imbibed since Gil's departure, she was wide awake. She couldn't help thinking that this would have been her wedding night, if Mr. Hartwell hadn't returned from the dead in such a timely fashion. She'd be lying in Neal Montgomery's arms at that very moment, no doubt, with her nightgown on the other side of the room, an unwitting bigamist.

Heat rushed through Emmeline, causing her to perspire from head to toe. For all her efforts to be modest and circumspect—teaching piano lessons, attending church services, marking her lost husband's passing in the accepted way—there could be no denying the truth—hers was a harlot's body. Her breasts yearned to be weighed in a man's hands, to be suckled and teased, and there was a melting ache in the deepest regions of her femininity that could not be denied. Her hips waited to cradle a man, and her long, shapely legs were poised to part even now.

But it wasn't Mr. Montgomery, the man she had almost married, who inspired these disgraceful thoughts. It was Gil Hartwell she wanted, now as always, and she wanted him with an anguish that was downright humbling.

In retrospect, she wondered if she would have been able to bear Mr. Montgomery's touch at all. His kisses had never made her feel the way Gil's did. Would Neal's caresses have ignited her senses? Would she have thrashed beneath him, like she had with Gil, and cried out in animal satisfaction while he appeased her?

Emmeline raised both hands to her cheeks in an effort to cool her burning face. It was no use telling herself not to think about Gil, and she couldn't work up any interest in anyone else.

After an hour, Emmeline rose, lighted a lamp, stripped off her nightgown, and bathed her fevered flesh in tepid water from the basin on the washstand. That done, she put on fresh drawers and a camisole, and then her favorite petticoat. Over these, she donned a cornflower-blue dress that brought out the color of her eyes. She brushed her hair, braided it, and wound the heavy plait into a loose knot at the back of her head. She took the porcelain brooch from her nightgown and pinned it to the high ruffled neck of her dress, then changed her mind and put the trinket away, very carefully, in her bureau drawer. After washing her teeth with salt and baking soda, Miss Emmeline sat down in the rocking chair next to her window and waited for the far-off dawn to come.

Gil made a bed in the fragrant grass beneath Emmeline's apple tree. Cupping his hands behind his head, he gazed up at the countless stars strewn across the endless Montana sky. This surely wasn't the homecoming he'd dreamed about all those years, but his time at sea had taught him some valuable lessons, one of which was that he needed almost nothing to survive.

Oh, yes, he wanted Miss Emmeline as much as he ever had, and he loved her even more. But he had his freedom now, and he knew the value of that as few men did. He could make some kind of life without her if that was the way the cards were dealt.

Gil hoped matters wouldn't come down to that, of course, that he and Emmeline would be able to find their way back to each other through the emotional wreckage. At the same time, he knew he'd get on if they didn't, and so would she.

One of the many things he loved about Emmeline was her strength.

Somewhere far off, a coyote howled and was answered by another animal. The creek whispered over its bed of smooth rocks as it always had, and a soft breeze rustled in the silvery leaves of the birch trees on the other side of the water. The sounds, so familiar and so long missed, soothed Gil's spirit, and he slept.

He dreamed, as he often did, of that night in Sydney Harbor when the light of the moon had turned the still waters to liquid opal. He remembered the fear, and the desperation, and saw the dark shadows gliding back and forth below, waiting. Waiting.

Gil broke out in a cold sweat, and he knew he was in the grip of the nightmare, but somehow he couldn't lift himself above it, into wakefulness. He'd gone over the side of the *Nellie May,* clinging to a rope, carrying nothing with him but the brooch he'd bought for Emmeline, resting on his tongue like the fare for a dead man's passage across the River Styx. His only garment was a pair of drawers, tied tightly at the waist with a drawstring.

The water was warm as an old maid's bath, and mirror-smooth, since the tide was out. He lowered himself into it, as other men had done before him, and would after him, trying not to think about the moving shapes below. In truth, he knew, there was more to fear from the two-legged predators patrolling the decks of the ship than from the legendary sharks. Gil had made two other attempts at escape over the course of his captivity, and his back, an unbroken expanse of scar tissue from the whippings he'd received for his trouble, was an ever-present testimony to the high price of failure. If he was collared again, he knew the captain would surely kill him, as an example to others who might be spinning some reckless scheme to get away.

He swam slowly, concentrating on absolute silence, praying inside his head. The shore was within fifty yards when Kenyon, the man swimming just ahead of Gil, went under the surface with one gurgling cry. Blood bubbled up from below, and Gil felt watery echoes of the graceful, rolling motions of the kill against his skin. The prayers gave way to soundless screams, and he did the only thing he could—he continued to move toward shore, blindly and without hope. Behind him, the carnage continued as other sharks gathered, and vaguely, as if from far in the distance, he heard men screaming, while others called mocking offers of salvation from the decks of the *Nellie May.*

Gil gained the beach, by some miracle, and lay sprawled in the sand, alternately shuddering and retching. As far as he knew, of the seven men who had begun the ordeal, he was the only one who had survived.

He awakened now, and was not surprised to find himself on his belly, with his arms spread wide over his head and his fingers digging into the dirt. His body invariably relived that night as vividly as his mind did when the nightmares came, and he rested under the apple tree for several long moments, trembling and fighting the need to weep. Those things, too, were part of the involuntary ritual.

When he'd collected himself sufficiently, Gil got to his feet, pulled on his trousers, and buttoned them. He stumbled to the creek, checked on the horse, and then knelt on the bank to splash cool water on his face. When the last remnants of the dream had dissipated like smoke, Gil found the flask in his saddlebags and drank deeply. After pissing in the tall grass over near the barn, he got back into his bedroll.

There was only one thing he could think of that would drive away nightmares better than cold water and whiskey, and that was a tumble with Miss Emmeline. He'd been celibate since the day he left her, and he had no intention of breaking his wedding vows now. He just hoped she'd be quick about deciding whether to take him back or not, because waiting was a lot harder, now that he could see and touch her and hear her voice. One hell of a lot harder.

Emmeline forced herself to have breakfast with Izannah and teach her nine o'clock piano lesson before she went out to the carriage house to hitch up the judge's surrey. She laid the satchel she'd taken from her grandfather's safe upon arising on the floorboard, securely against one foot, and took off.

There were less direct ways to reach Gil's property than by driving south on Main Street, but Emmeline was not given to deceit. Furthermore, she harbored no illusions that, by taking elaborate precautions, she could stem the flow of gossip. The speculative stares and hesitant waves she received as she passed through town were proof that she was right.

She had barely put Plentiful behind her when a rider

appeared, and she pulled up on the reins as Neal came to a halt beside her. He tipped his hat and smiled, but the look in his eyes was less than cordial.

"Good morning, Miss Emmeline," he said.

Emmeline fidgeted on the hard seat of the surrey while her ancient dapple-gray mare, Lysandra, bent her head to graze at the side of the road. "Good morning, Mr. Montgomery," Emmeline replied. "Was there something you wanted?"

Neal leaned, with deceptive indolence, on the pommel of his saddle. "Common decency prevents me from answering that question honestly," he told her. "I suppose I don't dare hope that you were on your way to the Circle M just now, to tell me you've decided to divorce Hartwell and marry me?"

Color climbed Emmeline's neck and throbbed in her cheeks, but she kept her shoulders straight and her chin high. "I have not made a decision one way or the other, where divorce is concerned. I do believe, however, that you and I were both saved from a tragic mistake yesterday."

He resettled himself in the saddle, an unnecessary motion, since he, like most men in that part of the country, had been riding so long that he was practically part of the horse. "Do you, now? Well, I happen to disagree completely. I'll wait, Miss Emmeline, until you come to your senses and accept the fact that you've thrown in your lot with a scoundrel."

Emmeline bit her lower lip and looked away for a moment. She had made up her mind, once and for all, not to marry Mr. Montgomery, but there was possibly some truth in his implication that she was allowing lesser instincts to guide her. "Please," she said with cool dignity and absolute sincerity. "Don't wait for me. You deserve someone better."

"There is no one better," he replied easily, and touched the brim of his hat again. "Good day to you, Miss Emmeline."

Emmeline did not answer, but instead reined poor Lysandra away from the lush grass and set the surrey moving again.

When Emmeline reached Gil's house, she found him straddling the apex of the roof, bare-chested in the June sunlight, wielding a hammer. Seeing her, he immediately reached for his shirt and pulled it on. He was agile as he moved down the inadequate ladder leaning against the front wall of the cabin, and she could easily imagine him climbing the rigging of a ship.

Gil was buttoning his shirt as he came toward her. His hair was mussed and his smile was tentative, almost cautious, as though he expected bad news. She supposed he'd had more than his share of that—provided his story was true.

Emmeline bent and picked up the small satchel that had been resting at her feet while Gil waited to help her down from the surrey. Even the act of placing her hand in his seemed wickedly intimate to her, and roused all the old, treacherous sensations.

She withdrew her hand quickly and clutched it to the grip of the satchel. "I wasn't able to care for the cattle and horses after you went away," she blurted out, "so I sold them. Since the livestock was yours, so is the money. Here it is."

Gil took the bag she thrust at him, but his expression revealed puzzlement. "You kept it all this time? But if you believed I was dead—"

"When it became obvious that you weren't coming back," Emmeline said, her voice rising a little before she managed to lower it to a more moderate tone, "I went back to live with my grandfather. He settled my affairs as best he could, considering his failing health, and when he died, I found the money in his personal safe, in a packet bearing your name."

Gil stared into Emmeline's eyes for what seemed like an eternity, then opened the satchel and reached inside, bringing out a stack of bills tightly bound with string. "I would have understood if you'd spent this on yourself," he said at length in a raspy voice. "What kept you from selling the land, Emmeline?"

She smoothed her skirts and then patted her hair, which

tended toward untidiness. "I knew it meant more to you than anything else in the world, and I couldn't bring myself to let go of it. I kept thinking I'd come back out here to live someday."

Gil smiled at Emmeline then, and though she remained somewhat nervous, she was more at ease after that. "I thank you for that," he said, "though I have to say you were only partly right. There isn't a parcel of land on this earth that means more to me than you do, including this one." Having said those pretty words, Gil had the good grace to turn away, so that Emmeline could blush in private.

After she'd recovered her composure, she lifted her skirts and followed him, even though good sense dictated that she ought to leave immediately. She simply couldn't trust her judgment when it came to Gil Hartwell. But the fact that he was her legal husband didn't mean she would fall into his arms and tell him all was forgiven. He had changed a great deal during their time apart, and so had she.

"This money will come in handy," he said, offering a nail keg for a chair. "As you can see, the place could do with some fixing up."

Emmeline looked around carefully, taking in the sunken roof, the broken fences, the weed-choked patch where her garden had been, long ago. She hadn't been back to the ranch since the day her grandfather had come to collect her and taken her away to his house in town. She'd always known there would be too many memories here, and that it would hurt like everything to see the property gone to rack and ruin, after all her and Gil's hard work. They'd had such dreams, such hopes.

Gil was leaning against the trunk of her beloved apple tree, his arms folded, the stack of bills protruding from his shirt pocket. "You look so sorrowful," he said. "What's going through that mind of yours?"

She lowered her head for a few moments, making busy-work of smoothing her skirts so he wouldn't see just how deep her sorrow ran. "I was thinking of dandelions," she said presently, fixing her gaze on the creek and the fine horse grazing beside it, "and how they turn to ghosts and blow away in the wind."

"Scattering their seeds over the land," Gil added gently. "Renewing themselves, the way all living things do." He came to stand before her, and touched her cheek with the lightest brush of his fingers before tilting her chin upward. The sun blazed behind him, blinding her to all but the shape of him, but she did not close her eyes.

"Tell me how to lift your spirits, Emmeline," he went on with quiet dignity. "I'll ride out if that's what you want. Hell, I'll make myself a pair of waxen wings and fly off into the sun. Just tell me how to please you."

The words were out before Emmeline had even guessed she would say them. "Hold me," she whispered. "Take me into your arms, Mr. Hartwell, and hold me tightly and don't let me go 'til I can really believe you're back."

Gil drew her slowly to her feet and into his embrace. It was bliss to nestle against him, as she had so long before, while her heart matched its pace to his. He smelled of old wood, summer grass, whiskey and hard work, and the scents lent substance to Emmeline's memories, and brought tears to her eyes.

He kissed her temple and spread his fingers wide over her back. She felt his desire, hard as tamarack against her lower belly, but he made no move to claim her as a husband claims a wife, nor did he speak. He just stood there, holding her, and for Emmeline the experience was a homecoming in and of itself.

She rested her forehead against his shoulder, and her tears wet his shirt. "I am so very afraid, Mr. Hartwell," she confessed in a low and wretched voice.

Gil cupped her face in his hands, the rough edges of his thumbs brushing the moisture from her cheeks. "Oh, darlin'," he said raggedly, resting his chin on top of her head. "Of what? Tell me what scares you."

Emmeline expelled a deep, shuddering sigh. "You do,"

she replied. "You and everything you make me feel. Dear God in heaven, Gil—to let myself love you again, and then lose you—"

"Shhh," he said. "I'm not going anywhere, ever again, unless you send me away."

Emmeline stepped back in his embrace, just far enough to look up into those impossibly blue eyes. "You said that before," she reminded him. "The day we were married. You mustn't make promises you can't keep, Gil."

He kissed her forehead, and an ancient and sacred yearning moved through Emmeline, weakening her. "You're not ready to hear my promises," he said, and there was grief in his voice, in his body, in his handsome face. Then, somehow, magically, he forced a smile, and closed his hand over hers. "Come and sit by the creek with me, Emmeline. Like you did when we were courting."

She allowed Gil to lead her past the ruined house and through the tall grass to the stream bank, and the sunlight danced like melted diamonds on the restless, whispering water.

"Take off your shoes," he commanded, beaming as proudly as if he'd created that pure, spring-fed creek himself, just for her amusement.

A strange intoxication possessed Emmeline, as if Gil had cast a spell over her. Whatever had lightened the mood, she was grateful.

She had worn slippers, instead of her usual practical black boots, with their many buttons, and she laughed as she kicked one away, then the other. The stream was ice cold, but she had always loved to wade in it and feel the smooth stones against the soles of her feet.

She made her way to the middle, where the water reached to her calves, and stood there reveling in the sheer irresponsibility of what she was doing. Gil watched her from the bank, grinning, his arms folded, his hair gleaming like onyx in the sunlight.

When Emmeline's feet went numb, she made her way reluctantly to the shore and sat down in the grass to stretch out her legs and wriggle her toes. Now that the judge was gone, and it was just her and Izannah, there were many demands on her time. She couldn't recall the last time she'd done anything so frivolous as to wade into a creek with her skirts hiked up.

Gil crouched beside her, and offered a bouquet of bright yellow dandelions, not yet turned to ghosts. She welcomed them as though they were orchids plucked from the Garden of Eden.

He sat down and pulled Emmeline's right foot onto his lap. She uttered a dreamy sigh as he began to rub that innocent extremity between his hands, restoring the circulation with such efficiency that she gave him the other foot as well. When she would have withdrawn, however, he took a gentle but firm hold on her ankles.

Emmeline braced herself by putting her hands behind her on the soft ground, and watched this beloved stranger curiously. It did not occur to her to feel fear; if there was one thing she was sure of, in all the universe, it was that Gil Hartwell would never hurt her. Not physically, at least.

Without speaking, he took the smallest toe on her right foot in his thumb and forefinger, and began to work it between them, his touch light and sure and sensual in a way Emmeline had not expected. He progressed, with infinite slowness, from one small digit to another, until he'd reduced all ten of them to the consistency of butter.

Emmeline closed her eyes and let her head fall back, feeling the sun on her face. Gil proceeded to caress her right instep, her arch, the protruding bone on the inside of her ankle. However innocent and undemanding his touch, Gil was seducing her, and she wasn't sure she would resist him. She was a tactile creature, shameless as a house cat, and it had been seven long years since she'd felt those light, leisurely strokes on her flesh.

She sagged backward into the deep, fragrant grass, expecting him to undress her, as he had done so many times before their parting, and make love to her on the creek bank, in the warm light of the sun.

Instead, Gil shoved her slippers back on, first one, then the other.

Emmeline sat up, stunned, disappointed, and more than a little insulted.

Gil's expression was grim. "I want you more than I ever have before," he said, "but I won't have you saying I seduced you. If you want my lovemaking, you'll have to ask for it."

Emmeline opened her mouth, then closed it again. She wasn't ready to ask, though she most certainly desired him, and the dichotomy was nearly overwhelming. Feeling spurned, she clambered awkwardly to her feet, her sodden hem and petticoats clinging to her legs and ankles. She shook a finger at him, but when she tried to speak, all that came out of her mouth was an indignant squeak.

Gil chuckled and stood up with considerably more grace than Emmeline had exhibited. "Take a breath," he said. "You look as though you're strangling."

Emmeline complied, and sucked in one outraged gasp. The mirth dancing in Gil's eyes incensed her, even as a part of her celebrated the easy ingenuousness of his laughter.

"The devil take you, Gil Hartwell," she managed to blurt, and then slogged off toward the waiting surrey.

Gil stopped her, taking a light hold on her shoulder and turning her to face him. "I'm not scorning you, Emmeline," he said, wearing a diplomatic expression now, made partly of amusement and partly of tenderness. "Please understand that. If I'd taken you just now—and God knows, I wanted to—you'd have hated me for it within the hour."

Emmeline sagged a little, for she could see the truth in his words. "How will I know," she asked in a small voice, "when I'm ready?"

Gil reached out, traced her lips with his fingertip. "You'll know," he assured her.

She searched his face and saw some of the old Gil there, and more of the new. In many ways, he was a stranger, this husband of hers. The man she remembered would have had her beside the stream, and gloried in her pleasure as well as his own. The old Gil wouldn't have thought beyond the moment, and in some ways, Emmeline missed that side of him.

"If someone had told me you were going to come back someday," she said softly, "I wouldn't have believed things could be so complicated. Did you know it would be like this?"

Gil's smile was infinitely tender and unspeakably sad. "I've learned to take life as it comes," he replied. "Six and a half years as a virtual slave makes a man patient, Emmeline, when it doesn't kill him."

She wanted then to put her arms around Gil, to give comfort instead of taking it. For the first time, it struck her that she'd been selfish, thinking merely of her own grievances, never really considering what might have happened to him. "Will you come for supper?" she asked, keeping her distance because she sensed he wanted that. "Tonight, I mean, at seven o'clock?"

Gil executed a stately bow. "I would be honored, Miss Emmeline," he replied. "Not to mention relieved to be spared my own cooking, if only for one night. Now, get yourself into that surrey and drive away before chivalry gives way to lust and I take you where you stand."

Although Emmeline did not find the latter idea entirely unappealing, she turned and hurried toward the surrey all the same, scrambling up into the seat before Gil could offer a hand and set her senses to rioting again.

"Seven o'clock," she said, gathering up the reins.

"Seven o'clock," Gil agreed, and stood watching as she drove off.

As soon as Emmeline was out of sight, Gil put away his tools, saddled his nameless horse, and set out for town. By his reasoning, when a man courted a woman—even when that woman was his wife—certain refinements were called for. Soap, for one, and a decent suit of clothes for another.

His appearance at the general store inspired murmured comments, especially since Miss Emmeline had probably just driven that silly-looking surrey of hers through town at a smart pace, but he didn't mind. Sooner or later, he'd have had to talk to folks and it was natural for them to be curious. His resurrection was probably the most interesting thing that had happened in Plentiful since the Sioux stopped taking scalps.

Gil found his neighbors friendly, if less than subtle in their efforts to find out whether or not he meant to fetch Emmeline from the judge's house and carry her back to his cabin over one shoulder. He kept his intentions to himself, not out of reticence but because he wasn't sure himself what he was going to do.

Emmeline was a desirable woman and, in the eyes of God and man, she was his wife. He wasn't made of stone, nor was he particularly noble, to his way of thinking. Which meant he might lose sight of his philosophy and good intentions one of these days, and show all the restraint of a wolf mounting its mate.

He bought a wagon and a mule before he left town, and stopped by the mill to order lumber for a new roof. Although he hadn't told Emmeline when she'd handed over the money for the stock she'd sold, probably to Montgomery, Gil had met with that banker friend in San Francisco before catching a stagecoach north to the Montana Territory. He had enough cash to repair the house and barn and buy the beginnings of a new herd.

Back home, he stripped off his clothes and waded into the stream, a bar of hard yellow soap in hand, and scrubbed himself clean from his scalp to the soles of his feet. He'd have preferred a tubful of hot water, but after all he'd been through since the night he was pressed into service aboard the infamous *Nellie May,* a cold bath was hardly cause for complaint.

Once he'd washed, Gil climbed out of the creek and dried himself with his shirt. Then, whistling, he got into the new duds he'd bought at the general store. He'd invested in four pairs of wool trousers and four chambray shirts, and it made him feel rich, having such an extensive wardrobe. Never mind that there was a hole in his roof and his barn was leaning to one side; a man could only attend to one matter at a time.

Emmeline was standing at the parlor window when Gil Hartwell arrived promptly at seven, in a buckboard pulled by a fine-looking mule. She backed away, lest he catch her watching him, and all but stumbled over a wide-eyed Izannah.

"Great Zeus, Emmeline," the girl whispered. "Just yesterday you were going to marry Mr. Montgomery. Now here you are inviting another man to supper!"

"Stop fussing," Emmeline said. "You sound like an old woman. And must I remind you—again—that Mr. Hartwell is my husband?"

"Becky Bickham says her father's going to preach against sins of the flesh tomorrow morning," Izannah confided, following Emmeline into the entry hall and right up to the front door. "I think you should attend, since the sermon is so obviously directed at you!"

Emmeline smiled distractedly, smoothing her brown sateen dress and patting her hair, which was already threatening to come tumbling down around her shoulders. " 'Sins of the flesh,' is it? I should think a situation like mine would call for a discourse on the evils of bigamy."

"Emmeline!" Izannah hissed, scandalized.

Gil's knock sounded at the door, and Emmeline held a finger to her lips and waited, as though she had to come from a great distance to admit him.

His smile was utterly disarming, and he carried a nosegay of wild violets and buttercups in one hand. Emmeline stared at Gil, hardly able to credit, even now, that he was back.

Izannah finally nudged her. "Good evening, Mr. Hartwell," the girl said cheerfully. "Won't you come in?"

"Thank you," Gil replied easily, and stepped past Emmeline. He offered the nosegay and she accepted it, blushing with shy pleasure, then excusing herself, in stumbling words, to go into the kitchen and put the tiny bouquet in water.

When she returned to the front of the house, Gil and Izannah were in the parlor. The girl sat at the piano, waiting for an invitation to play, while Gil stood beside the polished instrument, smiling down at her. Emmeline felt a surge of jealousy and was instantly ashamed. Izannah was a shameless flirt—she'd batted her lashes and flashed her dimples at Mr. Montgomery many a time—but she was only seventeen, after all, a mere child.

"Perhaps you wouldn't mind favoring us with a song," Emmeline said to her cousin, to make up for uncharitable thoughts. "Izannah is my most promising student."

There was a smile in Gil's eyes as he looked at Emmeline.

"I'm going to make some man a wonderful wife," Izannah chirped.

Gil didn't laugh at this announcement, and Emmeline would be forever grateful.

"I should think you'd want to make some sort of life for yourself first," she pointed out mildly, though her first instinct was to grab the girl by the throat and throttle her. Emmeline met Gil's eyes as Izannah began to play a Mozart sonata. "We have relations in the East," she said, as if he didn't know all about them. "Our great-aunt Margaret has offered to take Izannah to Europe next spring."

"It wouldn't be half so interesting as Plentiful," Izannah chimed, over the delicate notes of her favorite recital piece. She turned that dazzling, dimpled smile on Gil. "What would you have done if you'd come back and found Emmeline married to Mr. Montgomery?"

Gil took the little imp's hand, lifted it from the keyboard, and kissed it lightly. "That's easy," he replied smoothly. "I'd have turned right around and courted you, Miss Izannah."

3

"WILL YOU BE IN CHURCH TOMORROW?" EMMELINE ASKED AT
the end of the evening as she said good-bye to Mr. Hartwell
on the front veranda. Even though the steps were hidden by
climbing roses on one side and a lilac bush on the other, she
wouldn't have dared to do or say anything untoward. The
neighbors were simply too vigilant, and there was enough
gossip going around as it was.

Gil stood with his hat in his hand and one foot on the
bottom step, looking up at her. "Just think how disappointed folks would be if I didn't turn up," he said, and his
mouth tilted upward at the corners in the slightest of grins.
"I don't have the heart to let them down."

Overhead, a canopy of stars glinted, undimmed by the
feeble glow of light that was Plentiful. There was a weighted
feeling in the air, as if a violent storm was coming, and yet
the warm breeze promised a hot day tomorrow. Emmeline
wanted to ask if Gil was sleeping inside the cabin, with its
gaping roof, but she didn't dare raise such a subject with
Mrs. Dunlap surely bending so far over the garden fence

that she might impale herself on the pickets. The old meddler was bound to be taking in every word.

"Well, good night then," Emmeline said clearly, so her neighbors would know Gil had gone home directly after supper.

Gil reached out, took her hand, and brushed his lips across her knuckles in a feather-light kiss that left Emmeline trembling. "Good night, Miss Emmeline," he said, with equal clarity, and turned to stroll, whistling, toward the open gate at the end of the limestone walk. His mule and buckboard awaited on the other side of the fence.

It was all Emmeline could do not to call him back, and damn the neighbors and their clacking tongues. But she had not survived seven difficult years by weakness, and her determination held against an onslaught of physical longings. Lifting her skirt slightly with one hand, her spine as straight as a broom handle, Miss Emmeline turned and swept back inside the house with her chin high.

Nobody besides Gil would have guessed that her heart was pounding against her rib cage like a Sioux war drum and her breathing was so quick and shallow she feared she would swoon.

Emmeline took a long, tepid bath in the kitchen that night, but the indulgence did nothing to settle her jumping nerves. There was only one thing, unfortunately, that would do that.

Resigned, Emmeline dried herself, put on her nightgown and wrapper, dragged the tub to the back door and across the mud porch, emptied it, and hung it on its peg on the outside wall. Then, carrying the lamp, she climbed the rear stairway and went to bed. Miraculously, she fell into a heavy, dreamless sleep.

The next morning, Emmeline awakened with puffy eyes, feeling thoroughly unrested. The weather was strange, the air heavy and charged with some sort of elemental anticipation. The sky, a fierce and brittle blue, looked as though the flight of one sparrow might shatter it like an eggshell and bring it tinkling down over all their heads in the tiniest shards and splinters.

Emmeline prepared herself carefully, because today, for the first time since her thwarted wedding day, she would face the whole town. She wore her most conservative dress, a brown serge trimmed in cocoa-colored braid and adorned only by Gil's brooch, pinned circumspectly to her bodice. To complete the somber ensemble, she added a bonnet to match her frock.

Izannah looked up from her oatmeal as Emmeline entered the kitchen by way of the back stairs. Normally, Emmeline would have eaten a substantial breakfast, for the Sabbath was a long day in Plentiful, beginning with two hours of preaching and singing and another of fellowship on the shady side of the churchyard. But today she did not trust her fretful stomach to contain even the simplest food.

"You look quite ghastly this morning," Izannah said with exuberance.

"Thank you," Emmeline responded, tugging on her gloves. She'd be the center of attention today, along with Gil, of course, and she dreaded the inevitable looks and questions with all her heart, for she was by nature a quiet and private person, happiest when left alone to mind her own affairs. "Could you hurry, please?" she asked Izannah pettishly, frowning at the clock. The mechanism inside wound itself audibly, preparing to strike the hour. "It is nearly nine, and only the vain and feckless keep the Lord waiting."

Izannah rolled her mirthful brown eyes and carried her cereal bowl to the sink. "It isn't the Lord that's waiting *this* morning," she pointed out. "I don't imagine *He's* in any suspense at all."

"Hush," Emmeline scolded, aware of a sudden warmth in her cheeks. "It's not fitting to speak so flippantly of holy matters."

"Oh, fuss and bother," Izannah muttered, arranging the skirts of her Sunday dress. A blue sateen with puffed sleeves

113

and understated ruffles at the bodice and hem, it was the most sedate garment the girl owned. "Every day but Sunday, you let the Lord go His own way with hardly a nod, while you go yours. If you ask me, you're nothing but a hypocrite, carrying on about being late to church."

Emmeline gave her cousin a none too gentle push toward the back door. "Reverend Bickham's sermon will be sufficient unto the day," she said briskly. "I do not require an additional one from you."

They walked through the rear garden to the alley, proceeding down a rutted road toward the white clapboard church at its end, converging with other families, small and large, as they went. Greetings were exchanged, as usual, but Emmeline did not miss the sidelong glances or the whispers behind gloved hands.

A cluster of men had gathered, as they did every Sunday, in the shade of the row of poplar trees planted to protect the church from harsh Montana winds. As subtly as she could, Emmeline searched the group for Gil. Instead, she found her gaze locked with that of Neal Montgomery.

Blast him, Emmeline thought uncharitably, lowering her head a little and hoping the wide brim of her bonnet hid her flushed face from prying eyes. Mr. Montgomery was no believer; that was why they had planned to marry in her garden, rather than before Reverend Bickham's pulpit. He was present only to nettle Emmeline and to fuel the fires of speculation.

Emmeline shot him a skewering look, and he tipped his hat and smiled benignly. She wondered why she hadn't noticed the man's ornery streak before.

"Do you think Mr. Montgomery would marry me, now that it turns out you're taken?" Izannah teased, making no effort to speak in a moderate tone. She was plainly enjoying the melodrama as much as anyone else in town.

Emmeline's response was tight-lipped. "No doubt he would," she replied. "And I must say, such a union would serve you both right."

A twitter went up from the women and girls; the men,

fortunately, were too far away to hear. Or so Emmeline devoutly hoped.

The church bell began to ring, drowning out any response Izannah might have been brazen enough to offer, and the congregation moved in a swell toward the open doors of the church.

Emmeline swept down the aisle with her chin held high and took her place in the same pew she always did. Members of her family had sat right there ever since the judge had come to Plentiful in pioneer days, a new-minted lawyer with a young bride and a surplus of high hopes. A little modesty on her grandfather's part then might have saved Emmeline some difficulty now, for she was smack in front of the church, where everybody could see her. Worse, she hadn't seen Gil, and wouldn't know whether or not he'd kept his promise to attend until after the services were over, since she wasn't about to turn around and scan the congregation for him.

During the first chorus of "Shall We Gather at the River," there was a stir of sorts, but Emmeline straightened her shoulders resolutely and did not look back. She simply sang with greater dedication, and then Gil appeared beside her, booming the words of the old song with amused enthusiasm. She felt heat pulsing at her nape and a peculiar, tumbling sensation in the pit of her stomach.

She looked at Gil out of the corner of her eye, and aligned her vertebrae one square above the next, all the way up her back. She felt jubilant, just because he was standing there, and at the same time she wanted to smack him over the head with her hymnal for the sideshow he'd made of her life.

After the song came a lengthy prayer offered by Reverend Bickham, a sincere if unimaginative man who probably would have gone right on preaching even if he stopped believing. Emmeline knew he relished the traditions and rituals of the faith, and agreed that such things had their place in a balanced life, whether one accepted every tenet of the philosophy or not. Beyond that, as Izannah had pointed out in the kitchen that morning, Emmeline generally minded her own business, with an eye to being kind, modest, honest, and patient, and expected the Lord to mind His.

She found herself wondering, as the prayer progressed, how Mr. Hartwell felt about God after his experience on the high seas. Assuming, of course, that he had indeed undertaken the voyage against his will, and not because he'd simply wished to avoid the responsibilities and constraints of marriage.

At long last, Reverend Bickham finished his earnest conversation with heaven and instructed the congregation to be seated. It was hot that morning, and the air was close inside the little church. There were muffled sighs of relief at the invitation to sit, especially from some of those for whom the Lord had provided especially well, and Emmeline, being light-headed and weak in the knees, shared in the sentiment.

The Reverend cleared his throat, then loosened his string tie with one hooked finger. His small eyes gleamed with conviction and purpose beneath his great beetle brows, and he fixed his gaze on Emmeline.

"Today's sermon," he announced, seeming to address Emmeline and Emmeline alone, "is rooted in the thirty-first chapter of Proverbs." He paused, a good man intent on his business, and then went on in a voice like thunder to demand, "Who can find a virtuous woman? *Who?*"

He made the feat sound downright impossible.

At Emmeline's elbow, Gil Hartwell chuckled, and there were whispers, shufflings, and shiftings in all the crowded pews.

Emmeline seethed in silence, engaged in a stare-down with the Reverend and determined, on pain of death, to prevail. The way the pastor and everyone else in town were behaving, Emmeline thought ruefully, any objective observer would have thought she had personally clipped Samson's locks or asked for the Baptist's head on a platter. Nobody had noticed, it seemed, that she had done nothing wrong.

Relentlessly, the sermon boomed on, like a runaway freight train on a downhill track. While Emmeline's name was not mentioned, only an idiot could have failed to see that every word was said for her benefit, in the plain hope of steering her ship wide of the shoals of sin.

She was so indignant by the end that she had made up her mind not to stay after for fellowship, even though that was the part of Sunday services she enjoyed most. There were limits even to Emmeline's strength, and after that sermon, she needed some time to herself.

Reverend Bickham said another prayer, and then there were more hymns. Emmeline sang by rote and stole occasional glances at Gil, of whom she was painfully aware. The heat intensified, but rolls of thunder could be heard now and then in the distance, and once in a while a flash of heat lightning glowed at the windows. When rain began to patter lightly on the roof, the stifling air cooled a little, and so did Emmeline's temper.

"There is one announcement before we close in prayer," Reverend Bickham said. Emmeline had the whimsical thought that he might cap off his rousing discourse against carnal sin by condemning her to wear a scarlet letter from that day forward. "I have received word that there will be a traveling evangelist coming our way soon. I hope you will all attend."

Emmeline sighed. Practically everyone for fifty miles around would turn out, simply because those gypsy preachers, with their tents and platforms and ringing voices, put on such a marvelous show. Folks took wagons and food, parlor chairs and blankets, and stayed for the duration of the spectacle, listening in spellbound delight to rancorous sermons about the wages of sin and the glories of salvation, singing along with the dearly familiar hymns, getting themselves saved and resaved, just for the sheer excitement of it all.

Emmeline didn't blame them, and in fact would have shared their enthusiasm at most any other time. Entertainments were few and far between on the plains of the Montana Territory, and most everywhere else in the West.

"Today's fellowship will be held inside the church building," the Reverend finished, "on account of that rain we've been praying for has finally arrived. Shout hallelujah, brothers and sisters!"

While the brothers and sisters were shouting hallelujah, Emmeline shoved past Gil Hartwell and marched herself down the aisle and the outside steps, paying no heed whatsoever to the soft, warm rain wetting her dress and spoiling her bonnet. Anger and humiliation propelled her across the yard, through the gate, and straight down the middle of the street, puddles and the mud Montanans call "gumbo" notwithstanding.

Gil caught up to her just as she was turning in to the alley, and held his handsome new suit coat over her head like a canopy. His shirt was saturated, front and back, revealing the splendid masculine chest beneath, and Emmeline felt yet another surge of heat.

How on earth was a woman to keep to the straight and narrow, she asked herself, when she was faced with subtle temptations at every turn?

Perhaps, she reflected bitterly, Reverend Bickham had been right, after all, in aiming that blistering sermon of warning directly at her. She could not deny, to herself at least, that she harbored wanton thoughts.

Emmeline allowed Gil to escort her all the way to the mud porch of the judge's house, where they stood under the slanting shingle roof, staring at each other, drenched and dripping. Gil had gotten the worst of it, of course, since he'd used his coat as an umbrella for Emmeline.

"You shouldn't have followed me here," she said, lamenting the muddy splotches lining the hem of her good brown dress. "I lost my temper and made a fool of myself by storming out that way, but there was no need for you to join in as well. The gossip will be even worse than before."

A smile lurked in Gil's blue eyes as he shook out his coat and hung it on the peg next to the one that supported Emmeline's bathtub. Then he reached out, bold as you please, peeled the sodden bonnet off her head, and set it on the bench beside the back door. "Gossip has its season," he said, "like everything else. Sooner or later, the good people of Plentiful will turn their busy tongues to some other subject."

"You only say that because you're a man," Emmeline responded, wiping her shoes before proceeding into the kitchen to put a kettle on to boil. "Men don't mind what folks say about them. In fact, something like this can only improve *your* reputation. For a woman, things are quite different."

Gil drew a chair from the kitchen table, turned it around, and sat astraddle of it, with his arms folded on the back. Even wet through to the skin, with his hair plastered to his head, he was at ease. He'd always had a gift for living in the moment, and it seemed he'd perfected that during his years of alleged captivity.

"What do you suppose folks are saying about us, right this minute?" he asked in a teasing voice.

Emmeline got the yellow crockery teapot down from a shelf, dumped in two scoops of loose-leaf orange pekoe, and leveled a frown at him. "It's not what they're *saying,*" she pointed out coolly. "After all, they wouldn't dare speak of such things in Reverend Bickham's presence, lest they get themselves a sermon of their very own. No, Mr. Hartwell, it's what they're *thinking* that mortifies me to the bone!"

"And what are they thinking?"

Emmeline flushed; it was a flaw she had often attempted to overcome, without significant success. "That by now you've ripped my clothes off—and your own, of course— and we're rolling about on the kitchen floor, our two bodies entwined in passion."

Gil's eyes twinkled, and he grinned that slight, one-sided grin of his. "Miss Emmeline!" he scolded, and then made a tsk-tsk sound with his tongue. "I'm surprised at you, crediting the townsfolk with an image like that when you so obviously conceived it all by yourself."

Emmeline went crimson and whirled away to shove wadded newspaper and bits of kindling into the cookstove. The cast-iron lid clanked in a satisfying fashion when she slammed it into place. "Did you follow me home just so you could torment me?" she demanded, and it was only after several deep breaths that she trusted herself to turn and speak to the man who was—and at the same time wasn't— her husband.

Elbows resting on the table, fingers steepled under his chin, Gil regarded her with both amusement and something else, something that kindled a flame deep down inside Emmeline, even as the fire caught and then blazed, crackling and fragrant, inside the stove. "No, ma'am," he said at long last, his voice low and smoky. "I came to remind you of the things we used to do on rainy Sunday afternoons. Like the picnics we had in the hayloft, just the two of us. And the times we played cards until the lanterns burned out . . ."

Emmeline remembered those times with bittersweet clarity. She had been so happy then, so impossibly happy. Perhaps, she reflected, turning away again to add wood to the fire, they'd tempted fate, taking such joy from so little. "We're not the same people now," she said shakily. "So much has happened since we were together."

She heard him push back his chair and rise, and her body went as taut as the strings on a violin when she realized he was moving toward her, then went slack again when he laid his hands on her shoulders.

"Emmeline," he whispered, and as she felt the warmth of his breath on her nape a shiver went through her that had nothing whatever to do with the clammy wetness of her dress. He turned her into his embrace, his arms lying loosely around her waist. "Whatever else you're thinking, you mustn't believe for a moment that I ever meant to leave you."

She blinked, and sniffled once, inelegantly. "You said you wrote letters, but I never got any," she said, and felt silly for the way she'd framed the words.

Gil sighed. "I sent half a dozen, Emmeline, but the circumstances weren't exactly ideal."

Emmeline simply looked at him for a long time. She wanted to believe, wanted to trust, but she knew the pain would be terrible beyond bearing if that trust turned out to be misplaced. She felt tired, used up, and very confused, for while her mind warned her to be cautious, her body yearned to submit to his in the old, uninhibited way. "You said you'd make love to me when I asked," she said, as thunder crashed directly over the roof of the house, like a reprimand from God, rattling the dishes in the cupboards and causing the unlighted lamp over the table to sway a little. "Will you do it now?"

"No," Gil said, his expression solemn, his thumbs making light circles on the indentations beneath Miss Emmeline's collarbone.

She felt her eyes widen. "Why not?"

"Because it's comforting you want, not lovemaking."

"They're not the same?"

"Not the way I intend to have you, they're not."

Emmeline knew a delicious shiver of anticipation, followed by a surge of profound irritation. "You are taunting me, sir, and I do not appreciate it."

He took her chin into his hand, and although his grasp was not hurtful, neither was it gentle. "When I have you, Emmeline," Gil said clearly, "there will be no petting and stroking and no pretty words. I've waited a long time, and when you offer yourself to me, and mean it, I'm likely to pull down your drawers and have you over a table or a sawhorse instead of a bed. And make no mistake, my love—practically everything I say and everything I do is calculated to make you want me as desperately as I want you."

She swallowed, overwhelmed. "You say shocking things, Mr. Hartwell," she gasped. She did not add that she liked hearing them, though she hadn't any modesty left. He'd made short work of that, just as he always had.

"Yes," Gil answered, so close to kissing her that she was already responding, already straining forward for his touch. Instead, he clasped her hand and pulled her out of the kitchen, away from the rear stairway, through the dining room, and onto the screened porch where she sometimes slept when the heat was unbearable. It was a private place, sheltered by trellises of climbing flowers and by the gray gloom of the rain.

Dimly, through the darkened screens, Emmeline glimpsed the colorful ghosts of her Chinese lanterns, dangling sodden and bright over the backyard like the stars of some strange planet.

Between the two cots she and Izannah used, Gil pulled Emmeline into his arms and kissed her so deeply, so thoroughly, that she gave a little whimper and sagged against him.

"You wanted comfort," he whispered hoarsely when the kiss was over, "and you shall have it. But my restraint has a price, Emmeline. Don't forget that." With that, remarkably, he began unbuttoning her dress, and she allowed it, standing still and docile while Gil Hartwell stripped her naked.

When he had done that, he removed his own clothes, and Emmeline saw plainly that he was ready for lovemaking and wondered how she could convince him that she desired to be taken, not just teased.

"I want you," she said tremulously. "I'm asking, like you said I'd have to do."

Gil pressed her gently onto one of the cots and lay down with her, partly covering her body with the solid, heated weight of his own. "No," he said, though it was clear that the word had cost him dearly. "Not yet, Emmeline. Not yet."

She ran her hand over his back and felt the scar tissue— and knew instantly, letters or no letters, that everything he'd said was true. He *had* been shanghaied and spent years at sea, a slave to an obviously cruel captain. "Oh, Gil," she whispered.

Gil flinched slightly, and closed his eyes for a moment.

Emmeline kissed his bare shoulder, wanting to soothe him in the only way she knew how. He pulled away from her, and in that moment Emmeline grasped another truth: She wasn't the only one who wasn't ready for the complete, utter, and explosive physical reunion. Gil was afraid, too.

After gazing down at her for a few seconds in silence, his

expression unreadable, Gil slid one hand from her hip to the sumptuous curve of her breast.

Emmeline whimpered as his thumb coursed back and forth across the sensitive nipple, ever so slowly, over and over again. Too breathless to speak, she watched his face, and saw that he seemed wonder-struck by the breast, stricken by its splendor. He made a circle around the areola with the lightest touch of his index finger, causing Emmeline to moan again, and then traced the length of each of the tiny blue veins, barely visible under the pale, translucent flesh.

A deep, primal shudder went through Emmeline when Gil finally bent his head over her and touched the aching nipple with the tip of his tongue. One arm was pinned against her side because of the narrowness of the cot, but her free hand went immediately to his hair and buried itself there, pressing him closer, urging him to devour what he had merely been sampling.

But Gil took his time. Each time he tasted the morsel, or rolled it between his fingers, or simply blew on it as though to put out a candle, he paused afterward and watched the involuntary responses his touch had aroused.

Emmeline grew quietly frantic and pleaded in soft, half-coherent words, but Gil would not appease her. He had apparently decided to seduce her by degrees, to focus his attentions on one part of her at a time, she surmised, remembering how he'd kissed her the first day, then stroked her ankles and feet the next. There was no telling when he'd reach the point he'd spoken of with such scandalous frankness in the kitchen, but Emmeline harbored a shameless and desperate hope that it would happen soon.

"Let me touch you," she said.

Gil shifted so that Emmeline could move her arm, but he was suckling in earnest by that time, and he did not lift his head. When she found his rod and closed her hand tightly around it, she felt his groan move through the tissues of her breast, and he drew harder on the nipple, and harder still.

Emmeline stroked him slowly, all the while writhing in a

storm of pleasure. With a cry, Gil freed himself and pressed her beneath him before falling to her other breast with the same hunger. She entangled her fingers in his hair and began to chant his name under her breath, a rhythmic and disconsolate plea.

He did not mount her, but instead reached down between their two bodies, enjoying her breasts all the while, to ply her with his fingers.

Emmeline went wild, so great, so consuming was her need, and Gil left her nipple at last to cover her mouth with his own and muffle her hoarse groans with his kiss. His fingers went still, and he left her mouth to speak gruffly into her ear.

"I will satisfy you, Emmeline," he said, his voice no steadier than hers would have been, "but you must not cry out."

She nodded her assent—at that moment, she would have agreed to practically anything—and he rolled off the cot to kneel beside it, parting her legs with one hand, stroking the tender flesh of her inner thighs almost reverently.

"Gil," she whispered, arching her back.

"You promised," he scolded. Then he parted the silken delta between Emmeline's legs, studied the treasure buried there for a few moments, and lowered his head and feasted.

Emmeline let out a long, low cry, and Gil reached up to cup one hand over her mouth. She rocked under his tongue, her hips rising and falling as he led them to do, and he teased her without mercy. While he was engaged in a series of fleeting nibbles, Emmeline's universe splintered into a many-petaled blossom of white light.

When it was over—her back still slightly arched in an instinctive quest for pleasure, her flesh still quivering with satisfaction—she watched in silence as Gil rose to his feet, found his clothes, and began to put them on. When he bent to kiss her lightly on the mouth, she caught her own musky scent on his skin.

"You'd better get dressed, Miss Emmeline," he said. "That teakettle is probably boiling by now."

Emmeline sighed and stretched. For the moment, she was at ease, but she knew her body only too well, and the effect that Gil's attentions had upon it. The benefits of his efforts would wear off soon enough and then, because he hadn't put himself inside her, she'd want him more than ever. What he'd done to her there on the sunporch was not meant to satisfy, but to prime her for a true conquering.

By the time Emmeline got back into her camisole and drawers, Gil was gone, and she had just reached the top of the stairs, carrying the rest of her clothes in her arms, when she heard Izannah call her name from the kitchen.

Emmeline pretended not to hear, and fled into her room, where she splashed herself with tepid water from the basin and wept inconsolably.

An hour later, when she'd collected herself enough to go downstairs and face her cousin, she found Izannah at the stove. Emmeline had put on a wrapper and nightgown, like a convalescent, while Izannah wore a flower-print poplin and was putting the finishing touches on a dinner of fried chicken, mashed potatoes, and corn.

"You let the teakettle boil dry," Izannah accused, but there was no rancor in her voice. She was watching Emmeline with a speculative, worried expression in her usually mischievous eyes. "Are you sick, Emmeline?"

There was coffee, and Emmeline got a cup and poured herself some. She would have preferred a stiff dose of the judge's brandy, but it was Sunday afternoon and still light outside. Besides, she thought with a sniff, if she indulged, Reverend Bickham would probably find out somehow and preach a roof-raising sermon on the evils of strong drink.

"No, pet," she said gently. "I'm not sick, just tired."

"I stayed away as long as I could," Izannah went on, carrying a steaming bowl of mashed potatoes to the table. When it was just the two of them, they always ate in the kitchen. "Since Mr. Hartwell followed you home and everything."

"That was thoughtful of you." Emmeline turned, pretending to watch the rain through the small window over the sink, so Izannah wouldn't see her face.

"He gave me a dollar to spend the afternoon with Becky," Izannah confessed, without a trace of repentance. "Some people would call that bribery, but to me it's a new hair ribbon and that book I've been wanting."

Emmeline smiled a very small smile, but said nothing.

A brief silence fell while Izannah carried the rest of the dinner to the table and Emmeline assembled her composure.

"Come away from that window and eat your dinner," Izannah said when the meal was ready.

Vaguely amused at the turnabout—it was usually she who gave orders and cooked—Emmeline obeyed, taking her customary place at the table. Izannah even offered grace, which was a relief to Emmeline, who felt reticent just then about approaching the Lord for any reason.

"I bet Mr. Hartwell would enjoy a meal like this," Izannah said, buttering a slice of bread. "But of course he's gone home already, hasn't he?" She tried to be subtle as she eyed Emmeline's disheveled hair, puffy eyes, and nightclothes, and failed.

"Yes," Emmeline replied evenly. "Mr. Hartwell has indeed gone home." Picking up a fork, Emmeline forced herself to smile. "You really are quite a cook, Izannah. This chicken smells delicious."

"Thank you" was the girl's response. "But I know flattery when I hear it. You're only trying to change the subject, so I won't ask why you're in your nightclothes if you're not even sick, or why Gil paid me to stay away from my own house all afternoon. As if I couldn't guess."

Emmeline continued to eat, for she hadn't had breakfast and the day, though only half over, had been a long and arduous one. "You must content yourself," she said grudgingly, making no effort to sustain her smile, "with your own speculations. Why should you be different from the rest of the town?"

"I don't understand why you don't just go and live with

him, or ask him to move in here, with us," Izannah pressed. Tenacity was one of her foremost qualities, a trait that would no doubt serve her very well in the wide world, but was nevertheless trying in Emmeline's kitchen.

"Even if the situation was that simple, which it most assuredly is not, I wouldn't simply move out and leave you all alone in this house. As for asking Mr. Hartwell to live here, well, I don't happen to want to, and besides, he wouldn't come anyway. Not with that stiff-necked pride of his. No, he'd never leave his ranch."

Izannah smiled like a cat with feathers sticking out of its mouth. "You've given the matter a great deal of thought, it seems to me."

Emmeline glared at her cousin. "I had seven years to consider the matter," she answered, spearing a drumstick from the platter of chicken.

"Do you believe that Mr. Hartwell was really and truly shanghaied?" Izannah asked mildly, still undaunted.

Emmeline recalled the smooth, thick scar tissue she'd felt under her fingers when she'd stroked Gil's back, and her appetite was gone. Surely receiving such savage punishment changed men in very fundamental ways, breaking some, making others bitter or cruel.

"I believe it all right," she said.

"Then why don't you take him back?"

Emmeline could not bring herself to admit that she'd tried, and been rebuffed. "It's more complicated than that," she told Izannah with conviction in response to her latest question, but in her heart of hearts, she had plenty of questions of her own.

4

GIL STOOD ALONE AT THE FOOT OF HIS OWN GRAVE, PONDERING the many paradoxes of life—and death. It is not given to every man, he thought with grim amusement, to read his name on a marble tombstone.

Heedless of the copious summer rain, as soft and warm as an angel's tears, Gil noted that Emmeline had elected to bury him in the family plot, facing the judge's resting place. This touched him deeply, for Emmeline was a woman to whom family was vitally important.

It was the empty space next to his own, though, that tightened his throat and twisted his heart into a painful knot, for she had plainly reserved that spot for herself. Emmeline must have loved him when she'd commissioned that stone, he realized, and with such devotion that she would have gladly lain beside him throughout eternity.

He wondered, with the semblance of a smile rooted in irony rather than humor, exactly where she would have planted Mr. Montgomery—had she married him, of course. She hadn't, and for that Gil, who had learned to expect little in the way of miracles, was wondrously grateful.

He folded his arms, his new clothes soaked and his hair dripping. His body, still throbbing for want of the satisfactions he had denied it on Miss Emmeline's screened porch, found some small mercy in the dousing, and was eased.

For a time, Gil considered the world and its ways. Then, as mystified as ever, he squatted to trace the letters of his name, chiseled with Old World precision onto the face of the fine stone. Below was his birth date, followed by that of his supposed death—in a tragic twist, the day he'd been shanghaied. In many ways, he had indeed perished then, so he supposed it was fitting that there should be a grave for his old self. He might have come here to mourn the Gil he had been in the innocent arrogance of his youth, believing himself invincible and feeling so damn certain of everything.

He smiled bitterly at the memory. "Rest in peace," he said, rising and laying a hand to the smooth, curved top of the headstone. And then he turned and walked through the puddles and the thick, claylike mud to his wagon. The mule stood shivering in the rain, head down.

Gil climbed into the box, pushed the brake lever down with one foot, and took up the reins. The mule, glad to be moving, slogged patiently over the slippery, rutted track, hauling his master home.

Gil did not come to town on Monday, or at least he didn't pay Emmeline a call, and she told herself that was for the best. The rain had stopped sometime in the night, but the shrubs and the grass were bejeweled with water droplets, quivering prisms flinging off light. After her ten o'clock piano lesson, Emmeline went out into the garden and carefully took down the Chinese lanterns, now mere globs of brightly colored pulp.

On Tuesday, Reverend Bickham came to call. He was a good man, attentive to his flock, and Emmeline gave him tea and tried to reassure him that her soul was safe in the bosom of the lamb. He departed in some doubt, she suspected, despite her efforts.

By Wednesday, the prairie grasses were lavish, nurtured to a dazzling shade of emerald by Sunday's rain, and Brother Joy arrived, with his wagons and barkers, and set up his gypsy camp just outside of town. The rhythmic sound of hammers rang through the weighted, fragrant air as the faithful pounded nails into the speaking platform inside the main tent.

Plentiful buzzed with delighted expectation, and Emmeline was pleased. For a little while, at least, people would talk about Brother Joy and his good friend, the Lord, instead of her. Like everyone else, she cooked extra food, and she and Izannah cleaned the house from top to bottom, even though it was unlikely that either Brother Joy or the Lord would come to call. All the while, Emmeline thought about Gil, alternately blessing and cursing him, wondering if he was eating properly and if he'd taken a cold from walking her home in the rain.

With disturbing regularity, she caught herself halfway to the carriage house, bent on hitching Lysandra to the surrey and driving out to see how Gil was faring. Each time, however, Emmeline turned around and marched right back to whatever task she had just abandoned. She'd played the fool as it was, letting that man kiss her the way he had in the parlor that first night, allowing him to stroke her bare ankles beside the stream, and, finally, submitting to him as he'd stripped her naked on the screened porch. Not for all the rubies in India would she go to him again, just asking to be cast off like some strumpet.

The problem was that her body burned for her husband's touch, and the flames of her desire threatened to consume her.

On Thursday afternoon, summoned by the blare of a trumpet loud enough to be Gabriel's own, a stream of wagons, horses, and pedestrians spilled out of Plentiful and onto the road leading to the open field where Brother Joy would conduct the preaching. Emmeline and Izannah, riding in the surrey with a picnic basket and blankets on the floor behind the seat, were among the pilgrims.

"I don't see why we can't camp out for the duration, like everybody else," Izannah complained, folding her arms. "We'll miss all the fun if we go home every night. How am I supposed to get saved, if I'm not even here when Brother Joy calls forth all the repentant souls?"

Emmeline wore simple clothes, fit for sitting on the grass, and a broad-brimmed hat, chosen to protect her delicate skin from the ravages of the late-day sunshine.

She did not deign to give her cousin so much as a sidelong glance. "You were saved last year," she said. "And the year before that. Surely it is as much a sin to bore the Lord as to ignore Him."

Izannah was determined, as always. "I feel the need," she said, "to be washed in the blood of the lamb."

"By all means, do so," Emmeline responded. "Just be back at ten o'clock so that we can go home."

"You are a pagan," Izannah accused.

"I must be," Emmeline replied, drawing the surrey to a stop at the edge of the field among a bevy of wagons and buggies. "Because just now, I have an intense longing to sacrifice you to the moon goddess. Ten o'clock, Izannah."

Izannah scrambled down from the surrey with a lack of grace meant to irritate. "Ten o'clock," she confirmed, her lower lip protruding slightly. "You won't be able to treat me like this, once I'm married. *Then* who will you persecute?"

Emmeline scanned the gathering from the shadows of her hat brim, looking for Gil. "I shall have to find another victim, I suppose," she answered in a distracted tone.

Izannah spotted a friend on the horizon and fled in high dudgeon, and Emmeline watched the girl's retreat with a smile. She hoped she wasn't being too arbitrary with Izannah, insisting on a curfew, but the fact was that people got caught up in the fervor of these events and sometimes did things that were unwise. There were always more than a few babies conceived in the tall grass and the little copse of birch trees down by the creek.

131

Emmeline had lifted the picnic basket from the back of the surrey and was busy hobbling Lysandra, who sometimes took it into her head to roam, when his shadow fell over her.

"Come to get yourself saved, Miss Emmeline?" Gil asked as she looked back at him over one calico-clad shoulder. Rising, she held her hat in place with one hand, and hoped he couldn't see that she was quivering inside like the jellied fruit tucked away in her basket.

She shook her head, smiling a little. "Once," she answered, "ought to be enough. And you, Mr. Hartwell? Are you here to be, as Izannah puts it, 'washed in the blood'?"

He shuddered at the thought, although he was smiling too. "I came for the spectacle of it," he said. "According to Jake Fleming down at the general store, Brother Joy plans to celebrate three days of bringing in the sheaves by setting off a fireworks display."

Not wanting to be petty, Emmeline refrained from pointing out that there was only one Jake Fleming in town, and one general store, thereby eliminating the need to clarify the matter. "And since you want to see the fireworks, you feel honor-bound to listen to the preaching first?"

Gil was wearing wool trousers, a white shirt, and suspenders, and he pushed his hands into his pockets and shrugged, regarding Emmeline with his head tilted slightly to one side. "I'd better tell the truth," he said, "lest God strike me down for a liar. I was hoping to find you here."

Emmeline felt a blush climb her neck to pulse in her cheeks, but she was pretty certain that the brim of her hat hid her face. She made a business of reaching for the picnic basket, only to have Gil step up close and take it from her.

"Will you sit with me, Miss Emmeline?" he asked.

Emmeline's heart was pounding, and her breathing, though silent, was too fast and too shallow. "I don't reckon I can stop you," she answered coolly, "without making a scene."

His laughter was a sweet, unexpected sound, wholly familiar, and just hearing it made her soul resonate and brought tears to her eyes. She offered her first, and last, prayer of the day in the silence of her spirit—*Whatever happens, or doesn't happen, thank You for sparing him.*

After Emmeline had set her jar of jellied fruit and crock of fried chicken in the cold creek with dozens of other jars and crocks, Gil put the basket inside a small, ramshackle shed, along with the rest.

They found seats on the long benches inside Brother Joy's main tent, near the back. Folks had been arriving since daybreak in order to get a good view of the platform, and the places up front had been taken for hours. A baby cried lustily on the far side, and a farmer's wife fainted, probably from a combination of heat and excitement. The invisible energy of anticipation swirled in the worshipers' midst, like Pentecostal fire just waiting to burst forth.

Emmeline, despite a long and settled relationship with the Lord, found herself shifting on the bench, partly because she was eager for the festivities to begin and partly because Gil Hartwell was sitting so close. She tried not to think of the way his thigh and upper arm pressed against hers, but it was a losing battle.

Finally, when the tent was packed and the tension was palpable, Brother Joy's personal choir trooped in, mounting the platform steps and solemnly taking their places in front of a portable pulpit. If their robes were a bit shabby and their hymnals dog-eared, nobody minded. They began to sing, accompanied by a wheezing organ balanced on a wheeled cart, and slowly, awkwardly, earnestly, Brother Joy's borrowed congregation joined in.

Somewhere during that first song, Gil took Emmeline's hand in his, and she didn't pull away. His touch made her too excited to trust her singing, so she simply listened.

Brother Joy, a large, strikingly handsome man in a frayed suit, delayed his appearance, like the showman he was, until his audience had been roused to a fever pitch, then took the pulpit. Not only was he an orator to be reckoned with, but he was fascinating to watch, now weeping without restraint for the sins of the world, now calling down the wrath of heaven, now pacing the platform, talking of fire and brimstone in a low but thunderous voice. His skin glistened with sweat, and his energy was boundless.

One hour passed and then another. During that time, Brother Joy preached almost without ceasing. Now and then he paused to douse himself, as if to drown the very fires of hell, with a ladleful of cold water from a bucket on one corner of the platform. The people of Plentiful were spellbound the whole while; some of them even toppled off their benches and onto the sawdust floor, overcome by a combination of the heat and the power of Brother Joy's preaching.

Emmeline barely blinked, even though she, like most everyone else in that tent, had heard every word before and knew every Bible passage by heart. It was Brother Joy's delivery that captivated her, and if anybody on earth could have talked her into getting saved again, Emmeline supposed he'd have been the one.

After a full three hours of preaching, Brother Joy showed no signs of tiring, but he took pity on his congregation—several of whom had already been carried out of the tent, revived, and brought back in again—and sent everyone out to "feast upon the loaves and fishes and ponder the word of the Lord."

Lacking loaves and fishes, the faithful spread blankets by the stream and ate ham sandwiches, fried chicken, and baked beans, along with cakes and pies of every kind. Women nursed babies in the shade of the birch trees, and small children sprawled under wagon beds, slumbering in the soft, sweet grass. Men smoked and spat and talked, Emmeline suspected, of matters unrelated to the Lord.

For all that, people took note that Gil Hartwell was sitting on Emmeline's blanket, sharing her picnic lunch, but she didn't care. Though he was apparently set on barring her from his bed, Gil was Emmeline's husband, by decree of the very God they were there to worship. It was right and good that they were together, even if Emmeline thought with sadness, it was only temporary.

When the food was gone—except for what had been put aside for supper, of course—a few of the most devout returned to the tent, jealous of their seats at the foot of the platform. Gil lay back on the blanket with a contented sigh, a piece of grass between his teeth, his hands cupped behind his head.

"I've been working real hard out at the ranch," he said presently, without looking at Emmeline. "There's a good roof on the house again, and I mean to start shoring up the barn on Monday morning."

Emmeline wondered what she was supposed to think. Was he telling her he wanted her to come and live with him as his wife, or just making idle conversation? "That's nice," she said.

Gil propped himself up on one elbow and tossed aside the piece of grass. "About last Sunday afternoon—"

Emmeline stiffened. The hat didn't hide the color in her face, and she was too indignant to give a damn. "I hardly think this is the place to discuss last Sunday afternoon!" she hissed.

"Damn it, Emmeline, we have to discuss it somewhere, sometime, and you haven't come near me since!"

Several heads turned, and Emmeline considered standing up, striding into the middle of the stream, and trying to drown herself. Unfortunately, she realized, some sincere soul would probably haul her ashore while she was still breathing.

"In case you've forgotten, Mr. Hartwell," she replied in an acid whisper, "a gentleman calls on a lady. The reverse is not acceptable!"

"Then why did you come out to my place last week and let me rub your feet?"

Emmeline distinctly heard a giggle from the next blanket, and shot the miscreant a look fit to curdle sweet cream. "I have had enough of this conversation," she told her husband.

Gil reached out and grasped Emmeline's wrist when she would have gotten to her feet and stormed away. His hold, while not painful, was too firm to resist without stirring a ruckus. "I apologize," he said quietly. His blue eyes flashed with an unholy fire and there was a tense edge to his jawline, giving Emmeline to believe that he wasn't actually sorry about anything.

"You are not forgiven," Emmeline said, in a voice that was barely more than a breath.

"That," replied Gil, "is the problem."

That afternoon, Emmeline's heart wasn't in the preaching. If it hadn't meant spoiling Izannah's fun, she would have packed up her blanket and basket, unhobbled Lysandra, and driven home. Instead, she sat numbly on the bench, beside Gil, considering what he'd said.

He really and truly had been kidnapped that night in San Francisco, seven years before, and there could be no doubt that he had suffered the agonies of the damned aboard a ship—the *Nellie May,* he'd called it. Such an ordinary, innocent-sounding name for a vessel maintained by the blood and sweat of slaves.

Gil had felt the bite of the captain's whip, not once but several times, and had worked his way back from Australia after his escape.

Emmeline knew all those things, and believed them with her whole heart, and yet Gil was right. She had yet to forgive him for leaving her, for putting her through years of grief, for robbing her of the babies that might have been born of their love. It was insane to resent a man for something he couldn't help, and yet she did. Her fury was as powerful as her passion; she wanted to mate with Gil with all the ferocity of a tigress in the jungle, but she also wanted to fling herself at him, claws bared, screaming and biting, kicking and crying.

She loved Gil and, at one and the same time, hated him.

The realization was devastating, and Emmeline did not know how to resolve the problem. One thing was certain, however—she could not go to this man she loved so desperately until she'd found a way to lay down her anger, once and for all.

Brother Joy ranted and thundered all afternoon, and through half the evening, too. It was almost dark when he called another truce between good and evil and the believers filed out of the tent. Bonfires were lit, and people ate their suppers and told stories about other revivals, who'd gotten healed, and how and who'd gotten saved and why.

Mr. Dillard, the postmaster, had been wrested from the grip of sin that very afternoon, before their very eyes, and the sight had been a memorable one.

Emmeline shared her supper with Gil, just as she had shared her lunch, but few words passed between them, and when the meal was over, she announced that she was going home. Izannah was waiting when she reached the surrey, followed by Gil, who'd insisted on carryiing the picnic basket and the blanket.

"Mrs. Bickham says I can stay with Becky and sleep in their tent," Izannah blurted. "Please, Emmeline—say it's all right! It's likely to be five years before there's another preaching like this one."

Emmeline was conscious of Gil, standing so close behind her, listening. He would know, if she granted Izannah's plea, that she would be home alone that night. On the other hand, to refuse would be both unkind and unfair, when the girl had such trustworthy chaperons as the Reverend and Mrs. Bickham.

"All right," Emmeline agreed with a sigh. "You may stay. But mind you don't do anything foolish."

Izannah thanked Emmeline with an exuberant kiss on the cheek, promised not to be foolish, and hurried away, with Becky, in search of adventure. Emmeline stood for a long time, watching them go.

Gil placed the basket in the backseat, along with the blanket, and crouched to remove Lysandra's hobbles. After tossing those into the rig as well, he came to stand next to Emmeline.

"I love you," he said in a grave and quiet voice. "When the last star winks out, you will still own my soul."

With that, he turned and strode into the darkness, leaving Emmeline standing mute beside her surrey, her heart falling into fragments.

Gil's ranch was not far from the field where Brother Joy had erected his tents, and Emmeline guessed correctly that he would have walked the short distance rather than hitching a mule to a wagon or saddling a horse. After collecting herself she set out along that curving, star-washed road in the surrey, and found him in five minutes.

He kept walking when she drew up beside him, though not at a fast pace and with his face was turned toward her, his expression questioning. He refused to speak first, which was, to Emmeline's way of thinking, rather ungentlemanly of him.

"I just wanted to say," she began awkwardly, as Lysandra trundled along the bumpy track, "that I love you very much."

Gil thrust his hands into his pockets and kept walking, his head lowered, obviously deep in thought. At last, he looked at her again. "That's the tragedy of it," he said. "This would be easier in some ways, for you at least, if I'd never come back. No, don't deny it, Emmeline. You would have been married to Neal Montgomery by now, and while you might not feel for him what you claim you do for me, I know you well enough to think you'd have made a success of the marriage. You'd agreed to it, after all, and so you must have been ready to share the man's bed."

An insight came to Emmeline. It was so simple; she should have seen it before, and would have, if she hadn't been so caught up in her own dilemma. "I think I'm not the only one with something to forgive," she said gently. "You're angry with me, aren't you—because you suffered so much, and you were faithful, and all you thought about was getting home to me. And when you got here, you found me about to marry another man. One you'd never liked."

The look he flung at her was mildly venomous. "I was celibate for seven years, Emmeline," he said with some bitterness. "Granted, I had no opportunity for intimate congress—at least not of the type I would have ever been able to live with—while I was aboard the *Nellie May*, but there were women in Sydney Town that I could have turned to after I escaped. But I had a wife, one I loved, and I wanted to honor my vows."

Emmeline ached for him. It could not have been easy, after all he'd been through, to forswear such elemental comfort, and while she was selfishly glad he had been true to her, she wouldn't have blamed him if he'd found temporary solace in another woman's arms. "Most men couldn't have managed that," she said softly.

He stepped onto the running board, and Emmeline scooted over on the seat so that he could climb in and take the reins. Despite this small overture, he was stiff with fury and hurt. "Did you lie with him, Emmeline?" he asked, drawing the surrey to a halt in the middle of the empty road. Cries of "hallelujah" echoed on the night breeze. "With Montgomery, I mean?"

"Of course not," Emmeline said. "He wasn't my husband yet. And if you'll recall, Mr. Hartwell, I wasn't intimate with you, either, until our wedding night."

Gil relaxed, ever so slightly, and she saw in his eyes, even in the shadow of the surrey's canvas roof, that he believed her. "I guess it isn't fair to hold what you *would* have done against you," he allowed.

Emmeline laughed, not from amusement but because of the sudden release of tension. "No," she said.

Tightening his grip on the reins again, Gil turned Lysandra in a slow circle and headed back toward Plentiful.

"I'll see you home," he said.

Emmeline sighed. "I wanted to see your new roof."

He chuckled. "You'd have seen the wrong side of it, if I had my way," he said. "And that wouldn't be right."

"Why not?"

"You know why not, Emmeline," Gil told her patiently. "We agreed to wait until we were sure we wanted to be together."

Emmeline slipped her arm through his and let her head rest against his shoulder. "Maybe waiting to be sure isn't the right thing to do, Gil," she ventured to say. "You might be sure one day, while I might not be sure 'til the next, by which time you might have changed your mind again. Perhaps we should just close our eyes, hold our breaths, and jump in."

The bonfires of the revival glowed in the night as they passed Brother Joy's burgeoning camp again. "Perhaps," Gil answered, but he sounded uncertain.

"Stay with me tonight," Emmeline said, before she could stop herself.

"I can't."

"Why not?" She hoped the terrible hurt she felt wasn't audible in her voice.

"Emmeline, what if we conceived a child?" he countered.

"That would be wonderful!"

"Not if we didn't stay together, it wouldn't."

Emmeline bristled a little, despite her best intentions. "You would leave us?"

There was a brief, painful silence. "I would never abandon you, let alone an innocent baby. God in heaven, Emmeline, I wouldn't let you out of my sight."

"Then what would be so dreadful about making a child together? After all, Gil, we're married, and married people do that kind of thing all the time."

She felt Gil tremble against her, felt his struggle to quell the emotion, whatever it was, that rocked him from within. "The ranch is in shambles," he said at long last, not looking at her but gazing straight ahead at the road. "I have no cattle, and it's going to be at least a year before the place is paying again. I've got nothing to offer a child, Emmeline. Nothing to offer a wife."

Emmeline didn't speak, but simply let her head rest against his shoulder. Her heart was full of love and sorrow.

Plentiful was dark and quiet, since most everyone in town was attending Brother Joy's revival meetings. Gil drove the surrey straight down Main Street and turned into the judge's driveway. Lysandra, who would have known her way home without any guidance, stopped in front of the carriage house and nickered, ready to be fed and watered and settled in her stall.

"I'll see to the horse," Gil said. "You go on inside."

Emmeline hesitated. "Will you be coming in? You can't very well walk all the way to your ranch in the dark."

"I'd be a poor excuse for a man," he replied good-naturedly, "if I couldn't take myself three miles, whether at noon or midnight."

"You could sleep right here, in the carriage house," Emmeline suggested. She was every bit as stubborn as Gil, maybe more so.

"Go inside, Emmeline," Gil repeated. He had unharnessed Lysandra and was leading her into the small barn. Like the animal, he knew the inside of that building so well that he didn't need a lantern. "Do whatever it is that you do before bed," he called back. "Make tea, let your hair down, say your prayers. Be *sure* to say your prayers."

Emmeline sighed and headed for the front gate, picnic basket in hand. She moved up the walk, mounted the steps, crossed the veranda, and opened the door.

The big house yawned around her, a safe place, full of shadows.

Emmeline set the picnic basket in the entry hall and started up the stairs.

The scent of pipe tobacco filled her nostrils, pungently aromatic, and for one insane moment Emmeline thought the judge had come back to haunt the front parlor, since the smell came from that direction. A second later, rationality returned, and Emmeline realized that someone else was in the house.

Angry rather than afraid, she swept into the parlor.

There, seated on the horsehair settee, bathed in a shaft of moonlight flowing in through the front window, sat Neal Montgomery. The tobacco in his pipe glowed bright red as he drew on it.

"What are you doing here?" Emmeline demanded.

Neal took his time answering, drawing on the pipe again, savoring the smoke, letting it out in a slow stream. "I was welcome in this house once."

"Not in the middle of the night, without even troubling yourself to knock at the front door!"

He rose from the chair, but instead of approaching Emmeline, he stood at the window, the gauzy curtains caught between his fingers, and looked out. "You haven't given him up. Hartwell, I mean. He's in your blood, it appears, like some noxious fever."

"I love him, if that's what you're saying," Emmeline answered. She felt vaguely alarmed, and yet she could not believe that Neal would harm her. He had courted her so patiently and, though naturally displeased, he'd seemed to take their broken engagement in his stride.

"Then you are a fool," Neal said, and turned to face her at last.

Before she had time to think, to read the expression on his face and the coiled tension in his body, he had crossed the room and taken her shoulders in his hands. "Let me go!" she gasped, stunned and offended. No one had ever touched her in anger before.

"Scream," Neal urged. He was so calm, as unearthly as a specter in the moonlit parlor. "Go ahead and scream, Emmeline, so that your precious husband will rush to your rescue."

Now, at last, when it was probably too late, she was afraid. Either Neal had changed, or she had never really known him in the first place.

"And when he does?" Emmeline asked.

Neal's smile was ugly. "I'll kill him," he replied.

"I won't allow it."

He caught her chin in a hard, bruising grip, and suddenly Emmeline knew Gil's kidnapping hadn't been a random act of fate at all. "You will do what I tell you to do," he breathed.

Emmeline stared up at him, wide-eyed, full of loathing, and a step beyond simple fear. "You," she said. "You had my husband shanghaied."

5

GIL SETTLED THE AGED MARE IN A STALL, WITH FRESH WATER IN the trough and a ration of oats in case a bellyful of field grass wouldn't sustain her, and strolled, whistling, out of the small barn. The sight of the darkened house gave him pause, and he wished, for one whimsical moment, that the walls were transparent. It would have been a singular joy to watch Miss Emmeline sitting at her vanity table, letting her hair down, brushing it with long, measured strokes, and, finally, winding the coppery strands into a thick plait. He'd seen her do that a hundred times in reality and a thousand times in his dreams, and he never tired of the sight.

Just imagining that simple, ordinary ritual filled Gil with a yearning of unreasonable depths, rooted far down in his soul. He shoved splayed fingers through his hair in frustration.

Emmeline was his wife, and for seven long years he had lived only to return to her. Now, miraculously, here he was, resurrected, back from the dead, close enough to call out to her. So why was he holding back, like a thirst-ravaged man denying himself water? All the while, the great unseen and unheard clock of the universe was ticking, and with every swing of the pendulum, there was another heartbeat used and gone, another moment lost forever.

Gil was through considering, he suddenly decided, through letting fear and pique stop him from living out whatever was left of this grand, brief gift he had been allotted—his life. He would waste no more of it.

He vaulted over the garden fence and started across the judge's front lawn. He'd batter down the door if he had to, and when Emmeline let him in, he would offer himself to her, like a knight swearing fealty to his queen. *You were right,* he would tell her, *it's time to close our eyes, hold our breaths, and jump.*

Gil bounded up the veranda steps and over to the door, making no effort to be quiet. If any of the neighbors had straggled home from the revival camp to hear him, then so be it. Maybe he'd carry Emmeline right out into the middle of the street in his arms and turn round and round, to let the watchers see that she was his.

She opened the door before he knocked, and though a shadow veiled her face, he sensed, even before she spoke, that something was wrong.

"Go home, Gil," Emmeline said in a strange, thin voice, gripping the edge of the door as though poised to fling it shut in his face. "Please."

"Come in," countered a masculine voice from behind her.

Gil's heart spun over several beats, like a flat rock whirling across a sheet of ice, and he felt the absence of his holster and pistol as a phantom weight against his hip. Normally, he would have been armed, but he'd left his Colt at home that morning, not expecting to need it at an all-day revival meeting. Now, the hairs on his nape were standing upright, and his gut told him that that big clock he'd been thinking about earlier might be about to run down.

He greeted the other man calmly, with a nod and a murmured "Montgomery." As Gil passed Emmeline on the wide threshold, however, he eased her behind him, out onto the veranda.

Any other female might have had the God-given good sense to run, but not Emmeline, Gil said to himself as he saw her try to get past him, back into the house.

"He's the one," she cried as Gil barred her way. "It was Neal who had you shanghaied."

The news did not surprise Gil; in fact, it seemed so glaringly obvious that he wondered why he'd never guessed it. "This is between Montgomery and me," he said firmly, his gaze locked with that of his old adversary. He did not turn to look at his wife. "You run along, Emmeline, and stay out of this."

"I'll get Marshal Scead," Emmeline said.

"You do that," agreed Gil. Scead was eighty-two if he was a day, and probably sound asleep in the town's single jail cell by now, if he wasn't out at the revival, getting himself saved. There hadn't been a crime in Plentiful, as far as Gil knew, since Billy the Kid had come through ten years before and refused to pay the blacksmith for shoeing his horse.

Montgomery held a pistol loosely in his right hand, and when he heard Emmeline clatter down the veranda steps to fetch the law, he aimed it square at Gil's middle and repeated himself in a cordial tone. "Come in."

Gil strained in every bone and muscle for a fight, but his mind was cool, almost detached. Miss Emmeline treasured her bric-a-brac and fancy furniture, and if they got to shooting and rolling around on the floor, things were bound to get blood-spattered, if not broken.

"We ought to settle this outside," he said.

Montgomery shrugged and gestured, with the glinting barrel of his pistol, toward the door. "You go first."

Well aware that Montgomery might simply shoot him in the back, Gil nevertheless led the way out onto the porch, then down the walk. At the gate, he paused and looked back. "If there's going to be a gunfight," he said, "you've got an unfair advantage."

The other man smiled and set the Colt on the square, flat top of a gatepost. "I don't need a gun to kill you," he replied. "I can do it with my bare hands."

Gil led the way into the silent street, which was lighted only by the glow of the moon and stars. Gas-powered streetlamps, while common in large cities, had not yet come to Plentiful.

They faced each other, Gil and Montgomery, in the middle of that dusty, unpaved road. While Gil supposed the scene had its comic side, he knew Montgomery truly intended to kill him, and was willing to die trying. Thinking of all Montgomery had cost him, by paying thugs to knock him over the head that night in San Francisco and then turn him over to a sea captain willing to pay for able-bodied men, Gil was filled with a cold, quiet rage.

"What made you decide to tell the truth now, after all this time?" he asked, standing just six feet from Montgomery, clenching and unclenching his fists, his only weapons, in preparation for the coming fight.

Montgomery cast a glance over one shoulder, toward the field where Brother Joy's tents were erected. There was a faint glow against the sky from the bonfires. "Old Dillard, the postmaster, got himself saved today," he said. He smiled and laid the spread fingers of one hand to his breast. "He was truly repentant."

Gil thought of his letters to Emmeline, scratched out a sentence at a time, on paper he'd stolen or traded his dinner for, posted by freemen in return for his whiskey ration. They might as well have been penned in blood, those missives, so great was the risk of writing them, and he'd written them without knowing whether even one would ever get through.

"Dillard was repentant," Gil repeated. He wanted to get the fight over with before old Marshal Scead showed up and got himself hurt. "Specifically, I guess, for pulling my letters to Emmeline out of the mailbag when they came to the stagecoach and turning them over to you."

"Exactly," Montgomery said with a smile. He'd taken a

cheroot from the inside pocket of his coat, along with a wooden match, which he struck against the sole of his handmade boot. The flame flared, and the scent of sulfur uncurled in the air. "I must say, Hartwell, you write a touching letter."

Bile rushed into the back of Gil's throat at the idea of Montgomery reading his tenderest and most private thoughts. Every word had been wrung from his soul, and had been meant only for Emmeline's eyes. "Let's get on with this," Gil said, opening his cuffs and rolling up his sleeves.

Montgomery drew on his cheroot, then expelled the smoke. He tossed the small cigar aside with a flip of one wrist, and in that same motion a derringer slipped into his palm.

"I'll put the Colt in your hand," he said smoothly, "and it'll look as though you drew on me." He shrugged. "An obvious case of self-defense."

Gil didn't argue that Miss Emmeline was bound to tell the truth of the matter, because he knew Montgomery would never give her the chance. Montgomery meant to kill Emmeline, too, and then testify that Gil had done it. Folks might believe a story like that, since most of them probably thought Gil had never cared about Emmeline in the first place, disappearing without a word as he had. Montgomery, now that Gil considered the matter, had probably done what he could to foster that assumption.

He lunged at Montgomery, letting out a low roar of desperation and fury as he landed on the other man. The derringer went off, and Gil heard the report, felt the bullet burrow deep into the flesh of his shoulder. But the explosive pain, rather than felling him, sent the power of a wounded grizzly surging through his system.

He and Montgomery rolled on the ground, struggling for possession of the derringer for what seemed to Gil an eternity, and then there was another shot. Montgomery stiffened, then went still, and Gil raised himself to his knees.

He was holding the derringer in both hands, still pointed

at Montgomery's dead heart, when Emmeline arrived, accompanied by Marshal Scead and a handful of heathens who'd no doubt been waiting out the revival in Kelly's Saloon.

Gil found Emmeline's pale face in the darkness, focused on it, and passed out.

When he woke up again, he was lying on the billiard table at Kelly's, and old Doc Blitter, the most devoted heathen of them all, was digging in his shoulder with what felt like a broken ax handle. There was blood everywhere, and the pain was so exquisite that it set Gil's head spinning and brought his supper surging up into the back of his throat.

"Don't go puking," Doc Blitter said, speaking around the lighted cigar dangling from his teeth. "That's all I need right now, you puking."

Emmeline was somewhere nearby, at the edge of a shifting fog. Gil heard the rustle of her skirts as she paced back and forth, stirring the filthy sawdust floor with her leather shoes. "You, sir," she said to the doctor, "are nothing but a butcher!"

"Maybe so," said Doc, digging deeper, "but I'm the only man within fifty miles of this shit-heel town who knows how to get a bullet out."

"Look at you," Emmeline went on, her voice rising note by note toward a shrill crescendo. "You're filthy. Why, even if you do manage to get the bullet out, he's bound to die of infection!"

Doc swore, tossed aside his cigar with a bloody hand, and reached for something. Gil watched in horror as the doctor upended a half-filled bottle of rotgut whiskey into his wound.

"This'll fix that," the physician said.

Fire blazed in the wound and sped through Gil's veins, and he lost consciousness again and dreamed he was back aboard the *Nellie May.* He'd relived the entire experience by the time he woke up again.

This time he was in a bed, with clean linen sheets lying

smooth against his skin. The pain was with him, a dull, incessant ache, as though his bones had been pried apart at the joints. Emmeline sat nearby in a rocking chair, tatting an edge onto a pillowcase.

Gil tried to say her name, but it came out as a croak, and left his throat raw.

As though lit from within, her face brightened when she looked at him, and she set aside her needlework and rushed over to pour water from a carafe on the bedside table and offer him some.

He took a careful sip and fell back onto his pillows, feeling as weary as if he'd just plowed a field without a mule. Looking up at Emmeline, he suddenly did not know what to say.

She stroked his forehead with a cool, light hand, and he marveled that so simple a caress could send such a sweet echo pulsing through his soul. "At least that horse doctor didn't kill you," she said, and sat down carefully on the edge of the mattress.

"I thought I dreamed that part," Gil said gruffly, with a grin that wavered on his lips. Hell, he thought, even his mouth was weak.

Emmeline shook her head. "It was quite real," she told him. She was holding his hand in her lap, her fingers intertwined with his. "Neal Montgomery is dead."

"I know," Gil said, and was surprised to realize that he felt sorrow. He had, after all, intended to kill the other man, in order to save his life and Emmeline's.

Her cheeks were pale as parchment. "Everybody knows it was self-defense, so there won't be any trial."

Gil let out a long sigh, because he'd been worried that the incident would be construed as murder, even though he'd taken a bullet in the shoulder himself. He brought his hand to his mouth, and Emmeline's with it, and brushed his dry lips over her knuckles. "'Everybody'? Tell me what *you* think, Emmeline, because that's all that matters to me."

She looked deep into his eyes. "I think we were both fools

to spend even one day apart," she said earnestly. "Why, we acted as if we had all the time in the world!"

He nodded. "I agree," he replied, and looked around the room at the bright wallpaper, the solid furniture, the lamps with their colorfully painted glass globes, the silver picture frames on the guest-room fireplace mantel. "You won't mind leaving the judge's house and coming back to the cabin with me?"

Emmeline's smile nearly blinded him. "Mind? I've got my things all packed, and the house is already up for sale."

"What about Izannah?" Gil asked.

"She and Becky Bickham are going back east," she answered. "They'll both spend a year traveling in Europe with our aunt. Once we've sold the property, Izannah and I will share the proceeds."

Gil nodded, but he was weary, and his concentration was flagging. "I believe I'll rest for just a minute," he said.

Emmeline bent and kissed his forehead, then rose and went back to her chair. He heard the comforting sound of the rocker as he drifted off to sleep, away from the pain. Slumber was a quiet, peaceful realm, no longer haunted, and he rested there, and healed, safe in the constancy of Emmeline's love.

One Month Later . . .

Emmeline stood alone on the veranda, wearing her doing-business hat and carrying her gloves. Gil's precious letters, retrieved from Neal Montgomery's desk by the marshal, were tucked safely in her handbag.

Izannah, dressed to travel, was beside her, tearful and yet eager to set out on the journey east. Mr. Connors, the stage driver, had agreed to bring the coach right to their door, in honor of the occasion, since he had to pass by the judge's front gate on the way to Missoula anyhow.

The house, along with most of its furnishings, belonged to a young doctor from Boston now. He and his family would live on the upper floor and use the lower one as a clinic and small infirmary.

Emmeline heartily approved, her opinion of Doc Blitter being what it was. And she knew she would not miss the many possessions she had sold or given away—Gil's letters and the brooch he had brought her were all she really cherished.

Still, the house had been her refuge, first as a child, then as a bride believing herself to be a widow. As eager as she was to go home to Gil and the little cabin beside the creek, she could not turn away from it without sentiment, and gratitude.

She laid one hand to the whitewashed siding, as if caressing a living creature. *Good-bye,* she said in the silence of her heart.

The arriving stagecoach made a great racket and Becky Bickham, waiting by the front gate with her parents and a good-sized trunk, called out to Izannah in an eager voice to hurry up. Emmeline smiled and turned toward the street with one arm around Izannah's waist.

"We'll go forward," Emmeline said firmly, "and not look back."

When they reached the gate, Izannah embraced her. The coach driver and Reverend Bickham were already loading baggage, while Mrs. Bickham wept into a much-mended handkerchief.

"I promise I'll write every week," Izannah said.

Emmeline kissed her cheek. "You'd better," she answered with a mock scowl. There was a flurry of good-byes after that, along with a few tears, and then Emmeline stood with the Bickhams watching the stagecoach trundle off toward Missoula, where the girls would board a train that would take them all the way to New England.

When the dust settled, Emmeline and the Bickhams said farewells to one another—they would meet again on Sunday morning, of course—and then Emmeline climbed into her overloaded surrey. She took up the reins, released the brake, and turned the rig toward her future.

Gil was standing in the doorway of the barn when she arrived, his shoulder in a sling, leaning on a pitchfork. He watched, with a slight, crooked smile, as she drew the surrey to a stop beside the creek and climbed down. Lysandra lowered her ancient head to the clear waters and began to drink noisily, and on both sides of the stream, Gil's cattle grazed in the rich grass.

"You are not supposed to be working," she scolded as she drew near. Reverend Bickham had organized a crew to make repairs on the barn, and there was wood chopped and stacked for winter. With the cattle Gil had bought from other ranchers, they had the beginnings of the ranch they dreamed of building together.

"And you're not supposed to be nagging," Gil said when she reached him. He set the pitchfork aside and drew her against him in a one-armed embrace. Their kiss was gentle at first, even cautious, and Emmeline's heart leaped, brimming with a new and ever-deeper love.

They were like newlyweds—although not in all ways, for they had agreed not to consummate their marriage until they could wake up together the morning after and go on with their lives.

Gil eased Emmeline into the barn, where the fresh hay was sweet-scented and prickly-soft, and kissed her again, this time with hunger. She responded by parting her lips to receive his tongue.

"Perhaps we should go inside," she gasped, breathless, when he finally allowed her to take air.

Gil nuzzled her neck and stroked her breast. "You've forgotten what I said, Miss Emmeline," he teased as she trembled under his touch, yearning to shed her dress and underthings and receive him completely. "I have no patience, this first time. I've waited too long to have you."

Emmeline flushed, but with pleasure, not embarrassment. She stepped away from him, and he watched her breasts rise as she reached up to remove her sensible hat and toss it aside. After that, she unpinned her hair and shook her head, causing the auburn tresses to fall, bouncing, to her waist. Then, like a temptress, Emmeline began unfastening the small buttons at the front of her dress. Presently she stepped out of the garment and stood before Gil in her petticoats, drawers, and camisole.

He pulled her to him with a low, impatient cry and wrenched the eyelet-edged camisole down, freeing her full, sumptuous breasts. He admired them, fondled them gently in his calloused hand, and then bent his head to take fierce suckle at a taut nipple.

Emmeline cried out in shameless pleasure when he pushed down her petticoats and literally tore away her drawers to cup her in a firm, possessive grip. The heel of his palm pressed against the nubbin of flesh he'd bared, and he made slow, tantalizing circles as he continued to feast on her breasts.

He kissed her again, and the two of them dropped to the hay and knelt facing each other. "Next time," he said hoarsely, "I'll take you like a lady. Right now, I want you in the swiftest and most primitive way I can have you."

Emmeline had been transformed from woman to she-wolf, and she turned on her hands and knees, offering herself to her mate. Gil opened his trousers, found the passage that waited to receive him, and thrust himself inside her with a fierce, almost anguished cry. She was ready, and set a brisk pace for him, whimpering low in her throat while he fondled her breasts and moved hard against her.

Just when she would have hurled back her head and groaned in satisfaction, he slowed himself, and dipped his head to plant light kisses along the length of her backbone. Emmeline shuddered and drew him back into the age-old rhythm that would appease them both. She reached back into his trousers and tickled him with her fingertips, and after that, they were both lost.

Their bodies collided hard, then harder, then harder still. Finally, with a great, mingled sob, they climaxed together, flexing and straining against each other until the last tremor had subsided. Then they fell into the hay, exhausted, to gather their strength for another bout of lovemaking.

After some time, Gil raised himself onto his good elbow and surveyed Emmeline's breasts greedily. She pushed him onto his back and straddled him, and they both laughed at her audacity. The laughter stopped, however, when Emmeline guided Gil inside her, and had him as thoroughly, as mercilessly, as he had had her. She was relentless, and rode him until he lay tamed beneath her, and then was seized by her own pleasure, and uttered a long, gasping shout as she came.

When at last it was over, Emmeline fell to her husband's chest, and he held her, murmuring words of love as she drifted slowly back from ecstasy. In time they were strong enough to untangle themselves and rise from the lush cushion of hay. Emmeline found her clothes and put them on, but her hair was spiky with straw, as was Gil's, and her hat had disappeared entirely.

Gazing at Gil, Emmeline felt suddenly shy. She'd been wanton, flinging herself into their lovemaking the way she had, behaving like some primitive creature and carrying on wildly enough to scare the cattle away.

She looked down, shaking her skirts with both hands.

Gil cupped her chin in his palm and raised her face. "I love you, Emmeline," he said, clearly and with purpose, as though speaking to someone who might not hear or understand what he was saying.

She stood on tiptoe and kissed him. "And I love you," she responded.

Gil took her hand and led her out of the barn and across the wide yard toward the cabin. Inside, sitting in the middle of the table, was a small box. "I couldn't afford to buy you one of these before," he said as Emmeline raised the lid and found a simple golden band inside. "Will you stay with me, and be my wife?" he asked. "'Til death do us part?"

"Longer," Emmeline replied, holding out her hand so he could slip the ring onto her finger.

It was a perfect fit.

LINDA LAEL MILLER began her writing career in 1983 with *Fletcher's Woman.* Named "The Most Outstanding Writer of Sensual Romance" by *Romantic Times,* Ms. Miller was nominated by the Romance Writers of America for an award for her thrilling *Wanton Angel.* The bestselling author's delightful novels include the exciting Corbin series, *Banner O'Brien, Corbin's Fancy, Memory's Embrace,* and *My Darling Melissa;* plus two romances set amidst the lush, rugged beauty of New Zealand and Australia, *Angelfire* and *Moonfire.* A heart-stirring trilogy features the adventures of the Chalmers sisters, *Lily and the Major, Emma and the Outlaw,* and *Caroline and the Raider*—and a wonderful homespun romance, *Daniel's Bride,* once again skyrocketed her onto the bestsellers list. Another series about the magnificent Quade family began with *Yankee Wife,* and continued with the intriguing *Taming Charlotte.* Now, *Princess Annie* adds to the fun with more high spirits and sparkling sensuality. Ms. Miller has also penned an enchanting contemporary romance, *The Legacy.* Linda Lael Miller lives near Seattle, Washington.

LINDA HOWARD

Lake of Dreams

1

*H*IS EYES WERE LIKE JEWELS, AQUAMARINES AS DEEP AND VIVID
as the sea, burning through the mist that enveloped him.
They glittered down at her, the expression in them so intense
that she was frightened, and struggled briefly in his grasp. He
soothed her, his voice rough with passion as he controlled her
struggles, stroking and caressing until she was once more
quivering with delight, straining upward to meet him. His
hips hammered rhythmically at her, driving deep. His power-
ful body was bare, his iron muscles moving like oiled silk
under his sweaty skin. The mist from the lake swirled
so thickly around them that she couldn't see him clearly,
could only feel him, inside and without, possessing her
so fiercely and completely that she knew she would never
be free of him. His features were lost in the mist, no matter
how she strained her eyes to see him, no matter how she
cried out in frustration. Only the hot jewels of his eyes
burned through, eyes that she had seen before, through
other mists—

Thea jerked awake, her body quivering with the echo of
passion . . . and completion. Her skin was dewed with

sweat, and she could hear her own breathing, coming hard and fast at first, then gradually slowing as her heartbeat settled into its normal pace. The dream always drained her of strength, left her wrung out and boneless from exhaustion.

She felt shattered, unable to think, overcome by both panic and passion. Her loins throbbed as if she had just made love; she twisted on the tangled sheets, pressing her thighs together to try to negate the sensation of still having him within her. *Him.* Nameless, faceless, but always *him.*

She stared at the dim early-morning light that pressed against the window, a graying so fragile that it scarcely penetrated the glass. There was no need to look at the clock; the dream always came in the dark, silent hour before dawn, and ended at the first approach of light.

It's just a dream, she told herself, reaching for any possible comfort. *Only a dream.*

But it was unlike any dream she'd ever had before.

She thought of it as a single dream, and yet the individual episodes were different. They—it—had begun almost a month before. At first she had simply thought of it as a weird dream, singularly vivid and frightening, but still only a dream. Then it had come again the next night. And the next. And every night since, until she dreaded going to sleep. She had tried setting her alarm to go off early, to head the dream off at the pass, so to speak, but it hadn't worked. Oh, the alarm had gone off, all right; but as she'd been lying in bed grumpily mourning the lost sleep and steeling herself to actually get up, the dream had come anyway. She had felt awareness fade, had felt herself slipping beneath the surface of consciousness into that dark world where the vivid images held sway. She'd tried to fight, to stay awake, but it simply hadn't been possible. Her heavy eyes had drifted shut, and he was there again . . .

He was angry with her, furious that she'd tried to evade him. His long dark hair swirled around his shoulders, the strands almost alive with the force of his temper. His eyes . . . oh, God, his eyes, as vivid as the dream, a hot blue-green

*searing through the clouds of mosquito netting that draped
her bed. She lay very still, acutely aware of the cool linen
sheets beneath her, of the heavy scents of the tropical night, of
the heat that made even her thin nightgown feel oppressive
. . . and most of all of her flesh quivering in frightened
awareness of the man standing in the night-shadowed bedroom, staring at her through the swath of netting.*

*Frightened, yes, but she also felt triumphant. She had
known it would come to this. She had pushed him, dared him,
taunted him to this very outcome, this devil's bargain she
would make with him. He was her enemy. And tonight he
would become her lover.*

*He came toward her, his warrior's training evident in the
grace and power of his every move. "You tried to evade me,"
he said, his voice as dark as the evening thunder. His fury
rippled around him, almost visible in its potency. "You played
your games, deliberately arousing me to the mindlessness of
a stallion covering a mare . . . and now you dare try to hide
from me? I should strangle you."*

*She rose up on one elbow. Her heart was pounding in her
chest, painfully thudding against her ribs, and she felt as if
she might faint. But her flesh was awakening to his nearness,
discounting the danger. "I was afraid," she said simply,
disarming him with the truth.*

*He paused, and his eyes burned more vividly than before.
"Damn you," he whispered. "Damn both of us." Then his
powerful warrior's hands were on the netting, freeing it,
draping it over her upper body. The insubstantial wisp settled
over her like a dream itself, and yet it still blurred his features,
preventing her from seeing him clearly. His touch, when it
came, wrenched a soft, surprised sound from her lips. His
hands were rough and hot, sliding up her bare legs in a slow
caress, lifting her nightgown out of the way. Violent hunger,
all the more fierce for being unwilling, emanated from him as
he stared at the shadowed juncture of her thighs.*

*So it was to be that way, then, she thought, and braced
herself. He intended to take her virginity without preparing
her. So be it. If he thought he could make her cry out in pain*

and shock, he would be disappointed. He was a warrior, but she would show him that she was his equal in courage.

He took her that way, pulled to the edge of the bed and with only her lower body bared, and the mosquito netting between them. He took her with anger, and with tenderness. He took her with a passion that seared her, with a completeness that marked her forever as his. And, in the end, she did cry out. That triumph was his, after all. But her cries weren't of pain, but of pleasure and fulfillment, and a glory she hadn't known existed.

That was the first time he'd made love to her, the first time she'd awakened still trembling from a climax so sweet and intense that she'd wept in the aftermath, huddled alone in her tangled bed and longing for more. The first time, but definitely not the last.

Thea got out of bed and walked to the window, restlessly rubbing her hands up and down her arms as she stared out at the quiet courtyard of her apartment building and waited for dawn to truly arrive, for the cheerful light to banish the lingering, eerie sense of unreality. Was she losing her mind? Was this how insanity began, this gradual erosion of reality until one was unable to tell what was real and what wasn't? Because the here and now was what didn't feel real to her anymore, not as real as the dreams that ushered in the dawn. Her work was suffering; her concentration was shot. If she worked for anyone but herself, she thought wryly, she would be in big trouble.

Nothing in her life had prepared her for this. Everything had been so *normal,* so Cleaverish. Great parents, a secure home life, two brothers who had, despite all earlier indications, grown up to be nice, interesting men whom she adored. Nothing traumatic had happened to her when she was growing up; there had been the tedium of school, the almost suffocating friendships youngsters seem to need, the usual wrangles and arguments, and the long, halcyon summer days spent at the lake. Every summer, her courageous mother would pack the station wagon and bravely set forth to the summer house, where she would ride herd on three energetic kids for most of the summer. Her father would drive up every weekend, and would take some of his vacation there, too. Thea remembered long, hot days of swimming and fishing, of bees buzzing in the grass, birdsong, fireflies winking in the dusk, crickets and frogs chirping, the plop of a turtle into the water, the mouth-watering smell of hamburgers cooking over charcoal. She remembered being bored, and fretting to go back home, but by the time summer would come again she'd be in a fever to get back to the lake.

If anything in her life was unusual, it was her chosen occupation, but she enjoyed painting houses. She was willing to tackle any paint job, inside or out, and customers seemed to love her attention to detail. She was also getting more and more mural work, as customers learned of that particular talent and asked her to transform walls. Even her murals were cheerfully normal; nothing mystic or tortured there. So why had she suddenly begun having these weird time-period dreams, featuring the same faceless man, night after night after night?

In the dreams, his name varied. He was Marcus, and dressed as a Roman centurion. He was Luc, a Norman invader. He was Neill, he was Duncan . . . he was so many different men she should never have been able to remember the names, and yet she did. He called her different names in the dreams, too: Judith, Willa, Moira, Anice. She was all of those women, and all of those women were the same. And he was always the same, no matter his name.

He came to her in the dreams, and when he made love to her, he took more than her body. He invaded her soul, and filled her with a longing that never quite left, the sense that she was somehow incomplete without him. The pleasure was so shattering, the sensations so real, that when she had awakened the first time and lain there weeping, she had fearfully reached down to touch herself, expecting to feel the wetness of his seed. It hadn't been there, of course. He didn't exist, except in her mind.

Her thirtieth birthday was less than a week away, and in

all those years she had never felt as intensely about a real man as she did about the chimera who haunted her dreams.

She couldn't keep her mind on her work. The mural she'd just finished for the Kalmans had lacked her customary attention to detail, though Mrs. Kalman had been happy with it. Thea knew it hadn't been up to her usual standards, even if Mrs. Kalman didn't. She had to stop dreaming about him. Maybe she should see a therapist, or perhaps even a psychiatrist. But everything in her rebelled against that idea, against recounting those dreams to a stranger. It would be like making love in public.

But she had to do something. The dreams were becoming more intense, more frightening. She had developed such a fear of water that, yesterday, she had almost panicked when driving over a bridge. She, who had always loved water sports of any kind, and who swam like a fish! But now she had to steel herself to even look at a river or lake, and the fear was growing worse.

In the last three dreams, they had been at the lake. *Her* lake, where she had spent the wonderful summers of her childhood. He had invaded her home turf, and she was suddenly more frightened than she could ever remembering being before. It was as if he had been stalking her in her dreams, inexorably moving closer and closer to a conclusion that she already knew.

Because, in her dreams, only sometimes did he make love to her. Sometimes he killed her.

2

THE SUMMER HOUSE WAS THE SAME, BUT ODDLY DIMINISHED BY time. Seen through a child's eyes, it had been a spacious, slightly magical place, a house where fun and laughter were commonplace, a house made for the long, glorious summers. Thea sat in her car and stared at it, feeling love and a sense of peace well up to overcome her fear at actually being here, at the scene of her most recent dreams. Nothing but good times were associated with this place. At the age of fourteen, she had received her first kiss, standing with Sammy Somebody there in the shadow of the weeping willow. She'd had a wild crush on Sammy for that entire summer, and now she couldn't even remember his last name! So much for true love.

Now she saw that the house was small, and in need of a paint job. She smiled, thinking that she could take care of that little chore while she was here. The grass was knee-high, and the swing, hanging from a thick branch of the huge oak, had come down on one side. Thea steeled herself and quickly glanced in the direction of the lake. The dock was in need of repairs, too, and she tried to concentrate on that, but the expanse of blue water stretching out beyond the dock brought a sheen of sweat to her forehead. Nausea roiled in her stomach and she swallowed convulsively as she jerked her gaze back to the house and concentrated instead on the peeling paint of the front porch.

Last night, he had killed her. The expression in those aquamarine eyes had been calm and terrifyingly remote as he held her beneath the cool lake water, his arms like steel as her panicked struggles decreased in strength, until her tortured lungs had given up their last precious bit of oxygen and she had inhaled her own death.

She had awakened in the early dawn, sweating and trembling, and known that she couldn't go on like this much longer without having a nervous breakdown. She had gotten up, put on a pot of coffee, and spent the next several hours overloading on caffeine while she made her plans. She had no work going on right now, so mapping out free time for herself was easy. It probably wasn't smart, since summer was when she made the bulk of her income, but it was easy. At an hour when she could reasonably expect her parents to be awake she'd called and asked their permission to spend a couple of weeks at the lake. As she had expected, they were delighted that she was finally going to take a vacation. Thea's brothers and their families regularly made use of the summer house, but for one reason or another, Thea hadn't been back to the lake since she was eighteen. Eleven years was a long time, but life had somehow gotten in the way. First there had been college and the need to work in the summer to finance it, then a couple of boring jobs in her chosen field that told her she had chosen the wrong field.

She had stumbled onto her career as a housepainter by accident, when she had been out of a job and desperate for anything that would bring in some money. To her surprise, despite the hot, hard work, she had liked painting houses. As time went on, more and more jobs came her way. During the winters she got some inside jobs, but she usually worked like a fiend during the summers, and simply hadn't been able to get away to join the family at any of their outings to the lake.

"But what about your birthday?" her mother asked, suddenly remembering the upcoming event. "Aren't you going to be here?"

Thea hesitated. Her family was big on birthdays. Now that her brothers were married and had children, with their wives and kids thrown into the mix, there wasn't a single month in the year when *someone's* birthday wasn't being celebrated. "I don't know," she finally said. "I'm tired, Mom. I really need a rest." That wasn't why she wanted to go to the lake, but neither was it a lie. She hadn't slept good for almost a month, and fatigue was pulling at her. "How would a delayed party sit with you?"

"Well, I suppose that would be okay," her mother said doubtfully. "I'll have to let the boys know."

"Yeah, I'd hate for them to pull a birthday prank on the wrong day," Thea replied in a dry tone. "If they've already ordered a load of chicken manure to be delivered to me, they'll just have to hold it for a few days."

Her mother chuckled. "They've never gone quite that far."

"Only because they know I'd do something twice as bad to them."

"Have fun up at the lake, honey, but be careful. I don't know if I like the idea of you being there all alone."

"I'll be careful," Thea promised. "Are there any supplies in the house?"

"I think there are a few cans of soup in the pantry, but that's about it. Check in when you get there, okay?"

"Check in" was code for what her father called Pick Up The Phone And Let Your Mother Know You're All Right So She Won't Call Missing Persons. Mrs. Marlow normally let her children get on with their lives, but when she said "check in" they all knew that she was a little anxious.

"I'll call as soon as I get to the grocery store."

Thea had kept her promise, calling in as soon as she

arrived at the small grocery store where they'd always bought their supplies for the summer house. Now she sat in her car in front of the house, frozen with fear at the nearness of the lake, while bags of perishables slowly thawed in the backseat.

She forced herself to breathe deeply, beating down the fear. All right, so she couldn't look at the water. She would keep her eyes averted as she unloaded the car.

The screen door creaked as she opened it, a familiar sound that eased the strain in her expression. The screened front porch ran all the way across the front of the house, and in her childhood had been occupied by a collection of mismatched Adirondack, wicker, and lawn chairs. Her mother had often sat on the porch for hours, sewing or reading, and keeping an eye on Thea and the boys as they frolicked in the lake. The porch was bare now; the Adirondacks and wickers were long gone, and she'd heard her mother say that the lawn chairs were stored in the shed out back. Thea didn't know if she would bother to get them out; she certainly wouldn't be looking at the lake if she could help it.

No, that wasn't true. She had come up here to face the fear the dreams had caused. If that meant forcing herself to stare at the water for hours, then that's what she would do. She wouldn't let this nighttime madness rob her of a lifetime of enjoyment.

When she unlocked the front door, the heat and mustiness of a closed house hit her in the face. She wrinkled her nose and plunged inside, unlocking and opening every window to let in fresh air. By the time she had carried in the groceries and stored the perishables in the refrigerator, the light breeze had gone a long way toward sweetening the air.

Out of habit, Thea started to put her clothes in the same bedroom she'd always used, but halted as soon as she opened the door. Her old iron-frame bed had been replaced by two twin beds. The room was much tinier than she remembered. A slight frown knit her brow as she looked around. The bare wood floors were the same, but the walls were painted a different color now, and blinds covered the window, rather than the ruffled curtains she'd preferred as a young girl.

The boys' room had always had twin beds—three of them, in fact—and she checked inside to see if that still held true. It did, though the number of beds had dwindled to two. Thea sighed. She would have liked to sleep in her old room, but probably her parents' room was the only one with a double bed, and she knew she'd appreciate the comfort even more. She had a queen-size bed in her apartment.

She felt like Goldilocks as she opened the door to the third bedroom, and she burst out laughing. Sure enough, here was the bed that was just right. The double bed was no more. In its place was a king-size bed that took up the majority of the floor space, leaving only enough room on either side to maneuver while making up the bed. A long double dresser occupied most of the remaining space. She would have to be careful about stubbing her toes in here, but she would definitely sleep in comfort.

As she hung her clothes in the closet, she heard the unmistakable creak of the screen door, heavy footsteps on the porch, and then two short, hard knocks on the frame of the open front door. Startled, Thea stood very still. A cold knot of fear began to form in her stomach. She had no idea who could be at the door. She had never been afraid here before—the crime rate was so low that it was almost nonexistent—but abruptly she was terrified. What if a vagrant had watched her unload the car, and knew she was here alone? She had already checked in with her mother, to let her know she'd arrived safely, so no one would expect to hear from her for another week or so. She'd told her mother that she intended to stay about two weeks. She could be murdered or kidnapped, and it might be two weeks or longer before anyone knew she was missing.

There were other houses on the lake, of course, but none within sight. The closest one, a rental, was about half a mile away, hidden behind a finger of land that jutted into the lake. Sammy What's-his-name's family had rented it that summer when she was fourteen, she remembered. Who knew who was renting it now, or if someone hadn't bothered with renting and had simply broken in.

She hadn't heard another car or a boat, so that meant whoever was on the porch had walked. Only the rental house was within realistic walking distance. That meant he was a stranger, rather than someone belonging to the families they had met here every summer.

Her imagination had run away with her, she thought, but she couldn't control her rapid, shallow breathing, or the hard pounding of her heartbeat. All she could do was stand there in the bedroom, like a small animal paralyzed by the approach of a predator.

The front door was open. There was another screen door there, but it wasn't latched. There was nothing to stop him, whoever he was, from simply walking in.

If she was in danger, then she was trapped. She had no weapon, other than one of the kitchen knives, but she couldn't get to them without being seen. She cast an agonized glance at the window. What were her chances of getting it open and climbing out without being heard? Given the silence in the house, she realized, not very good.

That hard double knock sounded again. At least he was still on the porch.

Maybe she *was* crazy. How did she know it was even a man? By the heaviness of the footsteps? Maybe it was just a large woman.

No. It was a man. She was certain of it. Even his knocks had sounded masculine, too hard to have been made by a woman's softer hand.

"Hello? Is anyone home?"

Thea shuddered as the deep voice reverberated through the house, through her very bones. It was definitely a man's voice, and it sounded oddly familiar, even though she knew she'd never heard it before.

My God, she suddenly thought, disgusted with herself. What was wrong with her? If the man on the porch meant her any harm, cowering here in the bedroom wouldn't do her any good. And besides, a criminal would simply open the door and come on in, would already have done so. This was probably a perfectly nice man who was out for a walk and had seen a new neighbor arrive. Maybe he hadn't seen *her* at all, but noticed the car in the driveway. She was making a fool out of herself with these stupid suspicions, this panic.

Still, logic could only go so far in calming her fears. It took a lot of self-control to straighten her shoulders and forcibly regulate her breathing, and even more to force her feet to move toward the bedroom door. She stopped once more, still just out of sight, to get an even firmer grip on her courage. Then she stepped out of the bedroom into the living room, and into the view of the man on the porch.

She looked at the open door, and her heart almost failed her. He was silhouetted against the bright light beyond and she couldn't make out his features, but he was big. Six-three, at least, with shoulders that filled the doorframe. It was only her imagination, it had to be, but there seemed to be an indefinable tension in the set of those shoulders, something at once wary and menacing.

There was no way she could make herself go any closer. If he made a move to open the screen, she would bolt for the back door in the kitchen. Her purse was in the bedroom behind her and she wouldn't be able to grab it, but her car keys were in her jeans pocket, so she should be able to dive into the car and lock the doors before he could reach her, then drive for help.

She cleared her throat. "Yes?" she managed to say. "May I help you?" Despite her effort, her voice came out low and husky. To her dismay, she sounded almost . . . inviting. Maybe that was better than terrified, but she was doubtful. Which was more likely to trigger an approach by a predator, fear or a perceived sexual invitation?

Stop it! she fiercely told herself. Her visitor hadn't said or done anything to warrant this kind of paranoia.

"I'm Richard Chance," the man said, his deep voice once again sinking through her skin, going all the way to her bones. "I'm renting the house next door for the summer. I saw your car in the driveway and stopped by to introduce myself."

Relief was almost as debilitating as terror, Thea realized as her muscles loosened and threatened to collapse altogether. She reached out an unsteady hand to brace herself against the wall.

"I—I'm glad to meet you. I'm Thea Marlow."

"Thea," he repeated softly. There was a subtle sensuality in the way he formed her name, almost as if he were tasting it. "Glad to meet you, Thea Marlow. I know you're probably still unpacking, so I won't keep you. See you tomorrow."

He turned to go, and Thea took a hasty step toward the door, then another. By the time he reached out to open the screen, she was at the doorway. "How do you know I'm still unpacking?" she blurted, tensing again.

He paused, though he didn't turn around. "Well, I take a long walk in the mornings, and your car wasn't here this morning. When I touched your car hood just now, it was still warm, so you haven't been here long. It was a reasonable assumption."

It was. Reasonable, logical. But why had he checked her car hood to see how hot it was? Suspicion kept her silent.

Then, slowly, he turned to face her. The bright sunlight glinted on the glossy darkness of his hair, thick and as lustrous as a mink's pelt, and clearly revealed every strong line of his face. His eyes met hers through the fine mesh of the screens, and a slow, unreadable smile lifted the corners of his mouth. "See you tomorrow, Thea Marlow."

Motionless again, Thea watched him walk away. Blood drained from her head and she thought she might faint. There was a buzzing in her ears, and her lips felt numb. Darkness began edging into her field of vision and she realized that she really *was* going to faint. Clumsily she dropped to her hands and knees and let her head hang forward until the dizziness began to fade.

My God. *It was him!*

There was no mistaking it. Though she'd never seen his face in her dreams, she recognized him. When he had turned to face her and those vivid aquamarine eyes had glinted at her, every cell in her body had tingled in recognition.

Richard Chance was the man in her dreams.

3

*T*HEA WAS SO SHAKEN THAT SHE ACTUALLY BEGAN LOADING ALL of her stuff back into the car, ready to flee back to White Plains and the dubious safety of her own apartment. In the end, though still trembling with reaction, she returned her supplies and clothes to the house and then resorted to her own time-honored remedy of coffee. What good would going home do? The problem was the dreams, which had her so on edge that she had panicked when a neighbor came to call and then had immediately decided, on the basis of his vivid eye color, that he was the man in her dreams.

Okay, time for a reality check, she sternly told herself as she nursed her third cup of coffee. She had never been able to see Marcus-Neill-Duncan's face, because of the damn mist that always seemed to be between them. All she had been able to tell was that he had long, dark hair and aquamarine eyes. On the other hand, she knew his smell, his touch, every inch of his muscled body, the power with which he made love. What was she supposed to do, ask Richard Chance to strip down so she could inspect him for similarities?

174

A lot of people in the world had dark hair; most of them, as a matter of fact. A lot of dark-haired men had vivid eyes. It was merely chance that she had happened to meet Richard Chance at a time when she wasn't exactly logical on the subject of eye color. She winced at the play on words, and got up to pour her fourth cup of coffee.

She had come here with a purpose. She refused to let a dream, no matter how disturbing and realistic, destroy her enjoyment of something she had always loved. It wasn't just this new fear of water that she hated, but what the dreams were doing to her memories of the summers of her childhood. Losing that joy would be like losing the center of her being. Damn it, she *would* learn to love the water again. Maybe she couldn't look at the lake just yet, but by the time she left here, she swore, she would be swimming in it again. She couldn't let her stupid paranoia about Richard Chance frighten her away.

It didn't mean anything that he had said her name as if savoring it. Actually, it did mean something, but that something was connected to his sexual organs rather than to her dreams. Thea knew she wasn't a raving beauty, but neither was she blind to her attractiveness to men. She was often dissatisfied with her mop of thick, curly, chestnut hair, despairing of ever taming it into any discernible style, but men, for reasons of their own, liked it. Her eyes were green, her features even and clean-cut, and the rigors of her job kept her lean and in shape. Now that her nerves were settling down, she realized that the gleam in those memorable eyes had been interested rather than threatening.

That could be difficult, considering that she had come up here to work through some problems rather than indulge in a summer fling with a new neighbor. She wasn't in the mood for romance, even of the casual, two-week variety. She would be cool and uninterested in any invitations he might extend, he would get the hint, and that would be that.

"Come."
She turned, and saw him standing under the willow tree,

his hand outstretched. She didn't want to go to him, every instinct shouted for her to run, but the compulsion to obey was a terrible need inside her, an ache and a hunger that he could satisfy.

"Come," he said again, and her unwilling feet began moving her across the cool, dewy grass. Her white nightdress swirled around her legs, and she felt her nakedness beneath the thin fabric. No matter how many layers of clothing covered her, he always made her feel unclothed and vulnerable. She knew she shouldn't be out here alone, especially with him, but she couldn't make herself go back inside. She knew he was a dangerous man, and it didn't matter. All that mattered was being with him; the propriety that had ruled her life suddenly meant less to her than did the wet grass beneath her bare feet.

When she reached him, they stood facing each other like adversaries, neither moving nor speaking for a long moment that stretched out until she thought she would scream from the tension of it. Like the predator he was, he had been stalking her for weeks, and now he sensed, with unerring instinct, that she was within his grasp. He put his hand on her arm, his touch burning with vitality, and a smile lightly touched his hard mouth as he felt her betraying quiver. "Do you think I will hurt you?" he asked, his amusement evident.

She shivered again. "Yes," she said, looking up at him. "In one way or another . . . yes."

Inexorably he drew her closer, until her flimsily clad body rested against him and the animal heat of his flesh dispelled the chill of the night air. Automatically she put her hands up to rest against his chest, and the feel of the rock-hard sheets of muscle made her breath catch. No other man she'd ever touched was as hard and vital as this—this warrior, whose life was based on death and destruction. She wanted to deny him, to turn away from him, but was as helpless as a leaf on the wind to defy the currents that swept her toward him.

He brushed his lips against her hair in an oddly tender gesture, one she hadn't expected from such a man. "Then lie *down with me," he murmured, "and I'll show you the sweetest pain of all."*

Thea awoke, the echoes of her own cries still lingering in the darkness of the bedroom. He had; oh, he had. She was lying on her back, her nightgown twisted around her waist, her legs open and her knees raised. The last remnants of completion still throbbed delicately in her loins.

She put her hands over her face and burst into tears.

It was more than disturbing—it was humiliating. The damn man not only took over her dreams, he dominated her body as well. Her entire sense of self was grounded in her sturdy normality, her good common sense. Thea had always thought of herself as *dependable,* and suddenly that description no longer seemed to apply. Because of the dreams, she had taken a two-week vacation right in the middle of her busiest time, which wasn't dependable. What was going on with her now defied common sense, defied all her efforts to understand what was happening. And it certainly wasn't *normal* to have frighteningly intense climaxes night after night, while sleeping alone.

Choking back her tears, she stumbled out of bed and down the hall to the bathroom, where she stood under the shower and tried to rid her body of the sensation of being touched by invisible hands. When she felt marginally calmer, she dried off and relocated to the kitchen, where she put on fresh coffee and then sat drinking it and watching the dawn progress into a radiantly sunny morning.

The kitchen was located at the back of the house, so the lake wasn't visible from the window, and Thea slowly relaxed as she watched tiny birds flitting from branch to branch in a nearby tree, twittering to each other and doing bird things.

She had to stop letting these dreams upset her so much. No matter how disturbing their content, they were still just dreams. When she looked at this rationally, the only thing about the dreams that had really affected her life was the unreasoning fear of water they had caused. She had come to the lake to work through that fear, to force herself to face it, and if she could overcome that she would be satisfied. Maybe it wasn't normal to have such sexually intense dreams, or for the same man who brought her such pleasure to kill her in some of those dreams, but she would handle it. Who knew what had triggered the dreams? They could have been triggered by her eclectic reading material, or some movie she'd watched, or a combination of both. Probably they would cease as mysteriously as they had appeared.

In the meantime, she had already wasted one day of her self-prescribed recovery period. Except for that one nauseating glance at the lake when she had first arrived, she had managed to completely ignore the water.

All right, Theadora, she silently scolded herself. *Stop being such a wuss. Get off your can and do what you came here to do.*

In an unconscious gesture of preparation, she ran her fingers through her hair, which had almost dried in the time she had spent drinking coffee and postponing the inevitable. She could feel the unruly curls, thick and vibrant, taking shape under her fingers. She probably looked a fright, she thought, and was glad there was no one there to see. For this entire two weeks, she could largely ignore her appearance except for basic cleanliness, and she looked forward to the freedom.

For comfort, she poured one final cup of coffee and carried it with her out onto the porch, carefully keeping her gaze cast downward so she wouldn't spill the hot liquid. Yeah, she thought wryly, that was a great excuse to keep from seeing the lake first thing when she opened the door.

She kept her eyes downcast as she opened the front door and felt the cool morning air wash over her bare feet. She had simply pulled on her nightgown again after leaving the shower, and the thin material was no match for the chill that the sun hadn't quite dispelled.

All right. Time to do it. Firmly gripping the cup like a lifeline, she slowly raised her eyes so that her gaze slid first across the floor of the porch, then onto the overgrown grass, and then down the slight slope toward the lake. She deliberately concentrated on only a narrow field of vision, so that everything else was blurred. There was the willow tree off to the left, and—

He was standing beneath the spreading limbs, just as he had in her dream.

Thea's heart almost stopped. Dear God, now her dreams had started manifesting themselves during her waking hours, in the form of hallucinations. She tried to blink, tried to banish the vision, but all she could do was stare in frozen horror at the man standing as motionless as a statue, his aquamarine eyes shining across the distance.

Then he moved, and she jerked in reaction as she simultaneously realized two things, each as disturbing in a different way as the other.

One, the "vision" was Richard Chance. The figure under the tree was a real human being, not a figment of her imagination.

Two, she hadn't realized it before, but last night she had been able to see her dream lover's face for the first time, and it had been Richard Chance's face.

She calmed her racing heartbeat. Of course her subconscious had chosen his features for those of the dream lover; after all, she had been startled that very day by the similarity of their eyes. This quirk of her dreams, at least, was logical.

They faced each other across the dewy grass, and a slow smile touched the hard line of his mouth, almost causing her heartbeat to start galloping again. For the sake of her circuits, she hoped he wouldn't smile too often.

Then Richard Chance held out his hand to her, and said, "Come."

4

WHAT LITTLE COLOR SHE HAD DRAINED FROM THEA'S FACE.
"What did you say?" she whispered.

He couldn't possibly have heard her. He was standing a
good thirty yards away; she had barely been able to hear the
one word he'd spoken, though somehow the sound had been
perfectly clear, as if she had heard it inside herself as well as
out. But the expression on his face changed subtly, to
something more alert, his eyes more piercing. His outstretched hand suddenly seemed more imperious, though
his tone became cajoling. "Thea. Come with me."

Shakily she stepped back, intending to close the door.
This had to be pure chance, but it was spooky.

"Don't run," he said softly. "There's no need to. I won't
hurt you."

Thea had never considered herself a coward. Her brothers
would have described her as being a touch too foolhardy for
her own good, stubbornly determined to climb any tree they
could climb, or to swing out on a rope as high as they did
before dropping into the lake. Despite the eerie similarity
between the dream and what he'd just now said, her spine

180

stiffened, and she stared at Richard Chance as he stood under the willow tree, surrounded by a slight mist. Once again, she was letting a weird coincidence spook her, and she was tired of being afraid. She knew instinctively that the best way to conquer any fear was to face it—hence her trip to the lake—so she decided to take a good, hard look at Mr. Chance to catalog the similarities between him and her dream lover. She looked, and almost wished she hadn't.

The resemblance wasn't just in his eyes and the color of his hair. She could see it now in the powerful lines of his body, so tall and rugged. He was wearing jeans and hiking boots and a short-sleeved chambray shirt that revealed the muscularity of his arms. She noticed the thickness of his wrists, the wrists of a man who regularly did hard physical work . . . *the wrists of a swordsman.*

She gasped, shaken by the thought. Where had it come from? What did she know about swordsmen? They weren't exactly thick on the ground; she'd never even met anyone who fenced. And even as she pictured the elegant moves of fencing, she discarded that comparison. No, by *swordsman* she meant someone who used a heavy broadsword in battle, slashing and hacking. A flash of memory darted through her, and she saw Richard Chance with a huge claymore in his hand, only he had called himself Neill . . . and then he was Marcus, and it was the short Roman sword he wielded—

No. She couldn't let herself think like that. The dreams were a subconscious fantasy, nothing more. She didn't really recognize anything about Richard Chance. She had simply met him at a time when she was emotionally vulnerable and off-balance, almost as if she were on the rebound from a failed romance. She had to get a grip, because there was no way this man had anything to do with her dreams.

He was still standing there, his hand outstretched as if only a second had gone by, rather than the full minute it felt like.

And then he smiled again, those vivid eyes crinkling at the corners. "Don't you want to see the baby turtles?" he asked.

Baby turtles. The prospect was disarming, and surprisingly charmed by the idea, somehow Thea found herself taking a couple of steps forward, until she was standing at the screen door to the porch. Only then did she stop and look down at her nightgown. "I need to change clothes."

His gaze swept down her. "You look great to me." He didn't try to disguise the huskiness of appreciation in his tone. "Besides, they might be gone if you don't come now."

Thea chewed her lip. The nightgown wasn't a racy number, after all; it was plain white cotton, with a modest neckline and little cap sleeves, and the hem reached her ankles. Caution warred with her desire to see the turtles. Suddenly she couldn't think of anything cuter than baby turtles. Making a quick decision, she pushed open the door and stepped out into the tall grass. She had to lift her nightgown hem to midcalf to keep it from dragging in the dew and getting wet. Carefully she picked her way across the overgrown yard to the tall man waiting for her.

She had almost reached him when she realized how close she was to the water.

She froze in midstep, unable to even glance to the right where the lake murmured so close to her feet. Instead, her panic-stricken gaze locked on his face, instinctively begging him for help.

He straightened, every muscle in his body tightening as he became alert in response to her reaction. His eyes narrowed, and his gaze swung sharply from side to side, looking for whatever had frightened her. "What is it?" he rasped as he caught her forearm and protectively pulled her nearer, into the heat and shelter of his body.

Thea shivered and opened her mouth to tell him, but the closeness of his body, at once comforting and alarming, confused her so she couldn't think what to say. She didn't know which alarmed her more, her nearness to the lake or her nearness to him. She had always loved the lake, and was very wary of him, but his automatic response to her distress jolted something inside her, and suddenly she wanted to press herself against him. The warm scent of his skin filled her nostrils, her lungs—a heady combination of soap, fresh air, clean sweat, and male muskiness. He had pulled her against his left side, leaving his right arm free, and she could feel the reassuring steadiness of his heartbeat thudding within the strong wall of his chest.

She was abruptly, acutely aware of her nakedness beneath the nightgown. Her breasts throbbed where they pressed against his side, and her thighs began trembling. My God, what was she doing out here, dressed like this? What had happened to her much-vaunted common sense? Since the dreams had begun, she didn't seem to have any sense at all. No way should she be this close to a man she'd just met the day before. She knew she should pull away from him, but from the moment he'd touched her she had felt an odd sense of intimacy, of *rightness,* as if she had merely returned to a place she'd been many times before.

His free hand threaded through her damp curls. "Thea?" he prompted, some of the alertness relaxing from his muscles. "Did something scare you?"

She cleared her throat and fought off a wave of dizziness. His hand in her hair felt so familiar, as if . . . She jerked her wayward thoughts from that impossible path. "The water," she finally said, her voice still tight with fear. "I—I'm afraid of the water, and I just noticed how close I was to the bank."

"Ah," he said in a slow sound of realization. "That's understandable. But how were you going to see the turtles if you're afraid of the water?"

Dismayed, she looked up at him. "I didn't think about that." How could she tell him that her fear of the water was so recent that she wasn't used to thinking in terms of what she could or couldn't do based on the proximity of water. Her attention splintered again, caught by the angle of his jaw when viewed from below. It was a very strong jaw, she noticed, with a stubborn chin. He had a fairly heavy beard; despite the evident fact that he had just shaved, she could see the dark whiskers that would give him a heavy five-o'clock shadow. Again that nagging sense of familiarity touched her, and she wanted to put her hand to his face. She wondered if he was always considerate enough to shave before making love, and had a sudden powerful image of that stubbled chin being gently rubbed against the curve of her breast.

She gave a startled jerk, a small motion that he controlled almost before it began, his arm tightening around her and pulling her even more solidly against him. "The turtles are just over here, about fifty feet," he murmured, bending his head down so that his jaw just brushed her curls. "Could you look at them if I stay between you and the lake, and hold you so you know you won't fall in?"

Oh, he was good. She noticed it in a peripheral kind of way. Whenever he did something she might find alarming— something that *should* alarm her, like take her in his arms—he immediately distracted her with a diverting comment. She saw the ploy, but . . . baby turtles were so cute. She thought about his proposition. It was probably a dangerous illusion, but she felt safe in his arms, warmed by his heat and wrapped up in all that muscled power. Desire began in that moment, a delicate, delicious unfurling deep inside her . . . or maybe it had begun before, at his first touch, and had just now grown strong enough for her to recognize it. Why else had she thought about the roughness of his chin against her body? She knew she should go back inside. She had already made the logical decision that she had no time for even lightweight romance. But logic had nothing to do with the wild mixture of reactions she had felt since first seeing this man, fear, panic, compulsion and desire all swirling together so she never knew from one minute to the next how she was going to react. She didn't like it, didn't like anything about it. She wanted to be the old Thea again, not this nervous, illogical creature she didn't recognize.

All right, so throw logic out the window. It hadn't done her much good since the dreams had begun anyway. She looked up into watchful aquamarine eyes and threw caution to the dogs, too, deciding instead to operate on pure instinct. "Maybe that would work. Let's try it."

She thought she saw a flare of triumph in those crystalline eyes, but when she looked more closely she saw only a certain male pleasure. "Let's go a couple of steps farther away from the water," he suggested, already steering her along with that solid arm around her waist. "We'll still be able to see the turtles. Tell me if we're still too close, okay? I don't want you to be nervous."

She chuckled, and was surprised at herself for being able to laugh. How could she not be nervous? She was too close to the water, and way too close to him. "If I were wearing shoes, I'd be shaking in them," she admitted.

He glanced down at her bare feet, and the way she was having to hold up her nightgown to keep it out of the wet grass. "There might be briers," he said by way of explanation as he bent down and hooked his other arm beneath her knees. Thea gave a little cry of surprise as he lifted her, grabbing at his shirt in an effort to steady herself. He grinned as he settled her high against his chest. "How's this?"

Frightening. Exciting. Her heart was thudding wildly, and that first pressure of desire was becoming more intense. She cast a look at the ground and said, "High."

"Are you afraid of heights, too?"

"No, just water." *And of you, big guy.* But far more attracted than afraid, she realized.

He carried her along the bank, taking care not to get any closer to the water, while Thea looked everywhere but at the lake. The most convenient point of focus was his throat, strong and brown, with a small vulnerable hollow beneath the solid knot of his Adam's apple. The close proximity of his bare skin made her lips tingle, as if she had just pressed them into that little hollow where his pulse throbbed so invitingly.

"We have to be quiet," he whispered, and eased the last few steps. They had left the relative neatness of the overgrown yard and were in a tangle of bushes and weeds that probably did contain briers. Given her bare feet, she was just as glad he was carrying her. The trees grew more thickly here, greatly limiting the view of the lake. "They're still here, on a fallen log lying at the edge of the water. Don't make any sudden moves. I'm going to let you down, very slowly. Put your feet on my boots."

Before she could ask why, now that she was perfectly comfortable in his arms, he withdrew his arm from beneath her legs and let her lower body slide downward. Though he took care not to let her nightgown get caught between them, the friction of her body moving over his could scarcely have been more enticing. She caught her breath, her breasts and thighs tingling with heat even as she sought his boot tops with her feet and let her weight come to rest on them. Nor was he unaffected; there was no mistaking the firm swelling in his groin.

He seemed more capable than she of ignoring it, however. He had both arms around her, holding her snugly against him, but his head was turned toward the lake. She could feel excitement humming through him, but it didn't seem to be sexual in nature, despite his semierection.

"There are seven of them," he whispered, his voice the husky murmur of a lover. "They're lined up on the log like silver-dollar pancakes with legs. Just turn your head and take a peek, and I'll hold you steady so you'll feel safe."

Thea hesitated, torn between her desire to see the little turtles and her fear of the water. Her hands were clutching his upper arms, and she could feel the hard biceps flex as he held her a little closer. "Take your time," he said, still whispering, and she felt his lips brush her curls.

She took a deep breath and steeled herself. Half a second later she convulsively buried her face against his chest, shaking, trying to fight back the rise of nausea. He cuddled her, comforting her with a slight rocking motion of his body while he murmured reassuring noises that weren't really words.

Two minutes later she tried again, with much the same result.

By the fourth try, tears of frustration were welling in her eyes. Richard tried to take her back to the house, but the

stubbornness her brothers were well acquainted with came
to the fore, and she refused to leave. By God, she was going
to see those turtles.

Ten minutes later, she still hadn't managed more than a
single peek before the panic and nausea would hit her, and
she was getting furious with herself. The turtles were happily
sunning themselves right now, but they could be gone in the
next second.

"I'm going to do it this time," she announced, her tone
one of angry determination.

Richard sighed. "All right." She was well aware that he
could simply pick her up and stride away at any time, but
somehow she sensed that he would stand there until she was
ready to give up the effort. She braced herself and began to
turn her head by slow degrees. "While you're torturing
yourself, I'll pass the time by remembering how I could see
through your nightgown when you were walking across the
yard," he said.

Stunned, Thea found herself blinking at the little turtles
for two full seconds while she reeled under the impact of
what he'd just said. When her head jerked back around,
there was more outrage than panic in the motion. *"What?"*

"I could see through your nightgown," he repeated help-
fully. A smile tugged at his mouth, and his crystalline eyes
revealed even more amusement as he looked down at her.
"The sun was shining at an angle. I saw . . ." He let the
sentence trail off.

She pushed at his arms in an effort to loosen them,
without results. "Just what *did* you see?"

"Everything." He seemed to enjoy the memory. He made
a little humming sound of pleasure in his throat. "You have
gorgeous little nipples."

Thea flushed brightly, even as she felt the aforementioned
gorgeous little nipples tighten into hard buds. The reaction
was matched by one in his pants.

"Look at the turtles," he said.

Distracted, she did just that. At the same time he stroked
his right hand down her bottom, the touch searing her flesh

through the thin fabric, and cupped and lifted her so that the notch of her thighs settled over the hard bulge beneath his fly. Thea's breath caught in her lungs. She stared blindly at the turtles, but her attention was on the apex of her thighs. She bit back a moan, and barely restrained the urge to rock herself against that bulge. She could feel herself alter inside, muscles tightening and loosening, growing moist as desire built to a strong throb.

He was a stranger. She had to be out of her mind to stand here with him in such a provocative position. But though her mind knew he was a stranger, her body accepted him as if she had known him forever. The resulting conflict rendered her all but incapable of action.

The little turtles were indeed the size of silver-dollar pancakes, with tiny reptilian heads and stubby legs. They were lined up on the half-submerged log, the water gently lapping just below them. Thea stared at the sheen of water for several seconds before she realized what she was doing, so successfully had he distracted her.

"Richard," she breathed.

"H'mmm?" His voice was deeper, his breathing slightly faster.

"I'm looking at the turtles."

"I know, sweetheart. I knew you could do it."

"I wouldn't want to go any closer, but I'm looking at the water."

"That's good." He paused. "As you learn to trust me, you'll gradually get over your fear."

What a strange thing to say, she thought. What did he have to do with her fear of the water? That was caused by the dreams, not him. She wanted to ask him what he meant, but it was difficult to think straight when he was holding her so intimately, and when his erection was thrusting against her more insistently with each passing moment.

Then something unseen alarmed the little turtles, or perhaps one of them simply decided he'd had enough sun and the others followed suit, but all at once they slid off the log and plopped into the water, one by one, the entire action taking place so fast that it was over in a second. Ripples spread out from the log, resurrecting an echo of nausea in Thea's stomach. She swallowed ānd looked away, and the sensual spell was broken.

He knew it, too. Before she could speak, he matter-of-factly lifted her in his arms and carried her back to the yard.

Remembering what he'd said about her nightgown, she blushed hotly again as soon as he set her on her feet. He glanced at her hot cheeks, and amusement gleamed in his eyes.

"Don't laugh," she muttered crossly as she moved away from him. Though it was probably way too late, she tried for dignity. "Thank you for showing me the turtles, and for being so patient with me."

"You're welcome," he said in a grave tone that still managed to convey his hidden laughter.

She scowled. She didn't know whether to back away or to turn around and let him get a good view of her rear end, too. She didn't have enough hands to cover all her points of interest, and it was too late anyway. She compromised by sidling.

"Thea."

She paused, her brows lifted in question.

"Will you come on a picnic with me this afternoon?"

A picnic? She stared at him, wondering once again at the disturbing blend of strangeness and familiarity she felt about him. Like the baby turtles, a picnic sounded almost unbearably tempting; this whole thing was feeling as if she had opened a book so compelling that she couldn't stop turning page after page. Still, she felt herself pulling back. "I don't—"

"There's a tree in a fallow field about a mile from here," he interrupted, and all amusement had left his ocean-colored eyes. "It's huge, with limbs bigger around than my waist. It looks as if it's been here forever. I'd like to lie on a blanket spread in its shade, put my head in your lap, and tell you about my dreams."

5

THEA WANTED TO RUN. DAMN COURAGE; DISCRETION DE-
manded that she flee. She wanted to, but her legs wouldn't
move. Her whole body seemed to go numb. She let the hem
of her nightgown drop into the wet grass, and she stared
dumbly at him. "Who are you?" she finally whispered.

He studied the sudden terror in her eyes, and regret
flashed across his face. "I told you," he finally answered, his
tone mild. "Richard Chance."

"What—what did you mean about your dreams?"

Again he paused, his sharp gaze still fastened on her so
that not even the smallest nuance of expression could escape
him. "Let's go inside," he suggested, approaching to gently
take her arm and guide her stumbling steps toward the
house. "We'll talk there."

Thea stiffened her trembling legs and dug in her heels,
dragging him to a stop. Or rather, he allowed her to do so.
She had never before in her life been as aware of a man's
strength as she was of his. He wasn't a muscle-bound hulk,
but the steeliness of his body was evident. "What about your
dreams?" she asked insistently. "What do you want?"

190

He sighed, and released his grip to lightly rub his fingers up and down the tender underside of her arm. "What I don't want is for you to be frightened," he replied. "I've just found you, Thea. The last thing I want is to scare you away."

His tone was quiet and sincere, and worked a strange kind of magic on her. How could a woman fail to be, if not reassured, at least calmed by the very evenness of his words? Her alarm faded somewhat, and Thea found herself being shepherded once again toward the house. This time she didn't try to stop him. At least she could change into something more suitable before they had this talk on which he was so insistent.

She pulled away from him as soon as they were inside, and gathered her tattered composure around herself like a cloak. "The kitchen is there," she said, pointing. "If you'll put on a fresh pot of coffee, I'll be with you as soon as I get dressed."

He gave her another of his open looks of pure male appreciation, his gaze sliding over her from head to foot. "Don't bother on my account," he murmured.

"Your account is exactly why I'm bothering," she retorted, and his quick grin sent butterflies on a giddy flight in her stomach. Despite her best efforts, she was warmed by his unabashed attraction. "The coffee's in the cupboard to the left of the sink."

"Yes, ma'am." He winked and ambled toward the kitchen. Thea escaped into the bedroom and closed the door, leaning against it in relief. Her legs were still trembling. What was going on? She felt as if she had tumbled down the rabbit hole. He was a stranger, she had met him only the day before, and yet there were moments, more and more of them, when she felt as if she knew him as well as she knew herself, times when his voice reverberated deep inside of her like an internal bell. Her body responded to him as it never had to anyone else, with an ease that was as if they had been lovers for years.

He said and did things that eerily echoed her dreams. But how could she have dreamed about a man whom she hadn't met? This was totally outside her experience; she had no explanation for it, unless she had suddenly become clairvoyant.

Yeah, sure. Thea shook her head as she stripped out of the nightgown and opened a dresser drawer to get out bra and panties. She could just hear her brothers if she were to dare mention such a thing to them. "Woo, woo," they'd hoot, snorting with laughter. "Somebody find a turban for her to wear! Madam Theadora's going to tell our fortunes."

She pulled on jeans and a T-shirt and stuck her feet into a pair of sneakers. Comforted by the armor of clothing, she felt better prepared to face Richard Chance again. It was a loony idea to think she'd met him in her dreams, but she knew one sure way of finding out. In every incarnation, her dream warrior's left thigh had been scarred, a long, jagged red line that ended just a few inches above his knee. All she had to do was ask him to drop his pants so she could see his leg, and she'd settle this mystery once and for all.

Right. She could just see herself handing him a cup of coffee: "Do you take cream or sugar? Would you like a cinnamon roll? Would you please remove your pants?"

Her breasts tingled and her stomach muscles tightened. The prospect of seeing him nude was more tempting than it should have been. There was something dangerously appealing in the thought of asking him to remove his clothing. He would do it, too, those vivid eyes glittering at her all the while. He was as aware as she that, if they were caught, he would be killed—

Thea jerked herself out of the disturbing fantasy. *Killed?* Why on earth had she thought that? It was probably just the dreams again—but she had never dreamed that *he* had been killed, only herself. And he had been the killer.

Her stomach muscles tightened again, but this time with the return of that gut-level fear she'd felt from the moment she'd heard his step on the porch. She had feared him even before she'd met him. He was a man whose reputation preceded him—

Stop it! Thea fiercely admonished herself. What reputation? She'd never heard of Richard Chance. She looked around the bedroom, seeking to ground herself in the very normality of her surroundings. She felt as if things were blurring, but the outlines of the furniture were reassuringly sharp. No, the blurring was inside, and she was quietly terrified. She was truly slipping over that fine line between reality and dreamworld.

Maybe Richard Chance didn't exist. Maybe he was merely a figment of her imagination, brought to life by those thrice-damned dreams.

But the alluring scent of fresh coffee was no dream. Thea slipped out of the bedroom and crossed the living room to stand unnoticed in the doorway to the kitchen. Or she should have been unnoticed, because her sneakered feet hadn't made any noise. But Richard Chance, standing with the refrigerator door open while he peered at the contents, turned immediately to smile at her, and that unnerving aquamarine gaze slid over her jean-clad legs with just as much appreciation as when she'd worn only the nightgown. It didn't matter to him what she wore; he saw the female flesh, not the casing, Thea realized, as her body tightened again in automatic response to that warmly sexual survey.

"Are you real?" she asked, the faint words slipping out without plan. "Am I crazy?" Her fingers tightened into fists as she waited for his answer.

He closed the refrigerator door and quickly crossed to her, taking one of her tightly knotted fists in his much bigger hand and lifting to his lips. "Of course you're not crazy," he reassured her. His warm mouth pressed tenderly to each white knuckle, easing the tension from her hand. "Things are happening too fast and you're a little disoriented. That's all."

The explanation, she realized, was another of his ambiguous but strangely comforting statements. And if he was a figment of her imagination, he was a very solid one, all muscle and body heat, complete with the subtle scent of his skin.

She gave him a long, considering look. "But if I am crazy," she said reasonably, "then you don't exist, so why should I believe anything you say?"

He threw back his head with a crack of laughter. "Trust me, Thea. You aren't crazy, and you aren't dreaming."

Trust me. The words echoed in her mind and her face froze, a chill running down her back as she stared up at him. Trust me. He'd said that to her before. She hadn't remembered until just now, but he'd said that to her in her dreams—the dreams in which he had killed her.

He saw her expression change, and his own expression became guarded. He turned away and poured two cups of coffee, placing them on the table before guiding her into one of the chairs. He sat down across from her and cradled a cup in both hands, inhaling the rich aroma of the steam.

He hadn't asked her how she liked her coffee, Thea noticed. Nor had she offered cream or sugar to him. He drank coffee the same way he did tea: black.

How did she even know he drank tea? A faint dizziness assailed her, and she gripped the edge of the table as she stared at him. It was the oddest sensation, as if she were sensing multiple images while her eyes saw only one. And for the first time she was conscious of a sense of incompletion, as if part of herself was missing.

She wrapped her hands around the hot cup in front of her, but didn't drink. Instead she eyed him warily. "All right, Mr. Chance, cards on the table. What about your dreams?"

He smiled and started to say something, but then reconsidered, and his smile turned rueful. Finally he shrugged, as if he saw no point in further evasion. "I've been dreaming about you for almost a month."

She had expected it, and yet hearing him admit it was still a shock. Her hands trembled a bit. "I—I've been dreaming about you, too," she confessed. "What's happening? Do we have some sort of psychic link? I don't even believe in stuff like that!"

He sipped his coffee, watching her over the rim of the cup.

"What do you believe in, Thea? Fate? Chance? Coincidence?"

"All of that, I think," she said slowly. "I think some things are meant to be . . . and some things just happen."

"How do you categorize us? Did this just happen, or are we meant to be?"

"You're assuming that there is an 'us,'" she pointed out. "We've been having weird dreams, but that isn't . . ."

"Intimate?" he suggested, his gaze sharpening.

The dreams had certainly been that. Her cheeks pinkened as she recalled some of the sexually graphic details. She hoped his dreams hadn't been mirrors of hers . . . but they had, she realized, seeing the knowledge in his eyes. Her face turned even hotter.

He burst out laughing. "If you could see your expression!"

"Stop it," she said crossly, fixing her gaze firmly on her cup because she was too embarrassed to look at him. She didn't know if she would ever be able to face him again.

"Thea, darling." His tone was patient, and achingly tender as he tried to soothe her. "I've made love to you in every way a man can love a woman . . . but only in my dreams. How can a dream possibly match reality?"

If reality was any more intense than the dreams, she thought, it would surely kill her. She traced a pattern on the tabletop with her finger, stalling while she tried to compose herself. Just how real *were* the dreams? How could he call her "darling" with such ease, and why did it sound so right to her ears? She tried to remind herself that it had been less than twenty-four hours since she had seen him for the first time, but found that the length of time meant less than nothing. There was a bone-deep recognition between them that had nothing to do with how many times the sun had risen and set.

She still couldn't look at him, but she didn't have to see him for every cell in her body to be vibrantly aware of him. The only other times she had felt so painfully alive and sensitive to another's presence were in her dreams of this man. She didn't know how, or why, their dreams had become linked, but the evidence was too overwhelming for her to deny that it had happened. But just how closely did the dreams match reality? She cleared her throat. "I know this is a strange question . . . but do you have a scar on your left thigh?"

He was silent for several moments, but finally she heard him sigh. "Yes."

She closed her eyes as the shock of his answer rolled through her. If the dreams were that accurate, then she had another question for him, and this one was far more important. She braced herself and asked it, her voice choking over the words. "In your dreams, have you killed me?"

Again he was silent, so long that finally she couldn't bear the pressure and glanced up at him. He was watching her, his gaze steady. "Yes," he said.

6

THEA SHOVED AWAY FROM THE TABLE AND BOLTED FOR THE front door. He caught her there, simply wrapping his arms around her from behind and holding her locked to him. "My God, don't be afraid of me," he whispered into her tousled curls, his voice rough with emotion. "I would never hurt you. Trust me."

"Trust you!" she echoed incredulously, near tears as she struggled against his grip. "Trust *you?* How can I? How could I ever?"

"You're right about that, at least," he said, a hard tone edging into the words. "You've lowered yourself to let me touch you, give you pleasure, but you've never trusted me to love you."

She laughed wildly, with building hysteria. "I just met you yesterday! You're crazy—we're both crazy. None of this makes any sense." She clawed at his hands, trying to loosen his grasp. He simply adjusted his hold, catching her hands and linking his fingers through hers so she couldn't do any damage, and still keeping his arms wrapped around her. She was so effectively subdued that all she could do was kick at his shins, but as she was wearing sneakers and he had on boots, she doubted she was causing him much discomfort. But even knowing it was useless, she writhed and bucked against his superior strength until she had exhausted herself. Panting, unable to sustain the effort another second, she let her trembling muscles go limp.

Instantly he cuddled her closer, bending his head to brush his mouth against her temple. He kept his lips pressed there, feeling her pulse beating through the fragile skin. "It wasn't just yesterday that we met," he muttered. "It was a lifetime ago—several lifetimes. I've been here waiting for you. I knew you would come."

His touch worked an insidious magic on her; it always had. The present was blurring, mixing with the past so that she wasn't certain what was happening now and what had happened before. Just so had he held her that night when he had slipped through the camp of her father's army and sneaked into her bedchamber. Terror had beaten through her like the wings of a vulture, but she had been as helpless then as she was now. He had gagged her, and carried her silently through the night to his own camp, where he'd held her hostage against her father's attack.

She had been a virgin when he'd kidnapped her. When he had returned her, a month later, she had no longer been untouched. And she had been so stupidly in love with her erstwhile captor that she had lied to protect him, and ultimately betrayed her father.

Thea's head fell back against his shoulder. "I don't know what's happening," she murmured, and the words sounded thick, her voice drugged. The scenes that were in her head couldn't possibly be memories.

His lips sought the small hollow below her ear. "We've found each other again. Thea." As he had the first time, he said her name as if tasting it. "Thea. I like this name best of all."

"It's—it's Theodora." She had always wondered why her parents had given her such an old-fashioned, unusual name, but when she'd asked her mother had only said, rather bemusedly, that they had simply liked it. Thea's brothers, on the other hand, had the perfectly comfortable names of Lee and Jason.

"Ah. I like that even better." He nipped her earlobe, his sharp teeth gently tugging.

"Who was I before?" she heard herself ask, then hurriedly shook her head. "Never mind. I don't believe any of this."

"Of course you do," he chided, and delicately licked the exposed, vulnerable cord of her arched neck. He was aroused again, she noticed, or maybe he'd never settled down to begin with. His hard length nestled against her jean-clad bottom. No other man had ever responded to her with such blatant desire, had wanted her so strongly and incessantly. *All she had to do was move her hips against him in that little teasing roll that always maddened him with lust, and he would take her now, pushing her against the castle wall and lifting her skirts—*

Thea jerked her drifting mind from the waking dream, but reality was scarcely less provocative, or precarious. "I don't know what's real anymore," she cried.

"We are, Thea. We're real. I know you're confused. As soon as I saw you, I knew you'd just begun remembering. I wanted to hold you, but I knew it was too soon, I knew you were frightened by what's been happening. Let's drink our coffee, and I'll answer any questions you have."

Cautiously he released her, leaving Thea feeling oddly cold and abandoned. She turned to face him, looking up at the strong bones of his features, the intense watchfulness of his vivid eyes. She felt his hunger emanating from him like a force field, enwrapping her in a primal warmth that counteracted the chill of no longer being in his arms. Another memory assailed her, of another time when she had stood and looked into his face, and seen the desire so plainly in his eyes. At that time she had been shocked and frightened, an innocent, sheltered young lady who had suddenly been thrust into harsh conditions, and she'd had only his dubious protection from danger. Dubious not because of any lack of competence, but because she thought she might be in greater danger from him than from any outside threat.

Thea drew in a slow, deep breath, feeling again that internal blurring as past and present merged, and abruptly she knew how futile it was to keep fighting the truth. As unbelievable as it was, she had to accept what was happening. She had spent her entire life—this life, anyway—secure in a tiny time frame, unaware of anything else, but now the blinders were gone and she was seeing far too much. The sheer enormity of it overwhelmed her, asked her to cast aside the comfortable boundaries of her life and step into danger, for that was what Richard Chance had brought with him when he had entered her life again. She had loved him in all his incarnations, no matter how she had struggled against him. And he had desired her, violently, arrogantly ignoring danger to come to her again and again. But for all his desire, she thought painfully, in the end he had always destroyed her. Her dreams had been warnings, acquainting her with the past so she would know to avoid him in the present.

Go. That was all she had to do, simply pack and go. Instead she let him lead her back to the kitchen, where their cups sat with coffee still gently steaming. She was disconcerted to realize how little time had passed since she had fled the table.

"How did you know where to find me?" she asked abruptly, taking a fortifying sip of coffee. "How long have you known about me?"

He gave her a considering look, as if gauging her willingness to accept his answers, and settled into the chair across from her. "To answer your second question first, I've known about you for most of my life. I've always had strange, very detailed dreams, of different lives and different times, so I accepted all of this long before I was old enough to think it was impossible." He gave a harsh laugh as he too sought fortitude in caffeine. "Knowing about you, waiting for you, ruined me for other women. I won't lie and say I've been as

chaste as a monk, but I've never had even a teenage crush."
He looked up at her, and his gaze was stark. "How could a
giggling teen girl compete?" he whispered. "When I had the
other memories, when I knew what it was to be a man, and
make love to you?"

She hadn't had those memories until recently, but still she
had gone through life romantically unscathed, the deepest
part of her unable to respond to the men who had been
interested in her. From the first, though, she hadn't been
able to maintain any buffer against Richard. Both mentally
and physically, she was painfully aware of him. He had
grown up with this awareness, and it couldn't have been
easy. It was difficult to picture, but at one time he had been a
child, and in effect he had been robbed of a normal
childhood and adolescence, of a normal *life*.

"As to how I found you," he continued, "the dreams led
me here. The details I saw helped me narrow down the
location. The dreams were getting stronger, and I knew you
couldn't be far away. As soon as I saw this place, I knew this
was it. So I rented the neighboring house, and waited."

"Where is your home?" she asked curiously.

He gave her an odd little smile. "I've lived in North
Carolina for some time now."

She had the definite feeling that he wasn't telling her the
entire truth. She sat back and studied him, considering her
next question before voicing it. "What do you do for a
living?"

He laughed, and there was tone at once rueful and joyous
in the sound, as if he'd expected her to pin him down. "God,
some things never change. I'm in the military, what else?"

Of course. He was a warrior born, in whatever lifetime.
Snippets of information, gleaned from news broadcasts,
slipped into place. With her inborn knowledge of him
directing her, she hazarded a guess. "Fort Bragg?"

He nodded.

Special Forces, then. She wouldn't have known where
they were based, if it hadn't been for all the news coverage
during the Gulf War. A sudden terror seized her. Had he

been in that conflict? What if he had been killed, and she had never known about him—

Then she wouldn't now have to fear for her own life.

Somehow that didn't mitigate the fear she felt for him. She had always been afraid for him. He lived with danger, and shrugged at it, but she had never been able to do that.

"How did you get leave?"

"I had a lot of time due. I don't have to go back for another month, unless something unexpected happens." But there was a strained expression deep in his eyes, a resignation that she couldn't quite read.

He reached across the table and took her hand. His long, callused fingers wrapped around her slimmer, smaller ones, folding them in warmth. "What about you? Where do you live, what do you do?"

The safest thing would be not to tell him, but she doubted there was any point in it. After all, he had her name, and he probably had her license plate number. If he wanted to, he would be able to find her. "I live in White Plains. I grew up there; all of my family lives there." She found herself rattling on, suddenly anxious to fill him in on the details of her life. "My parents are still alive, and I have two brothers, one older and one younger. Do you have any brothers or sisters?"

He shook his head, smiling at her. "I have a couple of aunts and uncles, and some cousins scattered around the country, but no one close."

He had always been a loner, allowing no one to get close to him—except for her. In that respect, he had been as helpless as she.

"I paint houses," she said, still driven by the compulsion to fill all the gaps in their knowledge of each other. "The actual houses, not pictures of them. And I do murals." She felt herself tense, wanting him to approve, rather than express the incredulity some people did.

His fingers tightened on hers, then relaxed. "That makes sense. You've always loved making our surroundings as beautiful and comfortable as possible, whether it was a fur on the floor of the tent or wildflowers in a metal cup."

Until he spoke, she'd had no memory of those things, but suddenly she saw the pelts she had used to make their pallet on the tent floor, and the way the wildflowers, which she had arranged in a metal cup, had nodded their heads in the rush of cold air every time the flap was opened.

"Do you remember everything?" she whispered.

"Every detail? No. I can't remember every detail that's happened in this life, either; no one does. But the important things, yes."

"How many times have we . . ." Her voice trailed off as she was struck once again by the impossibility of it.

"Made love?" he suggested, though he knew darn well that wasn't what she had been about to say. Still, his eyes took on a heated, sleepy expression. "Times without number. I've never been able to get enough of you."

Her body jolted with responding desire. Sternly she controlled it. It would mean her life if she gave in to the aching need to become involved with him again. "Lived," she corrected.

She sensed his reluctance to tell her, but he had sworn he would answer all her questions, and his word was his bond. "Twelve," he said, tightening his hand on hers again. "This is our twelfth time."

She nearly jumped out of her chair. Twelve! The number echoed in her head. She had remembered only half of those times, and those memories were partial. Overwhelmed, she tried to pull away from him. She couldn't keep her sanity under such an overload.

Somehow she found herself drawn around the table, and settled on his lap. She accepted the familiarity of the position, knowing that he had held her this way many times. His thighs were hard under her bottom, his chest a solid bulwark to shield her, his arms supporting bands of living steel. It didn't make sense that she should feel so safe and protected in the embrace of a man who was so much of a danger to her, but the contact with his body was infinitely comforting.

He was saying something reassuring, but Thea couldn't concentrate on the words. She tilted her head back against his shoulder, dizzy with the tumult of warring emotions. He looked down at her and caught his breath, falling silent as his gaze settled on her mouth.

She knew she should turn away, but she didn't, couldn't. Instead her arm slipped up around his neck, holding tightly to him as he bent his head and covered her mouth with his.

7

THE TASTE OF HIM WAS LIKE COMING HOME, THEIR MOUTHS
fitting together without any awkwardness or uncertainty. A
growl of hunger rumbled in his throat, and his entire body
tensed as he took her mouth with his tongue. With the ease
of long familiarity he thrust his hand under her T-shirt and
closed it over her breast, working his fingers beneath the lace
of the bra cup so his hand was on her bare skin, her nipple
beading against his palm. Thea shuddered under his touch,
a paroxysm of mingled desire and relief, as if she had been
holding herself tightly against the pain of his absence and
could only now relax. There had never been another man for
her, she thought dimly as she sank under the pleasure of his
kiss, and never would be. Though they seemed to be caught
in a hellish death-dance, she could no more stop loving him
than she could stop her own heartbeat.

His response to her was as deep and uncontrollable as
hers was to him. She felt it in the quivering tension of his
body, the raggedness of his breathing, the desperate need so
plain in his touch. Why then, in all of their lives together,

had he destroyed her? Tears seeped from beneath her lashes as she clung to him. Was it *because* of the force of his need? Had he been unable to bear being so much at the mercy of someone else, found his vulnerability to be intolerable, and in a sudden fury lashed out to end that need? No; she rejected that scenario, because one of her clearest memories was of the calmness in his aquamarine eyes as he'd forced her deeper into the water, holding her down until there was no more oxygen in her lungs and her vision clouded over.

A teardrop ran into the corner of her mouth, and he tasted the saltiness. He groaned, and his lips left her mouth to slide over her cheek, sipping up the moisture. He didn't ask why she was crying, didn't become anxious or uneasy. Instead he simply held her closer, silently comforting her with his presence. He had never been discomfited by her tears, Thea remembered, past scenes sliding through her memory like silken scarves, wispy but detectable. Not that she had ever been a weepy kind of person anyway; and when she *had* cried, more often than not he had been the cause of her tears. His response then had always been exactly what it was now: he'd held her, let her cry it out, and seldom veered from his set course, no matter how upset he'd made her.

"You've never compromised worth a damn," Thea muttered, turning her face into his shoulder to use his shirt as a handkerchief.

He effortlessly followed her chain of thought. He sighed as his fingers gently kneaded her breast, savoring the silkiness of her skin, the pebbling of her nipple. "We were always on opposite sides. I couldn't betray my country, my friends."

"But you expected *me* to," she said bitterly.

"No, never. Your memories are still cloudy and incomplete, aren't they? Sweetheart, you made some difficult decisions, but they were based on your own sense of justice, not because I coerced you."

"So you say." She grasped his wrist and shoved his hand out from under her shirt. "Because my memory is cloudy, I can't argue that point, can I?"

"You could try trusting me." The statement was quiet, his gaze intent.

"You keep saying that." She stirred restlessly on his lap. "Under the circumstances, that seems to be asking a bit much, don't you think? Or am I safe with you, as long as we stay away from water?"

His mouth took on a bitter curve. "Trust has always been our problem." Lifting his hand, the one that had so recently cupped her breast, he toyed with one of her wayward curls. "On my part, too, I admit. I was never certain you wouldn't change your mind and betray me, instead."

"Instead of my father, you mean." Suddenly furious, she tried to struggle out of his lap. He simply tightened his arms, holding her in place as he had many times before.

"Your temper never changes," he observed, delight breaking through the grimness of his mood.

"I don't have a temper," Thea snapped, knowing full well her brothers would instantly disagree with that statement. She didn't have a hair-trigger temper, but she didn't back down from much, either.

"Of course you don't," he crooned, cuddling her closer, and the absolute love in his voice nearly broke her heart. How could he feel so intensely about her and still do what he did? And how could she still love him so much in return?

He held her in silence for a while, his heartbeat thudding against the side of her breast. The sensation was one she had felt many times before, lying cuddled on his left arm so his right arm, the one that wielded his sword, was unencumbered.

She wanted this, she realized. She wanted *him,* for a lifetime. For forever. In all their previous lifetimes, their time together had been numbered in months or even mere weeks, their loving so painfully intense she had sometimes panicked at the sheer force of what she was feeling. They had never been able to grow old together, to love each other without desperation or fear. Now she had a vital decision to make: should she run, and protect her life . . . or stay, and fight for their life together? The common sense that had ruled her life, at least until the dreams had disrupted everything, said to run. Her heart told her to hold to him as tightly as she could. Maybe, just maybe, if she was very cautious, she could win this time. She would have to be extremely wary of situations involving water. With the perfection of hindsight, she knew now that going to see the turtles with him had been foolhardy; she was lucky nothing bad had happened. Probably it simply wasn't time, yet, for whatever had happened in the past to happen again.

Things were different this time, she realized. Their circumstances were different. A thrill went through her as she realized that this time *could* be different. "We aren't on opposing sides, this time," she whispered. "My father is a wonderful, perfectly ordinary family man, without an army to his name."

Richard chuckled, but quickly sobered. When Thea looked up, she saw the grimness in his eyes. "We have to get it right," he said quietly. "This is our twelfth time. I don't think we'll have another chance."

Thea drew back from him a little. "It would help if I understood why you did . . . what you did. I've never known. *Tell* me, Richard. That way I can guard against—"

He shook his head. "I can't. It all comes down to trust. That's the key to it all. I have to trust you. You have to trust me . . . *even in the face of overwhelming evidence to the contrary.*"

"That's asking a lot," she pointed out in a dry tone. "Do you have to trust me to the same extent?"

"I already have." One corner of his mouth twitched in a wry smile. "The last time. That's probably why our circumstances have changed."

"What happened?"

"I can't tell you that, either. That would be changing the order of things. You either remember or you don't. We either get it right this time, or we lose forever."

She didn't like the choices. She wanted to scream at him, vent her fury at the mercilessness of fate, but knew it wouldn't do any good. She could only fight her own battle, knowing that it would mean her life if she failed. Maybe that was the point of it all, that each person was ultimately responsible for his or her own life. If so, she didn't much care for the lesson.

He began kissing her again, tilting her head up and drinking deeply from her mouth. Thea could have reveled in his kisses for hours, but all too soon he was drawing back, his breath ragged and desire darkening his eyes. "Lie down with me," he whispered. "It's been so long. I need you, Thea."

He did. His erection was iron-hard against her bottom. Still, for all the intimacy of their past lives, in *this* life she had only just met him, and she was reluctant to let things go so far, so fast. He saw her refusal in her expression before she could speak, and muttered a curse under his breath.

"You do this every time," he said in raw frustration. "You drive me crazy. Either you make me wait when I'm dying to have you, or you tease me into making love to you when I know damn well I shouldn't."

"Is that so?" Thea slipped off his lap and gave him a sultry glance over her shoulder. She had never given anyone a sultry glance before, and was mildly surprised at herself for even knowing how, but the gesture had come naturally. Perhaps, in the past, she had been a bit of a temptress. She liked the idea. It felt right. Richard's personality was so strong that she needed *something* to help keep him in line.

He glowered at her, and his hands clenched into fists. If they had been further along in their relationship, she thought, he wouldn't have taken no for an answer, at least not yet. First he would have made a damn good effort at seducing her—an effort that had usually succeeded. Whatever his name, and whatever the time, Richard had always been a devastatingly sensual lover. But he too felt the constraints of newness, knew that she was still too skittish for what he wanted.

Stiffly he got to his feet, wincing in discomfort. "In that case, we should get out of here, maybe drive into town for lunch. Or breakfast," he amended, glancing at his wrist-watch.

Thea smiled, both amused and touched by his thoughtfulness. Being in public with him did seem a lot safer than staying here. "Just like a date," she said, and laughed. "We've never done that before."

It was a delightful day, full of the joy of rediscovery. After eating breakfast at the lone café in the small nearby town, they drove the back roads, stopping occasionally to get out and explore on foot. Richard carefully avoided all streams and ponds, so Thea was relaxed, and could devote herself to once again learning to know this man she had always loved. So many things he did triggered memories, some of them delicious and some disturbing. To say their past lives together had been tumultuous would have been to understate the matter. She was shocked to remember the time she had used a knife to defend herself from him, an encounter that had ended in bloodletting: his. And in lovemaking.

But with each new memory, she felt more complete, as the missing parts slipped into place. She felt as if she had been only one-dimensional for the twenty-nine years of her life, and only now was becoming a full, real person.

And there were new things to discover about him. He hadn't been freeze-dried; he was a modern man, with memories and experiences that didn't include her. Occasionally he used an archaic term or phrasing that amused her, until she caught herself doing the same thing.

"I wonder why we remember, this time," she mused as they strolled along a deserted lane, with the trees growing so thickly overhead that they formed a cool, dim tunnel. They had left his Jeep a hundred yards back, pulled to the side so it wouldn't block the nonexistent traffic. "We never did before."

"Maybe because this is the *last* time." He held her hand in his. She wanted to just stare at him, to absorb the details of his erect, military bearing, the arrogant angle of his dark head, the stubborn jut of his jaw. Panic filled her at the thought of this being the end, of losing him forever if she didn't manage to outwit fate.

She tightened her fingers on his. That was what she had to do: fight fate. If she won, she'd have a life with this man she had loved for two millennium. If she lost, she would die. It was that simple.

8

THE NEXT MORNING, THEA LAY MOTIONLESS IN THE PREDAWN hour, her breath sighing in and out in the deep, easy rhythm of sleep. The dream began to unfold, as long-ago scenes played out in her unconsciousness.

The lake was silent and eerily beautiful in the dawn. She stood on the dock and watched the golden sun rise from behind the tall, dark trees, watched the lake turn from black to deep rose as it reflected the glow of the sky. She loved the lake in all its moods, but sunrise was her favorite. She waited, and was rewarded by the haunting cry of a loon as the lake awoke and greeted the day.

Her child moved within her, a gentle fluttering as tiny limbs stretched. She smiled, and her hand slipped down to rest atop the delicate movement. She savored the feel of that precious life. Her child—and his. For five months now she had harbored it within her, delighting in each passing day as her body changed more and more. The slight swell of her belly was only now becoming noticeable. She had been in seclusion here at the lake, but soon her condition would be impossible to hide. She would face that problem, and her father's rage, when it became necessary, but she wouldn't let anything harm this child.

She still woke up aching for the presence of her lover, weeping for him, for what might have been had he been anyone else, had she been anyone else. Damn men, and damn their wars. She would have chosen him, had he given her the chance, but he hadn't. Instead he had simply ridden out of her life, not trusting her to love him enough. He didn't know about the new life he had left inside her.

The dock suddenly vibrated beneath her as booted feet thudded on the boards. Startled, she turned, and then stood motionless with shock, wondering if she was dreaming or if her longing had somehow conjured him out of the dawn. Faint wisps of mist swirled around him as he strode toward her. Her heart squeezed painfully. Even if he wasn't real, she thanked God for this chance to see him so clearly again—his thick dark hair, his vibrant, sea-colored eyes, the muscular perfection of his body.

Five feet from her he stopped, as suddenly as if he had hit a wall. His incredulous gaze swept down her body, so clearly outlined in the thin nightgown that was all she wore, with the sun shining behind her. He saw her hand resting protectively on the swell of her belly, in the instinctive touch of a pregnant woman.

He was real. Dear God, he was real. He had come back to her. She saw his shock mirrored in his eyes as he confronted the reality of impending fatherhood. He stared at her belly for a long, silent moment before dragging his gaze back up to hers. "Why didn't you tell me?" he asked hoarsely.

"I didn't know," she said. "Until after you'd gone."

He approached her, as cautiously as if confronting a wild animal, slowly reaching out his hand to rest it on her belly. She quivered at the heat and vitality of his touch, and nearly moaned aloud as the pain of months without him eased from her flesh. Couldn't he sense how much he had hurt her? Couldn't he tell that his absence had nearly killed her, that only the realization she was carrying his child had given her a reason to live?

And then she felt the quiver that ran through him, too, as his hands closed on her body. Pure heat sizzled between them. She drew a deep, shaky breath of desire, her body softening and warming, growing moist for him in instinctive preparation.

"Let me see you," he groaned, already tugging her nightgown upward.

Somehow she found herself lying on the dock, her naked body bathed in the pearly morning light. The discarded nightgown protected her soft skin from the rough wood beneath her. The water lapped softly around her, beneath her, yet not touching her. She felt as if she were floating, anchored only by those strong hands. She closed her eyes, giving him privacy to acquaint himself with all the changes in her body, the changes she knew so intimately. His rough hands slipped over her as lightly as silk, touching her darkened, swollen nipples, cupping the fuller weight of her breasts in his palms. Then they moved down to her belly, framing the small, taut mound of his child.

She didn't open her eyes, even when he parted her legs, raising her knees and spreading them wide so he could look at her. She caught her breath at the cool air washing over her most intimate flesh, and the longing for him intensified. Couldn't he sense how much she needed him, couldn't he feel the vibrancy of her body under his hands? Of course he could. She had never been able to disguise her desire for him, even when she had desperately tried. She heard the rhythm of his breathing become ragged, and glowed with the knowledge of his desire.

"You're so lovely, it hurts to look at you," he whispered. She felt one long, callused finger explore the delicacies between her legs, stroking and rubbing before sliding gently inward. Her senses spun with the shock of that small invasion; her back arched off the dock, and he soothed her with a deep murmur. And then she felt him moving closer, positioning himself between her legs, adjusting his clothing, and she lay there in an agony of anticipation waiting for the moment when they would be together again, one again, whole again.

He filled her so smoothly that he might have been part of her, and they both gasped at the perfection of it. Then the time for rational thought was past, and they could only move together, cling together, his strength complemented by her delicacy, male and female, forever mated.

Thea moaned in her sleep as her dream lover brought her to ecstasy, and then became still again as the dream altered, continued.

The water closed over her head, a froth of white marking the surface where she had gone under. The shock of it, after the ecstasy she had just known with him, paralyzed her for long, precious moments. Then she thought of the baby she carried, and silently screamed her fury that it should be endangered. She began struggling wildly against the inexorable grip that was tugging her downward, away from air, away from life. She couldn't let anything happen to this baby, no matter what its father had done. Despite everything, she loved him, loved his child.

But she couldn't kick free of the bond that dragged her down. Her nightgown kept twisting around her legs, instead of floating upward. Her lungs heaved in agony, trying to draw in air. She fought the impulse, knowing that she would inhale only death. Fight. She had to fight for her baby.

Powerful hands were on her shoulders, pushing her deeper into the water. Despairing, her vision failing, she stared through the greenish water into the cool, remote eyes of the man she loved so much she would willingly have followed him anywhere. He was forcing her down, down, away from the life-giving air.

"Why?" she moaned, the word soundless. The deadly water filled her mouth, her nostrils, rushed down her throat. She couldn't hold on much longer. Only the baby gave her the strength to continue fighting, as she struggled against those strong hands, trying to push him away. Her baby . . . she had to save her baby. But the darkness was increasing, clouding over her eyes, and she knew that she had lost. Her last thought in this life was a faint, internal cry of despair: "Why?"

Helpless sobs shook Thea's body as she woke. She curled

on her side, overwhelmed by grief, grief for her unborn child, grief for the man she had loved so much that not even her destruction at his hands had been able to kill her feelings for him. *It didn't make sense.* He had made love to her, and then he had drowned her. How could a man feel his own child kicking in its mother's belly, and then deliberately snuff out that helpless life? Regardless of how he felt about her, how could he have killed his baby?

The pain was shattering. She heard the soft, keening sound of her sobs as she huddled there, unable to move, unable to think.

Then she heard the Jeep, sliding to a hard stop in the driveway, its tires slinging gravel. She froze, terror running like ice water through her veins. He was here. She should have remembered that he had the same dreams she did; he knew that *she* knew about those last nightmarish moments beneath the water. She couldn't begin to think what he was trying to accomplish by repeating her death over and over through the ages, but suddenly she had no doubt that, if she remained there, she would shortly suffer the same fate again. After that last dream, there was no way he could sweet-talk her out of her fear the way he had done before.

She jumped out of bed, not taking the time to grab her clothes. Her bare feet were silent as she raced from the bedroom, across the living room, and into the kitchen. She reached the back door just as his big fist thudded against the front one. "Thea." His deep voice was forceful, but restrained, as if he were trying to convince her she wasn't in any danger.

The deep shadows of early dawn still shrouded the rooms, the graying light too weak to penetrate beyond the windows. Like a small animal trying to escape notice by a predator, Thea held herself very still, her head cocked as she listened for the slightest sound of his movements.

Could she slip out the back door without making any betraying noise? Or was he even now moving silently around the house in order to try this very door? The thought of opening the door and coming face-to-face with him made her blood run even colder than it already was.

"Thea, listen to me."

He was still on the front porch. Thea fumbled for the chain, praying that her shaking hands wouldn't betray her. She found the slot and slowly, agonizingly, slid the chain free, holding the links in her hand so they wouldn't clink. Then she reached for the lock.

"It isn't what you think, sweetheart. Don't be afraid of me, please. Trust me."

Trust him! She almost laughed aloud, the hysterical bubble moving upward despite her best efforts. She finally choked the sound back. He'd said that so often that the two words had become a litany. Time and again she had trusted him—with her heart, her body, the life of her child—and each time he had turned on her.

She found the lock, silently turned it.

"Thea, I know you're awake. I know you can hear me."

She opened the door by increments, holding her breath against any squeaks that would alert him. An inch of space showed, gray light coming through the slot. Dawn was coming closer by the second, bringing with it the bright light that would make it impossible for her to hide from him. She didn't have her car keys, she realized, and the knowledge almost froze her in place. But she didn't dare go back for them; she would have to escape on foot. That might be best anyway. If she were in the car, he would easily be able to follow her. She felt far more vulnerable on foot, but hiding would be much easier.

Finally the door was open enough that she could slip through. She held her breath as she left the precarious safety of the house. She wanted to cower behind its walls, but knew that he would soon break a window and get in, or kick down the door. He was a warrior, a killer. He could get in. She wasn't safe there.

The back stoop wasn't enclosed, just a couple of steps with an awning overhead to keep out the rain. There was a screen door there, too. Cautiously she unlatched it, and began the torturous process of easing it open, nerves drawing tighter and tighter. Fiercely she concentrated, staring at the spring coil, willing it to silence. There was a tiny creak, one that couldn't have been audible more than a few feet away, but sweat dampened her body. An inch, two inches, six. The opening grew wider. Eight inches. Nine. She began to slip through.

Richard came around the side of the house. He saw her and sprang forward, like a great hunting beast.

Thea cried out and jumped backward, slamming the kitchen door and fumbling with the lock. Too late! He would come through that door, lock or not. She sensed his determination and left the lock undone, choosing instead an extra second of time as she sprinted for the front door.

The back door slammed open just as she reached the front. It was still locked. Her chest heaved with panic, her breath catching just behind her breastbone and going no deeper. Her shaking, jerking fingers tried to manipulate the chain, the lock.

"Thea!" His voice boomed, reverberating with fury.

Sobbing, she jerked the door open and darted out onto the porch, shoving the outside screen door open, too, launching herself through it, stumbling, falling to her knees in the tall, wet grass.

He burst through the front door. She scrambled to her feet, pulled the hem of her nightgown to her knees, and ran for the road.

"Damn it, listen to me!" he shouted, sprinting to cut her off. She swerved as he lunged in front of her, but he managed once again to get between her and the road.

Despair clouded her vision; sobs choked her. She was cornered. He was going to kill her, and once again she was helpless to protect herself.

She let her nightgown drop, the folds covering her feet, as she stared at him with tear-blurred eyes. The gray light was stronger now; she could see the fierceness of his eyes, the set of his jaw, the sheen of perspiration on his skin. He wore only a pair of jeans. No shirt, no shoes. His powerful chest rose and fell with his breathing, but he wasn't winded at all, while she was exhausted. She had no chance against him.

Slowly she began to back away from him, the pain inside her unfurling until it was all she could do to breathe, for her heart to keep beating. "How could you?" she sobbed, choking on the words. "Our baby . . . *How could you?*"

"Thea, listen to me." He spread his hands in an open gesture meant to reassure her, but she knew too much about him to be fooled. He didn't need a weapon; he could kill with his bare hands. "Calm down, sweetheart. I know you're upset, but come inside with me and we'll talk."

Angrily she dashed the tears from her cheeks. "Talk! What good would that do?" she shrieked. "Do you deny that it happened? You didn't just kill me, you killed our child, too!" Still she backed away, the pain too intense to let her remain even that close to him. She felt as if she were being torn apart inside, the grief so raw and unmanageable that she felt as if she would welcome death now, to escape this awful pain.

He looked beyond her, and his expression shifted, changed. A curious blankness settled in his eyes. His entire body tensed as he seemed to gather himself, as if he were about to spring. "You're getting too close to the water," he said in a flat, emotionless voice. "Come away from the bank."

Thea risked a quick glance over her shoulder, and saw that she was on the edge of the bank, the cool, deadly lake lapping close to her bare feet. Her tears blurred the image, but it was there, silently waiting to claim her.

The unreasoning fear of the lake gnawed at her, but was as nothing when measured against the unrelenting grief for her child. She changed the angle of her retreat, moving toward the dock. Richard kept pace with her, not advancing any closer, but not leaving her any avenue of escape, either. The inevitability of it all washed over her. She had thought she could outwit fate, but her efforts had been useless from the very beginning.

Her bare feet touched wood, and she retreated onto the dock. Richard halted, his aquamarine gaze fastened on her. "Don't go any farther," he said sharply. "The dock isn't safe. Some of the boards are rotten and loose. Come off the dock, baby. Come to me. I swear I won't hurt you."

Baby. Shards of pain splintered her insides, and she moaned aloud, her hand going to her belly as if her child still rested there. Desperately she backed away from him, shaking her head.

He set one foot on the dock. "I can't bring that child back," he said hoarsely. "But I'll give you another one. We'll have as many children as you want. Don't leave me this time, Thea. For God's sake, let's get off this dock."

"Why?" Tears were still blurring her vision, running down her cheeks, a bottomless well of grief. "Why put it off? Why not get it over with now?" She moved back still more, feeling the boards creak and give beneath her bare feet. The water was quite deep at the end of the dock; it had been perfect for three boisterous kids to dive and frolic in, without fear of hitting their heads on the bottom. If she was destined to die here, then so be it. Water. It was always water. She had always loved it, and it had always claimed her in the end.

Richard slowly stepped forward, never taking his eyes off her, his hand outstretched. "Please. Just take my hand, darling. Don't move back any more. It isn't safe."

"Stay away from me!" she shrieked.

"I can't." His lips barely moved. "I never could." He took another step. "Thea—"

Hastily, she stepped back. The board gave beneath her weight, then began to crack. She felt one side collapse beneath her, pitching her sideways into the water. She had only a blurred, confused image of Richard leaping forward, his face twisting with helpless rage, before the water closed over her head.

It was cool, murky. She went down, pulled by some unseen hand. The darkness of the dock pilings drifted in front of her as she went deeper, deeper. After all the terror and pain, it was almost a relief for it to end, and for a long moment she simply gave in to the inevitable. Then instinct took over, as irresistible as it was futile, and she began fighting, trying to kick her way to the surface. But her nightgown was twisted around her legs, pulling tighter and tighter the more she struggled, and she realized that she had caught it in the broken boards. The boards were pulling her down, and with her legs bound she couldn't generate enough energy to counteract their drag.

If she could have laughed, she would have. This time, Richard wouldn't have to do anything. She had managed to do the deed herself. Still, she didn't stop fighting, trying to swim against the pull of the boards.

The surface roiled with his dive, as he cut through the water just to her left. Visibility was poor, but she could see the gleam of his skin, the darkness of his hair. He spotted her immediately, the white of her nightgown giving away her position, and he twisted his body in her direction.

Anger speared through her. He just had to see it through; he couldn't let the lake do its work without his aid. Probably he wanted to make certain she didn't fight her way free.

She put up her hands to ward him off, redoubling her efforts to reach the surface. She was using up all her oxygen in her struggles, and her lungs were burning, heaving with the need to inhale. Richard caught her flailing hands and began pushing her down, down, farther away from the light, from life.

Thea saw his eyes, calm and remote, every atom of his being concentrated on what he was doing. She had little time left, so very little. Pain swirled inside her, and anger at the fate that was hers, despite her best efforts. Desperately she tried to jerk free of him, using the last of her strength for one final effort. . . .

Despite everything, she had always loved him so much, beyond reason, even beyond death.

That was an even deeper pain: the knowledge that she was leaving him forever. Their gazes met through the veil of murky water, his face so close to hers that she could have kissed him, and through the growing darkness she saw her anguish mirrored in his eyes. *Trust me,* he'd said repeatedly. *Trust me . . . even in the face of overwhelming evidence to the contrary. Trust me. . . .*

Trust him.

Realization spread through Thea like a sunburst. Trust. She had never been able to trust him, or in his love for her. They had been like two wary animals, longing to be together, but not daring to let themselves be vulnerable to the other. They hadn't trusted. And they had paid the price.

Trust him.

She stopped struggling, letting herself go limp, letting him do what he would. She had no more strength anyway. Their gazes still held, and with her eyes she gave herself to him, her love shining through. Even if it was too late, she wanted him to know that in the end, no matter what, she loved him.

She saw his pupils flare, felt his renewed effort as he pushed her down, all the way to the bottom. Then, without the weight of the boards dragging at her, he was able to get enough slack in the fabric of her nightgown to work it free of the entangling wood. The last bubble of air escaped her lips as he wrapped his arm around her waist and used his powerful legs to propel them upward, to the surface and wonderful oxygen, to life.

"God, please, please, oh God, please." She heard his desperate, muttered prayer as he dragged her out of the water, but she couldn't respond, couldn't move, as she flopped like a rag doll in his arms. Her lungs weren't quite working; she couldn't drag in the deep, convulsive breaths that she needed.

Richard dropped her on the grass and began pounding her on the back. Her lungs jerked, then heaved, and she coughed up a quantity of lake water. He continued to beat her on the back, until she thought he would break her ribs.

"I'm . . . all . . . right," she managed to gasp, trying to evade that thumping fist. She coughed some more, gagging.

He collapsed beside her in his own paroxysm of coughing, his muscular chest heaving as he fought for air.

Thea struggled onto her side, reaching for him, needing to touch him. They lay in the grass, shivering and coughing, as the first warming rays of the sun crept across the lake to touch them. Convulsively he clasped her to him, tears running down his cheeks, muttering incoherently as he pressed desperate kisses to her face, her throat. His big body was taut, shaking with a tension that wouldn't relent. He rolled her beneath him, jerking the sodden folds of her nightgown to her waist. Thea felt his desperate, furious need, and lay still as he fought with the wet, stubborn fabric of his jeans, finally getting them open and peeling them down. He pushed her legs open and stabbed into her, big and hot and so hard that she cried out even as she held him as tightly as she could.

He rode her hard and fast, needing this affirmation that they both still lived, needing this link with her. Thea's response soared out of control and she climaxed almost immediately, crying out with the joy of having him there with her as she clung to him with arms and legs. He bucked wildly, shuddered, and she felt the warm flood of his orgasm within her, then he fell onto the grass beside her.

He lay there holding her for a long time, her head cradled on his shoulder, neither of them able to stop touching the other. He smoothed back her unruly tumble of curls; she stroked his chest, his arms. He kissed her temple; she nuzzled his jaw. He squeezed and stroked her breasts; her hands kept wandering down to his naked loins. She imagined they made quite a picture of debauchery, lying there on the ground with her nightgown hiked to her waist and his jeans down around his knees, but the sun was warm and she was drowsy, her body replete with satisfaction, and she didn't much care.

Eventually he moved, kicking his legs free of the damp jeans. She smiled as he stretched out, blissfully naked. He had never been blessed with an overabundance of modesty.

But then, it was almost a crime to cover up a body like his. She sighed with her own bliss, thinking of the naughty things she planned to do to him later, when they were sprawled out in that big bed. Some things required a mattress rather than grass. Though those pelts had been wonderful . . .

"All those times," she murmured, kissing his shoulder. "You were trying to save me."

His vivid eyes slitted open as he gathered her closer. "Of course," he said simply. "I couldn't live without you."

But you did. The comment died on her lips as she stared at him, reading his expression. His eyes were calm, and accepting. Emotion swelled in her chest until she could barely breathe, and tears glittered in her eyes. "Damn you," she said shakily. He *hadn't* lived. Each time, when he had failed to save her, he had remained there with her, choosing to share her death rather than live without her. This had been his last chance as well as hers, and theirs. "Damn you," she said again, thumping him on the chest with her fist. "How could you do that? Why didn't you *live?*"

A slow smile touched his lips as he played with one of her curls. "Would you have?" he asked, and the smile grew when she scowled at him. No, she couldn't have left him in the water and gone on living. She would have remained with him.

"You little hellcat," he said contentedly, gathering her against his chest. "You've led me on quite a chase, but I've caught you now. We finally got it right."

Epilogue

TWO DAYS LATER THEA AND RICHARD WERE SITTING OUTSIDE IN the swing, which he had repaired, contentedly watching the lake. Her bare feet were in his lap and he was massaging them, saying he wanted to get in practice for when she was big with pregnancy and would need such services. Both of them were absurdly positive that their first lovemaking had been fertile, and her happiness was so intoxicating that she felt giddy.

Her fear of the water had disappeared as suddenly as it had formed. She hadn't been swimming yet, but that was more because of Richard's anxieties than her own. Whenever they walked, he still positioned himself between her and the water, and she wondered if he would ever relax his vigil.

Plans. They'd made a lot of plans for their life together. For one thing, she would be moving to North Carolina. Her warrior wasn't just "in" the Special Forces—he was a lieutenant colonel. Since he was only thirty-five, that meant he had a lot of time left to reach general, which was probably inevitable. Thea rather thought she would have to give up painting houses; it just wasn't the thing for a general's wife to do. The murals, though, were something else. . . .

For now, though, they were selfishly enjoying getting reacquainted with each other, hugging every moment of privacy to themselves. They had cleaned up the yard, and this morning they had started preparing the house for its new coat of paint. Most of the time, though, they had spent in bed.

She tilted her face up to the sun, and gently cupped her hand over her belly. It was there. She knew it was. She didn't need either drugstore or lab test to confirm what she felt in every cell of her body. Too tiny almost to be seen, as yet, but indubitably there.

Richard's hand covered hers, and she opened her eyes to find him smiling at her. "Boy or girl?" he asked.

She hesitated. "What do you think?"

"I asked first."

"Let's say it together. You go first."

His mouth opened, then he stopped and narrowed his eyes at her. "Almost got you," she said smugly.

"Smart-ass. All right, it's a boy."

She twined her fingers with his, sighing with contentment. "I agree." A son. Richard's son. The baby who had died with her had been a daughter. She blinked back tears for that child, wondering if it was forever lost, or if it too had been given another chance.

"She'll have another chance," Richard whispered, gathering Thea close. "Maybe next time. We'll know."

Yes, they would. Each night, her memory became more complete as the dreams continued. Richard still shared them, and they would awaken to find their bodies locked together, ecstasy still pulsing through them. They were linked, body and soul, the past revealed to them as it was to only a few lucky people.

They heard the cars before they could see them, and Thea sat up, swinging her feet to the ground. Richard stood, automatically moving to place himself between her and whoever approached. Thea tugged on his belt and he looked around, a sheepish look crossing his face as he realized what he'd done.

"Old habits," he said, shrugging. *"Real* old."

Then the three cars came into view, and Thea watched in astonishment as her entire family drove up. It took her a moment to realize. "Today's my birthday!" she gasped. "I'd forgotten!"

"Birthday, huh?" He looped an arm over her shoulder. "How about that. That makes you . . . thirty, right? I have to tell you, this is the oldest you've ever been. But you're holding up good."

"Thank you so much." Grinning, she caught his hand and began tugging him forward. She'd see if he was so sassy after being overwhelmed by her family. Nieces and nephews were spilling out of open doors, running toward her, while adults unfolded themselves at a slower pace. Lee and Cynthia, Jason and June, and her mom and dad all approached a bit warily, as if afraid they had intruded on a romantic getaway.

"I didn't realize you'd brought company with you, dear," her mom said, looking Richard up and down with a mother's critical assessment.

Richard laughed, the sound low and easy. "She didn't," he said, holding out his hand to Thea's father. "My name is Richard Chance. I'm renting the house next door."

Her father grinned. "I'm Paul Marlow, Thea's father. This is my wife, Emily." Polite introductions were made all around, and Thea had to bite her lip to keep from laughing out loud. Though her father was perfectly relaxed, and both Cynthia and June were smiling happily at Richard, her mom and brothers were scowling suspiciously at the warrior in their midst.

Before anything embarrassing could be said, she slipped her arm through Richard's. "Lieutenant Colonel Richard Chance," she said mildly. "On leave from Fort Bragg, North Carolina. And, for the record, my future husband."

The words worked a sea change in her more pugnacious relatives. Amid a flurry of congratulations and squeals, plus tears from her mother, she heard her father say reflectively,

"That's fast work. You've known each other, what, four or five days?"

"No," Richard said with perfect aplomb. "We've known each other off and on for years, but the timing wasn't right. Everything worked out this time, though. I guess it was just meant to be."

LINDA HOWARD is one of the best-loved romance authors writing today. She is a three-time winner of the "Maggie" award, and has won Readers Choice and Readers Favorite awards from *Romantic Times* and *Affaire de Coeur,* along with several other awards from Waldenbooks and B. Dalton.

While she writes category books for Silhouette, her full-length novels are published by Pocket Books. They include *A Lady of the West, Angel Creek, Touch of Fire,* and *Heart of Fire,* published in 1993, which prompted daily calls and letters from avid fans eager to know when her next full-length novel would be available. Look for *Dream Man* in August 1995 and *After the Night* in December. Both contemporary love stories, they're worth the wait!

Ms. Howard lives in Alabama with her husband, Gary, who is a professional tournament-bass fisherman.

KASEY MICHAELS

Role of a Lifetime

Prologue

The only thing is to keep working, and pretty soon they'll think you're good.

—Jack Nicholson

Y OU CHEEKY BEAST!"

Michael Casey saw the slap coming, but he didn't turn away. Nor did he lose his smile, even as he willed himself not to rub at his stinging face. He only watched in appreciation as the waitress, or barmaid, or whatever these Brits called full-breasted young blondes in low-cut peasant blouses, retreated to the bar without so much as a backward glance.

Ah, women, Casey thought as he drained his mug of dark English ale and slapped it down onto the table. How he loved women. In all their shapes, all their sizes, all their teasing little ways. He considered himself an appreciator of women, if there was such a word; maybe even a connoisseur.

"Stung yer good, didn't she, ducks?" a deep, gravelly female voice asked, and Casey looked up as a cherublike, ruddy-faced old woman slipped, uninvited, into the only other chair at the table. "Oi bin watchin' yer, lad, from over

233

there, in the corner, an' seen it all. Stealin' kisses like a raw lad. Fer shame! Wot yer think yer doin', anyways?"

Casey looked at the old woman, who was dressed in more colors than the NBC peacock. If he didn't know better, he'd think she was a gypsy, when she was probably nothing more than a local eccentric hitting on him for a free glass of ale. "Looking for love in all the wrong places?" he suggested after a moment, then winked and grinned, for he couldn't help himself. He had been born to please women. All women. It was his gift. Maybe even his curse.

The chubby cherub didn't smile back at him, which was unusual, for he had always scored high with older women—older women, teenage boys, the entire X Generation. Even older men. No one was immune to the Michael Casey grin. His demographics proved it. His eleven-mil-a-picture contracts proved it.

"Such a pretty smile on such a sad man," the grotesque cherub said, shaking her gray head as she stared at him, giving him an unsettled feeling. "Yer're lookin' all right, dearie, but for what? Fer somethin' or someone ta fill up that empty place inside yer? Someone ta make yer real, and not jist the man everyone sees? Yer don't even know if yer are missin' somethin', do yer, not fer certain? But Oi does. Oi does. Yer came ta the right spot, almost. Almost. Oh, boyo, wot I see," she ended, her voice taking on the eerie lilt of the omniscient. "Wot I see!"

Casey frowned, as the cherub reached across the table to touch him, her shiny-skinned arthritic hand, each finger banded by at least two rings, strangely strong and grasping.

"Okay, I give up," he responded, trying for bravado and knowing he'd failed. "The naive American hereby agrees to be fleeced by the wily English gypsy. What do you see? And how much is it going to cost me to find out?"

"Listen now, Michael Casey, and listen well, fer Oi'll only say it the onct." The gravelly voice was low, intent, yet shut out all the louder noises in the dark, crowded pub. The fingers that traced over his palm felt hot and dry and branding, their very heat somehow translating to a chilling shiver that ran down his spine.

She closed her rheumy brown eyes, took a deep breath, and pronounced: "So many gifts. So little understanding. Years to travel afore you find your true love. I see danger. Danger in the water. A pond . . . a stream . . . a brook? Danger, learning, love everlasting. Keep the hickory branch close."

She took another deep breath, opened her eyes, then released his hand, turning her own palm-up, and all the noises in the pub were audible again. "That'll be a fiver, mate, seein' as how Oi've sworn off the drink now that Oi'm old an' not so steady on m'feet," she said brightly, suddenly all business.

Casey, wishing like hell for a scriptwriter who could furnish him with some sort of snappy comeback, briskly rubbed his palms together, trying to wipe away the gypsy's touch, along with her words. "You're good," he said flippantly. "Damn good. Pushed all the right buttons. Although you only knew my name because you've seen one of my movies, or read one of the newspaper stories about the film we're shooting here. Right?"

She said nothing, only kept her hand extended, her dark eyes revealing less than her suddenly silent, unsmiling mouth. And another shiver ran down Casey's spine.

He decided he'd had enough of the village pub for his first night in jolly old England. As a matter of fact, he'd probably had enough of England, although he would be here for another two months, at the least.

How could he have been so drawn to this place, to this particular script, that he had landed himself in such a backwater when he knew he was happiest in the center of action? Knew he could tell himself he was happy, fulfilled, when he was careful to keep himself surrounded by all the trappings of his unexpected success? Why had he felt this burning need to film on location, and to take such a career risk in his determination to play the role of the Earl of Ambersley?

And why did he feel, *know,* that this strange old woman not only knew of all his unspoken questions, but had answers for them as well? Not that he would ask her. Oh, no. He wasn't that drunk!

"Yeah, well," he said as he stood up and pulled some bills from his pocket, slipping one into the gypsy's hand and tossing another on the table for the barmaid. "Not that it hasn't been fun, but I'm out of here."

"Not yet, boyo," the gypsy said, her laugh a dry cackle as she folded the bill and slipped it into her bodice. "But yer will be. Yer will be. Oi'll be seein' yer when yer gets back—iffen ye've learned anythin', that is."

He left the pub in a purposely slow, unhurried gait, not allowing himself to break into a jogging trot until he had passed out of the light of the last lamppost on his way back to Ambersley Hall.

By the time he had poured his fourth drink from the bottle that sat beside his bed, he had forgotten the gypsy and remembered only that he was Michael Casey, movie star. . . .

1

"Fasten your seat belts. It's going to be a bumpy night."

—Bette Davis, in *All About Eve*

JILLY A'BRUNZO, LONGTIME COSTUME DESIGNER TO THE STARS, leaned back on his haunches, his lips clamped down tight on a dozen or more straight pins. "That takes care of it, Mr. Casey," he mumbled around the dangerous hardware. "The sleeve is perfect now." His knees creaked as he rose to assist the actor out of the midnight-blue claw hammer tailcoat. "We'll do the evening jacket now, if you want."

"Later, Jilly," Michael Casey said offhandedly as he took a single step closer to the full-length mirror and struck up the pose Geoffrey, his personal-gesture coach, had told him was reminiscent of the perfect Regency gentleman: chin high, shoulders back, one knee slightly bent, one freshly manicured hand raised negligently to his chest, a studied look of pained boredom doing nothing to mar the dark handsomeness of the face that had launched a thousand fan clubs spanning four continents.

Not half bad. No one could tell that he had barely slept last night. *Not bad at all,* Casey concluded, taking in the sight of himself as he stood dressed in not only the claw hammer tailcoat but also a muted ivory shirt and neck cloth, skintight waistcoat, fawn pantaloons, and nearly knee-high custom-made soft leather boots. *And it sure beats hell out of a fry cook's apron.*

But something was missing. "Jilly—shouldn't I be carrying something? A hat? A cane?"

The costumer winced. "Yes, sir," he admitted, pulling the pins from his mouth. "You'll be wearing something called a curly-brimmed beaver when you go outside, and you'll be carrying a cane. But both those things are still back in the States. If I had known, if someone had told me earlier that you wanted all your costumes waiting for you in England a full two weeks before we began shooting, I would have—"

"Never mind, Jilly," Casey broke in impatiently, walking over to the large four-poster bed to pick up the battered Louisville Slugger that looked so out of place lying on the broacade coverlet. "But I do want to spend some time getting used to this costume. It's the one Beau Lindsey wears the day he returns to Ambersley Hall, and the first change I have in the movie."

He swung the baseball bat up onto his shoulder. "Maybelline here can play understudy to the cane while I take a tour of the rest of this barn. My plane got in late yesterday, and I spent most of the evening in the village."

"I quite understand, Mr. Casey," Jilly said, picking up his pincushion. "Again, please accept my apologies."

Uh-oh, Casey thought, *Jilly's pissed. I gotta stop taking myself so seriously. I think I might be getting a reputation for being difficult.*

He didn't want to be difficult. He just wanted, needed, to be *right.* It was no secret in the industry that Michael Casey had his own way of getting into character, a sort of "immersion process" that had seen him working the night shift at a local diner for three weeks before filming his last movie and riding with the Los Angeles SWAT team for the picture before that one.

Not that any of Casey's movies were great anywhere except at the box office. Just shoot-'em-up, bang-bang blockbusters, that's all they were. Except for this one. This one was supposed to be different. In this one, the shoot-'em-up and bang-bang would take a backseat to the story—at least for a while. *Ambersley* was going to show Michael Casey's growth as an actor.

And I'm believing that crap. That'll teach me to read press clippings. Yeah, well, just as long as the public believes it.

"Jilly?" Casey smiled, the famous, female knee–melting Michael Casey dimple coming into play. "The costumes are great. You're doing a hell of a job. I just want you to know that."

"Thank you, Mr. Casey! You may leave now. Oh, dear, that's not what I wanted to say. I mean, you go see the house and, um, and I'll just stay here and lay out the costume you'll be wearing for the final fight scene."

"Oh, yeah. The one where I start out crawling over the beach looking for Alexandra Deverell," Casey said, his nearly photographic memory zeroing in on the finale even as he mentally ran over his lines for the opening scene. "Do me a favor, Jilly, and double-check that the left sleeve is breakaway. The last time I needed my shirt ripped off the damn seam had been double-stitched. We needed three takes before the scene played right."

He pointed the barrel of the bat at the costumer. "And no zippers, even if they're to be hidden. I want everything to be authentic, understand? I'm counting on you walking away with an Oscar for costume design on this film, Jilly. No slipups. Let's not forget the second *Die Hard* flick. Willis is still fielding bad jokes about those West Coast pay phones in a D.C. airport."

"Of course, Mr. Casey," Jilly said, standing up very straight and pushing out his nonexistent chest.

Knowing he had just blatantly appealed to the man's vanity, and sure he had just put that same man firmly on his side, Casey left the small bedroom that had been set aside for his personal use for the duration of the filming and headed for the split stairs that led to the ground floor of the tenth Earl of Ambersley's sprawling, pink-brick country estate.

The earl, whose need for ready cash had conveniently pushed aside any thought that renting out his family home to a bunch of uncouth American filmmakers intent upon telling the story of his ancestor's derring-do might be considered déclassé, had already decamped to the Monaco casinos for the duration of the shoot, leaving the house vacant except for a skeleton staff, none of whom were in evidence at the moment.

The house was immense and, thanks to the Ambersleys' lack of money, still furnished very much in the way of an early nineteenth-century estate. It was perfect for the movie, and Casey could hardly wait for the filming to begin.

In two days the remainder of the advance crew would descend on the estate, armed with lights, booms, and miles of electrical cords—their job being to block out areas of the rooms that would be used for interior shots. Already, a half dozen trailers had been crowded into a small area behind the stables, close enough to be used as dressing rooms and distant enough from the action so that they would not be visible in the camera lens. The director would set up shop in the nearby village, where rushes would be run each night after filming, and both local inns had been engaged for the six-week duration of the shoot.

But now, for today, and for several more days if he ignored the camera and setup crews, Casey had Ambersley Hall pretty much to himself. He had time to steep himself in the clothes, the atmosphere, the lines he would say, the emotions he would have to bring to the role, to the screen. *Ambersley* was still to be an adventure film, an action-thriller, but this was *his* film, *his* baby, *his* chance to prove that he could do more than single-handedly defeat three dozen villains and save the girl—all in 122 minutes. Sort of Errol Flynn's *Captain Blood* meets Mel Gibson's *Lethal Weapon,* with a little schmaltz thrown in for the ladies—or so Casey saw the project.

They'd all laughed, at first, when Casey had brought the *Ambersley* project to the studio. But a few months later Gibson had done *Hamlet,* and not fallen on his face. And then Michael Keaton did *Much Ado About Nothing,* right after raking it in at the box office with another *Batman* flick. Did anyone dare to say that Michael Casey would fail where Gibson and Keaton had triumphed?

Not when it was Michael Casey's money that was paying for *Ambersley,* Michael Casey who was executive producer of the film, Michael Casey who was taking all the chances and putting money in the pockets of a crew that numbered over a hundred, not to mention the salaries of three dozen actors as well. No. No one had complained. And they wouldn't. Not in this lifetime!

Especially when everyone knew American women would flock to the theaters to see the handsome Michael Casey in tight pants.

Casey turned to his left as he descended the last step and walked toward the main drawing room, an immense, high-ceilinged chamber that would have the cinematographers drooling. He strolled into the room at his ease, then inclined his head to greet, in absentia, his fellow characters. "Lord Brooks, Sir Charles—Miss *Dev*-er-ell?" he intoned in his newly acquired bored English drawl. "Charmed. Utterly charmed, I am sure."

He didn't bother watching for his marks as he rehearsed the remainder of the scene, for no one had yet taped them to the faded carpet, but concentrated only on attitude, on mood, as he did his best to crawl into the skin of Beau Lindsey, Sixth Earl of Ambersley, spy extraordinaire.

He could feel the persona of the sixth earl descending on him, oozing into his pores, transforming him from movie star to hero of the Napoleonic Wars, creating inside himself the dual personalities of a man who was outwardly a buffoon and secretly the hatchet man and enforcer of the War Office's edict to weed out a Bonapartist spy who had been responsible for the deaths of hundreds of British soldiers.

It took three run-throughs before Casey was satisfied that he understood the scene, by which time he was looking curiously at the paneled walls of the drawing room, wondering if one of the many secret passages Beau Lindsey had used to slip out of the mansion could be hidden behind the painted wood.

Secret passages. Damn, but he was a sucker for mysteries. Not puzzles, he told himself, remembering the gypsy after he'd thought he'd forgotten her. Just mysteries. Besides, it might be fun to crawl around inside the walls for a while. At least until lunchtime. Maybe Midge worked the lunch-hour crowd?

Hefting Maybelline onto his shoulder once more, he began an inspection of the room, pushing on wooden medallions decorating the mantel, then peeking behind picture frames to see if a hidden hinge might operate a sliding panel or some such inventive hiding place.

Nothing.

Not in the drawing room, or the music room, or the morning room, or the—wait a minute! *The library!* There were always secret passages hidden behind bookcases. Every Vincent Price movie had at least one. And *Young Frankenstein*—there had been a secret passage behind a bookshelf in that movie, the mechanism sprung by lifting a candle from a wall-mounted sconce. *"Put the candle back!"* That had been the line that had sent him into mild hysterics when he'd seen the film in his hometown Philadelphia theater, Casey was sure of it.

Convinced he was at last hot on the trail of adventure, Casey headed to the back of the house, having already learned from the set drawings where the library was located. Sure enough, the room was lined floor to ceiling with bookcases. There was even a curving set of steps that led to a small loft which was also lined with bookcases. The place was a fucking Library of Congress.

Momentarily defeated, Casey wandered the room aimlessly, tapping Maybelline against the odd interesting bit of wood carving, but with no luck. Until he climbed to the loft, that is, where small carved lions' heads decorated the shelf dividers along the back wall, each of the lions grimacing, it seemed to Casey, at the pain those small brass rings shoved through their noses must have caused.

"Nah, too obvious," he said, ready to turn away. But then he stopped. He'd come this far, hadn't he? Why not give it a shot?

He struck pay dirt with his first good pull on the third lion nose from the left, when the bookcase immediately slid back and to the right, as if someone had just oiled the hinges that morning.

Casey looked behind him, down into the center of the library, then shrugged and stepped forward into the exposed space, employing Maybelline to clear the way of cobwebs. He had gone no more than three feet when he smiled, knowing he had been duped. No wonder it had been so easy to find the secret passageway. It wasn't a passageway at all! It was nothing more than a small hidey-hole, as he believed such places were called. A claustrophobic room not much bigger than a coffin, and twice as cold.

He had already turned to leave, knowing Jilly would burst into tears if he got dirt on his costume, when it happened.

The bookcase slid left and forward, back into place, leaving Casey trapped behind the wall!

"Jesus H. Christ!" Casey exploded, cursing the darkness because it was better than advertising his own stupidity. *Now* what was he going to do? Scream for help? Oh yeah. That'd be good. He could just see the *Variety* banner— *Casey Cooped, Crying!*

"This is taking method acting too far, buddy, even for you," he growled, hating the fact that his voice echoed rather thinly around him. He stood very still for several moments, trying to "feel" the direction in which he was standing, at last making a half turn and deciding that he was now facing the back of the bookcase. Placing his hands on the rough wall, he began searching for some sort of latch, or handle, or *something* that would serve as a trigger for the mechanism that held the bookcase in place.

After all, if there was a way in, there had to be way out. It only made sense.

At least Casey hoped so.

After five minutes of running his hands along all four seams of the bookcase, and beginning to wonder how long a person could live without fresh air, Casey was about ready to employ Maybelline as a battering ram when his fingers touched on a small round knob near the low ceiling.

His heart pounding, he turned the knob and then squinted as the bookcase slid back and daylight entered the small, hidden room nearly as rapidly as Casey departed it, only to watch in mingled awe and amazement as the bookcase slid back into place once more. "That's a damned death trap," he said aloud, trying to calm himself. "Special Effects will love it."

And then, tiring of adventure, and getting pretty sick of the high white neck cloth that seemed intent upon choking him, Casey descended the spiral steps and started back down the corridor, planning on climbing the main stairs two at a time and getting himself the hell out of costume before heading into the village.

"Lord Ambersley? Is that you? Why, this is a shock—um, that is, a *surprise,* isn't it? You weren't expected for another fortnight."

Casey stopped in his tracks, cocking his head to one side before performing a slow about-face in the direction from which the female voice had come.

And then he smiled.

"Now, this is interesting," he said, walking slowly toward the young actress standing just outside the door to the music room. He circled around her, considering her period costume and the exemplary way the tallish, dark-blond female filled it out. Jilly had been right on target in choosing to accentuate her firmly rounded breasts with that lace business around the bodice.

She was fine-boned, her slightly slanted eyes and cleanly sculpted features reminding him a bit of Jodie Foster—on a bad hair day, that is. That straggly topknot had to go, and he made a mental note to tell the hairdresser. "You look somehow familiar. Who do you play, honey?" he asked, always open, as she most certainly knew, to a little on-location romance with a willing ingenue.

" 'Play'? *'Honey'?"* the actress responded in what Casey considered a really good impression of cultured English tones. She lifted one sculpted eyebrow a fraction. "I beg your pardon, for I do not believe I understand. Although I most heartily agree that we are as if actors upon a stage, my lord. We two are commencing upon a farce in the near future, aren't we?"

Casey nodded. "Good line, babe, and a passable delivery," he said, tucking Maybelline beneath his arm. "But it definitely sounds like one of Alexandra Deverell's, not yours. Don't go stepping on Sheila's toes, or she'll have those lovely green eyes skewered on a *Spago* toothpick."

The actress took a step backward, then slapped at Casey's hand as he reached out to untie her topknot. "Sheila? Who on earth is Sheila? Good Lord, everything I've heard is true, and more. You're not simply blockheaded—you're completely insane! I *am* Alexandra Deverell, as if you didn't know. Papa sent my miniature to you in America last year. And I must say, your accent is atrocious, but that is what will come from living amidst savages all these years, I suppose."

"Improvisation, huh?" Casey countered, deliberately stepping back into character. "Very well, *Miss Deverell,* I'm willing to play along. It might be fun." Remembering Geoffrey's tutoring, he made her an elegant "leg," nearly dropping Maybelline in the process. *I'll have to give Geoff a call. I need more work with canes,* he told himself as he rose from the bow.

"I see ours will be an interesting marriage, Miss Deverell," he commented, holding out an arm to her, then guiding her into the library when after a brief frown she placed her hand on his forearm. "Tell me, what brings you to Ambersley Hall today? As you said, I was not expected for another two weeks."

Now let's see her get out of this one! Casey thought, smiling. *Or will she give up and admit she's here, and already in costume, in order to get the jump on anyone else who might be planning to become Michael Casey's love interest for the next six weeks? It's not a bad idea, offering herself as my foil while I ease myself into the mood, into the character of Beau Lindsey, Sixth Earl of Ambersley. Got to hand it to the girl. She's damned inventive!*

"I—I was simply checking to make sure Tilden had everything in hand for your arrival," she said, avoiding his eyes. "Lord Brooks's communication to Tilden was adamant that the estate be perfect, you understand. As if I care, one way or the other," she ended quietly, obviously speaking only for her own benefit.

"Tilden? Oh, yes, the family butler. And Lord Brooks, Ambersley's trusted adviser," Casey said, motioning for her to seat herself before he went to the window, staring out over the gardens. *Good. Can't see the trailers from this window either.* "That leaves us with Quickly, Edwardine, James Williard, the lovely Louisa—and your dear papa, of course, Sir Charles Deverell."

He turned about to face her. "Now let's see if you can use all the major players' names in the same sentence. Come on, honey, I'm giving you the chance to impress the hell out of me. Then it'll be my turn, and I can show you the secret chamber. It's nothing great, but it beats the bejesus out of anything else I've seen today."

"How—how do you know about Edwardine? And—and *Quickly!* Nobody knows about Quickly!"

Casey was beginning to feel bored. Not Regency hero bored, but Michael Casey bored—which, as any of his associates would have been happy to volunteer (out of earshot of the great man, of course), was considerably more dangerous.

"Look, babe," Casey said, sighing. "Fun's fun and all that, but now you're becoming a drag, if you know what I mean. What do you say we get out of these clothes and go into the village for a beer?"

The actress shrank back in her seat, her emerald-green eyes wide as she glared at him. "Get undressed and drive into the village? I—I . . . Confound it all, Ambersley, I don't know how you know about my maid, or about Quickly, but to suggest that we *disrobe,* and—and drive into the village? My God, man, are you *mad?"*

"Not yet, but I'm getting there. For the moment, I'm just a little sick of this particular game. However, that doesn't mean there aren't other games we could play." Casey walked to the center of the room, hefting Maybelline as he took up his classically flawed batting stance, which was the single reason he was Hollywood's darling rather than All-Star second baseman for the Philadelphia Phillies. He threw her a look over his shoulder, his patently sexy Michael Casey look, calculated to melt women at the kneecaps. "If you're interested, get back to me. If not . . . well, I'll see you around the set, okay?"

And then he turned his back on her and began to recite.

" 'There was ease in Casey's manner as he stepped into his place,' " he said, quoting from Ernest Thayer's famous poem—from Michael Casey's too-close-to-the-bone nemesis of a poem, so that he often employed the lines as a joke against himself, thereby deflecting his critics. " 'There was pride in Casey's bearing and a smile on Casey's face.' "

He turned to grin once more at the actress, who was sitting, openmouthed, on the very edge of her seat. *Works every time,* he thought with satisfaction. *Impresses the hell out of them!* " 'And when responding to the cheers he lightly doffed his hat,' " he continued, tipping an imaginary baseball cap in his audience's direction, " 'No stranger in the crowd could doubt 'twas *Casey* at the bat.' "

"Tilden? Oh—*Til*den? Where are you, Tilden?" the actress called out weakly, rising from the chair and beginning to ease toward the doorway. *"Tilden!"*

Isn't she ever going to give it a rest? Casey wondered, looking toward her in disgust.

Holding Maybelline back over his shoulder once more, with his legs spread and his weight leaning back onto his right foot, Casey continued, " 'Ten thousand eyes were on him as he rubbed his hands with dirt, Five thousand tongues applauded when he wiped them on his'—woman, would you for the love of heaven *shut up!*"

How was a man supposed to concentrate on his lines when some ridiculous female insisted on screaming like a rock star groupie? And the least she could do was scream *his* name, and not that of the Ambersley butler—as if some guy who'd been dead for over a hundred and fifty or so years would be able to hear her.

Reluctantly, Casey came out of his stance and followed after the actress as she continued out into the hallway, still bellowing for Tilden.

"Now look, babe," Casey bit out, catching up with her, grabbing her elbow to keep her in one place, "enough's enough. I'll personally pay your flight back to the coast, but as of now you're officially off this picture. There's only enough room on the set for two egos—mine and Sheila's."

"There you go again! Sheila! Who is this Sheila person? Some light-skirt you've already secreted in the village, no doubt. Oh, never mind—because it doesn't matter a fig to me if you have ten mistresses, a thousand! And furthermore, Lord Ambersley, I don't care if you're rich as Croesus and marrying you will save my ungrateful father from the poorhouse, for I wouldn't bracket myself to you if you were twice as wealthy. Now, unhand me, sirrah, let me go *at once!*"

Casey had never considered himself to be particularly insightful or patient when it came to women—Woo 'em, bed 'em, leave 'em laughing, that was his motto—but there was something about this one, something about the genuine fear in her lovely green eyes, that kept him from merely saying something sarcastic and then leaving her where she stood. Not taking the chance of releasing his restraining grip on her arm, he gave her his most convincing, innocent smile and led her back into the library.

"Let's start over, honey, shall we, with none of the usual Hollywood crapola to get in the way?" he suggested, laying

Maybelline on a chair before perching himself on one corner of the large mahogany desk. "I'm Michael Casey, and you're . . ."

"Oh, very well. I suppose it would only be simple Christian charity to accommodate you. I'm Alexandra Dev—*what* did you say? Michael Casey? An Irishman? Then you're *not* Lord Ambersley?" She collapsed into the seat she had occupied earlier, one hand pressed to her lovely breast as she gave a weak smile. "Oh, my stars, don't I feel above everything silly!"

Casey was beginning to believe he had stumbled into a bit of mischief. "No, I'm not Ambersley," he told her, "although I'm sure he'll be sorry he missed you. He grabbed a jet for Monaco three days ago." He pushed himself away from the desk. "Did he forget to tell you he canceled some masquerade party or something?"

Her beautiful features became mulishly indignant. "There you go again! Just when I think you're going to make some sort of sense, you start rambling on and on, making entirely *no* sense at all. That's how it is with people who show dimples when they smile. The dimples make you think they're nice, but then they go and do something perfectly horrid, so that you kick yourself, remembering that appearances are almost always deceiving."

"Now, honey—" Casey began, flashing his particular dimple once more, only to be cut off mid-cajol.

"Be quiet if you please, Mr. Casey, and let me think! And I must warn you, if you address me as your 'honey' one more time, I fear I may just do you a violent injury. Honey. *Babe.* Such disgusting appellations—but then you *are* Irish, aren't you? Your nationality is so prone to informal familiarity." She shook her head. "If only I could understand how you know about Quickly."

"He's in the script," Casey reminded her coldly, once again deciding that she was what he had originally believed her to be—a bit actress on the make. "Quickly was the smuggler Ambersley picked up to help him capture the spy, only—"

"Oh, my God! You know Quickly is a free trader? But, how? Nobody knows that. Nobody except—"

"Yeah, yeah. Don't bother going through the whole story line, okay? Nobody knew about Quickly but Alexandra Deverell, who had been getting her kicks running with the smugglers while waiting for her globe-trotting hero of a fiancé to come home from America and marry her to his fortune. Look," Casey concluded, going over to the window once more, "could you do us both a favor and take a hike now? I don't know why you insist upon calling yourself Alexandra Deverell, but—what the *hell?*"

Casey threw open the window, then pressed his palms on the windowsill as he peered toward the stables. He hadn't seen any of the trailers when he'd looked earlier, but now he noticed that he also couldn't see any of the overhead electrical wires that were going to have to be shot around when they filmed the stable yard scenes.

What idiot had given the order to remove the poles and lines? Did they think he was made of money, that he could afford such extravagant expenses as laying underground electrical wires?

Leaving the window, he stomped over to the French doors that led onto the patio, taking Maybelline with him, fully intending to wave the bat in George's face when he found the head electrician. "Take your act on the road, babe," he tossed over his shoulder at the almost forgotten female. "I've got to go kill somebody."

Only there was nobody to kill.

There was nothing but gardens, and the stables in the distance, and a few extras wasting time pruning roses—and in costume, no less. Was Jilly out of his tiny mind, issuing costumes two weeks early?

He stopped walking. *Wait a minute,* his brain warned him. *Something's wrong.*

Scary kind of wrong.

Eerie kind of wrong.

He swallowed, and the action hurt, for his throat felt suddenly tight, restricted, as was his breathing.

Then he had it. He knew what had stopped him. *There were no trailers parked behind the stables.*

He whirled about in a full circle, trying to regain his bearings. Where did those trailers go? They had been there an hour ago. The electrical poles and lines had been there an hour ago. An hour ago—before he had practiced his lines in the drawing room, then gotten himself locked behind that damned bookcase.

And there was more. Not only weren't there any trailers, but the grassy space they had occupied was now cluttered with small wooden buildings, one of which looked suspiciously like an old-fashioned "outhouse," reminiscent of those he had seen in his youth when he'd toured an Amish farm with his fifth-grade class.

Casey felt his heart beginning to pound in his chest, its jackhammer-quick beat making it even more difficult to breathe, to think. *"Surprise!"* he could almost hear Dick Clark chortling. *"Michael, you've been caught by our hidden cameras. How does it feel to be yet another celebrity tricked by one of our famous practical jokes?"* Casey closed his eyes. He had never much liked Dick Clark. People were supposed to age, damn it. Who did he think he was, Dorian Gray?

"Are you all right, Mr. Casey?" the young woman who had called herself Alexandra Deverell asked from somewhere behind him. "You don't look very well. Perhaps I should find Tilden and have him send for Dr. Williard."

Casey wheeled about sharply, his famous sky-blue eyes now narrowed menacingly as he grabbed onto her shoulders. "All right, lady. Fun's fun, but this goes beyond playing jokes on the boss. I want the truth, and I want it now. What's your name? Who hired you to keep me occupied while they moved the trailers?"

"I—I've told you and told you," she said, vainly trying to remove his hand from her left shoulder. "My name is Alexandra Deverell. Now, please, Mr. Casey, let me go. I think that at the least I should call Tilden to assist you to a bedchamber. You're obviously experiencing an emotional overset of some sort."

"Oh, my God," Casey breathed quietly, doing his best to make some sense of the totally senseless. "Oh, my God. It's not Dick Clark. He'd have been out here by now, grinning and expecting me to be a good sport. Damn—why couldn't it have been Dick Clark?"

"Mr. Casey?"

He ignored her, instead casting his gaze left and right, trying to get his bearings. As he looked, he rambled, hardly aware he was speaking to anyone but himself. "If it's not a trick, a joke—then this is actually happening. I'm actually here, *now*. But when is *now*? Goddamn! I've heard about stuff like this. *Back to the Future*—one and three were good, but two was pretty lame. And that one with the blonde— what's her *name*, for crying out loud? Kathleen-something. *Turner*. That's it. Kathleen Turner. A little old to play a teenager, but that's Hollywood for you. As long as you're A-list, you do what you want. *Peggy Sue Got Married*. Yeah, I remember now. But those were movies. Just movies. Christ, Casey, get a grip!"

But a grip on what?

"If the Jodie Foster look-alike is who she said she is, if she isn't acting at all, but actually playing it straight, and if she really can't understand how I know about Tilden, and Quickly, and even Edwardine—" He felt a nervous, almost protective tightening in his groin area, and a sickening hole gaping wider and wider in the pit of his stomach. "Oh, God. *Oh my God!*"

"Mr. Casey! You're beginning to frighten me! I'll have to ask you to stop this at once, or else I should be forced to—oh, well."

Casey felt his head slam to the left as a hand came up and gave him a stinging slap on the right cheek. He glared down at the young woman, tempted to hit her back. Instead, he gave her a single, mighty shake.

"All right, Miss Deverell, we'll play it your way. I'm Beau Lindsey, Sixth Earl of Ambersley, just arrived from America to wed and bed you—not necessarily in that order—then single-handedly save the world. Bang-bang, shoot 'em up, cut—that's a print. Now, as I'm being so congenial, perhaps you will give me the date."

"Bang-bang?" she echoed, then frowned. "The date? Why, it's Tuesday, of course. The fourth of May. But—but you said you were Michael Casey. I don't understand. Why did you lie to—"

He gave her another shake. "May the fourth—of what year, Miss Deverell? What is the year?"

"There you go again!" she protested hotly, finally succeeding in breaking free of him. "Leave it to Papa to betroth me to a lunatic! It's 1813, of course. Unless you'd prefer it to be some other year, Mr. Casey—my lord. I'm sure I would be amenable to such a suggestion, as it is always best to humor the mentally afflicted—at least until Tilden can knock you senseless. He used to indulge in fisticuffs in his youth, you know, and if he once bested Gentleman Jackson —although I think the man is fudging it when he makes that claim—I'm convinced he would make short work of you, Mr. Casey. Um—my lord."

Casey staggered back into the library, noticing for the first time that there was no telephone on the desk and no cabinet containing a television—although there had been both before he had taken his detour behind the bookcase.

He picked up Maybelline, cradling the bat close against his chest as he sank into a chair. Madly, *crazily,* a line from *Johnny Dangerously* crept into his addled brain, and he said softly, and to no one in particular, " 'I've been thinking about taking up smoking. This clinches it!' "

2

"What we've got here is a failure to communicate."
—Strother Martin, in *Cool Hand Luke*

ALEXANDRA KEPT THE FIREPLACE POKER FIRMLY IN HER FIST AS she watched the lunatic pull on the small brass ring, then stepped back a pace in mild shock as the bookcase slid back and to the right, exposing a small, dark space.

"See?" the lunatic said, grinning at her in a way that made her feel sorry for him. "I told you this was a secret passage."

"Yes," she concurred gently, leaning forward to take a quick peek into the darkness. "I suppose you could call it that. My congratulations, for I've run tame in this house all my life and never knew it was there. You have a right to seem so proud of yourself. And you believe that you—" she hesitated, clearing her throat, "that you traveled through time by stepping into that space? How, how terribly *interesting,* I'm sure." *Where was Tilden when she needed him? Drat the hollow-legged man for trying to drink up the French brandy she'd brought him all in one sitting!*

"You don't believe me," the man who variously called

254

himself Michael Casey and Beau Lindsey, Sixth Earl of Ambersley, declared, his lower lip coming forward in a comically childish, oddly endearing pout. What a stubborn fellow he was, she thought, and very much impressed with himself, even when he was so obviously frightened.

"No, I don't believe you," she answered him levelly. She might be willing to coddle a lunatic, but she was not about to deliberately lie to one. "I am not so hen-witted, however, as to be set against learning new things. Why, it was difficult to put any credence into the thought of balloon flight, but it is a fact. However, traveling across time? Really, Mr. Casey, I don't believe you should judge me too harshly for having reservations about the exercise."

"Mary Shelley would have bought it," he went on, "her and her whole gang—Byron and those other dope addicts. That's how *Frankenstein* was written, you know. Opium pipes all around, then off to write. You look like you've never heard of the book, which I guess would mean it hasn't been written yet. But I don't blame you for not believing me. I wouldn't believe it either. But it happened. I got stuck behind this damned bookcase, and ended up in 1813. Nothing else makes any sense—not that anything I've said does. Now, if I've figured it right, all I've got to do is go back in, let the door shut, and I'll be back in my own time—at which *time,* Miss Deverell, I'm going to personally nail the damned thing shut."

"Then I imagine this is good-bye, Mr. Casey," Alexandra said dryly, trying her best not to giggle. Really, he was a most attractive gentleman, for a lunatic. "Do have a pleasant journey."

Still holding onto the brass ring, having twice explained that the door might slide shut too soon if he didn't, he turned to look at her oddly, almost sadly, then stepped into the opening, the bookcase quickly moving back into place behind him.

Alexandra lowered the poker and leaned a shoulder against the wall, patiently counting aloud from the number one as she waited for him to appear again, which he did just as she was about to say "sixty."

"Oh, back so soon?" she teased, tilting her head as she tried once more not to laugh, this time not succeeding half as well in her attempt to remain serious. "Is it conceivable that there was something you forgot? Perhaps you should have muttered some incantation first?"

He glowered at her, brandishing the wooden club almost menacingly. "Damn it! Strike one."

"Strike one? That's an odd sort of incantation," Alexandra repeated in confusion. "I suppose it means something profound, but I am afraid I am at a loss as to just what that is. And now, Mr. Casey, or whoever you are, may I assume that are you willing to have Tilden summon Dr. Williard? Or perhaps you'd like to trip on down to the water's edge, just to see if you can part the channel from here to Calais?" And then she broke down and giggled at her own wit.

The lunatic figuratively pinned her to the wall with his cold blue gaze. "You want to know something, Alex, honey? You're beginning to get on my nerves. And for God's sake, don't send for Williard. He's the last man we need right now," he bit out, rudely brushing past her and descending the spiral steps to the main floor of the library.

Once there, he did what Alexandra considered the oddest thing—not that she didn't include everything he had already said and done within the realm of the truly bizarre. He stood in the middle of the carpet just as he had done earlier, his legs spread wide apart, the odd club held two-handed at shoulder level, closed his eyes, and said as if reciting once more, "'And now the leather-covered sphere came hurtling through the air, / And Casey stood a-watching it in haughty grandeur there. / Close by the sturdy batsman the ball unheeded sped; / "That ain't my style," said Casey. "Strike one," the umpire said.'"

His arms came down to his side, his hands still clutching the menacing club, and Alexandra hastened to join him, certain that he was going to collapse at any moment. "Are you all right?" she asked in real concern, laying a hand on his arm.

He turned his head slowly and looked down at her, for he was exceedingly tall—rather attractively tall, she realized. And those eyes! Why, he had shown no such inclination to handsomeness in the likeness that hung in the drawing room. Of course, he had only been six when he'd sat for the portrait.

Alexandra sighed, realizing that she was beginning to believe he actually was Beau Lindsey—which would be horrible. How was she supposed to reconcile herself to marriage with a positively dotty creature who clearly belonged in Bedlam? Not that her papa would care. Money was money, no matter where it came from. And if she could produce a male heir who was even halfway sane, why, Papa would be in alt!

"It's just as well, I suppose," the stranger with two identities said after a moment, pulling her back from her depressing thoughts as he tossed the club to the floor and led her to a dark burgundy leather couch, then sat himself down beside her. "I didn't really want to leave anyway. The trades say I'm only out for myself, but I'm not completely single-minded. I have feelings. I mean, considering the fact that you're going to die when you try to help Ambersley catch the spy, it doesn't seem fair that I don't stick around and see if I can help you."

"Well, yes, I suppose there is that," Alexandra said before her head shot up. *"What* did you say?"

His grin was infectious. "Just checking to see if you've been listening, babe," he said, taking her hands in his—after removing the poker from them, that is. "Now, look. I know this is difficult to believe, but work with me a minute, all right? Just for now, for this moment, pretend that I'm telling the truth. Pretend that I am Michael Casey, actor, and I'm starring in a movie—a play, to you—about the life and times of Beau Lindsey. All right?"

Alexandra nodded, listening, while at the same time

giving serious consideration to the notion of swooning. She was going to die? Impossible! She had only just begun to live. And yet, he had known about Edwardine, and Quickly as well. Why was she beginning to believe him now—when he was dealing her such horrible news? "You've already said all of that," she reminded him. "You've already told me that that's how you know about things you shouldn't know. But I still don't see how—"

"I traveled through time when I went behind that damned bookcase!" he nearly shouted, frightening her.

"Please, sir, I refuse to listen to you if you will persist in bellowing," Alexandra told him, striving to control her own emotions. Damn! Did he have to be so sincere, so that she had no choice than but to believe him? "I can hear you perfectly well when you speak in normal tones. Now, speak slowly and distinctly, why don't you, and we'll see if we can yet muddle through this."

Shockingly, he dared to wink at her. "A little British stiff-upper-lip stuff, huh, Alex? I'll have to practice that. All right, all right," he continued when she glared at him. "Look, honey, I don't know how, I don't know why, but you have to believe I'm telling the truth. Damn. If Jilly had only taken a shortcut and put a zipper in these pants."

"'Zipper'? What a strange word. Whatever is a zipper?"

"It's something that would have proved that I—wait a minute. Scratch the zipper. Right now I've got to figure out why I'm here, and the hell with anything else. But maybe I already know what's going on. Maybe, just maybe, it's one of those cosmic blips, the kind with a moral. I could have been sent here to save you. I know it's not a very original plotline; Christ, it's already been used on the small screen. But it's possible."

He squeezed her fingers until they hurt. "That's it, honey! That's got to be it. And who could be better for the job? I know the plot, I know the players. I even know the lines. It'll be a piece of cake."

"Cake," Alexandra repeated. "That's it. You're hungry. If I can find something for you to eat, possibly then you'll—"

"Damn it, Alex, would you listen to me? I'm here for a reason. Some twisted, character-building lesson in humanity, and humility, or something like that. And maybe I have been getting a big head lately. You know, minor league baseball player one day, box office idol the next. You lose perspective after the ten thousandth fan letter. I mean, women send me their underwear, for crying out loud! But I'm getting ahead of myself, aren't I, babe?"

"Personally," Alexandra countered, "as you've asked, I think you're far more than ahead of *yourself.* You're also miles ahead of *me,* for I haven't been able to understand more than every second word."

"It's simple, Alex. I'm here to save you, to do a good, redeeming deed. Because I do believe in God, in a higher power. I wasn't *born* cynical, you know. And then, after I've saved you, when I go behind that bookcase again, I'll be zapped back to my own time. As someone said on another television show—I did a guest shot once; early in my career, you understand—'I love it when a plan comes together!' Hey, what do you want from me, shoot-from-the-hip originality? I'm not Robin Williams, you know."

Then, seemingly caught up in his own joy, he leaned forward and kissed her, square on the mouth.

It was becoming rather tedious, slapping this man, but Alexandra did it again anyway—only to have him laugh at her.

"You are the most odious, offensive, *unmanageable* man it has ever been my misfortune to encounter," she told him succinctly, picking up the poker as she gingerly rose to her feet, "and for the life of me I cannot understand why on earth I am still listening to you. Now, once and for all—who are you?"

"I'm Michael Casey," he responded, smiling as he stood, and seemingly twirling a nonexistent mustache. "Failed minor league second baseman and star of *Hellfire,* top-grossing picture of the decade. Adored by millions, owner of a brand-new beach house in Malibu, and the time-traveling lead in the upcoming blockbuster *Ambersley,* which is based on the life and times of one Beau Lindsey, swashbuckling hero and all-around good guy. In short, Miss Alexandra Deverell, at least for the duration, I'm your new guardian angel. I've come from the future to save your lovely skin."

And then he frowned, his broad shoulders slumping. "Aw, face the facts, honey. *I've* had to."

"It's fortunate the real Ambersley had several personal trunks sent on ahead," Alexandra said, pulling open the doors of the large wardrobe in the main bedchamber. "We can only hope that his clothes will fit you."

Casey reclined at his ease on the wide tester bed in the Sixth Earl of Ambersley's private apartments, his arms crossed behind his head as he lay propped against a mound of satin-covered pillows. Looking at the pair of knee breeches Alexandra was holding up, he remarked idly, "At least we won't have to worry about the pants being too short and showing my anklebones. I haven't worn high-waters since I got taller than my brother and Mom couldn't give me any more of his hand-me-downs."

And then he grinned at Alexandra Deverell. Pretty Alexandra Deverell. His buddy, his pal; his good-hearted, good-natured, *believing* Miss Alexandra Deverell.

Well, maybe terming her "good-natured" was pushing the envelope. But at least she had reluctantly begun to believe him, once presented with the single unalterable fact of the portrait of a six-year-old future Earl of Ambersley—a dark-haired, vacantly grinning miniature monster with decidedly *brown* eyes. That one piece of evidence, coupled with Casey's otherwise unexplainable knowledge of Edwardine and Quickly, and added to Alexandra's declaration that she most definitely did not believe in the existence of either warlocks or sorcerers, had at last convinced her that he wasn't lying to her: he had traveled across time.

The additional fact that Alexandra Deverell didn't like him, even a little bit, just made the whole thing more interesting.

"God, Alex, I'm tired, like I'm suffering from jet lag—

which, in some twisted way, I suppose I am. But so far so good, don't you think? So you really believe Tilden bought it—that I'm Ambersley?" Casey asked, idly watching as Alexandra checked some nearby drawers for—*drawers?* What did Regency men call their B.V.D.'s? "He didn't seem to question my presence earlier at the dinner table. What was that breaded stuff anyway?"

"'Breaded stuff'?" Alexandra asked, looking at him blankly. "Oh, you mean the rabbit, don't you. You seemed to enjoy it."

"Rabbit!" Casey bolted upright on the bed. "I thought it was veal, without the Parmesan. Damn, babe, I don't eat rabbits."

She pushed an errant lock of hair out of her eyes as she crossed to the bed and gingerly sat down. They really were going to have to do something about that hair, he said to himself. "You do now, my lord," she pointed out, smiling. She was a real looker when she smiled; less Jodie Foster and more Alexandra, he thought, as if that explained it. "And I shouldn't be in this room. It's only because Tilden is still half in his cups that he hasn't burst in here, planting you a facer for daring to compromise me. That and the fact that, to the rest of the world at least, we have been betrothed almost from the cradle."

She stood again, looking toward the window and the rapidly failing light beyond it. "I must return to Deverell House. Papa won't take the medicine for his gout unless I stand over him threatening to cut off his port for a fortnight."

A sudden panic replaced Casey's temporary feelings of comfort. "You—you're *leaving* me? Here? Alone? What am I supposed to do now?" He was reminded of Scarlett O'Hara, feeling himself ready to bleat out, "Where will I go? What will I do?"

As if she had heard his thoughts, and as if she had seen the movie that wouldn't be made for more than a hundred and twenty or thirty-odd years, Alexandra replied calmly, "We'll think about that tomorrow, my lord. For now, with Tilden drinking in his quarters, and the rest of the staff at a minimum, you'll be safe enough here in your bedchamber. Just nod yes and no to questions, and wait for me to return. I'll be back here early, probably before Tilden so much as draws your bath. We'll have to get you a valet, won't we?" she added consideringly. "The remainder of the staff we've hired won't arrive for another week, more's the pity. And then there's seeing about readying a chamber for Lord Brooks, and—"

Casey quickly climbed down from the high bed, chasing after Alexandra as she continued enumerating her inventory of problems. "Let's backtrack to the most important thing," he said, interrupting her. "Although it leaves a lot to be desired, that thing you called a water closet wasn't so bad. But there was no shower in there—no tub. Am I really supposed to expect Tilden to drag a bathtub in here tomorrow?"

Alexandra cocked her head to one side, as if in thought. "Is that how you moderns arrange it? The bathtub in the same room as the water closet? How curious," she murmured, then shook her head. "No. I don't believe that would work. One would miss being close by the fireplace, you understand, when winter comes. Well, whatever. We'll discuss tubs tomorrow as well. Good night, *my lord.*"

She turned to leave him, so that he couldn't help reaching out to grab her by the elbow. "You're not going out with Quickly tonight, are you?" he asked, looking at her closely to judge whether or not her coming answer might be a lie. "I've got enough grief right now without you playing at smuggling."

Alexandra smiled even as she pried his fingers from her forearm. "Why, my lord, how you flatter me. Anyone would think you were worried for me."

"Not for you," Casey countered honestly, wishing Alexandra were the fainting, giggly sort instead of the Regency version of a smart-mouthed, liberated woman. But at least she wasn't stupid. God knows what would have happened to him earlier if Alexandra had been a stupid woman. "I'm worried for *me*. If you get killed I might be stuck here forever. As an exercise in role-immersion, this is fine, maybe the best thing that's ever happened to me. By the time I get back to my own time I'll have Beau's role down cold. However, honey, like they say—your time might be a nice place to visit, but I sure as hell wouldn't want to live here."

Her smile disappeared, and Casey unexpectedly sensed his personal sun sliding beneath the horizon. "Well, there's no danger of me getting a swelled-up head, now is there, my lord? Don't worry. I will not be with Quickly tonight, thus jeopardizing *your* future. I've much too much to think about before I see you again tomorrow."

"We both do," Casey countered, doggedly trying to detain her by stepping in front of her as she turned toward the door once more. It wasn't as if he was afraid to be alone or anything; he'd just miss the smell of her perfume once she was gone, that's all.

"For instance," he blurted out, grabbing at the first thought that came into his mind, "when is this wedding supposed to take place? Wait a minute! I think I remember you saying something about the real Beau Lindsey showing up here in another two weeks. Is that all the time we have? Because you're supposed to die the night before the wedding, you know."

She slid her gaze away from his. "You will persist in talking about that, won't you. But, yes, the wedding is to take place a week after the earl's arrival here at Ambersley Hall—three weeks from tomorrow, to be precise about the thing. Lord Brooks was most adamant about the date when he wrote to me." Then she brightened. "We've plenty of time, if you really mean to help me. After all, if you can journey through time, the simple rescue of one lone female shouldn't be all that difficult."

"You bet. A walk in the park." Casey leaned forward impulsively and kissed her on the cheek. Her skin was baby-soft, and slightly warm to the touch. "Never fear, my lady, Casey's here," he added huskily, sliding his arms around her waist.

He could see the gentle motion in her slim throat as she swallowed before answering. "I am Miss Deverell, not 'my lady.' As my betrothed, you may be so informal as to address me as Alexandra. Not honey, not babe, and not Alex. *Alexandra*. You, however, are my lord Ambersley, or Ambersley, or—as we are being informal, *Beau*. The real earl hasn't been called Beaumont since his infancy, you understand, while Lindsey, the family name, is rarely used in conversation. And, even though we are supposed to be married soon, you are to refrain from kissing any part of my anatomy save my hand—and that only when it is offered to you. Do you understand?"

He eased himself closer, until he could feel his hips pressing against hers. "Damn, there's nothing sexier than a beautiful woman with an authentic British accent. I'd much rather you called me Casey when we're alone, by the way," he said, tilting his head as he concentrated on the soft pink fullness of her lips. "And, honey, I have to tell you, there's many a spot on your anatomy I'd like to kiss, but your hand isn't anywhere near the top of the list."

She didn't shrink from him, only rolled her eyes and sighed. "I see I'm going to have to hit you again, *Beaumont*," she said with all the maidenly starch of a spinster schoolteacher, then sighed in a patently false, long-suffering way. "How prodigiously fatiguing."

Casey had been born with the ability to know when to attack and when to back off, to try again another day. He backed off now, dazzling her with a quick flash of his famous dimple as he put a small, reassuring space between them. "Sorry, Alex—I'm too used to adoring fans, I suppose. However, I suggest you get the hell out of here now, for I'm a desperate, lonely, displaced man, and God only knows what I'm capable of doing in search of a little comfort."

That last line came from his third movie, *Nobody Home*. In it he had played a Vietnam veteran released after a ten-year stay in a Cambodian prison camp who returns home to find his wife married to another man. The line had

worked on the female lead, and he was fairly certain it
would work again now.

"Fustian! What unalloyed drivel! Oh, all right, my lord—
Casey," Alexandra protested, then surrendered, as Casey
stared sadly, soulfully into her eyes, knowing he'd won.
"Papa, Edwardine, and I will arrive here at Ambersley Hall
before noon tomorrow, packed up and prepared to bear you
company until the wedding, or my death, whichever comes
first. We won't let my father in on our little secret, because
he'd have you transported to Bedlam immediately, and
because he wouldn't understand what we were saying in any
case. But," she pushed on, holding out her arms to ward him
off as he grinned and tried to embrace her, "don't go reading
anything remotely romantic into this, Casey. The roof of
Deverell House has sprung quite a few leaks this spring, and
a temporary change of residence does have a certain quixot-
ic appeal. And now, once again—good night, my lord."

Casey, convinced he should be content with this first
small victory, stepped forward to open the door to the
hallway. "Good night, my sweet love—that's a line from the
script, you understand, so I'm fairly certain the term was
used in your day." He leaned against the doorjamb, his arms
folded, one booted foot crossed over the other, as Alexandra
brushed by him, her cheeks hot. "Dream of me."

"Ha!" she exclaimed over her shoulder, giving a depreca-
tory toss of her badly coiffured head. "Just what I need after
a day like today—nightmares!"

Casey watched her move toward the double stairs, admir-
ing the sweet, singing sway of her hips, then stepped inside
his bedchamber, locking the door behind him in case Tilden
decided to do a bed check. Raising his eyes to the ceiling, he
murmured, "Beaumont, old buddy, you may have been a
first-class hero, but you were also a grade-A ass. Let me tell
you something—that is one *hell* of a woman!"

Then, still feeling sadly out of place, but unable to worry
about it too much at the moment, and still clad in Jilly's
authentic-looking costume, he hopped onto the high bed,

once again stretched out with his arms folded behind his head, and almost immediately fell into a deep sleep.

A sleep that was interrupted several times by the haunting words of a cherubic-looking gypsy who'd told him, "So many gifts. So little understanding. Years to travel afore you find your true love . . ."

A gray, somewhat soggy dawn had come, to Alexandra's weary mind, no more than an hour after she had at last found a light, troubled sleep. Even now, clutching her father's arm as she steered Sir Charles Deverell's corpulent, gout-cursed frame toward the relatively safe harbor of the Ambersley Hall morning room, she had to stifle a yawn.

She had wanted to linger a while longer over her toilette before climbing into the coach beside Sir Charles for the one-mile trip to Ambersley Hall. But Edwardine had deserted her in order to pack a few trunks, so that Alexandra knew her hastily put up hair made her appear as if she had been dragged backward through a hedge. And her gown? Well, the brown had never been her favorite, but it did button down the bodice, as her favorite sprigged muslin did not.

Not that she worried about her appearance. Hardly. She had weightier matters on her mind than whether or not the arrogant, overbearing, frightfully *forward* gentleman awaiting them in the morning room would cast his haunting blue eyes over her in admiration. In point of fact, she didn't care a fig what Michael Casey thought of her!

She straightened her posture as she and Sir Charles neared the door to the morning room, determined to blight Casey with her regal bearing. Then she remembered the dimple. That intriguing, infuriating, compellingly attractive dimple. The dimple, and the kisses. Those unexpected, unforgettable kisses. The next time she was about to pity the man, consider him a helpless victim of some capricious portal in time, she would have to remember his reprehensible, forward behavior. For the man wasn't a victim. He was a menace!

"Oh, the devil with it. I'll just have to deal with matters as I go along," she muttered with feeling, waiting as Tilden opened the door to announce that Sir Charles and Miss Alexandra Deverell had come to see his lordship, Earl of Ambersley.

"Alex! Come on in and sit down!" Casey called out affably from his seat at the head of the table, the sensual rumble of his voice curling her toes inside her slippers. "The bacon's a little odd, but good, although I'd steer clear of the kippers if I were you. Brutally ugly-looking things, aren't they? Sleep well?"

He didn't stand when she and Sir Charles entered, showing her that he was either insufferably arrogant or brick-stupid, but only waved them both to chairs as he sipped from his coffee cup, the outrageously long lace of his cuff nearly coming to grief in his coddled eggs. Didn't he know he wasn't to dress so formally in the country? Yes, a valet was certainly in order, although bringing yet another person onto the scene might be dangerous. She sighed. But he did look wonderful; she'd have to hand him that.

"Sir Charles!" Casey exclaimed as Tilden assisted the older man, who needed a second chair upon which to prop his heavily bandaged left foot. "How terribly decent of you to agree to bear me company until the wedding. Sink me, but I've been dreading the thought of rattling round this huge pile alone until my blushing bride might share my childhood home. And begin filling it up with a few of our own brood, eh what?"

Our own brood? Eh, what! Sink me? Alexandra rolled her eyes in mingled despair and amusement. And was that Casey's idea of how the King's English was spoken? What a dreadful accent; it was even worse than his natural, rather unnervingly hypnotic, unique tone and accent, the one he had quite proudly informed her was "half South Philly, half old Robert Redford movies"—whatever that meant.

"Already talkin' of settin' up your nursery? God's eye-teeth," Sir Charles exclaimed, slapping his knee, "if you ain't the downy one, Ambersley! Takes me back to the days with your dear father, rest his larcenous soul. The pair of you cut from the same cloth—always out adventurin', leavin' this place with only a skeleton staff for dog's years. And you're the picture of him, too—the very picture!"

Alexandra bit the inside of her cheek as she and Casey exchanged glances, Alexandra knowing that her toad-eating father was putting it on too thick and rare, and Casey smiling triumphantly, as if he had just stuck his thumb into a tart and pulled out his very own ripe plum. *Actors!* She said to herself, reflecting that whatever century they hailed from, they all appeared to share the same insufferable conceit.

"Thank you, sir," Casey said with a slight inclination of his head, the action marred only by his seeming inability to keep a halfway solemn expression on his face. "I have often heard it said that I resemble dear Papa. I miss him so. Looking into a mirror is, at times, my only solace."

Alexandra rolled her eyes again, this time in disgust. She was sitting between a brace of fools, one a money-mad old reprobate, and the other simply reprehensible on all counts, and she could not remain there a moment longer.

"If you two gentlemen will excuse me," she said from between clenched teeth, rising out of her chair, "I believe I need some fresh air." She held out her hands as Casey, lounging at his ease, made no move to play the gentleman and stand up until she had quit the room. "No, no," she protested archly, "don't get up, my lord. Far be it from me to discommode you."

"Got her hair in a twist over somethin', don't she?" she heard her father remark around a mouthful of jam-spread toast as she swept out of the room. "That's what happens to these long-in-the-tooth virgins. Leave 'em too long on the shelf and they turn sour. Always flyin' into the boughs over any little thing. Mark my words, Beau, and bed her now— sweeten her up a tad, else you'll rue the lapse on your wedding night."

Her cheeks flaming, Alexandra broke into a near run, not wanting to hear whatever horrible thing Casey said in reply to her father's crude suggestion. Turning to her left once outside the morning room, she trotted through the music room and out onto the patio overlooking the gardens, hoping to hide herself in the shrubbery until she could regain her composure.

"Come to tumble the spinster, have you?" she said cuttingly not fifteen minutes later when Casey discovered her sitting behind a large bit of topiary, passing the time shredding a few loose leaves into soggy green bits. "I'll say one thing for you, my lord; you're nothing if not obedient."

"Put a sock in it, Alex," Casey said affably if incomprehensibly as he sat down beside her, splitting his coattails before he did so, just like a true gentleman, and not a time-traveling actor whose English sounded as if it were a foreign language. "How do you stand him?" he asked after a moment, looking at her with something she believed to be dangerously close to sympathy—which was the last thing she needed, because kind words always made her cry.

"Papa?" she asked rhetorically, avoiding Casey's mesmerizing blue eyes. "He's no more or less than any other man, I suppose. If I were a son, he would have pushed me into the military. As it is, I can only be of use to him if I marry into a fortune. The coup of Sir Charles's life was getting me betrothed to Ambersley, and we've been living on the expectation this past dozen or more years. I must marry Beau, or else Papa's creditors will descend like buzzards— which would serve him right, you know."

She turned to look at Casey, not knowing why his opinion mattered, but desperate to hear it in any case. "Do you think I'm an unnatural daughter, to not like my own father? I love him, I suppose, even though he doesn't love me and makes no bones about that fact, but I really don't like him above half."

Casey reached out to push a stray lock of hair out of her eyes, his slight touch against the skin of her temple sending a curious shiver down her spine. "I remember something a great actor, Henry Fonda, said in a movie—*The Best Man*, I think it was. He said, 'He has every characteristic of a dog except loyalty.' That pretty much sums up your father, I think. So, no, honey: I don't blame you for not liking him."

"Th-thank you, Casey," she said. "And since you're being so kind, I won't mention that your strange speech in the morning room left much to be desired."

"You didn't like it? Some of the lines were from the script for *Ambersley,* and I thought I handled the scene well, even after you ran away and left me hanging out to dry." He shrugged, reminding her of a naughty child caught doing something wrong, but not necessarily repentant. "Yeah, well, everyone's a critic. So what was it, Alex? My accent? My hand motions? Maybe that 'sink me' line was too much?"

"No, I don't think so. I didn't mean you weren't good. It's just that you sounded different than you did yesterday. I'm sure you did just fine. Really." Then, before he could ask any more questions, Alexandra prudently changed the subject. "But now I suppose we should get down to cases. How—how am I supposed to die? Last night, when I couldn't sleep, I thought that, if I just stayed away from the place where I died, then I wouldn't be killed."

His eyes clouded slightly, and she wondered if the mention of her coming death had served to remind him of his own perceived predicament. If he could not save her, he believed, he would be trapped in her time forever. As he was clearly not going to be able to explain the existence of *two* Lord Ambersleys, that thought could not be reassuring.

He took hold of her hand and pressed it to his lips, kissing her palm, which she had not expected, and sending another curious shiver down her spine, a reaction she had reluctantly begun to enjoy. "There's no easy way to say this, I guess, so I'll just give it to you quickly. Bottom line, babe—you were found stretched out on some rocks near the shore, dead of a knife wound to the heart."

"A knife?" Alexandra felt another shiver skip down her spine, but this time it was definitely without pleasure. Being knifed did not sound like a particularly pain-free death. "Very well, I am to be murdered, most probably on the stretch of rocky beach Quickly uses to launch his smuggling boats out to the yawls, for that is the only beach I ever walk," she said, sighing as she attempted to erase any emotion from her response. "Let us proceed. Do you know who killed me?"

Casey nodded. "It was the spy. Beau kills him, of course. Then he and his true love, Louisa Hatfield—April Clairborne plays her in the movie; she's an unknown, but I felt we needed a new face—go to London with Lord Brooks. Louisa is a smaller part, the innocent beauty Beau rescues somewhere in France, with Sheila doing you in the lead. Nobody plays a great death scene like Sheila, although she likes to chew the scenery sometimes."

"Louisa Hatfield?" Alexandra repeated dumbly, mentally sorting through Casey's rambling explanation, and seeking out the salient points. What a sweet man. He was only rambling because talk of her death made him uncomfortable. Why, anyone would think he was beginning to like her!

"Yeah, that's right. Louisa comes to Ambersley Hall with Beau. He doesn't bring her from America, though, because he really hasn't been there. He's been spying for Lord Brooks and his pals at the War Office all over Europe. When he hits London, good old Beau is given the royal-hero treatment, and he and Louisa live happily ever after—fade to black, run the credits up from the bottom of the screen, don't trip over the popcorn cups on your way out of the multiplex."

Casey laid a hand on her shoulder. "Sorry, honey. I wish I hadn't had to tell you, but if we're going to change history I figured you had to know what happened."

Alexandra slapped his hand away, feeling herself growing very angry, almost dangerously angry, with the whole, entire world. "Isn't it enough that I die? Did he have to have planned to marry me when he was already in love with this Louisa person?" She lowered her voice an octave and said, "Ah, my fiancée is dead. Too bloody bad, but lucky for us, eh? Let's tuck her up with a shovel, my dear—no need to go into black gloves, for she was only a plain spinster already at her last prayers—then we'll toddle off to the city and see if we can still procure vouchers for Almacks."

"Aren't you being a little hard on the guy, Alex?" Casey asked, looking down the path as if he had just caught sight of something, or someone. "It isn't as if you could have expected him to love a woman he'd never really met."

Alexandra sighed, her anger leaving her, to be replaced by a nagging sadness, a feeling that she had not yet experienced enough of life to face the prospect of leaving it. Why, she, unlike Beau, had never even been in love! "It's not that, Casey. It's just the futility of it all. Think about it. Except for Quickly and Edwardine, there will be no one to weep for me, will there? Papa will mourn the loss of a fortune, I know, but it isn't quite the same thing, is it."

She turned to Casey, putting her hands in his. "Casey, you've got to save me, if for no other reason than I want to see Beau Lindsey's face when I tell him I wouldn't marry him if he was next in line to the throne. Then, after Papa recovers from his apoplexy in time to be toted off to debtors prison, I do believe I shall go to London and become a fashionable impure. I hear they have very nice lodgings and are gifted with the loveliest jewelry. Casey?"

"Later, honey," he answered vaguely. "I think we've got company."

Alexandra followed the line of Casey's pointing finger and smiled. "Oh, it's Dr. Williard. I wonder what brings him out here—unless he went to Deverell House to check on Papa and the servants sent him here."

"Williard?" Casey repeated, any lingering traces of his affected British accent dying a quick death. "Now, this ought to be interesting."

"Why?" Alexandra could sense that Casey was—as they wrote in all the worst marble-backed novels—girding his loins for battle. "What does your movie script have to say about James?"

"Not a whole hell of a lot, honey," he responded, pinning a dimple-edged smile on his handsome face as he rose to greet Williard, who was still some distance away. "But I do remember one of his lines. 'Terribly sorry, dearest Alexandra, but you have become expendable,' or words to that effect—just before he buries the knife in your chest."

Alexandra looked at the doctor, an unprepossessing man of indeterminate years and barely memorable looks or intellect. "James is the spy?" she whispered almost to herself, her entire body growing cold. "I'd as soon believe Tilden has sworn off French brandy!"

3

"I'd love to kiss you, but I just washed my hair."

—Bette Davis, in *Cabin in the Cotton*

HE WAS DRESSED IN BLACK FROM THE TOP OF HIS SILK SCARF—
tied head to the tips of his booted toes. The trousers were
interestingly snug as they stretched over his powerful thighs,
the black silk shirt full-sleeved and rather "blousy" as it
tucked into the narrow waistband. His boots, showing the
strain of being Casey's only footwear this past week—
as Beau Lindsey's feet were a good two sizes smaller—
added just the right touch of the dramatic, while the scarf
supplied a little of that well-known Hollywood flair for the
overdone.

Casey would have blackened his face and hands with
burnt cork, the better to camouflage himself in the darkness,
but Alexandra had put her foot down, demanding that he
either "be serious about this thing, Casey, or I shall go
without you. The scarf is bad enough!"

"Have you looked at yourself sufficiently," Alexandra
asked now without rancor, "or would you like me to have

274

Edwardine fetch you a hand mirror, so that you might turn about and admire yourself from both fore and aft?"

Casey grinned into the full-length mirror, watching as Alexandra slipped down off the bed while simultaneously shoving her hair up inside the black knitted cap she had called a "toque." Her long straight legs were a marvel in slacks—*trousers.* The knitted fisherman's sweater—at least that was what Casey saw it as—had been designed with her flat rib cage and generously full breasts in mind. And her classic features, once her usually haphazardly arranged hair had been pushed out of the way, would have done a young Katharine Hepburn proud.

A real aristocrat—that was Alexandra Deverell, her demeanor that of a queen whether she was calmly taking the air in the Ambersley gardens on the arm of the deadly Dr. Williard or preparing to head out to the beach to meet with the local smugglers. Sheila could never do this extraordinary woman justice, not if she had twenty takes of each scene.

"No, I'll pass on the mirror, Alex," Casey said as he picked up Maybelline, taking a moment to peer into a darkened corner of the bedchamber, where Edwardine sat stuffing her mouth with sugarplums. The maid looked straight out of central casting, complete with three chins, oversized mobcap, and a wart on the end of her nose. He'd already made a mental note to tell Makeup about the wart, but he doubted if the character actress picked to play the part could arrange her features to project such natural, bovine stupidity as did the real Edwardine.

"'I'm ready for my close-up, Mr. DeMille,'" Casey teased, striking a haughty pose, then bowed, using Maybelline to motion for Alexandra to precede him toward the door to the hall.

"More inane babbling, Casey?" Alexandra questioned him, shaking her head. "Some people are known to quote Shakespeare, you know. Now, please, follow me—and do be quiet so that we don't wake my father."

Giving a jaunty, pointed-pistol-finger farewell salute to Edwardine, who looked at him blankly, Casey called out,

"Hasta la vista, baby," screwed his features into a frown of solemn gravity meant to show his recognition of the seriousness of the coming adventure, and fell into step behind Alexandra.

As they tiptoed down the candlelit hallway past Sir Charles's bedchamber and headed toward the kitchens, Casey reflected on the events of the past week, even as he admired Alexandra's physical form as she preceded him down the narrow, twisting servant stairs.

And what a unique seven days it had been! Dredging up memories of old Errol Flynn and Stewart Granger movies he had seen on cable, and employing lines of dialogue that seemed to fit at the time—although Alexandra had rolled her eyes at him more than once as he occasionally slipped snippets of *Ambersley, Casablanca,* and even *Mrs. Doubtfire* into the conversation—he had convinced James Williard that the Sixth Earl of Ambersley was a dedicated, non-threatening twit.

Not that he'd gained any really useful information from the good doctor in return. The man was as dull as *Brady Bunch* reruns, and not nearly as deep. He just didn't fit the image of a spy, let alone a cold-blooded murderer of beautiful, defenseless women—which, Casey had decided, probably meant the traitorous bastard was very good at his job.

Casey would have been content to stick close to Alexandra until Williard did something to tip his hand, then take the doctor out with a good right cross, but Alexandra was scheduled to meet with Quickly tonight to pick up her share of booty from their last run, and any change in plans might make Williard suspicious. Besides, he figured he needed as much help as he could get before he acted, needed to enlist someone else who cared for Alexandra—and Quickly was, or so she had told him, the closest thing to a friend she had.

Casey had been racking his brain all week, looking for a way to get Alexandra to himself for a while—away from Ambersley Hall, and her crudely suggestive father, and the drunken Tilden, and the moronic Edwardine, and most especially, the curiously hovering Williard.

They needed to talk, he and Alexandra. They needed to be honest with each other, to explore the reasons why their eyes seemed to so often meet in silent understanding, shared humor, and even unspoken longing. And, most important, he needed to understand why the thought of returning to his own time, of leaving Alexandra behind, had kept him dragging his feet all week and making up excuses for not confronting Williard.

Casey knew he had never felt this way about a woman before, never before felt this crying need to touch her, to smell her, to listen to her laughter, to anticipate her frowns.

Not that she did any more than put up with him, humor him—and that, it seemed, only because she needed him to save her skin so that she could kiss Ambersley and her uncaring father good-bye and head for London to become some fat old lord's mistress.

"I still think Quickly might shoot you on sight, you know, since he doesn't have much respect for what he calls 'gentry morts,'" Alexandra whispered, mulishly stopping just at the door leading into the kitchen garden. "Are you quite sure you don't want to rethink this research expedition, Casey? Why don't you just go back upstairs, get out of those clothes—and most especially that *ridiculous* scarf—and stop pretending that meeting with desperate smugglers is akin to any of the sort of make-believe nonsense you tell me you do in that place, that *Hollywood.*"

"What?" Casey responded, grinning at the way she hid her concern for him beneath a thin layer of sarcasm. "And give up showbiz?"

Then he sobered, taking her arm and pulling her close against him. "Alex, honey, I have a confession to make," he said, his voice low and husky. "I'm through researching my role for *Ambersley,* and have been for days. Tonight has nothing to do with any movie."

"I thought not," she responded, smiling. "You're only

doing it so you can wear that ludicrous scarf. Truly, I've never in my life encountered such a vain man. Although you do look rather dashing in it, I must say."

"I do?" Casey grinned, then gave her a quick shake. "Would you forget the scarf! Damn it, Alex, I'm trying to be serious here! I'm tagging along tonight because I may need Quickly's help with Williard. I can't take the chance of going this one alone, babe, take the chance of anything happening to you—and not because I'm worried about myself. It's a weird concept, I admit, Michael Casey not putting himself first, but it's true. I have to get everything right on the first take. Babe, you're the best, most honest thing to happen to me since Little League, and I'd never be able to live with myself if something happened to you."

Alexandra wet her lips, driving him wild—although he doubted she knew it—and looked up at him intently. "Is that another quote from one of your theatrical productions, Casey? For if it is, and if you are only playing a May game on me, in the way you have been teasing Papa and Doctor Williard so shamelessly all week, I truly believe I might just hate you."

Good old Alex! A real cut-to-the-chase sort of woman. "Does this feel like I'm playing games?" he asked, then captured her mouth in a hard, searing kiss.

"You—you surely do pick your moments, don't you, Casey?" Alexandra gasped out when, still embracing her, he finally released her from the kiss.

Chuckling softly, Casey leaned forward to nuzzle her throat, her long, smooth, sweet-smelling throat. "There could be other moments, Alex—tonight . . . tomorrow . . . and for as much time as we might have."

"Casey?" Alexandra whispered against his ear. How he adored the way she said his name.

"Hmmm? Are you going to tell me how much you like this? I know I'm having the time of my life." He continued to nuzzle her throat, finding that she tasted as good as she smelled. Like spring. Like flowers. Like his woman.

"In truth, Casey, I am enjoying myself most thoroughly,"

she said with a hint of indulgent amusement in her cultured English voice. "And while I wouldn't mind overmuch if Quickly were to grow whiskers waiting for me on the beach, and I would most definitely not be averse to retiring upstairs to listen to more of your empty flattery and to begin my short, sure-to-be-exciting life of sin before I am murdered, I do feel that I must inform you that Maybelline is hitting me on the shin and that the intermittent thumping is growing prodigiously painful, as well as intrusive on my delicious, rather decadent mood."

"A simple 'Move it, you jerk,' would have done it," Casey told her, laughing as he took hold of her hand and led the way into the kitchen garden, stopping on the narrow brick path only long enough to say, "I could grow to really care for you, you know. And it scares the hell out of me, babe, because I think that would mean I'm finally growing up, at the ripe old age of thirty-three."

"We've been living in each other's pockets for a week. I should think we would have to either hate each other by now or feel some attraction for each other. And you're *grateful* to me, Casey, just as I am to you," Alexandra said reasonably, although he thought he detected a slight catch in her voice. "I'm your lone anchor in a strange world, and your only hope of returning to your own, if your explanation for your time voyage is to be believed. Conversely, you are *my* hope that history can be changed and I will not soon die on the beach. I would imagine it is natural for us to feel kindly toward each other."

Casey stopped on the path, turning to glare at her. "That's bull, Alex," he bit out angrily. "If it wasn't, we could cover our thank-yous with a Hallmark card. I'm not grateful to you—I want to make love to you. *Badly.* Now come here, and I'll prove it."

"Not now, you idiot!" she warned, pushing him away. "Or have you forgotten that Quickly is waiting for me? If you want to ask his help, I don't think it wise to keep him waiting."

"Ah, she called me an idiot," Casey crowed to no one in

particular. "Now I know she likes me." He stepped to the side of the brick path and motioned for Alexandra to lead the way to the beach. "All right, woman, move it! I've got big plans for the rest of the night, and our local freeloader isn't a part of them."

"That's free *trader*, Casey," Alexandra informed him as she brushed past him. "I have no idea what a free *loader* is."

"Whatever," Casey responded, his heart light as he fell into step behind her. "As to freeloaders, Hollywood is full of them, all of them looking to kiss ass, er, kiss *feet* if they think there's something in it for them. Freeloaders, hangers-on, opportunists, bootlickers . . ."

"Oh, you mean toadeaters, encroaching mushrooms, and the like," Alexandra said, shrugging. "Goodness, Casey, you should try to take Papa with you when you travel back to your own time. He'd be right at home in this Hollywood of yours."

He means to make love to me, Alexandra screamed silently, although still smiling bravely as Casey squeezed her hand in his, assisting her as they stepped gingerly over the rocky beach, aided only by the light of a quarter moon.

Even worse, she was seriously considering tumbling most willingly into bed with the man. Very seriously considering it. Running with the local smugglers paled in comparison with the adventure she was contemplating now. Die a virgin? That was an insult she would simply not allow!

Alexandra was so engrossed in thoughts of her anticipated debauchery that she nearly tripped over Quickly, who seemingly appeared from nowhere to block the rocky path.

"Yer wuz ta come alone," he said menacingly.

"This is the Earl of Ambersley," Alexandra told him nervously. "He's a friend, Quickly, I promise."

"That's him? The earl?" the free trader growled, doing his utmost to look fierce, which was rather difficult, as Quickly stood a full head shorter than Alexandra, and was twice as round. "That 'is worship? Bloody silly-lookin' cove, what with 'is 'ead all tied up loik a bleedin' washerwoman. An' who's 'e plannin' fer ta whack with that great club?"

"Anyone who doesn't like it, that's who," Casey declared softly, stepping in front of Alexandra. Then, looking over his shoulder at her, he muttered, grinning, "About my scarf—is it going to be a running gag for the rest of the night, or do you think we can put it to rest now?"

Alexandra shrugged, not understanding what he was talking about. "Oh, stop posturing, you two," she then warned as the men glared at each other once more.

She was suddenly weary of this whole business, and more than a little angry with Casey for not seeming able to take anything seriously for more than a few moments. Why she had brought him with her tonight was still beyond her comprehension—as was the reason she had ever taken up with the smugglers in the first place.

No, that last part wasn't true. She had begun running with the free traders for the sheer excitement of the thing, and had never given a thought to anything as involved, or as potentially dangerous, as *spying*. Providing her greedy father with French brandy had been only the transparent excuse she had employed to soothe her conscience, as she had finally admitted to herself last night at the dinner table, when that man had nearly reduced her to tears by asking Dr. Williard if he believed her hips wide enough to bear heirs.

Yet Casey believed the smugglers could be quite innocently involved in transporting military secrets across the channel to Bonaparte. And Casey had come with her tonight, armed with information from that damnable script he kept talking about, to save her from herself.

Needlepoint, she decided, shaking her head. *Why couldn't I have been interested in needlepoint? Or watercolors?*

"You may keep my share of the last run with the earl's compliments, Quickly," she informed the smuggler even as a half dozen other men sidled out of the rocks to peer curiously at Casey. "We only came to tell you that his lordship, as he understands your reasons for free trading and appreciates that you have to find ways to feed your families, will not deny you the use of his beach. However, he also wants it made clear that his future wife is no longer a part of your operation."

"What? I couldn't have said that myself?" Casey groused, although she noticed that he had lowered Maybelline to his side, reducing the threat of being set upon by this motley crew of easily violent men.

"Yer'll let us keep on usin' the caves ta 'ide the booty till we can move it on inland?" Quickly asked, eying Casey warily. "Yer ain't bin 'ere fer ever so long, so's that we wuz startin' ta think o' the place as iffen it wuz ours."

"And you may continue to use it with my compliments," Casey responded, bowing to the smugglers, which might have done him a world of good if he hadn't added, "although I guess I should ask you if you'd think twice from now on if any suspicious-looking strangers ask you to allow them to cross to or from France on your boats. Spies, you know. Second, and most important, I want to ask your help in—"

"Spies, is it!" Quickly roared, obviously insulted that anyone, even an earl, might question his loyalty to the crown. The smugglers all took a single, menacing step forward. "Oi'll blacken both yer pretty-boy blue daylights fer thinkin' we'd have truck with any froggie spies! We jist takes a fella—"

And then, just as Alexandra believed she was about to witness the worst, the inconceivable happened. From up above them, just at the edge of the overhanging bluff, there could be heard the sound of firearms being cocked and raised to shoulders. The shoulders of half a dozen or more of the local Preventive Service out on a regular patrol, she decided, and most probably alerted to Quickly's presence as a result of his angry retort to Casey's suggestion.

Their leader called out for the smugglers to lay down their arms and prepare to surrender, a proudly proclaimed directive that resulted in the free traders melting back into the darkness in less than a single, startled blinking of Alexandra's eyes.

"Halt, I say!" the officer repeated . . . just as Casey grabbed Alexandra's hand and began pulling her back along the path . . . just as a volley of rifle fire and the stinging spit of shot against stone turned the rocky beach into a battle zone . . . just as Alexandra heard Casey's short, succinct curse and felt him flinch for a moment before throwing her up and over his shoulder and running . . . running . . . running.

"Ouch! Damn it, babe, would you be careful?"

Alexandra sat back on her haunches, for she had been kneeling over him as he laid on the bed in his chamber, and glared at him. "Oh, stop being such an infant," she admonished, pushing a stray lock of hair out of her eyes. "I have to get this material away from the wound so that I can inspect it, but the blood has dried fast to the fabric."

Casey lifted his head and pressed his chin against his left shoulder, trying to take a peek at his wound. There was a lot to be said for breakaway sleeves, and even more to be said for special effects artistry that gave the indication of a wound where none really existed. "I gotta stop thinking I'm in another movie," he said ruefully, dropping back against the pillows. "Those bastards were using real bullets!"

She began soaking the material of the sleeve with warm water, slowly easing the silk away from his wound. "Yes, Casey, they were using real bullets. And if you hadn't insulted Quickly so that he forgot himself to the point of raising his voice, those real bullets would have remained safely inside their chambers. I only wonder how the revenue officers could have guessed that we would be on the beach tonight, as we were only there to divide the goods, not go on a run. Ah, there we go—and look, it's barely a scratch!"

Casey raised his head again and took a look. It appeared as if a shallow, three-inch-long furrow had been dug into his upper arm as the bullet whizzed by him. It wasn't the sort of wound that would give him a "ticket home" if he were in the army, but there certainly was enough blood to impress *him*. He grinned up at Alexandra. "I guess I'll live," he said, then sat up to watch as she cleaned the wound with a foul-smelling lotion before wrapping his arm in a bandage.

"Only because you seem to lead some sort of charmed life," Alexandra pointed out, clearing the bed of towels and basins, then sitting on the edge of the mattress, shaking her head. "We're just fortunate we didn't have to call Dr. Williard in on this. However would we have explained it?"

Casey positioned himself behind Alexandra, bracing his good arm against the mattress as he leaned forward to nuzzle her neck. "We could have told him we'd had a lovers' spat and you tried to blow a hole in me with one of my own dueling pistols. I do have dueling pistols, don't I?"

She laid her head back against his bare chest. "Oh, thank you, sir. So gallant of you, my lord Ambersley—telling everyone your shrew of a fiancée has taken to violence."

"Yes, but I would also have told them that I'd deserved shooting, having suggested we anticipate our marriage vows, or whatever you call it."

"Marvelous. Not only am I to be a shrew, but a prude into the bargain. Casey, you say the most romantic things. And just when I've all but decided to become a fallen woman."

"All but decided, Alex? You're doubting my expertise in that age-old area of seduction? Now I *am* wounded." He maneuvered himself back against the pillows, taking her with him until she was lying entirely on the bed, her head resting against his uninjured shoulder, her cool, soft cheek soothing, yet exciting, against his heated, naked flesh. "I save your life—"

"After putting it in jeopardy—"

"I get shot—"

"You get *yourself* shot—"

"And all you can do is critique my romantic perform-ance? Here I am, shot, in excruciating pain, most probably dizzy from enduring such a great loss of blood, and you want to condemn me without so much as a full run-through of the scene?"

"Now you've lost me," Alexandra said, looking up at him, "although I can't say I'm not used to it. However, I do think we ought to talk about those revenue officers. It *was* as if they were expecting us, wasn't it?"

"They weren't revenue officers," Casey said succinctly, beginning to unbutton the front of Alexandra's dressing gown, which she had quickly changed into in case anyone heard them and came to investigate what they were doing up and about after midnight. She knew that being discovered in her black trousers and sweater would not have been good, but if Sir Charles were to find her in Casey's chamber, and dressed only in her nightrail and dressing gown, he would probably call for a champagne toast!

"They weren't revenue officers?" Alexandra asked, putting her hand on Casey's, stopping him just as he was getting to the more interesting buttons. "And how, pray tell, would you know that?"

"The script for *Ambersley,* remember?" he countered, using his index finger to trace the soft curve beneath her right breast, delighting in her quick, nervous shiver. "The spy, our good friend Williard, kept the local smugglers in line by using his own men—dressed up like revenue officers, of course—to harass the hell out of them and keep them from making some of their runs, just so they'd be receptive to taking his money when he wanted them to carry the occasional traveler to Calais. The traveler, saying he wanted to visit his oppressed French family, carried the information to Bonaparte. In other words, babe, the traveler was—is—a courier."

Alexandra sighed, moving closer to him as he went back to the business of opening the rest of her buttons. "This is getting too complicated, Casey."

"Not really, honey," he assured her. "As a matter of fact, you figured it out on your own eventually. Maybe you would have even started putting two and two together tonight, if I hadn't been there to get in the way. That's why you went down to the beach the night of the next run, to warn Quickly that he was involved in treasonous acts—and got yourself killed. Beau arrived too late to save you, but he did kill Williard, then go to London to be congratulated, etcetera, etcetera. You know, except for all the shooting, explosions, and my duel with Williard's character at the end, I guess Alexandra is the real hero of the story. Damn, no wonder Sheila didn't mind dying. Did I mention that you were in love with Quickly?"

She sat up so abruptly that Casey found himself clutching his wounded arm, watching in something akin to awe as a circle of brilliant, blue-edged white stars floated around his head. "In love with—good Lord, isn't it enough that I die in this stupid play of yours? *Quickly!* Of all the ridiculous, far-fetched—"

Casey pulled her back down onto the mattress, levering her onto her back, so that her long hair became a living, honey-dark fan around her beautiful face—a face just now screwed up into a furious scowl. "I'll make them do rewrites if that's what you want, babe, I promise," he said, laughing as her bottom lip pushed forward in a pout. "Although I should tell you that, in the movie, Quickly is a lot more handsome and dashing than our resident smuggler."

"Well," she said, beginning to smile as she reached up to shyly slip her fingers through the mat of hair on his chest, "if he's handsome and dashing, I suppose I could become resigned to being portrayed as a tragic heroine. As long as the real me *does* get to live."

"That's my girl," Casey congratulated her, lowering his head slowly, his wound forgotten as he concentrated on Alexandra's smiling mouth, the feel of her soft breasts beneath the careful weight of his chest, the knowledge that her long legs and smooth stomach were only a whisper or two of flimsy material removed from his touch.

"Tell me you love me, Michael Casey, even though it's a lie," Alexandra said huskily, her eyes growing wide as her dressing gown fell away and he slid the strap of her nightrail down to capture her breast in his hand. "If I'm really going to go through with this, I need you to tell me that you love me."

"I love you, Alexandra Deverell, even if it's a lie," he said softly as he concentrated his gaze on her full, moist lips.

And then, to his great surprise, as he kissed her, Casey trembled—not from any weakness caused by his wound, but with the first very real fear he had ever experienced.

Fear that he might hurt this glorious woman as he took her, as he aided her in passing through the doorway between curiosity and completion.

Fear that desire as strong as this might be dangerous— dangerous to his peace of mind, his comfortable life, his the-hell-with-it ability to make love to a woman, any woman, and then walk away.

Fear that the lie she had begged him to recite wasn't really a lie at all.

Sex by candlelight had its drawbacks, the major one being that he could see Alexandra's slowly bared body only as a series of glimpses of golden skin and enticing shadows. But the glory he discovered beneath his practiced, skillful hands had him shutting his eyes in any event, and behind those closed lids his imagination created a picture of physical beauty so profound he could have been struck blind in an instant and yet never forget the image that now alternately teased and tortured his mind.

"I'll try not to hurt you," he heard himself promise into her ear as he nuzzled her, the tip of his tongue tracing the soft curves of skin, his teeth lightly tugging on the velvety lobe, his warm breath deliberately provocative, purposely provoking.

"I swear I won't hurt you," he vowed a moment later, as Alexandra held on to his shoulders while she tipped her head to one side and gave his seeking mouth access to her lovely long throat . . . her creamy breasts . . . the mind-bending dip just at her waist.

"Never hurt you, never hurt you." He whispered the correction, stroking her inner thighs, moving his hand ever upward. Slowly, carefully, timing his every progression to follow a heartbeat after her every sigh, her every slight relaxation of tautly held muscles.

"Casey?" she breathed in clear astonishment as at last he reached his goal—his hand slipping completely between her thighs, his fingers finding, and stroking, the silky softness that was ready for him, even if Alexandra, in her virginal apprehensions, was not. "Oh, Casey—what? What are you—*oh Casey!*"

He was a master, practicing his trade. He knew just how to touch her. Just where, and just how hard, how fast, to move his talented fingers. When to tantalize, when to drift closer to the heart of her. When to lightly probe. When to withdraw.

With his mouth positioned over one pebble-hard nipple, his tongue teased, enticed, circled, licked, before he allowed himself to take full possession of her glory, suckling at her, inflaming her until she arched her back in her attempt to keep him from stopping, from leaving her now that he had made her body sing with pleasure, with need.

When it happened, how it had come to happen, he would never know. But, suddenly, the master became the pupil. Even as he continued his lovemaking, Alexandra's untutored passion transferred itself to him, and he felt his own body, his own passion, begin to spiral toward completion. Like a raw teenager, he nearly lost control. Him. Michael Casey. The man who enjoyed sex, enjoyed women, but never let the power slip out of his hands.

Those hands began to shake as Alexandra pressed her heels into the mattress, lifting her hips to his touch. His mouth went dry when he heard her soft moans just above his ear, felt her warm breath against his hair. He pushed his hard, heated body closer against her side. *Closer.* He would never be close enough, even once he was inside her. Deep inside her. Taking her to the threshold, and beyond.

He was an eager boy again, unsure of himself, nervous, his entire energies concentrated on Alexandra. On what would please Alexandra. On how to bring her the magic . . . how to make that magic last.

For the moment.

For as many moments as they had.

For forever.

He raised his head, reluctant to look into her eyes, knowing without knowing why that when he did he would be lost.

And there it was. In her tear-wet eyes. In her tremulous smile. There it was. All he had ever believed the South Philly kid turned baseball player turned actor would never know. All the empty spaces were suddenly full.

So many gifts. So little understanding. Years to travel afore you find your true love.

"I forgot," he rasped quietly, stroking Alexandra's cheek, running a finger over her full bottom lip. "I didn't understand, and I forgot. I just didn't listen. I didn't get it."

"Casey?" Her soft green eyes showed her confusion, clouding the passion that had burned so brightly only a moment ago. "What—what's wrong?"

He eased himself between her legs, concentrating on those eyes, those trusting, troubled eyes. "Nothing, babe," he told her as he pushed into her, slowly, carefully, dealing gently with the thin barrier that would keep them from being one. "For the first time in my life, everything's right."

And then, as he kissed her, as her arms came up to hold him, and he began to move inside her, Casey knew for certain why he had traveled through time.

The warm halo of candlelight turned the wide bed into an island of pleasure floating in an endless sea of darkness, a special paradise . . . and the man who had for so long believed in nothing came to understand that, where there is love, nothing can be considered impossible.

Nothing . . . not even taking Alexandra with him when he traveled back to his own time . . .

Alexandra awoke to the sound of screaming, immediately recognizable as coming from Edwardine, who was standing in the hall, but yelling loudly enough that Alexandra could have sworn her maid had climbed into bed with Casey and herself sometime during the night.

"Her's gone! Her's gone!" Edwardine wailed. "M'puir missy's gone! Kilt, most like!"

"I'm right here, Edwardine, not killed at all, although the thought of *committing* mayhem is just now crossing my mind," Alexandra said wearily as she leaned against the hastily thrown open door, feeling as if she had been able to leap into her dressing gown and cross the room in a single bound—only sparing a moment to glare at the helplessly giggling man who remained sprawled most comfortably on the bed. "What's that you're holding? It looks like one of his lordship's curly-brimmed beavers."

The maid looked down at her hand, saw the hat, and dropped it as if it showed signs of turning into a deadly adder and biting her. "Oh, laws! He throwed it at me—"

"Who threw it at you, Edwardine?" Alexandra asked as she picked up the hat and wearily propelled it, and the still sniffling maid, into the bedchamber.

Edwardine stopped in her tracks, staring bug-eyed at Casey, who was just shrugging into a clean shirt, his pantaloons on, but not yet buttoned. "His worship," she said blankly. "Not *this* his worship, but the new one. He jist throwed it at me, and Oi jist catched it. Oi didn't think—"

"Now there's a news bulletin, babe," Casey said, winking at Alexandra.

"Tilden's got his cape, yer see, an' none o' the footmen wuz about, so's that's how Oi come by that thing," Edwardine explained, pointing at the curly-brimmed beaver. "Missy, you weren't never *sleepin'* in here, was yer?"

Casey draped a companionable arm around the maid's shoulder and walked her toward the door. "Naw, Edwardine, Miss Deverell wasn't sleeping in here. She was waiting for a bus. Weren't you, babe? Now, dear woman, what do you say you tell us who our company is, so we can go downstairs and say hello to him."

"'Him,' yer worship?" Edwardine asked as she gaped up

at Casey, showing all the signs of a badly smitten female. "Oh, *him!*" she then blurted, giggling. "He said he was Lord Brooks, yer worship—sir!" Edwardine informed him, ducking down to slip out from under Casey's arm, then racing toward the hallway, her usually pasty-pudding cheeks flushed from her close contact with the handsome Earl of Ambersley.

"Lord Brooks? Ah, yes. My London benefactor, the guy who's been sending me all over Europe to spy for the government. The plot thickens! I wonder if good old Beau's ever met Lord Brooks face-to-face," Casey remarked coolly, running a hand through his hair as he turned to face Alexandra. "In the script, they meet for the first time at Ambersley, having kept in contact only through letters up until that point, from the time the earl took over spy duties from his deceased father. Yeah, well, Alex, I have a feeling convincing his lordship that I'm Beau Lindsey isn't going to be as easy as faking out Sir Charles and Dr. Williard."

"Casey—?" Alexandra began, truly frightened. What would happen to the man if Lord Brooks were to take one look at him and scream, "Impostor!"? She loved this man, really loved him. Not that she would burden him with a declaration of that love. She wanted him to remain here with her, but not if it meant he would be stuck in some prison for impersonating Lord Ambersley. He had to be free to return to his own time, even if her heart would break the moment he left her. "Oh, Casey!"

"Come on, honey, look flattered," Casey prodded when she couldn't say any more, dropping a kiss on her forehead as he walked past her to give a mighty tug of the bellpull that would summon Tilden and hot water for his morning ablutions. "You're about to see Michael Casey's first Oscar-worthy performance! While Tilden's shaving me I think I'll rehearse my acceptance speech. Nothing off-the-wall, no political causes to push. Just a simple, humble string of drivel. Let's see—I want to thank the Academy . . ."

"Casey!" Alexandra shouted, knowing he was rambling on and on in order to relax her, but was in reality pushing

her very close to the edge of physical violence. "Lord Brooks shouldn't be here yet. Not according to either his letter to me *or* your blessed script. What are we going to do?"

Casey was already stripping out of his shirt, wincing slightly as he moved his injured arm. "Do? Well, for starters, babe, I think you might consider getting dressed. Much as I think you've never looked better, especially with your hair hanging down like that, Tilden might not be equally impressed."

"Oh, damn and blast!" Alexandra exclaimed, pulling the edges of her dressing gown together over her nakedness, then quickly retreated to her own bedchamber.

4

*"It's a hundred and six miles to Chicago, we've got a
full tank of gas, a half pack of cigarettes, it's dark,
and we're wearing sunglasses."*

—John Belushi, in *The Blues Brothers*

OF ALL THE GIN JOINTS IN ALL THE TOWNS IN ALL THE WORLD
. . . he has to walk into mine," Casey grumbled, then smiled
sheepishly. "Sorry, just doing a little fractured Bogart from
Casablanca. So, what do you say, honey? Do you think he
bought it?"

Alexandra collapsed onto the leather couch in the library,
feeling as if she were a horse who had just been ridden hard
and put away wet. "'Bought it'?" she repeated distractedly
as she watched Casey pace the carpet, then said, "Oh, never
mind. You mean, did he believe you're really Beau Lindsey?
I don't know, Casey, I honestly don't know. He's even worse
in person than he is in his letters. So arrogant, so conde-
scending and brusquely autocratic. In short, a typical English peer."

"Yeah," Casey answered, pausing at the drinks table to pour each of them a glass of wine. "He reminds me a lot of F. Murray Abraham in *Amadeus*—only not quite as carefree. And that business about India, when I couldn't remember the name of that pasha, or whatever he was—" He shook his head. "Nope, Oscar hopes aside, I don't think I can carry this one off. He's a tougher audience than your father and the rest of them."

Casey handed Alexandra one of the glasses, then tossed back his own in a single gulp and drawled, grimacing, "The bloody pasha? Sink me, Brooks, old man, but I haven't the foggiest!"

Alexandra, still frightened, blinked back tears, wishing she could think of something brilliant to say, something that would make everything better. But when she opened her mouth all that came out was, "I know to stay away from the beach now, and from Dr. Williard as well, so you don't have to worry about me. In point of fact, you've already saved my life. You've done what you were sent here to do. I can leave for London at any time. Do you think it's time for another try at the bookcase?"

"Huh?" Casey asked, looking at her strangely, as if he had been deep in thought and missed what she'd said. "Sorry, I wasn't listening. Alex. . . ." he said, running a hand through his hair, unconsciously confirming what she had thought: he hadn't been paying her the slightest attention. But he was really terribly handsome when he was distracted, even adorably so. "Alex, I met this gypsy the night before I traveled through time."

He could have said any number of things that might have surprised her, but none more so than what he had just said. "I beg your pardon?"

His grin was sheepish. "Yeah. I guess I should explain myself." He sat down beside her, taking her hands in his. "For starters—remember all that business about my acting career? Forget it. Let me tell you about the real Michael Casey. To put it bluntly, babe, I'm a jerk. A nobody. Just a guy from the old neighborhood who happened to be in the right place at the right time. I was playing minor league ball and the team was hired to do a few days' work as extras for a baseball movie. I was never going to make the big leagues. It's my swing. It stinks. Casey at the bat at his worst. Anyway, when one of the speaking actors got beaned with a pitch, the director picked me to take his place. Three weeks later I was in Hollywood. The camera loved me, or so the director said."

She reached out to touch his cheek. "I don't understand any of this, Casey. What are you trying to say? And why now?"

"I'll explain in a minute, but first let me say this before I lose my nerve." He frowned, looked out the window, then looked at her once more. "I'm a fake, babe," he told her quietly. "I couldn't play ball, and I can't act. I just sort of fell into it, just the way I fell into traveling through time. I've been faking it for years, relying on luck—and the dimple, I guess—and hoping like hell nobody would catch me. And the gypsy saw it. I think Brooks did, too."

"Poor, darling Casey," Alexandra soothed, wondering why he should be so upset to be likening himself to Beau Brummell, the Prince Regent, and nearly every titled peer she had ever heard of. They all had "fallen into" their situations. They were all of them relying on their luck, their money, their looks—until Napoleon Bonaparte cast his greedy eyes over their little island. Then a great number of those dandies and Corinthians and the rest of those deep playing, skirt-chasing young exquisites had gone off to fight, becoming soldiers, and heroes, and even martyrs. Just as Casey was rising to the occasion in trying to save her life.

"You are what you are, Casey," she told him. "And that, my dear, dear man, is much better than you suppose yourself to be. Now, tell me about the gypsy. What did she say to you?"

Casey leaned over and kissed the tip of her nose, sending shivers of love, of desire, skipping down her spine. "She told me I'd find you, for one thing."

"She did? However did she do that?"

She could see him searching his mind, mentally reviewing all that the gypsy had said. "'So many gifts,' she said, probably referring to the way I backed into acting. 'So little understanding.' Boy, did she have that one right!"

"Go on," Alexandra urged as Casey looked ready to set himself off on another round of introspection, which might be a good idea, but one she would rather he dealt with later, not now.

"'Years to travel afore'—she said 'afore,' not '*be*fore'—'you find your true love.'" He kissed her again, this time on the lips. "Do you get it now? I wasn't sent here to save you—or maybe I was, but that wasn't the only reason. And it goes way beyond just having me learn some kind of lesson. I was sent here so that *you* could save *me*. Save me from myself, I suppose. Anyway, I'm here. You're here. The gypsy had it exactly right. Because I do love you, Alex. I really do."

"I believe I might like this gypsy," Alexandra said, tears stinging her eyes.

"Don't tell her, or she'll ask for more money," Casey teased, then frowned. "But we'll talk about all the rest of it later, once we're safe. I have a plan—did I mention that I have a plan?"

"No, you failed to mention that. But I will hold you to a more romantic declaration of love at some later date."

"You got it," Casey promised, kissing her yet again—an action that showed all the signs of becoming a highly enjoyable pastime. He sat up straighter. "But now listen to this—to what I started to tell you in the first place. The gypsy talked about Lord Brooks. Damn it! I can't remember exactly what she said, which shows how much she got to me, because I have a good head for remembering dialogue. But I sure do remember that she warned of danger. Danger in the water, then mumbled something about streams, and *brooks*. The way I see it, good old Lord Brooks is going to figure out I'm not the real Ambersley. It'll all hit the fan then, and I'll be stuck here forever, probably in some really lousy jail. If they don't hang me as a spy."

"Oh, dear." Alexandra sighed, looking across the room and out the window, unconsciously mimicking Casey's earlier attempt at avoiding looking imminent danger squarely in the eye. "Then it is obvious, Casey: you have to leave now."

"No. And that's what I've been trying to say to you—what I've been thinking about since last night," he said, his voice low, strangely silky, and eminently convincing. *"We* have to leave now. I'm taking you with me."

"You're taking . . . you want me to . . . not you remaining here, but *me* going with . . . well!" Alexandra stammered, feeling her cheeks flush. "What a singularly remarkable notion. I had always thought that either you would go, or you would stay. The notion of *my* traveling through time never occurred to me."

"It occurred to me, babe," he said, pushing her back against the cushions, his hands running lightly over her upper body. "And I knew it for certain last night, after you fell asleep in my arms. I liked that, liked having you close. Having you with me all through the night."

She frowned up at him. "Isn't that what lovers do? Stay the night with each other?"

His smile was self-mocking. "Not me. Not until last night. Now, listen to me, and I'm sorry if I don't sound romantic. Alexandra Deverell—I'm not ready to either lose you or leave you, so I'm taking you back to the future. Jesus, babe, I sound like a movie even when I don't want to sound like a movie! What I mean is this—I'm taking you to my time with me, if you'll say you want to go."

"You're right, Casey. That wasn't in the least romantic." She eased her body closer to his. "And I was wondering if you were going to ask me, or just keep *telling* me."

He grinned. "I think I'm telling you, babe. You're coming with me. To my time, to London, and, somehow, to America. I'll want to keep the place in Malibu, but we'll buy a real house in Beverly Hills. Yeah—Beverly Hills. Swimming pools—movie stars! I'm even going to marry you, let you make an honest man of me—which is a good thing, because I want kids, you know. At least three. Now, what do you think of that?"

And the man said he wasn't going to be romantic? Silly, vain, adorable creature! Alexandra was silent for some time, wondering if anyone could be happier than she was at the moment and not expire of the heady emotion.

"Damn! I haven't convinced you, have I? Why can't I dredge up some lines from an Oscar-caliber script that would say it all in a passionate, heart-thumping monologue that would leave you melting in my arms, and every woman in the darkened theater weeping happily into her Kleenex?"

"Who *is* this Oscar you keep prosing on about? Oh, never mind. You're the most impossible, headstrong, impulsive, *incomprehensible* man I've ever met, Michael Casey," Alexandra declared at last, her heart singing, "but, as I am unfortunate enough to have fallen deeply in love with you—and as I've never before in my life seen someone so very much in need of a commonsensible, levelheaded keeper—I suppose I'll go with you."

"Then again," Casey said softly as he leaned down to kiss her, "who needs a script?"

Several "heart-thumping" moments later, just as Alexandra was wishing the two of them back in Casey's bedchamber, he broke off the kiss and pulled her to her feet, stooping only to pick up Maybelline. "What do you say we continue this behind the bookcase before Lord Brooks comes poking around, asking more questions I can't answer. That was the plan, wasn't it—getting the heck out of here? God, Alex—I love you! I can't believe how much I love you!"

"And I love you, Casey," Alexandra said, sighing yet again. Oh, dear. Why had she been born such a *responsible* creature? She couldn't blame Casey for not thinking of it—after all, he was an American, and not from this troubled time. But she was English, and she knew she had to do her duty.

"Dearest, darling Casey," she said gently. "I can't leave just yet. Something still has to be done about Williard, for he can't be allowed to continue running around loose, selling secrets to the French. And then there's the problem of Lord Brooks, and explaining a second Earl of Ambersley. . . ."

"Damn. You're right. Can't leave any loose plot threads, can we. Otherwise we'll really screw up the old history books." Casey propped Maybelline against the side of the desk, locked the door to the library, and sat down beside Alexandra. "All right, honey, let's put our heads together. Between us, we should be able to rework our plans and still get out of here today."

Over the next few hours, they did put their heads together —their heads, their lips, their eager bodies—but in the end, even hampered by the yearnings of their newfound love, they came up with a workable plan.

It would be a lie, of course. Nobody would believe the truth.

All they had to do was expose James Williard as the traitor by penning a note to Lord Brooks informing him of that fact, explain that the *real* Lord Ambersley would be arriving in a few days, a supersecret arm of the government having sent an "impostor" ahead of him to ferret out the aforementioned spy, and reporting that, lastly, said impostor and Miss Deverell have agreed to vacate the premises and renounce her betrothal in exchange for a healthy allowance doled out quarterly to one Sir Charles Deverell for the remainder of his life.

"I do love him, in a way," Alexandra said, peering over Casey's shoulder as he wrote down a reasonable amount for Sir Charles's allowance, then scribbled his signature at the bottom of the page, handing her the pen so that she could add her own name. "And it's not as if he'll miss me."

"And, dear heart," Casey added, folding the letter and placing it squarely in the center of the desk, "it's not as if we've altered history all that much. You had no future here, Williard was going to be caught anyway, and Ambersley is still going to be welcomed back to England as a hero, and still be free to marry his Louisa."

Alexandra took one last look around the library, sighing. "I suppose it's time to go then, isn't it?"

"Almost. But first, there's something I've always wanted to do. It's not like I've been named MVP of the World Series, but it'll do." Casey picked up Maybelline and held the bat high in the air, Alexandra thought, as if it were a valuable trophy that had just been handed him to commemorate a victory of some sort.

"Michael Casey," he intoned importantly, "you've just arranged to catch a spy, thereby saving the British Empire for the monarchy. Watta-ya gonna do now?" He lowered Maybelline, grinning, and drew Alexandra close, pressing her head against his shoulder. "Why, I think we'll go to Disney World! But first," he ended, his voice reverting from teasing to serious as he kissed her forehead, "what say we head for the bookcase, okay, babe? Scared?"

She nodded. "A little," she admitted, then smiled up at him. "But terribly excited all the same. Do you think your mother will like me?"

"Like you? She'll probably send up flares that I've finally decided to settle down. She thinks I've gotten a swelled head over the last couple of years—and you and I both know she's right. Not that *you'll* ever let me get away with anything, will you, Alex? But we won't tell Mom that you've come to America through time—although I doubt if it would bother her if you flew in from another planet. She just wants more grandchildren."

"And you love me?"

"And I love you," Casey said firmly, gifting her with a glimpse of his resolve-melting dimple. She'd believe anything, as long as he smiled at her that way. He took her hand, hoisted Maybelline onto his shoulder, and started for the circular staircase. "Now, as we used to say in the old neighborhood—let's make like a shepherd and get the flock outta here!"

"Casey! I don't believe you should speak that way in my presence," she cautioned him without real rancor as she led the way up the staircase, then stood back as he pulled on the brass ring, holding her breath as the bookcase slid away, exposing the small chamber.

"After you, my lady," Casey said, holding onto the brass ring until she stepped into the darkness, then following after her just as the panel began to slide closed once more.

They stood close together in the pitch-black chamber, saying nothing until Alexandra admitted wryly, "I feel prodigiously ridiculous, Casey."

"I know," he said, chuckling. "It's just like being in an elevator. Stand facing front, please, your mouth shut, and pretend you don't notice that everyone's doing just what you're doing—watching the numbers light up and praying the damn thing won't go crashing to the basement, turning you all into a short stack of pancakes."

"If you say so, Casey. But I thought you said it was cold in here. It's not. It's depressingly stuffy."

"Yes," Casey answered, his voice sounding muffled in the airless chamber. "It is, isn't it. I hate saying this, but that's not good. It wasn't cold the first time I tried to get back to my own time." She could sense that he was stretching up toward something as he said, "I think that damn poem is still haunting me."

She heard a soft "click," and the bookcase slid away, allowing them to step back into the library. She looked down into the main area of the room to see the note Casey had written still lying on the desk. "Oh, dear," she said quietly, looking at him.

Casey brushed past her, quickly descending the spiral staircase and brushing past the desk to peer out the window, most probably hoping to see something that wouldn't be there for another 182 years. "Damn it! That's two!"

Alexandra watched in fascination as Casey took a deep breath, hoisted Maybelline onto his shoulder once more, and began to recite bitingly, "'With a smile of Christian charity great Casey's visage shone;/He stilled the rising tumult, he bade the game go on;/He signaled to the pitcher, and once more the spheroid flew;/But Casey still ignored it, and the umpire said, "Strike two."'"

"Casey? Darling?" He had acted this way the first day, when Alexandra had thought him daft, and it didn't strike her as a particularly good sign now. She laid a hand on his arm, trying to get his attention. "Are you all right?"

"Yeah, I was just thinking. Reciting that poem sometimes helps me to concen— *That's it!*" He turned to her and grabbed her at the shoulders, pulling her close as he gave her a short, hard kiss. "Casey *ignored* it, Alex. That's what I'm doing. I've missed something. I'm still missing something. Some weird *something* that is keeping me here. Keeping us both here. I've been putting too much credence into that damned script, when it hasn't been right *yet*. Quickly's nowhere near to being anyone's love interest, your father's a dead loss instead of the sweet old guy he is in the script, the real Ambersley isn't looking too swift at the moment if he could overlook you for some other woman, and it wouldn't be a stretch to see our friend Brooks—another hero in the script—swiping candy from babies. As a matter of fact, the only guy who looks honest—nerdy, but honest—is Williard. Alex, I think it's time we had a talk with the good doctor!"

"My boy! Alexandra, dear child of my heart. There you are, my two cooing turtle doves, even holding hands. Ah, what a treat for these old eyes. Doctor? What d'ye say— shall we put you down for a birthin' late next winter?"

Casey squeezed Alexandra's fingers reassuringly as they walked into the small bricked clearing at the center of the gardens. "Dear Sir Charles, have I told you yet what a major pain in the ass you are?" he inquired politely, his words wiping the satisfied smile from the older man's face. "And, if you hope to gain a penny from my marriage to your daughter, I suggest you get the hell out of here—now."

"Casey . . ." Alexandra hissed under her breath, although she did nothing to stop her father as he hauled his bulky frame to a standing position, stood with his mouth gaping widely for a moment, then beat a hasty retreat back to the house. She felt no real need to watch him go.

"Shh, Alex, don't stop me now. I think I'm on a roll," Casey whispered back to her, motioning for Williard to seat himself once more, as the doctor had risen from one of the stone benches when he saw Alexandra. "No old movie lines this time, babe, because now I'm mad. Fighting mad. This one's going to be pure South Philly, straight from the shoulder, up close and damned personal."

He walked up to the doctor, idly wondering how the guy would look in a plaid jacket—a fully loaded plastic pocket protector stuck in his breast pocket—and pointed Maybelline at Williard's chest. "I'm going to put all my cards on the table, Doc," he began, watching the man for any sign that he might be entertaining thoughts of reaching for a weapon. "I'm not Beau Lindsey."

The doctor leapt to his feet. "You—you're not—"

"Shut up and listen," Casey said pithily. "And for crying out loud—sit down! You'll learn more that way. I'll tell you when you can talk. And no, I'm not Ambersley. He won't be here until the end of next week, his mistress in tow. But relax, I'm still one of the good guys—'God, King, and Country' and all that crap. And I'll go you one better than that. *You're* not Dr. Williard. Or, if you really are a doctor, you're only using it as your cover. You're a spy for the War Office or something, aren't you, Williard, old sock?"

"And you?" Williard's watery blue eyes narrowed, and he suddenly looked worlds more intelligent, and cunning, than he had before. "Would I be far off the mark if I were to suggest that you're one of Lord Liverpool's personal staff? I've heard that our esteemed prime minister has his own coterie of agents."

Casey shrugged. "All right, if it makes you happy: I'm one of Liverpool's men," he said, figuring the familiar name sounded good. "His top man, actually. *Nobody's* heard of me—I'm that much of a secret."

"God's teeth, the place is soon going to be knee-deep in spies! We're all tripping over each other with that idiot's absurd demands for all this hole-and-corner secrecy," Williard exploded, standing up and extending his hand.

"You're here on Liverpool's orders, to check up on my reports on Brooks. Get the traitor out of the way before our fair-haired hero lands—and hands all his latest intelligence information over to Brooks? Yes, that makes sense. I've had my suspicions for a long time, but this is the first I've learned that Liverpool is finally paying attention to my missives. Thank God you didn't think *I* was the traitor. We could have ended by blowing off each other's heads!"

"Lord Brooks is the spy? Not Dr. Williard?" Alexandra exclaimed, tugging on Casey's arm. "Well, that would explain everything, wouldn't it, Casey? His lordship is very highly placed in Liverpool's government. He certainly must know about Dr. Williard, about Dr. Williard's suspicions of him, and he probably has plans for Ambersley to get the man out of the way the moment he arrives here from the Continent. After all, Ambersley *trusts* Brooks, so that he'd be sure to do what he says."

"Excuse me—" Dr. Williard interjected, only to be ignored.

"Especially after his fiancée is found murdered on the beach, Dr. Williard standing nearby, perhaps even with the bloody knife in his hand," Casey added, his brain shifting into ever-higher gears as each new thought accelerated his deductions. "Maybe you never knew anything, babe. Maybe you were just a handy victim."

The doctor was on his feet once more. "Bloody knife? I say, my good fellow! Miss Deverell! *Excuse* me—"

"That's what I like best about you, Casey," Alexandra put forth without rancor. "Your always-high opinion of my insightfulness. Why, I'm surprised, with my limited intuition, that I have seen anything past the end of my nose in dog's years."

"If I might interrupt!"

"Sit," Casey ordered offhandedly, then took Alexandra's hand. "No, seriously, babe. Your runs with Quickly often put you on the beach at night, alone, where you'd be easy to kill. You might have gone out on one last run the night before the wedding, perhaps after finding out about Louisa.

You were angry, not thinking clearly, not being careful? Brooks probably waited for you in the dark, knifed you, then lured Williard to the beach with some story about you having fallen from the bluff or something equally lame, having already arranged for Ambersley to stumble over the body—and the spy. Bingo-bango! Williard is discredited and very dead, Brooks is safe again, and Ambersley, none the wiser, sets off for London to be named a hero."

"D-dead?" The good doctor sat down.

"So," Alexandra offered, "if we tell the doctor everything, and he can arrest Brooks, Ambersley will come home to all his problems solved, including having me out of the way so that he can marry Louisa—if the bookcase works now that we've solved the last mystery. The spy will have been caught, the information to Boney stopped, and history changed for the better." She frowned. "Although not that much, I suppose. You did tell me that we eventually won the war."

"That's why we couldn't leave. We had to save not only you and me, but Williard as well—and get rid of Brooks before he could do any more damage. Ambersley isn't a real bang-bang, shoot-'em-up hero at all. As a matter of fact— the guy was sort of a schmuck, wasn't he?" He ran a hand through his hair, remembering the movie in which he was slated to star. "Man, is this thing ever going to need rewrites. Thank God a lot of the movie takes place in flashbacks, in France, where Ambersley was a *real* hero. We'll be heading there after we shoot the scenes on the estate. You ever been to France? You'll love it, babe, honest. The Eiffel Tower, the—"

"Now *that* is quite enough!" Williard exploded, hopping to his feet once more. "I loathe interfering in what is by all indications a singularly engrossing conversation—but what in God's name are you two talking about? I was condemned as a French spy—and a *murderer?* When, and by whom? And you said I am to be killed by the Earl of Ambersley? Mr. Casey, or whoever you are . . . Miss Deverell—I believe you owe me some sort of explanation."

Casey slid a comforting arm around the smaller man's shoulders and gave him a bracing shake. "An explanation, Jimmy, old sport? I agree, and you shall have one—not that you'll believe the half of it. The important thing, I suppose, is that you, my good man, are about to become a card-carrying hero, probably with a title in it if you play your cards right—although in the movie version I think we'll let Ambersley take all the credit. You can live with that, can't you?" he ended, winking at Alexandra.

"Dear, *dear* Doctor Williard—James," Alexandra said soothingly, "don't try to fight it. I warn you, Mr. Michael Casey has a strange way of always winning in the end."

"Thanks, babe," Casey said, and then he began telling Dr. James Williard a story that he, even more than a week into it, was still having difficulty believing himself.

It was nearly teatime before Alexandra and Casey headed for the library once more, this time more fully prepared for their journey across the centuries.

For one thing, Casey, remembering Jilly A'Brunzo, had dressed himself in costume once more. Alexandra, in turn, had packed up a small satchel of her favorite things: a garnet necklace that had been her mother's, a small watercolor of Deverell House, her grandmother's recipe for freckle cream, the toque she had worn when she had gone adventuring, and practical things like her toothbrush and powder, two changes of undergarments, some lavender toilet water, and a light cape—just in case 1995 proved chilly.

She had told a sobbing Edwardine that she was off to Gretna Green with her beloved, one Michael Casey, gifting the woman with all her remaining pin money and the advice to remove herself from Deverell House and seek employment in more congenial surroundings.

Having said their farewells to Dr. Williard, who had promised to summon assistance from the village and then go hunting for Lord Brooks—an exercise, he assured them, that would end with his lordship locked up in the local guardhouse before dusk—Alexandra held tightly to Casey's hand as he employed Maybelline to push open the door to the library, and they both stepped inside.

"Ah, you're here. Mr. Michael Casey, I believe the name is, if I have correctly deciphered your signature. And Miss Deverell as well. How accommodating of you both," Lord Brooks said from his seat behind the desk. "Now, Tilden, my good fellow, if you will be good enough to close the door?"

Casey swung around in time to see the Ambersley butler pushing the door shut, then standing in front of it, his beefy arms crossed against his broad chest. "Wot?" the butler snapped. "Did yer think Oi stayed here all this time just ta polish all that bloody silver in an empty house? Want me ta tie 'em up fer yer, my lord?"

"Tilden!" Alexandra exclaimed. "You're a traitor, too? How could you? And after all that brandy I brought you!"

"Let him alone, babe," Casey warned her, inclining his head toward Lord Brooks, who still sat at the desk, a lethal-looking pistol in one hand, Casey's damning note in the other. "This one's all my fault. I should have realized that Brooks couldn't have been in this alone, not unless he'd wanted to personally ride down from London every time he had a secret to sell to France. But Tilden's the least of our problems, isn't he, my lord."

"Dear me, yes," his lordship agreed almost genially, uncoiling his tall, lanky, well-dressed frame from the chair and perching himself on the edge of the desk. "Although I must admit that it was Tilden who first alerted me to a possible problem. A most timely note addressed to me in London concerning some boots that didn't fit—isn't that it, Tilden? It wasn't much, as questions go, but enough to bring me to Ambersley Hall a few days early, just to be certain Tilden hadn't turned into an imaginative old woman on me. Can you conceive my consternation when I first met you and you had so little knowledge of our long, if distant, relationship? And then there is the matter of this garbled letter," he ended, tossing the paper onto the desktop. "Shame, shame, Mr. Casey. Not only an impostor, but a considerable troublemaker as well. Although this note incriminating dear Dr. Williard might prove useful."

Casey cursed softly, wanting to kick himself for forgetting to destroy the damning letter.

"Should I tie 'em up *now?*" Tilden asked, standing so close behind Casey that he could smell the man's brandy-soaked breath. "He's still holdin' that evil weapon."

Weapon? What weapon? Oh, yes. Tilden was talking about Maybelline. His bat. His best friend. His stick. The old hickory . . .

Keep the hickory branch close.

The gypsy's last warning belatedly slammed into Casey's consciousness. Jesus! How had he forgotten?

A single squeeze of her hand had to serve as Casey's only signal to Alexandra that she should follow his lead; then he turned about on his heels, employing the great Michael Casey smile as he embarked on the role of his lifetime. "'Evil weapon,' Tilden?" he repeated, shaking his head. "It's nothing of the sort, and totally harmless. You're looking at a Louisville Slugger, made of solid hickory. It's a *bat,* you understand—you play a game with it. Shall I show you?"

The butler tipped his head to one side. "A game?"

"Tilden," Lord Brooks murmured quietly, but with heavy censure.

"Oh, let him show you," Alexandra implored, stepping between Casey and Lord Brooks, shielding Casey from the pistol while placing herself directly in the line of fire. "You're going to kill us either way. Why shouldn't Tilden have a little frolic first? Why, Mr. Casey even recites as he plays this game. It's wondrous to behold, truly, and I imagine the Prince Regent will be enthralled to have some new diversion at court."

Alexandra's mention of the Prince Regent seemed to turn the trick, and Lord Brooks said, "Very well. I am nothing if not civilized. Demonstrate this game, Mr. Casey. Then we will all take a stroll onto the beach. Tilden is prodigiously strong, but I see no need for him to have to carry your bodies all the way to the cave, where the dear, soon-to-be-departed Dr. Williard will be summoned to treat your injuries—sustained in a fall from the bluff, you understand —and end by being arrested for your murders. Mr. Casey, you may proceed, for the moment, as this might prove amusing. But, please, I warn you: do not bore me."

Casey didn't need any further prodding to do his best. With a wink to Alexandra as he gently maneuvered her to one side—closer to the circular stairs—he picked up a round marble paperweight and tossed it to Tilden, telling the man to hold it in front of him at arm's length, his palm flat.

Then, doing his best not to grin at this small success, he slowly raised Maybelline to his shoulder, spread his feet into his usual flawed batting stance, and intoned importantly: " 'The sneer is gone from Casey's lips, his teeth are clenched in hate, / He pounds with cruel vengeance his bat upon the plate.' "

He hit Maybelline's barrel against the carpet a time or two and took a quick practice swing that stopped just short of the marble paperweight—but seemed to impress Tilden, who had never seen Lenny Dykstra's powerful stroke—and continued passionately, his voice building to a crescendo, " 'And now the pitcher holds the ball . . . and now he lets it go . . . /And now the air is shattered . . . *by the force of Casey's blow!'* "

Tilden went down like a stone as Maybelline's full barrel slammed into his ample gut, but Casey didn't stand there to admire his work. He tucked Maybelline's length flat against his own stomach with both hands and, using a stunt he'd learned for *Hellfire,* executed a perfect backflip, ending by wheeling in a half circle and whipping Maybelline out in a wide arc in a move that sent the pistol flying from Lord Brooks's hand.

"Alex!" Casey shouted, glaring at Lord Brooks, just daring the man to move, then punched him square in the jaw anyway, just because he wanted to. Lord Brooks slid to the floor, dazed.

"Yes, Casey?"

"That ought to keep them both in one place until Williard can get here with the posse. Damn! Remind me never, *never* to do my own stunts again." Casey shook his hand, sure he had cracked a knuckle, but not caring if he had. He picked up the letter he had written, that most incriminating letter, and stuffed it into his pocket. "Okay, babe—make like a shepherd!"

Alexandra didn't need any further explanation, hiking up her skirt with one hand as she clutched the satchel in the other, and succeeding in reaching the loft moments before Casey could join her.

A quick tug on the brass ring opened the door, their personal portal through time, and the two of them tumbled into it, collapsing against each other as the bookcase slid closed and sealed them inside the dark, *cold* compartment.

Casey found Alexandra's mouth with his own, crushing her against him as he kissed her, rejoiced with her, gloried with her, and even, after some moments, laughed with her.

"You were magnificent, you know," Alexandra said, touching his cheek as they stood in the darkness, the world forgotten.

"Yeah, I was, wasn't I? I may have to think about a career in acting. Although most of the credit goes to Maybelline," Casey quipped, turning his mouth into her palm. "Are you ready?"

She pushed herself closer against him, and he could feel the shiver that raced through her body. "What—what if you're wrong? What if we open the door and Tilden is standing there?"

"You have a point, I suppose," Casey said, prying himself free of her convulsive grip in order to reach up and locate the knob that would open the door to the future—or to their deaths. "But as the only alternative is to stay here until we either freeze or run out of air, I don't think we have a whole lot of choice."

Alexandra stood on tiptoe beside him, pulling his hand

away from the knob. "The poem, Casey," she asked, "It seemed to work for us this time. How—how does it end?"

He winced, wishing she hadn't asked. And then, shrugging, he said, "You told me to use an incantation the first time I tried this, remember? Well, let's try it now, all right, honey? I'll give you the last stanza, then we'll pull the knob—together."

He could sense that she nodded her head. Giving her one last kiss, and gripping Maybelline in preparation for fighting their way out of the library if Tilden and Lord Brooks were on the other side of the bookcase, he said quietly, reluctantly, "'Oh, somewhere in this favored land the sun is shining bright, / The band is playing somewhere, and somewhere hearts are light; / And somewhere men are laughing, and somewhere children shout'—"

Oh, God, please, Michael Casey prayed. *Not for me, but for Alex. For Alex. Please. Just this once, don't let Casey strike out.* He pushed Alexandra behind him protectively, took a deep breath, and pulled on the knob. The bookcase silently slid open, letting in sunlight, and fresh air, and the most beautiful sight of all—that of Jilly A'Brunzo reclining on the couch on the floor below them, sipping a beer and watching a soccer game on the television set.

"Casey?" Alexandra whispered from behind him.

Thank you, God. Thank you! Tears stinging his eyes, Casey turned to her, to the woman who had come into his life so unexpectedly, the woman who had shown him the reality he had lost sight of since becoming a movie star, the woman he would love and cherish forever.

He slid his arms around Alexandra's shoulders as he repeated triumphantly, "'And somewhere men are laughing, and somewhere children shout'—and, damn it, babe," he ended, laughing, as he led Alexandra Deverell out into the bright light of his world, the world they would share, "from now on, that's good enough for me!"

Epilogue

"Ouuuu-aaaah!"

—Al Pacino, in *Scent of a Woman*

*A*MBERSLEY HAD PREMIERED THE PAST FALL TO PACKED HOUSES, two thumbs up from Siskel and Ebert, and ecstatic sighs from Michael Casey fan clubs all over the world, who seemed to love their hero even more now that he was a husband and, wonder of wonders, the doting father of newborn twin daughters.

It hadn't been easy, getting identification for one "Alexis Devon," and it hadn't been all that legal when they'd finally managed it, but all of that was behind them now as they sat in front of Barbara Walters in their Beverly Hills living room, taping a segment for the newswoman's annual pre-Oscar television special. Maybelline, cracked and taped thanks to its collision with Tilden's belt buckle, but still Michael Casey's trademark, and never out of sight for long, was propped against one arm of the couch.

"You've been nominated for an Oscar, you're under contract for a sequel to *Ambersley* and will be leaving for

England next week to begin filming near Ambersley Hall, the gorgeous home you bought for your wife as a wedding present—"

"Yes, Barbara, and we were lucky to get it," Casey interrupted. "Have you heard the story? While we were filming *Ambersley,* the tenth earl met a beautiful red-haired croupier in Monaco and married her on the spot. With the estate unentailed, and the earl looking for some ready cash, Alex and I were able to buy the whole thing, including Deverell House, which adjoins Ambersley on one side. It's very picturesque. We even have a small gypsy encampment on the property, don't we, babe."

"He's speaking of Ramona—although one sweet old *possible* gypsy does not constitute an encampment. But we adore Ambersley Hall, Barbara," Alex put in, "and have left it much as it was when we bought it. Although there were certain renovations we felt necessary, isn't that right, darling?"

"We made some changes in the library, Barbara, at Ramona's suggestion," Casey informed her, his expression curiously amused. "Nothing much. Just a matter of hammering home a couple of nails, really."

"How wonderful. But to continue—you're up for an Oscar, you bought the estate where *Ambersley* was filmed, you have two darling babies, *and* you've just been voted this year's most romantic couple by *People* magazine. Life doesn't get much better, does it. Michael, there's only one question I've never found an answer to in my research. How did you two meet, anyway?" Barbara asked, clutching a sheaf of notes as she leaned forward in her seat, as was her custom when she asked personal questions.

"That's such a boring story, Barbara," Casey said easily, squeezing Alexandra's hand as they sat close together on the overstuffed couch. The entire room was comfortably, cozily furnished in Alexandra's dearly loved Laura Ashley prints and English Country furniture. "Are you sure you wouldn't rather ask me what sort of tree I'd pick to be, if I was

313

suddenly turned into a tree? Which color I'd be, if I were a color? What sort of vegetable I'd be, if—"

"Is he always such a tease, Alex?" the newswoman broke in, turning away from Casey. "No, don't answer that. Why don't *you* tell me how you two met."

Alexandra looked to Casey, and he nodded, their unspoken communication shining out through the cameras, giving the watching world a small glimpse into their remarkable closeness, their obvious love for each other.

"Well, Barbara," Alexandra said in her cultured English accent, a hint of mischief in her beautiful green eyes, "to be perfectly forthright, it all began in 1813, when Michael first met Alexandra Deverell. . . ."

"Oh, you two!" Barbara exclaimed, laughing. "Poor Alex! I should have known Michael would corrupt you. All right, all right, I know when I'm beaten. I'll try another question. Michael, I've asked all my interviewees for this show the same final question—have you practiced an acceptance speech in case you win the Oscar tonight? You should have, you know, for you're heavily favored for your performance in *Ambersley.*"

Casey lifted Alexandra's hand to his lips and kissed her fingertips, facing her as the camera zoomed in for a close-up. "What would I say?" he asked, his famous voice low and husky with emotion. "Why, Barbara, I imagine I'd say what I say every day: Alex, babe, everything I am, everything I ever hope to be, I owe to you. Only to you. Thank you, babe. Thank you for loving me."

"Well, I surely can't think of anything else to add, boys," Barbara told her crew with a satisfied sigh after a long silence during which Alex and Casey continued to smile into each other's eyes. "Cut it here, that's a wrap!"

KASEY MICHAELS, author of more than forty novels, has been described by *Romantic Times* as "one of the romance genre's most beloved authors" and "a powerhouse writer." *Affaire de Coeur* calls her writing "so real you can almost hear her characters breathe." Winner of the Romance Writers of America's prestigious RITA award and the recipient of the *Romantic Times,* Waldenbooks, and Bookrak awards, Ms. Michaels has appeared frequently on television, including the *Today* show. Her most recent work for Pocket Books, *The Secrets of the Heart,* is to be followed by *The Passion of an Angel,* which will be published in October 1995. Other Pocket Books include *The Legacy of the Rose, The Bride of the Unicorn, A Masquerade in the Moonlight,* and *The Illusions of Love.* Ms. Michaels resides in eastern Pennsylvania, with her husband and four children. She appreciates hearing from readers; you may write to her care of Pocket Books, 1230 Avenue of the Americas, New York, NY 10020.

CARLA NEGGERS

Tricks of Fate

1

THE FOG, THE WIND, AND THE DAMP COLD WERE NOT, IN SAM
Archer's mind, a sign of good things to come.

He kept silent as the car made its way up the long,
meandering, utterly decrepit driveway. Eaton Halliwell was
at the leather-covered wheel. He was an old-fashioned
confidential assistant to Sam's rich uncle, very correct in
manner and bearing, upright, ethical, of an indeterminate
age. Sam had tried to talk him out of this ridiculous
escapade up the California coast. He had failed.

"You cannot bring a vehicle of any kind," Eaton Halliwell
had told him in the elegant front parlor of Dryden Archer's
San Francisco home. "Not a car, not a truck, not even a
motor scooter or a bicycle—or Rollerblades, for that matter. Of course," he had gone on, a rare glint of humor in his
old eyes, "you wouldn't be able to Rollerblade where you're
going."

Halliwell swerved to avoid a crater-sized pit in the gravel
driveway. Ancient oaks and shrubbery grew wildly on either
side, their branches swirling and shifting in the wind and

fog, contributing to a feeling of eeriness Sam immediately dismissed as absurd. He was up in wine country, within half a day's drive of downtown San Francisco. Any sense of isolation was in his head.

But two weeks without a car. Without a telephone or a fax machine or a computer. Without, for the love of God, a simple transistor radio.

The ghost, apparently, disapproved.

"It—er—only seems to tolerate running water and minimal electricity," Halliwell had explained.

"Does it?" Sam had replied mildly. He did not believe in ghosts. He wouldn't, however, be the least surprised if his late uncle did. Dryden Archer had always been something of a kook, although still an Archer to the core and thus a man who looked after his own interests.

"The terms of Mr. Archer's will are very precise," Eaton Halliwell had continued. "You must stay at the old Liberty House for two weeks—fourteen full days—without modern transportation or conveniences before you are permitted to sell it. If you refuse or renege, the house and vineyards will be donated to one of Mr. Archer's favorite charities."

Halliwell had declined to specify *which* charity. Dryden Archer had had a variety of fruitcake causes he supported, and his definition of charity and Sam's were two entirely different things.

Sam had accepted the challenge. Come fifteen days from now, the house and vineyards would go on the market.

Halliwell eased the car around an overgrown mass of something, and Sam sat forward, peering through the fog as his home for the next two weeks came into view.

He shuddered.

The Liberty House was a sagging, peeling, cracked Victorian monstrosity. Lord, but it would be an interminable two weeks. His uncle was probably up on his cloud having a hell of a laugh.

If he were dead. Sam already had his doubts. It wasn't like Dryden Archer to arrange something he would find as entertaining as this knowing he wouldn't be around for the show. Sam hadn't attended the funeral: his uncle's will had stipulated there was to be no funeral.

Halliwell pulled the car up to a dilapidated front porch. Steps and floorboards were missing. Others appeared rotted. The front door itself . . . well, Sam could see he wouldn't need a key.

No wonder people said the place was haunted.

The ghost even had a name. Cassandra Belle Liberty. She had founded Liberty Vineyards a hundred years ago, as one of the first women wine makers in California. She had lost her vineyards to an Archer. Sam didn't know the details. Until his uncle's death last week, he hadn't even realized the old vineyards were still in family hands. He did know, however, that Cassandra Belle hadn't been the first woman wronged by an Archer. Or the last.

Halliwell turned off the engine. "You could change your mind," he said.

"That's what Uncle Dryden expected, isn't it?"

Halliwell's refined features remained placid. If he knew, he would never say what Dryden's intentions were. That the two had remained friends for more than fifty years never ceased to amaze Sam. Eaton Halliwell was every bit as upright and honorable as his employer and friend was not.

"I'll stay," Sam said. "Just be here two weeks from now to pick me up."

The old man shrugged. "As you wish."

Sam climbed out, the cold and dampness of the air almost a relief after the drive north from San Francisco, yesterday's flight up from San Diego. Civilization. He lived on the water and worked in a modern building with telecommunications on the cutting edge of technology. He could reach virtually anywhere in the world through computer networks, faxes, messenger services, telephones, even the age-old telegram.

But not from here, of course. He could reach no one from this place. No one could reach him.

Halliwell got the trunk open. Sam removed his duffel bag, his boxes of food and drink, his books, his sleeping bag, his camp-style cooking utensils and supplies. He had bottled water in the backseat, just in case. Matches. Flashlights. Batteries. He'd tried to sneak in a hibachi and some charcoal, but Halliwell had vetoed them. Cassandra Belle, the ghost, wouldn't approve.

Here he was, Samuel J. Archer, a prominent criminal defense lawyer, being treated like a twelve-year-old caught with candy bars at summer camp.

"Well, that does it," Halliewell said when Sam had heaped his supplies onto the front porch. "I'll be off now. If you change your mind, it's a five-mile walk into the village. You have my number."

"I won't change my mind. I wouldn't give Uncle Dryden the satisfaction. Are you sure the old codger's dead? I think he'd have tried to figure out a way to be around for this one."

"I scattered his ashes myself."

Ashes. With Dryden Archer, Sam would have preferred to see the body.

A gust of wind off the rolling, overgrown grounds penetrated right to his bones. Or maybe it was just dread that had him shuddering. Eaton Halliwell seemed unaffected by the chill in the air. He climbed back into his car. "Will there be anything else, Mr. Archer?"

Sam glanced dubiously at the house, its gabled mansard roof in desperate need of repair. A wonder if it didn't leak. "No. Nothing."

"Then I'll be off." He gave Sam a dry smile. "Enjoy Cassandra Belle."

"Well, Halliwell," Sam said, "if I've got to put up with a ghost, it might as well be female."

From her second-floor window, Cassandra Liberty watched with deep consternation as the expensive sedan crept back down the driveway.

Why had it left the dark-haired man behind?

He was standing in the middle of the driveway, his arms crossed on his chest as if he, too, were wondering why he'd been left. He wore a black roll-neck sweater and jeans, and he seemed tall and strongly built. Just what she needed.

Suddenly he turned and stared up at her window, and Cassandra shot backward, startled by his quick movement and the intensity of his narrowed eyes.

And by an uncomfortable prick of familiarity. His angular features, his probing expression, his arrogant stance reminded her of someone. She couldn't say who.

She frowned, thinking. No. She'd never seen him before. She would have remembered.

Dropping to her creaky iron-framed bed, she debated how she should proceed with a visitor on the premises. Should she trot downstairs and greet him? Grab a poker in case he was not of the best character? Grab what she could, slip out the back, and go home to San Francisco and forget this whole business?

Of course, she had no car. Dryden Archer had insisted.

Was her visitor his doing?

"What to do, what to do."

It was midafternoon, cold, damp, dreary, as it had been since her arrival the previous evening. She had been relatively unconcerned about Dryden Archer's conviction that the house and vineyards were haunted. The ghost, after all, was supposed to be one of her ancestors—her namesake, the turn-of-the-century wine maker Cassandra Belle Liberty.

She had slept peacefully and spent much of the day exploring the rambling house, and, despite the bad weather, had ventured outside. Long-neglected and abandoned by their Archer owners, Liberty Vineyards lay in a remote but picturesque part of the warm, narrow valleys of California wine country. Cassandra was eager to explore the rest of the property.

But now, exhausted by weeks of overwork, she'd put on a nightgown of flannel-backed white silk, feeling quite feminine and Victorian as she anticipated a long afternoon nap to the soothing sounds of the wind and the rain.

She hadn't counted on a strange man venturing into her midst.

"Maybe you should have," she muttered aloud.

It had been dangerous even to talk to Dryden Archer,

much less *like* him. He had the Archer roguish charm, the Archer arrogance, the Archer zest for risk and adventure. He'd had a proposition for her. A business proposition, he said. He wanted her to catalog and appraise a wine cellar he had recently discovered at her great-great-aunt's old house and vineyards.

With Dryden Archer, of course, there had to be a catch. She had to agree to spend two weeks there, alone, without transportation or modern conveniences or communication with the outside world, not even a newspaper.

If she did, in addition to her regular payment for her work and expertise, she could claim five bottles of Liberty wines, if any remained in good condition. He must have known money alone wouldn't have persuaded her to agree to such a bizarre arrangement, especially with an Archer.

She heard footsteps pounding up the front porch. Rising carefully so as not to make any noise, she sidled back over to the window. The porch roof, however, blocked her view of the front entrance. She tiptoed to her door and listened. Hearing nothing, she pushed the door open and ducked quietly into the hall. She was barefoot. Her long, copper hair hung down her shoulders. Ordinarily she kept it pinned up or pulled back, but not when napping, not when she was supposed to be alone in an empty, hundred-year-old house.

She went down the hall, across a threadbare floral runner, and, holding her breath, peered over the balcony.

The front door creaked, banged open, and a duffel bag was hurled onto the entry floor.

Cassandra froze. Surely the dark-haired stranger wasn't moving in. *Surely* he wasn't.

Her heart thumping, she tiptoed back into her room, grabbed the wrought-iron poker from her marble fireplace, and quickly returned to the balcony. Dryden Archer hadn't said anything about a housemate.

The front door opened. The man from the driveway stood on the threshold with a box of groceries in his arms and stared up at her. His eyes were probing, narrowed, suspicious. "What the hell?"

Cassandra gasped, about-faced, and fled down the hall and into her room. She shut the door firmly behind her and pushed a chair in front of it and collapsed on the bed, poker still in hand.

No. It couldn't be. Dryden Archer *wouldn't*.

"The place is cursed, Cassandra. Only you—Cassandra Belle's youngest descendant—can change that. If you go out there and find eternal love within the boundaries of Liberty Vineyards, she'll lift the curse and finally rest in peace herself. And we Archer men will have a chance at happiness for the first time in a hundred years."

Dryden Archer talk. More of his babble. Cassandra had barely paid attention.

She should have known better. Dryden Archer was a rich eccentric—an adventurer and a scoundrel with a knack for making money, like all Archer men. If he felt her falling in love would lift some crazy curse, *naturally* he would have a candidate in mind.

She simply never would have imagined it would be Samuel J. Archer himself.

Nah, Sam thought. *No way.*

First the window, now the balcony. It must have been a trick of his imagination. Something with the light. Fatigue. Given the prospect of two weeks alone in a purportedly haunted house, without the amenities to which he'd become accustomed, it was not beyond reason that he'd conjure up a copper-haired woman in a lacy white nightgown.

Of course, the poker had been a bit of overkill.

"She was a figment of your imagination, Sammy my boy," he muttered, dumping his sleeping bag atop the rest of his stuff. "She was not a ghost."

A pity, in a way. That copper hair and creamy skin, that slim body, its silhouette clearly visible beneath the nightgown. He'd conjured up worse images, for certain.

The entry was huge, in the center of the rambling house. To his left was a drawing room, done in a large, faded floral print in shades of rose, burgundy, and deep green. Lacy, dingy curtains hung on the windows, and there were lots of clunky, overstuffed chairs and sofas. To his right was a living room, dark and dreary, largely unfurnished.

Leaving his stuff for the moment, Sam ventured into the tattered drawing room, through an archway leading to a dining room with more floral wallpaper and heavy furnishings. The feminine decor must have been to appease the ghost, since none of Liberty Vineyards' Archer owners could have had a woman long enough to make her mark.

"Ghosts," Sam muttered, disgusted with himself for having forgotten for a moment that they didn't exist. The floral decor was probably just in keeping with the house's Victorian style.

He headed out into a hall that, if he turned left, would take him back toward the rear of the house, where he saw glimpses of a bathroom and kitchen. There'd be time enough for that. If anything could send him screaming back to San Diego, it would be the kitchen and the variety of vermin that could congregate there. He knew how to cook. He'd done a lot of it in college and law school. He just hadn't done much since.

He went back to the entry, checking out the living room. There was a fireplace, a window seat, and double doors that led to a wood-paneled library. He lingered in the doorway. No floral wallpaper, no lace curtains. Just a couple of leather chairs, a leather couch, library-type wooden tables and bookcases, and a fireplace. He could carve out a corner for himself here, bury himself in one book after another.

Uncle Dryden, God rest his soul, had insisted Sam carry no cash or credit cards. Halliwell had checked. "There's nowhere to spend money in any case," he had added, as if that would make Sam feel better.

Returning to the entry, he decided he ought to venture upstairs—copper-haired woman or no copper-haired woman—and choose a bedroom.

He grunted to himself, grabbing up his duffel bag and hoisting it over one shoulder. "It's going to be a long two weeks."

He started up the stairs.

A door creaked behind him, off toward the living room, and he thought he heard footsteps. A cold shiver ran right up his back, and he whirled around, nearly dropping his duffel bag.

She was there, in the living room doorway. The shining copper hair, the creamy skin, the lacy white nightgown, the bare feet. The beautiful figment of his imagination.

He could see the outline of her nipples under the white fabric, utterly real.

Her eyes were teal-colored, wide and black-lashed. Intelligent. They fastened on him.

She spoke. "So you're Sam Archer." Her voice was throaty, as if it hadn't been used in a while. "I should have been expecting you."

Not since he was eight years old and had inadvertently stepped on a snake had Sam been so damned close to screaming and running. He tightened his grip on his duffel bag. *You don't believe in ghosts.*

"Who are you?" he demanded.

"Cassandra Liberty."

That was all he needed to hear. He wasn't going to scream and he wasn't going to run, but damned if he was going to stand there and talk to . . . to whatever she was. He had to get his wits back. He about-faced and marched up the stairs, determined not to look back until he was absolutely certain he was beyond seeing things. He didn't believe in ghosts. He hadn't *seen* a ghost. Either Eaton Halliwell's drivel had affected him the wrong way or the copper-haired woman was his uncle's doing, part of some elaborate scheme of his.

Cassandra Liberty.

"Uh-uh. That woman's been dead a hundred years. She is not downstairs in the goddamned entry."

He didn't stop until he'd reached the second floor. There, he glanced over the balcony. If he'd conjured her up, he'd be all right in a few minutes. If not—well, he'd see to it she quit her ghost act.

But he saw nothing but his gear and the eerie light angling

in through the filthy windows, heard nothing but the sound of the wind, howling now, outside. Sam steadied himself. What the hell kind of coward was he, running from some damned alleged ghost.

He grunted. Running wasn't the problem. *Seeing* a ghost was the problem. Of course, if anyone could go to his reward and talk some poor bastard on the next cloud to haunting this godforsaken place, it was Dryden Archer.

But Cassandra Liberty? She'd been a premier wine maker late in the last century, a rare woman in the business. An Archer had ruined her. She'd promised to haunt the lot of them—at least the males. For a hundred years, every Archer man who'd encountered trouble in romance had blamed Cassandra Liberty.

And Archer men *did* have a way of making a mess of their romantic lives. Uncle Dryden, himself the son of an Archer not known for his monogamous nature, had never had an enduring relationship. Affairs and the occasional near marriage, but nothing that he could sustain. Sam's own father was no better. He'd left his mother when Sam was in grade school and never was able to settle down with one woman. Still, Sam was less inclined to blame some long-dead wine maker than some innate Archer quirk. He had promised himself he would be different. But he wasn't sure he was.

He would have to find an old photograph of Cassandra Liberty. There had to be one around here somewhere. He'd see if she had copper hair and teal eyes and skin like fresh cream. Even if the photo was black-and-white, he'd be able to tell if she and the woman downstairs, in the window, on the balcony, bore any resemblance to each other.

Then he'd deal with his "ghost."

"Well, Halliwell," Dryden Archer said later that evening, drink in hand, "I must say, it's never felt so good to be alive. The deed is done?"

Eaton Halliwell nodded, matter-of-fact as always. "Miss Liberty and young Mr. Archer have both arrived at Liberty Vineyards."

"Sam can't wait to get these two weeks over and sell the place, can he?"

"I expect not."

Dryden sipped his Scotch. He knew he'd asked a lot of Halliwell, a straight arrow if there ever was one. But, then, he always had asked a lot of Halliwell. "He shed any tears for me?"

"Not in my presence, I'm afraid."

"The man's not in touch with his emotions," Dryden said with conviction. "Well, maybe the next two weeks will change that. I've got plans for Liberty Vineyards and that damned ghost is interfering with them. I want her out."

Halliwell settled back in his bone-colored leather chair, gazing into his untouched drink. "Mr. Archer—"

"Dryden. For God's sake, man, it's been fifty years."

Only the faintest of smiles. "Yes, I suppose it has. But I must say—I must say, sir, that your nephew and Cassandra Liberty are a most unlikely pair."

Reluctantly, Dryden had to agree. But he was a gambler and an optimist—and he owed Sam a chance at real happiness, never mind that Dryden himself stood to make a profit if all went well. And all *would* go well. If the curse wasn't broken within the year, the ghost—that relentless witch Cassandra Belle—would take over the house for all time and there'd be no getting rid of her.

And no hope for Archer men.

Dryden Archer fervently believed in ghosts.

I curse the lot of you. May not one of you find romantic happiness, ever.

She'd meant it, too.

Dryden supposed an argument could be made that he was using his nephew. Scheming and manipulating, as was the wont of Archer men. Yet surely, he thought, Sam would thank him in the end.

The doorbell rang. Halliwell got it, returning to the study in a moment. "It's your architect, sir."

"Good, good. Let him in."

All inhibitions about manipulating his nephew and young Cassandra Liberty vanished as he eagerly greeted the man who would help him transform Liberty Vineyards into a profit-making enterprise, once Cassandra Belle's curse was lifted.

2

By EVENING, SAM KNEW HE WASN'T DEALING WITH A GHOST. HE was dealing with a squatter.

He stood in the middle of the large, airy bedroom from whose window he had spotted her upon his arrival. The lacy white nightgown was cast off on the bed. A T-shirt from a popular Napa Valley vineyard hung over the iron footboard. He'd nearly tripped over a pile of exercise clothes: unitard, crumpled white socks, sneakers. The leather suitcase propped up against the antique marble-topped dresser was battered and old, but there was no mistaking the underwear flung on a pathetic drying rack for anything a Victorian lady would have worn.

Not a tidy squatter, whatever her identity or her purpose in being there.

She did bear a striking resemblance to Cassandra Belle Liberty, the purported ghost of Liberty Vineyards. Sam studied the portrait of her above the fireplace mantel. The copper hair and teal eyes were the same as those of his squatter, but the Cassandra Liberty of a century ago was squarer in the face, with no discernible sense of humor.

Maybe it was just the style of the era in which the portrait had been painted, but she had an eat-nails-for-breakfast look that, Sam figured, might easily have persuaded someone as susceptible to such things as Dryden Archer that she was haunting the place.

A small, framed oval photograph atop the mantel offered a no-less-forbidding image of the woman who had built Liberty Vineyards and lost them to an Archer.

The bedroom door creaked open. Everything in the house, Sam had discovered, creaked.

His copper-haired squatter appeared in the doorway. She'd changed from her nightgown into heavy black leggings and a multicolored tunic that was mostly the same teal color as her eyes. Her cheeks were rosy, as if she'd just come from outside, never mind the miserable weather.

She followed his gaze to the portrait. "That's Cassandra Belle Liberty."

"I know. I'm surprised my uncle allowed her portrait to be hung in the house."

"He didn't. I found it in storage in the wine cellar."

"Who are you? You're no damned ghost. If Dryden put you up to pretending to haunt the place in an effort to force me out, you can forget it. I don't respond well to his tricks, and I'm not going anywhere."

She frowned. Her hair, Sam noticed, hung down her back in a thick, messy braid. She was perhaps in her late twenties, younger than the woman in the portrait. "He did no such thing. He hired me to appraise the wine cellar. We have a deal."

Sam felt a prick of suspicion—and curiosity. "What deal?"

"That's between Dryden Archer and me."

"Then you don't know." Sam moved toward the door, his guard up. "Or maybe you're just pretending not to know."

Her teal eyes half-closed on him. "Know what?"

"My uncle died last week."

"No!" She grabbed hold of the doorjamb, the rose draining from her cheeks. "Oh, I'm so sorry. No, I didn't know. What happened?"

Her shock seemed genuine, but Sam was accustomed to dealing with people—clients, witnesses, even fellow attorneys—quite good at faking shock, grief, surprise. And given what he knew of Dryden Archer and what he didn't know of this woman, he remained wary.

"He died in his sleep last Friday."

Supposedly, he added privately. This woman's presence did not ease his suspicion that his uncle just might be up to another of his schemes.

"I had no idea." Her voice was soft, pained. "I don't—I didn't know him well, but what I knew, I liked."

Most people did. Dryden's charm was notorious. "How long have you been here?"

"Just since last night."

"Does your 'deal' with my uncle still stand now that he's dead?"

She thought a moment, her expression unreadable. "Yes, I'm sure it does. We have a written contract. Mr. Halliwell is the one who was to see to the details—that I kept up my end of the agreement and so forth."

Sam moved a few steps closer, noting that her eyes remained leveled on him. He guessed she was intelligent, astute, and just as wary of him as he was of her. "Miss Liberty—if that is your name—you might as well know that I intend to stay here for the next two weeks. So I think you should explain what you're doing here."

"What do you get if you stay here?"

"We're not talking about me right now."

Her eyes narrowed even more, questioning, suspicious. Anyone who knew Dryden Archer more than ten minutes learned to be wary of any "deal" he offered. There was always a catch. But she tossed her head back, steadying her gaze on him. "My deal with Mr. Archer was fairly straight-forward. I'm to examine the wine cellar, catalog its contents, and appraise its value."

"You're a wine expert?"

"Of sorts. I'm more of a wine historian. I edit a wine review out of San Francisco."

"And your real name?"

She leaned against the doorjamb, as if utterly unconcerned by his presence. "Cassandra Liberty is my real name. Cassandra Belle was my great-great-aunt."

Hell, Sam thought, his fists tightening at his sides. She *had* to be Dryden's doing. "You know she lost the vineyards to an Archer?"

"Of course."

"You don't hold a grudge?"

She shrugged. "What's past is past."

A self-contained woman, Cassandra Liberty. No doubt she could be as forbidding as her namesake. But he didn't believe her. "So you can finish your business in a day or two and be off?"

Her composure faltered, but she hung on to it, straightening against the doorjamb. "It's not that simple."

Sam sighed. *Dryden,* he thought, *you sneaky bastard.* "My uncle insisted you stay here two weeks, didn't he? Without transportation or any method of communicating with the outside world. Is that right?"

She let out a breath. "That's right."

"Why did you agree? Because this place was founded by one of your ancestors?"

"I have a personal as well as a professional interest in Liberty Vineyards, yes." She drew away from the doorjamb, tugging the covered rubber band from what was left of her braid. It was an effective way of avoiding his eyes. "But I would never have agreed to such an arrangement without some sort of added perk, besides money and curiosity. If I stay, your uncle promised me five bottles of Liberty wine if I find any in good condition."

"They'd be worth a fortune, wouldn't they?"

She shot him a look of pure annoyance. "That's not my first concern. I've only seen pictures of Cassandra Belle's wines—the bottles, the labels. And I've only heard of her artistry as a wine maker—her instincts, her skill. If I could see a bottle, touch it, *taste* the wine . . ." She broke off and took a deep breath, then smiled, embarrassed. "Well, it seemed worth two weeks without a phone or a car."

Her enthusiasm was so genuine, so infectious, Sam had no doubt she was telling the truth. He just wondered if she knew his uncle would never have made the offer if there weren't something in it for him. Dead or alive, Dryden Archer was a man unaccustomed to doing anything just to be nice, decent, or honorable.

Nevertheless, Liberty wine or no Liberty wine, Sam wasn't convinced that his uncle and Cassandra Liberty didn't have something up their sleeves, with him as their intended victim. "Did my uncle mention a ghost?" he asked mildly.

"We didn't get into it in great detail, but I know Cassandra Belle is supposedly haunting the house and vineyards."

She was dissembling. Sam was trained and experienced in making such judgments, and he knew Cassandra Liberty wasn't telling him everything.

He leaned forward and leveled his eyes at her, just as he would have a witness he wanted to intimidate. "I don't believe in ghosts."

"Well, Mr. Archer," she said with a sudden amused, wholly captivating smile, "you could have fooled me."

He gritted his teeth and breezed past her. He would get settled, and then he would inform Cassandra Liberty that, since the vineyard would no doubt be his in two weeks, she could fetch her wine and go.

"Oh, Mr. Archer."

He stopped on his heels and turned.

She was still in the doorway, raking her braid loose with one hand. "You must be getting something for your two weeks here. Mind telling me what?"

"Liberty Vineyards."

Her teal eyes deepened, but gave away nothing. "You've

inherited Liberty Vineyards? I suppose it makes sense, seeing how you're an Archer." Her tone suggested a low opinion of Archers. "Thinking of giving up lawyering and becoming a wine maker?"

As if he never would. As if he *couldn't*. As if he hadn't the brains, the talent, the will. The personality. Of course, Cassandra Liberty would know what a mess the previous Archer owners had made of her great-great-aunt's legacy.

Sam shook his head, refusing to give in to defensiveness. "I have no intention of doing anything with this place but sell it as soon as possible. Unfortunately, my uncle's will stipulates that I can't sell until I've stayed here two weeks under these draconian conditions."

"Ah," she said, "the profit motive. I shouldn't have wondered." She smiled coolly, and added, "You being an Archer and all."

He didn't return her smile. "What do you know about Archers?"

"More than I care to," she said breezily—and evasively.

A wine historian and descendant of Cassandra Belle Liberty, Sam reasoned, would likely know a thing or two about Archers. He wondered if she knew they blamed Cassandra Belle for their romantic missteps. No doubt. The Cassandra Liberty in front of him looked as if she would make it a point to know as much as she could before venturing into a deal with any Archer, much less rich, eccentric Dryden Archer.

"Perhaps," Sam said, "you should take your wine and go."

"And violate my contract? No way. According to my deal with Dryden, the wine isn't mine unless I stay here two weeks."

"I'll cancel the damned contract when I get back—"

She shook her head, adamant. "My agreement was with your uncle. I'm sticking to it."

For five damned bottles of wine. Sam gave her a grudging smile. "You don't trust me, do you, Ms. Liberty?"

"Not a chance," she muttered, and whirled into her bedroom, shutting her door firmly.

Cassandra very badly wanted the wine. If not, she would have packed her bags and hiked to the village and been done with Samuel J. Archer.

Would he try to sabotage her deal with Dryden? No, she thought. He couldn't. She had it in writing. Stay here two weeks, and the wine was hers.

Seeing a ghost wouldn't have rattled her more than Sam Archer had. Dryden had been manageable. Aging, charming in a roguish way, straightforward in his dealings with her.

"Right," she grumbled, making her way down the back stairs to the butler's pantry. "So how come his nephew's here?"

In the end, Dryden had proved himself thoroughly Archer. He had deliberately, without warning her, arranged for her and his nephew to spend these two weeks together in some outrageous hope they'd fall in love and end Cassandra Belle's curse on Archer men.

Hah.

But she tempered her anger, reasoning that Sam Archer's presence could just be a coincidence. Dryden Archer was dead, God rest his soul. He couldn't have known he had only days to live. He couldn't have planned for his nephew to fulfill the terms of his will during the same two weeks she was appraising the Liberty Vineyard wine cellar.

No, Cassandra corrected herself. He was an Archer. He would think he could do anything.

She heaved an aggravated sigh, then pushed her way through a swinging door into the kitchen. It was a big, open room that had pre-World War II cabinetry and slightly post-World War II appliances. Cassandra could almost imagine June Cleaver at the refrigerator.

Instead Sam Archer was.

Matters were not going to be helped, she thought, by her response to him. It was physical, it was immediate, it was relentless. Of course it would be. She had a knack for being hopelessly attracted to the wrong sort of man, and nobody could be more wrong than an Archer. She'd done her research. She'd already known a fair amount about Archers, since they were a prominent California family and had bankrupted Liberty Vineyards. But once Dryden Archer had made his proposal, Cassandra had decided it would behoove her to know as much as she could about modern-day Archers, of whom Samuel J. was one of the more conspicuous.

He glanced around at her. "Evening."

His eyes were clear and penetrating, a surprising blue. She had expected them to be dark. She didn't know why. She couldn't remember the color of his uncle's eyes.

She saw that the pine table in a windowed alcove of the kitchen was set for two.

He followed her gaze and grinned. "Since you're not a ghost, I figured you had to eat."

His subtly self-deprecating humor surprised her, seeing how Archers were known for their high opinion of themselves. They didn't like making mistakes, and thinking she might be a ghost had been a very big mistake.

"I'm heating up a couple of thin-crust pizzas I brought and tossing together a salad," he went on. "It's nothing fancy, but there's plenty for two."

"Thank you. That sounds wonderful."

She sat down at the table and watched Sam Archer pull together dinner. Her initial impression of him was proving exactly on target. His features weren't so much handsome as arresting, in that roguish Archer way. He was obviously very fit, with long, well-muscled legs, a broad chest, and strong arms. His smile could be whatever he wanted it to be. He was a man very much in control of himself.

Cassandra groaned inwardly. And he liked to be in control of his surroundings, too, and the people in them. He was *Samuel J. Archer.*

How couldn't Dryden have known what a bad match they

would make? How could he have thought she would find "eternal love" with his damned nephew?

She wouldn't mention to Sam his uncle's prattle about ending Cassandra Belle's curse. He wouldn't believe in curses any more than he did in ghosts. And no point, she thought, in bringing up love and romance when they had two whole weeks to get through.

"I took the second shelf in the refrigerator," Sam said, "and the cabinet in the corner."

His mundane statement pulled Cassandra from her brooding. She was thinking about keeping him out of her bed and he was thinking about keeping her out of his food. *A little perspective works wonders, Cassandra.* She smiled to herself. "That's fine."

"But help yourself," he added. "I brought enough to feed an army. Figured there wouldn't be much else to do around here besides eat, sleep, hike, and read."

She duly noted his use of the past tense. Perspective indeed. *Do not presume to know what an Archer is thinking.* "I take it you have no trials pending?"

His vivid blue eyes leveled on her as he glanced over from the scarred counter, where he was preparing a salad. She felt her mistake but wasn't sure what it was. "I always have trials pending," he said, "but I have competent co-counsel and staff. I assume Dryden told you all about me?"

So that was it. He wanted to know what she knew about him. She picked at a paper napkin next to a green plastic plate he must have brought. "I've read about you in the papers, Mr. Archer."

"Sam. We're housemates."

Lucky me, she thought. Nothing in his words, actions, or bearing indicated he knew about Cassandra Belle's "curse" and his uncle's recommended cure. She couldn't imagine Sam Archer allowing himself to be manipulated by anyone —or being very happy about it if anyone somehow managed to.

He offered her a glass of wine. Cassandra accepted.

339

"Not going to check the label?" he asked.

"I'm a wine historian, not a wine snob."

But when he brought her a glass, she automatically eyed the red wine's color, then sniffed it. A decent merlot she decided, if perhaps a little too full-bodied. She took a sip.

With a rush of heat, she realized that Sam was watching her closely. "What, is it rotgut?" he asked.

"Not at all. It'll do fine with pizza."

He laughed, unoffended. "A ringing endorsement. So," he said casually, moving back to the counter, "what have you read about me?"

She shrugged. "You're a prominent defense lawyer in San Diego for rich, white-collar criminals."

He whacked a cucumber in two. "My clients aren't criminals until convicted in a court of law." His tone was mild, neither defensive nor pompous, despite her attempt to provoke him. "We Americans have a long-standing tradition of the presumption of innocence."

"The average guy who robs a gas station can't afford your fees."

He arranged slices of cucumber on the salad and brought the bowl over to the table. "The average guy *accused* of robbing a gas station," he corrected. "No, he probably can't afford my fees, but I do pro bono work."

She leaned back in her chair, assessing him as she sipped her wine. It was going to be a rough two weeks. Good thing it was a big house with a lot of land. "Ever defend an Archer?"

He'd returned to the stove, using a dish towel as a potholder to remove the two small pizzas from the archaic oven. He slid them onto the stove top, casting her a look that gave away nothing of what he felt, thought. No wonder he was a nightmare for the prosecution. "No."

But she'd made her point. She'd let him know she was aware of the Archer reputation. They were adventurers and scoundrels who had a gift for making money. Sam Archer, respected attorney though he was, was no exception. According to her research on living Archers, his idea of a vacation was climbing the sheer, vertical rock face of some mountain. Two weeks in a neglected, abandoned vineyard wouldn't try his survival skills. He was a shrewd investor, supposedly worth millions. He wasn't married. Like all Archer men, he wasn't cut out to be a husband and father—not that it stopped them from trying. And no curse was to blame; of that Cassandra felt certain. Archers had been rogues and scoundrels long before Cassandra Belle had wished them ill. They were the cause of their own unhappiness.

Sam served the pizza and poured more wine, and Cassandra helped herself to salad. Dinner was companionable enough, despite the jumble of emotions and physical sensations that had her all tied up. She would simply need a little time to adjust to the man's presence, she told herself.

They discussed living arrangements. He had taken a bedroom at the opposite end of the house from hers, and he requested the library as his personal space, for reading. Cassandra took that as a hint she should not expect a checkers partner. She would be on her own—a relief.

"I would think," he went on, "it would be sensible to have breakfast and lunch on our own and dinner together."

The legalistic mind at work, Cassandra thought. She'd figured they'd just wing such things. "Sounds good to me."

Afterward, she provided fudge brownies from her favorite San Francisco deli for dessert. They had them in the drawing room. None of the lamps—what few there were—had a bulb over sixty watts, leaving much of the huge room in shadows. Between that and the howling wind, Cassandra felt how isolated she was. Yet she wasn't afraid. She was reasonably confident that Dryden Archer, whether dead or alive, would never have set her up for two weeks with a dangerous lunatic.

Sam tried to make himself comfortable in the tattered overstuffed chair. "If you're a wine historian and a Liberty, you must know something about the woman who built this place."

"Some, but not as much as I'd like. She was a very private person, almost reclusive, and didn't leave much of a written record—letters, diaries, that sort of thing. I'm writing an article on her. If I can find enough information, I'd like one day to do a book. She had a tremendous feel for the blend of science and artistry that goes into any great wine."

"Unlike the Archer who took over her vineyards."

"True. Not only did he lie and scheme to gain control, but then he quickly lost interest and bankrupted Liberty Wines."

Sam propped one foot up on his knee, eying her. "That's why she's haunting the place." He gave Cassandra a faint smile. "Supposedly."

She carefully sipped her milk, grateful she'd had no more than a glass and a half of wine. When dealing with an Archer, she knew, a Liberty needed to keep her wits about her. "Wouldn't you in her position?"

"If I were a ghost, I'd find something besides a crumbling house and overgrown grapevines in the middle of nowhere to haunt."

"She loved this house, the land—"

He waved her off. "A hundred years ago, maybe this place was worth haunting. Now, it's a wreck. I'll be lucky to sell it without having to pay to demolish the house."

Cassandra sat forward, horrified. "You wouldn't sell to someone who'd tear down the house! You couldn't—"

"Cassandra," he said with ill-concealed impatience, "I'll sell this place to the first buyer who meets my price."

"That's disgusting." She got to her feet, anger and frustration burning in her stomach, stiffening her spine. "But I suppose such an attitude on the part of an Archer is to be expected. Why didn't your uncle sell the place when he inherited it?"

Sam's only reaction to her outburst was to settle back in the chair and fold his hands across his flat abdomen. "He said Cassandra Belle wouldn't let him."

"But you believe she's dead and gone and has no say."

"Correct."

"Well," she said, thoroughly disgusted with him, and with

herself, for being so intrigued by him, "I'm going to bed. If Cassandra Belle is haunting the place, I hope she pays you a visit."

He yawned—probably, Cassandra figured, just to show how concerned he was about ghosts. "Ordinarily I'm not too worried about things that go bump in the night. But," he went on, the intense blue of his eyes deepening as he pinned his gaze on her, "I guess it depends on what's causing the bumping."

Her cheeks flamed instantly, as if he'd touched them. He grinned, without innocence. She quickly departed for the stairs. What fool, she thought, tries to have the last word with an Archer male?

After a restless night and an even more restless day, Sam found Cassandra in the stone-hewn wine cellar late in the afternoon. She had spent most of the day there while he had explored the overgrown vineyards, a picturesque tree-lined stream, a crumbling brick winery building. It was an incredibly beautiful spot, in spite of the lack of improvement in the weather. It was still windy, thick with fog, chilly. When he'd come inside, he'd made himself a cup of coffee and sat down with a book.

But he couldn't concentrate. He was preoccupied with his mysterious copper-haired housemate and his uncle. Ghoulish and suspicious as it was, Sam wanted more proof of Dryden Archer's death, especially now that Cassandra Liberty had waltzed into the picture. Halliwell's assertion that he'd scattered his employer and old friend's ashes himself just wasn't good enough. As far back as Sam could remember, he had fallen into his uncle's traps.

But how would Dryden Archer benefit—dead or alive—from having his nephew and Cassandra Belle Liberty's great-great-niece under the same roof?

It was dark and cool in the basement wine cellar, where hundreds of wines from the past century were carefully stored. Dryden had inherited the place five years ago, but the ghost and the old man's disinterest had prevented him from doing much more than minimally maintaining it and paying the taxes.

Cassandra was squatted down amidst a row of dusty wine bottles, a steno pad and pencil in hand, her hair pinned up haphazardly. Her slim figure was hidden beneath an oversized flannel shirt and a threadbare denim vest. She glanced up at him. "You look like you need a nap, Sam," she said with an amused grin. "Didn't sleep well last night?"

"The wind kept me up."

"Oh. I didn't hear it."

She wouldn't admit it if she had. "I suppose you didn't hear all the creaks and groans, either."

"Nope."

"Old houses," he said dismissively.

"I'm sure." She leaned forward onto her knees, peering at a wine bottle but not touching it. "Of course, Cassandra Belle might have seen to it that only you—the Archer in her midst—were disturbed and left me alone."

Sam dropped down beside her. "You don't believe this place is haunted any more than I do."

"Did I say I didn't believe in ghosts?"

She was baiting him, Sam knew, amusing herself at his expense, and he ignored her. "What are you doing?"

"Examining the cork. If it's sound, there's a chance the wine might still be good. I look for signs of deterioration, crumbling, softness."

"That's not good, I assume."

"A deteriorated cork lets in oxygen, and that ruins the wine. For old wines, like these, a sound cork is absolutely essential." Concentration furrowed her brow as she made a notation in her steno pad, the scratching of her pencil the only sound in the cool stillness. "Next I'll check the condition of the bottle, the variety of the wine, the vintage. Certain wines hold their peaks longer than others. Whites are meant to be drunk young, of course, but reds and sparkling wines can remain wonderful long after they've been bottled, and many naturally improve with age. Proper storage makes a huge difference. This cellar is perfect. Even temperature, no drafts."

Her enthusiasm and excitement were almost palpable, making everything about her seem alert, alive. Sam had only a modest interest in wine beyond drinking it.

She flipped her steno pad shut and got to her feet, wincing with stiffness. "That's enough for one day. The must and dust get to my sinuses after a while. Is it still miserable out?"

"Worse than yesterday."

She grinned. "Cassandra Belle knows an Archer's on her territory."

Sam rose beside her, noticing a cobweb stuck in her hair. He debated brushing it off, then wondered why the hell he was debating something he ordinarily would have done as a matter of course, without thinking.

Because, pal, it's dangerous to do anything as a matter of course with Cassandra Liberty.

Last night, tossing and turning, hearing every noise and howl of the wind, he'd thought of her deep teal eyes, the shape of her hips—his mouth on hers. Hell, he didn't need any damned ghost to keep him awake.

"What are you looking at?" she asked sharply, frowning at him.

"You've a cobweb in your hair." Then he caught it between his fingers and flicked the sticky mess onto the floor. He'd barely touched her.

She brushed a hand along the spot where the cobweb had been, picking out any remaining strands. "So long as no spider's crawling around—"

"Would you like me to look?"

"No, that's okay."

She spoke quickly—a little too quickly, Sam felt. She shot toward the door to the main part of the rambling cellar. So, he thought, she would rather risk a spider in her hair than his fingers. Interesting.

"Are you coming?" she asked, her hand holding the string

to a naked lightbulb that was hanging above the door. As everywhere else in the house, the lighting in the wine cellar was bad.

Sam smiled to himself. "Yes."

She waited for him to walk past her into the doorway before she tugged on the string, plunging the wine cellar into complete darkness. Only the light on the stairs in the adjoining section of the cellar alleviated the pitch black. Sam could just make out Cassandra's silhouette. He could hear her soft breathing. He wondered if she regretted switching off the light.

Without a word, she started toward the door a few feet away, but something caught her toe, sending her tripping forward.

She landed sprawled against his chest, and he caught her up by the waist, steadying her. It was an automatic move, done without thinking. She gripped his arm as she caught her balance.

"Thank you," she murmured.

But she didn't move. Neither did he. He noticed the silence, the absolute stillness.

Her mouth was already close to his, easy to find in the near darkness.

Kissing her was the most natural and inevitable thing Sam had ever done. Her lips were cool from her hours in the wine cellar. Nothing he'd imagined last night had prepared him for his reaction to her. It was as if he'd been flung off a cliff and was free-falling, not knowing where he'd land or if he'd ever be the same again.

Cassandra drew back, stiffening in his arms, then pulling herself from them. She muttered, "Oh, dear," and fled toward the light.

She took the stairs so fast Sam hardly heard her feet hit. He remained in the darkness. He would need a bit longer to pull himself together.

Nothing was certain anymore, he thought, except that it was going to be a very interesting two weeks.

3

I HAVE A TENDENCY TO FALL FOR CADS, ROGUES, AND RAKES," Cassandra explained over dinner. She'd showered, calmed herself, changed clothes, and resolved not to kiss Samuel Archer again.

His thick eyebrows raised. "And which am I?"

She smiled. "All of the above. You're an Archer."

"Ah."

His tone was dry as he sampled his wine, a chardonnay she had tucked in among her things before leaving San Francisco. She'd done tonight's cooking: salmon and asparagus over fresh linguine, salad, and French bread. They would run out of good fresh stuff before long.

"Cassandra," Sam went on, serious, "if you didn't want me to kiss you—"

"Was it you who kissed me? I thought I kissed you. And that's the problem." She set down her wineglass, trying to be honest and frank without embarrassing herself. "You see, you're not at all right for me."

"You know that already?"

"Yes. Absolutely."

He eyed her closely, everything about him reminding her of how much she'd enjoyed kissing him and being kissed back. It just wouldn't do. She had to be strong. She had to be responsible.

"Cassandra, it was only a kiss."

"Only a kiss." She laughed, raising her wineglass. "And if we'd ended up in bed, it would have been 'only sex.' A little fun. A toss in the hay. Physical release. A natural result of our being alone together and attracted to each other."

Sam blinked, clearly amused. "And that would have been bad?"

She drank some of her wine, then set her glass down, hard. "There, I rest my case. Relationship, commonality, emotional intimacy—they would never come before sex, would they?"

"Are we speaking theoretically here?"

She groaned. "I'm serious! I am explaining to you why I don't date, kiss, or sleep with your type. Not that you want to sleep with me or I want to sleep with you—I just—I'm just trying to explain—" She broke off, cursing silently. *God, you idiot. Keep digging and soon you'll be fully buried.* She licked her lips, drank some more wine, regrouped. "I think we should call a truce."

Sam Archer was obviously enjoying himself immensely. "One little kiss doesn't call for a truce."

"We've been together just over twenty-four hours. We have thirteen days to go. If we don't set up some boundaries now—well, I've already told you I have a weakness for cads. And you, being an Archer, would . . . I don't mean to be insulting, but I think you know what I'm trying to say."

"You're here, I'm here—why not make the most of it?"

"That's pretty much it in a nutshell."

"What if you've misjudged me? What if I'm not as attracted to you as you think I am?"

She tossed her head back. "Are you saying if I climbed into your bed tonight, you'd boot me back down the hall?"

His eyes darkened, narrowing on her with an intensity

that left her mouth dry and her body tingling. He swirled his wine in his glass, not drinking it. "Okay, Cassandra." He took a quick gulp of wine. "Spell out your rules of engagement."

"Simple. You keep your distance, I'll keep mine."

"Not specific enough."

"All right. We're housemates. Any contact we might have—meals together, that sort of thing—isn't to be construed as a 'date.' We don't touch each other unless by accident or if in imminent physical danger. We respect each other's privacy."

"And if things should happen?"

"'Things'? What things?"

He smiled. "Relationship, commonality, emotional intimacy."

"I'm not holding my breath, and neither," she said, spinning linguine onto her fork, "should you."

"No cads, rakes, and rogues in your life."

She shot him a look. "That's my goal."

He grinned, a gleam coming into his eyes that gave him a deliberately rakish look. "Well, whatever, this cad, rake, and rogue would rather have you for a housemate than some Victorian ghost."

"Which you now know for sure I'm not. Ghosts don't get cobwebs in their hair, and they don't trip over cracks in cement."

He eased back in his chair, stretching out his long legs. "I suspect they also don't kiss back."

Cassandra felt an unwelcome heat spread up into her cheeks, but she managed a wry smile. "Who knows? We've got two weeks, Sam. Maybe Cassandra Belle will let us both know just what a ghost *does* do."

Dryden Archer was not one to panic, but the headline that appeared in the business section of the morning paper four days after he'd sent his nephew into wine country almost did him in.

Dryden Archer to Restore Liberty Vineyards

"Where do you suppose they dredged up that one?" he demanded of Eaton Halliwell. "It's supposed to be hush-hush."

Halliwell shrugged. They were at the breakfast room in Dryden's sunroom, the Golden Gate Bridge wafting in and out of the fog in the distance. "The architect, your bank, that wine expert at the university you consulted. An indiscreet secretary. There are innumerable possibilities."

"You're no help," Dryden muttered in disgust.

"At least the article says you could not be reached for comment."

Dryden glared at him to make certain he wasn't getting a kick out of the delicate situation in which his employer found himself, but Halliwell's face was as composed as ever. The article had included a brief recap of Liberty Vineyards' colorful founder and the subsequent—and disastrous—Archer takeover.

"There's no mention of the curse," Dryden said.

"Quite true."

Halliwell didn't believe Cassandra Belle Liberty or anyone else was haunting her defunct vineyard and sagging house. He hadn't said as much—Eaton Halliwell was wiser than to argue against one of his employer's pet theories—but Dryden knew a skeptic when he saw one.

It didn't matter. Sam and Cassandra would fall in love, and that damned ghost would retire to the heavens where she belonged. With the curse lifted, Dryden could rehabilitate the vineyards and renovate the house. His nephew would be happy. If Sam had any residual irritation with his uncle for having pretended to be dead, all would be forgiven when he realized that but for Dryden's cleverness he would have been doomed to a life of romantic misery, like his father and grandfather before him. Like Dryden himself.

But there'd be no chance for forgiveness, love, or an unhaunted vineyard if Sam didn't stay put long enough for Cassandra Liberty to work her magic, as Dryden was confident she would. Fifty years ago, he might have fallen in love with her himself.

"If my nephew sees this story, I'm doomed." Dryden sipped his espresso, staring at the offending headline. "He'll march down here and have my head on a platter. You've dealt with him, Halliwell. You know what he's like. No profit, no interest."

Halliwell seemed unworried. "I informed him he was not to read any newspapers during his sojourn at Liberty Vineyards. Considering he would have to hike five miles into the village to get one, not to mention violate the terms of your will, I think it's highly unlikely he'll see the article."

"I hope you're right. He's never had a sense of humor when it comes to me and my projects."

"That's because your projects usually involve manipulating him in some way," Halliwell put in mildly.

Dryden had to allow that he was right. He *had* used his nephew on a variety of occasions. "You know damned well he would never have gone up there if he knew I was alive and there wasn't any profit in it for him." He added defensively, as if Halliwell was not yet aware of the fact, "We're not a close family, you know."

"Closer than you think, I believe." Halliwell got to his feet, his own espresso consumed. "Let's hope no reporters decide to go out to the vineyards and take pictures. Sam would be certain to ask questions."

Dryden shuddered. "Maybe I should post you out there just in case."

But Halliwell, as was his custom when Dryden tested his loyalty and common sense beyond their reasonable limits, pretended not to hear him as he removed himself from the breakfast room.

The weather refused to improve. For four days Cassandra was largely confined to the house and wine cellar, with only brief interludes outdoors and with nothing to distract her but Samuel J. Archer.

"I think Cassandra Belle's making her opinion known of an Archer staying under her roof," she said, having invited herself into the library, where Sam was staring out a tall window at the windy, rainy side yard.

His gaze fell on her, his eyes grayed by the fog and rain. "I think it's a protracted low that everyone else in the area has to endure as well."

"How do you know? You haven't been off the grounds."

"Cassandra, your great-great-aunt has no control over the weather. She died seventy-five years ago."

His skepticism only made her more stubborn. "Something's got to be responsible for the rough nights you've been having."

He looked away from her. She could see his fatigue in the shadows and angles of his face, could sense it in his moods. "I'm not used to the noises old houses make at night."

"I don't hear any noises."

He scowled and returned to his high-backed leather chair and his book, yet another account of the Battle of Gettysburg. He seemed to alternate between it and various thrillers—and the occasional nap. Cassandra had a couple of books going, but she had her work in the wine cellar to occupy her. Ordinarily she didn't disturb Sam in the library. She wasn't one to poke sticks at tired, caged lions.

But she was bored. Just plain bored.

He flipped a page, apparently not distracted by her presence.

"Pickett's Charge still a bloody disaster?" she asked, just to make conversation.

"I'm still on the first day." He glanced up at her, mildly curious. "You know about Pickett's Charge?"

She shrugged. "I saw the movie." But he kept his eyes pinned on her, as if he knew she was being flip, and she relented. "Okay, okay. I did the tour of the battlefield one year. It gave me the chills. I'll never forget looking out at those rolling fields and imagining the carnage. Have you ever been?"

"When I was fourteen. My father was living in Washington that year and had me out, and we went together. It's one of the reasons I went into law."

"Not for the money?"

He ignored her halfhearted sarcasm. "I remember lying awake that night, struggling to make sense of it. For the first time I really *felt* the value of the Constitution and the rule of law. It made sense to me on an emotional level, not just an intellectual one. Knowing their value and feeling it are two different things."

Cassandra drew away from the window and its uninspiring view, struck by his words but unwilling to show it. Without waiting to be invited, she flopped onto a chair, its leather so cold she almost jumped back up.

"So now you're a high-profile defense lawyer making heaps of money," she said.

Sam would not be provoked. "I believe in a defendant's right to competent counsel—"

"Which you are."

"Yes, I am."

Cassandra gave him a long look. "I'll bet prosecutors have dartboards made up with your picture on the bull's-eye. Doesn't anything rattle you?"

"You don't want me to answer that, Cassandra."

His voice was husky, his eyes a deep, smoky blue. She shifted in her seat, no longer cold. What he'd been doing and thinking the past four days, she could only guess. "You have to admit you've defended some serious scoundrels."

"I've defended people convicted of major felonies, yes. That's my role in the system. Without it, the system wouldn't work. I believe in the presumption of innocence. I believe in the burden of proof resting with the state. Otherwise we risk sliding backward into tyranny."

The wind and rain whipped and slashed at the windows, adding to the feeling of isolation. Cassandra tucked her feet up under her. Sam had a nice fire going. She wasn't in any hurry to leave. "Is all this noble talk for my benefit, because I accused you of being a typical Archer? Aren't you just a tad cynical about our judicial system?"

"I'm pragmatic and I can be hard-nosed when I need to be, and I don't like manipulating or being manipulated. I don't like the problems I see. But if I become cynical, I'll quit."

"Never mind the fat fees?"

He leaned forward, mockingly conspiratorial. "If I'm a typical Archer, Cassandra, I don't need the money."

"Well, an Archer certainly wouldn't be in law for reasons of nobility and honor. My bet is you like the adrenaline rush of the courtroom and just won't admit it."

He threw back his head and laughed.

"What?" she demanded, not sure if she should be embarrassed or annoyed.

"'The andrenaline rush of the courtroom'? Shows what you know about lawyers and white-collar crime." Before she could think of a comeback, he changed the subject. "But tell me about your day. Find any interesting wines?"

She took the bait. No point goading an Archer into anger, even if it would alleviate her boredom. "Some that would have been interesting fifty years ago but are long past their peak now. I've found a number that have potential, and a few that are real finds. But I don't want to distract you from your reading." She popped up off her chair. "If you get bored, I have a checkers set."

"Checkers?"

He seemed mystified. She smiled. "You know: little black and red disks, 'king me'? Checkers."

"Yes, I know. I didn't think anyone played anymore."

"I do. I also brought a Scrabble board, jacks, and a deck of cards."

His eyes narrowed suddenly, suspiciously. "Sounds as if you were expecting company."

"Just Cassandra Belle," she said, and whirled out of the room.

The drawing room was cold, drafty. The wind seemed louder there. She flopped onto a lumpy sofa and pulled a musty afghan over her. For four days Sam Archer had kept his word and hadn't touched her or tried to touch her—or, so far as she could tell, even thought about touching her. Her physical attraction to him, however, hadn't abated. It was just as strong and relentless and distracting as it had been that first day. But now, to her distress, she was battling an emotional attraction as well.

She *liked* the man.

It was all wrong.

"Cassandra?"

She jumped, startled. He was looming in the doorway, an imposing presence even in Cassandra Belle's huge house.

Cassandra swallowed. "Yes?"

"Still up for a game of checkers?" He ventured into the drawing room, casting eerie shadows. "Of course, you have to keep an eye on us cads, rogues, and rakes—we're tempted to cheat if we start to lose."

She swung up off the couch to fetch her board. "Not to worry. A Liberty is always on her guard against a cheating Archer. And if *I* cheat," she said, grinning at him over her shoulder, "you'll never know it."

Sometime after midnight, a loud, sharp noise jerked Sam from a deep sleep. His eyes wide open, he stared at the shadows dancing on his ceiling. It hadn't been a dream. It hadn't been an old-house creak. It hadn't been the wind.

"Cassandra," he muttered.

And he didn't mean Cassandra Belle. Despite his harrowing nights, Sam told himself, he still didn't believe in ghosts.

With a groan of impatience and frustration, he threw back his sleeping bag and slid out of bed, pulling on a pair of shorts and a sweatshirt. Creeping about the dark, chilly, isolated house in his skivvies held no appeal.

He ventured out into the hall. His heart wasn't pounding. His hands weren't clammy. Whatever the source of the noise, he was totally unworried about either Cassandra Liberty. One had been dead a long time, and the other—the other, he thought, was very much alive.

Feeling his way in the darkness, he crept down the hall toward his housemate's room. He was determined to find out what she was holding back. In their days together, in their rambling conversations about life and politics and food and wine and the proper rules for checkers, Sam had become increasingly convinced that Cassandra Liberty hadn't told all, that there was more to her presence at Liberty Vineyards than just work and wine.

She had facts he didn't have. Information. *Something.* He never liked operating without the full story. When he *knew* someone was withholding information. In any given situation, Sam wanted all the facts—good, bad, or ugly. He'd been blindsided too many times when someone, friend or enemy, decided he didn't need to know something.

Cassandra obviously still didn't trust him. She didn't trust herself when she was with him. He had sensed her qualms about being in close physical proximity to him during their round of checkers. Whenever she started to lower her guard—usually when she was winning—she would catch herself and back off. They would retreat to neutral ground. She would talk about the history of California vineyards, seeming to show more interest in the people who grew and harvested the grapes than in the wine itself. When she hinted at her own hopes and dreams, she would stop herself.

No point confiding in a cad, a rogue, and a rake, Sam said to himself with grim amusement.

He had garnered the basics of her life. Her father was a sommelier in a San Francisco hotel, her mother the manager of a prestigious wine shop. Like Cassandra, neither parent was a wine snob. They didn't believe, she said, a wine was necessarily bad because it was popular or inexpensive. She lectured at various local colleges on the history of wine, she wrote, she occasionally appraised old wine cellars.

She had a collection of wine bottles and labels.

She lived on Telegraph Hill.

Details of her inner life remained a mystery. Sam had

found himself wondering what bastard had put her off men, because it now seemed to him that her view of men as "cads, rogues, and rakes" extended to the gender in general, and not just Archers.

The wind howled and whistled in the giant old oaks outside, blowing so viciously he could feel its sting in the hall. The temperature seemed to drop. There was no moon, no stars to guide him, all shrouded by the persistent clouds.

Up ahead, he saw that the door to Cassandra's room was cracked, a light on.

So she was up. Perhaps he should have crept from bed and investigated his bumps in the night sooner.

He beelined for the light, then rapped on the half-opened door. Cassandra was sitting up in bed, a book on her lap. She glanced up. She had on her white Victorian nightgown, a contrast to the dark, coppery hair tumbling down her shoulders.

"That wasn't you?" he asked.

"What wasn't me?"

"That noise. Don't tell me you didn't hear it."

She looked mystified. "I'm afraid I didn't."

"How long have you been awake?"

"Just a few minutes. I could tell I wasn't going to go back to sleep right away, so I decided to read a while."

"The noise must have awakened you and you just didn't realize it."

"Actually, it was a dream." Color rose to her cheeks, obviously unbidden. She waved a hand, shutting her book. "But never mind."

Suddenly Sam didn't want to never mind. He wanted to hear about her dream. He wanted to know everything about Cassandra Liberty. She looked cozy and rested beneath her layers of blankets. His sleeping bag seemed meager in comparison.

"Sam—are you sure you're hearing noises?" She studied him with an alertness, an incisiveness, that undermined her claim to have been awake only a few minutes. "Maybe you're restless because you just lost your uncle. Your subconscious could be trying to force you to deal with your grief."

"I don't believe Dryden's dead."

The moment he'd said them aloud, Sam knew his words were true. It wasn't a question of denial. If Dryden Archer was dead, he was dead.

But he wasn't.

Dryden Archer was alive.

Cassandra fastened skeptical eyes on him. "But didn't Eaton Halliwell indicate he'd scattered your uncle's ashes himself?"

"Halliwell would lie for my uncle. He wouldn't like it, but given the right circumstances, he'd do it."

"Why would Dryden do such a thing? I know he was an Archer and therefore capable of almost anything so long as there was a profit or a woman in it for him—" She stopped, glaring at Sam. "Well, it's true."

"I don't deny it."

"But faking his own death—that's pretty low."

"Even for an Archer?" Sam grinned, more amused by Cassandra's Archer talk than insulted. The reputation of Archer men was not unearned. "It's not beyond Dryden, I assure you. How long have you known him?

"We met about six weeks ago."

Sam studied her, trying to see beyond the creamy skin and deep, luminous eyes and his own reaction to her, which was becoming increasingly difficult to ignore. He hoped to hell he wasn't falling in love with her. He needed to ignore his confused feelings and concentrate on finding out who Cassandra Liberty was—and not who he wanted her to be.

"How did you meet?" he asked.

"For heaven's sake, it's the middle of the night. Couldn't we discuss this in the morning?" But she sighed before he could answer, her impatience only thinly disguised. "He called me. We had lunch, discussed the possibility of my appraising the wine cellar. I think hiring a descendant of

Cassandra Belle's appealed to him. We met a few times after that to go over details. He didn't come up with the offer of the bottles of Liberty wine and the unusual conditions for getting them until our last meeting."

"That was last week?"

"Yes, apparently not long before he . . . died."

"And you agreed to his conditions," Sam said, the chilly night air taking its toll. "Because you wanted the wine."

"The wine isn't as important to me as what it symbolizes. I've been fascinated by Cassandra Belle and this place since I was a little kid. They're a part of my family mythology." She paused, assessing him a moment. "And yours, too, I suspect."

It had been handy, Sam supposed, to have a ghost on whom to blame one's romantic miseries. Not that he'd indulged in such avoidance of responsibility. But he wasn't going to bring up hauntings now, not with the wind whistling and howling and the rain lashing at the windows. "Dryden gave you no indication of why he wanted you here for two weeks?"

"No."

She'd turned her attention back to her book and flipped a page. Sam squinted at her. He was experienced in cross-examination. Much of his success depended on his ability to determine if a witness, or a client, was lying.

His instincts told him Cassandra Liberty was lying.

"If you don't mind," she said airily, "I need to get back to sleep."

Sam hesitated, debating whether to confront her. Patience, too, was a key component of his success. "I'll see you in the morning, then."

"Sleep well."

She was eager to be rid of him, it seemed to Sam. He lingered in the shadows just outside her door. "You wouldn't be the cause of the bump in the night that just woke me up, would you?"

She looked up sharply. "What's that supposed to mean?"

"It means I hope you aren't pretending to haunt this place in an attempt to drive me out. Because it won't succeed."

"Why would I want to drive you out?"

"I don't know." He gave her a long look. "Something you and Dryden cooked up. He needs me here for two weeks, and I can't figure out why."

Cassandra leaped out of bed, her nightgown twisted around her knees. She tugged it down and bounded over to the door, as angry as if he'd thrown a bucket of cold water in her face. "If you're implying I'm helping your uncle fake his death—if you think *I'm* lying to you—" She sputtered, choking on her own fury. "How dare you!"

Sam grinned. He couldn't help himself. "It's a gift."

Her spine went stiff. "I couldn't stand being as suspicious about everything as you are."

"Oh, but you are." He moved back into the doorway, but she didn't back off, instead thrusting her chin up at him as he came closer. He could feel the rawness of his fatigue, the heavy, aching weight of his desire for her. When Eaton Halliwell had driven him up the pitted, neglected driveway of Liberty Vineyards, two weeks had seemed an eternity. Now it seemed like no time at all. "You don't even trust *yourself.*"

"It's you I don't trust, Samuel J. Archer."

"No it isn't. Maybe at first it was, but not now."

He watched her swallow. Watched her breasts as she fought for air, for composure, against his unrelenting gaze. *Let her suffer,* Sam thought. *Let her want me as much as I want her.* "I'm trying—" She licked her lips, a kind of torture for him. "I'm trying to avoid disaster."

"Cassandra."

"I think you should go back to bed."

"Cassandra, who was the bastard who made you afraid of your own longings?"

The wind and rain continued to lash at the windows, filling the house with the smell of the cold and the damp and the wildness of the night. Sam thought she wouldn't answer.

And he knew he wouldn't force her to give him something she was unprepared to give.

"It was a long time ago," she said suddenly, softly. "Not years and years, but a while. I'm over him. He was—it's so clear to me now how wrong he was for me. He wanted me for a time. And then he didn't. It's as simple as that."

Sam's eyebrows raised in doubt. Nothing was ever as simple as that.

She straightened, pushing back her tangled hair with one hand. "Well, he also lied and cheated and made promises he had no intention of keeping, but that goes with the territory. It was a learning experience. I resolved not to be as precipitous in matters of the heart. I understood I have a sort of fatal attraction to the wrong sort of man."

"We're all individuals, Cassandra. It's dangerous to generalize." The windows behind her groaned and creaked against the onslaught of the weather, as if protesting his words. Sam didn't back off. "And it's unfair."

She leveled her eyes at him, not backing off either. "Maybe. But it's safer."

"Is it?"

This time she didn't answer.

He sighed, knowing he had pushed her far enough for one night. Raising his hand toward her, he brushed the silken line of her jaw with one finger, as if to prove to her—and to himself—that he could touch her without wanting more. But he did. He wanted to scoop her up and carry her back to her bed and make love to her all night, all day.

"Good night, Cassandra."

Before he turned, he saw the flash of disbelief in her eyes. He started down the dark hall. Maybe there'd be no more strange noises. Maybe he'd sleep.

He doubted it.

"Sam." Her voice penetrated the darkness, its calm at odds with the storm raging outside. "It's quieter in my room."

He turned, but didn't move toward her.

In the shadows, he could see her half smile. "The ghost doesn't seem to bother me."

He walked back to her in the doorway and traced her mouth with his fingertips. She didn't draw back. "Cassandra, I want to make love to you. I can't make it any plainer than that."

"You don't have to make it plainer," she said steadily. "It's enough." She caught his wrist in one hand and kissed his fingertips, then drew his arm around to the small of her back as she pressed herself to him. "Just love me tonight, Sam Archer. And let me love you."

Pounded by the fierce wind, the windows shuddered and groaned in their weak frames as he and Cassandra fell into her bed together, shedding clothes, casting them onto the floor. Sam reveled in the feel of her warm, lean body, the smoothness of her skin, the softness of her breasts. He found her mouth in the darkness. She must have switched off the lamp. Or maybe he had, although he didn't remember doing it.

Their kiss was long, languorous, deep. Emotion and physical need, lust and romance melded together, as inseparable as the wind and rain. His hands and mouth roved over her body. He felt her pulse quickening, and his own not far behind.

"Yes," she whispered. "Yes . . ."

She cried out with the gusting wind and slashing rain when their bodies came together, becoming a part of the storm. They raged with it, their lovemaking as wild and unpredictable and fierce as anything the night skies could offer up.

Afterward, when the silence and the stillness had finally come, Sam brushed his lips across Cassandra's copper hair, smelling it as she snuggled against him, exhausted, dreamy. "I told you it was quieter in my room," she murmured.

He said nothing, listening to the silence in amazement. The storm had blown itself out. There wasn't so much as a breeze. Soon the stars might even come out.

Cassandra Belle?

No. He didn't believe in ghosts. Even if from what he knew of Cassandra Belle Liberty, she'd have cooked up a good storm at the thought of an Archer making love to one of her descendants.

But there were no more strange noises that night, and no more wind and rain. Still, Sam didn't sleep.

4

DRYDEN ARCHER *WAS* MANIPULATING HIS NEPHEW, AND CAS-
sandra knew why. Sam was supposed to fall in love with her,
thus lifting Cassandra Belle's curse on Archer men and
prompting her to quit haunting Liberty Vineyards. Unlike
his nephew, Dryden Archer did believe in ghosts.

He wasn't being a romantic. He was an Archer, after all.
Self-interest had to work into his motives somewhere.

Which meant Sam was probably right and his uncle was
alive.

She would have to tell Sam what she knew about Dryden,
the curse, and why the two of them "happened" to be under
the same roof.

Cassandra threw back her covers, deliciously aware of her
body, the warm, bright sun angling into her room. She had
no regrets about last night. None at all. She'd been vaguely
aware of Sam slipping out of bed, but had been unable to stir
herself—in part, she suddenly remembered, because after
the weather had cleared, they'd conjured up another storm
between them.

An Archer. Dear God, she was falling in love with an *Archer*.

She smiled to herself, amused and unafraid.

Yawning, she leaned over her marble-topped dresser to peer at herself in the cracked oval mirror. What did a woman look like after making love to Samuel J. Archer at dawn?

Her heart leaped.

No.

He'd found the letter. Laser-printed on Dryden Archer's letterhead, it lay atop a stack of her folded underwear, stark and accusatory.

She had quite forgotten until this moment that, Dryden Archer being Dryden Archer, he'd mentioned the curse in their written agreement.

"In addition to her payment for her work appraising the Liberty Vineyards wine cellar, Cassandra Liberty will be entitled to five bottles of any Liberty wine she finds, provided she remains on the grounds for two weeks without transportation or modern conveniences, thus providing all Archer men the opportunity for the curse against them to be lifted."

Sam had spotted the letter, read it, and jumped to his own conclusions.

And very likely his conclusions were not complimentary to either her or his uncle.

Groaning, she tore open her door and ran out onto the balcony. "Sam—Sam, we need to talk!"

But he was gone.

She searched downstairs, upstairs, the wine cellar. She checked outside. Not a man who liked to be manipulated, Samuel J. Archer. And not a man, she was coming to believe, who liked to manipulate others.

"How very un-Archer of him," Cassandra muttered, but there was more desperation than humor in her tone.

She had to think. If she were Sam Archer and believed she'd been lied to and manipulated, what would she do?

Leave. I wouldn't even bother packing.

But if he'd stuck to the terms of his uncle's will, he would have come to Liberty Vineyards without cash or credit cards. Even if he were to make the five-mile hike to the village, it wouldn't be easy to rent a car or jump on a bus.

"You're not thinking," Cassandra said aloud, already grabbing her windbreaker and heading out the door. "Sam Archer wouldn't go anywhere without money. He'd cheat first."

She started down the driveway, grateful for the sun and the clean, cool air. Sam had a good head start on her, but she wasn't worried. He wasn't the sort to go unnoticed in a small village. Someone would have seen him, would have noted his movements. It might take a little time, but Cassandra was confident she would catch up with him.

Sam heard the footsteps pounding down the driveway behind him, but he didn't turn around. Let her lose her breath chasing him down. She deserved a stitch in her side. Deserved to twist her ankle in one of the ruts and pits in the old driveway.

The miserable little liar. It made no sense—none at all—that he was in love with her.

In love with her. Such a simple statement for so complicated a feeling. He was warm where before he had been cold, confident where he'd been uncertain, strangely unafraid—in spite of his anger, in spite of not knowing what Cassandra Liberty and Dryden Archer had up their dirty sleeves.

His father, always afraid, always uncertain, must have never felt the kind of solid, unreasoning, unrelenting love Sam felt for his teal-eyed liar, his copper-haired wine historian, his checker-playing beauty. For that, he could only feel pity for the man.

"Hey," she called, "wait up!"

He kept moving. God, he was mad at her.

"Sam—Sam, I was going to tell you this morning at breakfast!"

He didn't break his stride. Once she caught up with him,

she had to walk at a near run to keep up with him. Her hair was a mass of copper tangles and her cheeks were flushed, but she wasn't as out of breath as he'd have wished. He remembered the exercise clothes heaped on her bedroom floor, convincing him he wouldn't be sharing the old house with a ghost. She liked to keep fit.

Well, so did he. He picked up his pace.

"You're going to San Francisco, aren't you?"

He gave her the merest glance. "Where I'm going is none of your concern."

"You're angry," she said, stating the obvious. "You found Dryden's letter. You know, dead or alive, he set you up."

"Oh, he's alive." On that point, Sam was crystal clear. "He's manipulating me to fall in love with you, and you knew it. You didn't tell me because you wanted to get your greedy little hands on the wine." He snarled in disgust, unable to believe he'd permitted himself to get sucked into another of Dryden's schemes. "Only my lunatic uncle would believe in a damned ghost's curse."

"*I* didn't believe in the curse. I barely paid attention when he yammered on about it."

Gravel crunched under his feet as Sam ground to a halt. "You didn't know he was sending me to fall in love with you?"

"I didn't know he was sending *anyone* to fall in love with me. My God, do you think I'm *crazy,* too? I wouldn't have come! I just thought that—at most—he *hoped* someone would come along and sparks would fly. It never in my wildest dreams occurred to me he would manipulate you into spending two weeks with me."

Sam searched her face, but nothing even hinted she was lying. "Why didn't you tell me?"

"I was going to, but when you said he was dead—well, what I thought was off-base. What if your presence was just a coincidence? I wasn't about to mention Dryden believed if I—Cassandra Belle's youngest living descendant—fell in love at Liberty Vineyards, the curse she supposedly placed

367

on all Archer men would be lifted. Frankly," she said, tilting her chin up at him, "I didn't want to give you any ideas."

"Why me?"

"Why did Dryden choose you? I'm not sure myself. I understood a Liberty had to find true love at Liberty Vineyards for the curse to be lifted—not that it specifically had to be with an Archer."

"Then presumably he could have sent the milkman, the postman, the local police chief?"

Sam thought he saw her stiffen. "Presumably."

He shook his head. "No, it couldn't have been just any man. It had to be me—an Archer. Otherwise the risk of failure in sending me was too high." Her breath caught at his words, and he smiled, adding, "Not that I'd fall in love with you, but that I'd come at all." He sighed. "I knew I should have insisted on seeing the body."

"So," Cassandra said, walking briskly at his side, "you have a way for us to get to San Francisco?"

"Before I left, I had my secretary wire money to the local bank and arrange for a rental car. Just in case."

She angled a grin at him. "You cheated."

"I was dealing with my uncle. Of course I cheated."

They came to the end of the driveway and walked out onto the road, a narrow, twisting, unpopulated stretch of California road. Cassandra offered him half a dry bagel. "I snatched it from the kitchen before I left. If you don't want to go to the trouble of renting a car, we can always take mine."

"You have a car?"

"Yes, I have a car. A friend drove it up and parked it in the village, just in case."

Sam caught her hand in his, grinning. "A woman after my own heart."

"It *was* rather Archer of me, wasn't it?"

Dryden Archer knew he was doomed. Doomed! Halliwell had just reported that Sam and Cassandra had collected money from the local bank and were headed south in her car. "I shouldn't have trusted either one of them," Dryden raged. "Liars. Cheats."

"I wouldn't be surprised, Mr. Archer, if they feel much the same about you."

"Me? What'd I do?"

Halliwell judiciously said nothing.

Dryden paced back and forth across the thick Persian carpet in his study. "I've got to get out of town."

"I'm afraid there's not enough time. I received word rather late. They've been gone since this morning."

"A couple of—"

He was cut off by the sound of pounding on the front door, followed by the angry boom of his nephew's voice.

"Open up, Dryden, or I'll beat down the damned door."

Cassandra Liberty, Dryden realized miserably, was his only hope of avoiding strangulation. Sam and she had had, what, five or six days together? *Surely* that had been plenty of time for romance to blossom.

Dryden opened the door himself. "Nephew! My God, it's good to see you. I suppose you're here because you've discovered that rumors of my death have been vastly exaggerated."

Sam scowled at his uncle and cast a nasty look at Eaton Halliwell. "Scattered his ashes yourself, eh, Halliwell?"

"They belonged to him," Halliwell replied mildly. "They were from the fireplace. I would never lie to you, Mr. Archer."

Cassandra Liberty ducked past the two Archer men into Dryden's study. She looked like hell—hair sticking out, shirt crookedly buttoned, no socks. Dryden eyed her with disappointment. She'd seemed so damned pretty last week.

He turned his attention back to his nephew. "Missed me when you thought I was dead, didn't you?"

"You"—Sam jabbed a finger at him—"are a liar and a lunatic."

"I might be a liar, but I'm no lunatic."

"Cassandra Belle. Ghosts. Curses. What nonsense."

"I don't know," Dryden said, watching Sam as he joined

Halliwell and Cassandra in the study. "You look like hell, Sam. I'd say you've been wrestling with a ghost the past few days and just won't admit it."

Sam glared over his shoulder at him. "Don't get me started."

Dryden was sweating. Cassandra, he saw, was at his rolltop desk, picking at his papers. Sam looked over her shoulder.

Halliwell's eyes drifted to his longtime friend and employer. Dryden licked his lips, dry and parched from nerves. There was no hope, and he and Halliwell both knew it.

"What's this?" Sam demanded sharply.

He had the architect's preliminary drawing for the restoration of Liberty Vineyards in hand.

"Now, Sam," Dryden said. "You're a defense lawyer. You have firsthand experience with what people do when they act first and think later."

But his nephew showed no sign of having heard him. He slammed down the drawing and balled his hands into tight fists, swinging around at his uncle. "You sneaky bastard! You set Cassandra and me up so you could restore Liberty Vineyards."

"No, no, Sam. I wanted the curse lifted so you could be happy."

Sam snorted in disbelief.

Cassandra was still at the desk, ignoring the bedlam around her as she grasped a yellowed page. Dryden couldn't imagine what it was.

Then he remembered.

"Oh," he said, swallowing hard.

Sam followed his gaze and turned just as Cassandra, pale as a ghost herself, looked up at them both. "Dryden—this is a letter from Cassandra Belle to herself. It's like a diary. Where did you get it?"

"Diary—hah! The woman didn't have any friends, so she had no choice but to write to herself."

"You mean there are more letters?"

Dryden shrugged evasively, but a warning look from Sam

370

prompted him to come clean. "I found a box of her papers—letters, mostly—when I inherited the vineyards. I never bothered with them until a few weeks ago."

Cassandra swallowed, clutching the old letter. "A *box* of Cassandra Belle Liberty's papers?"

"They're yours," Sam blurted to Cassandra.

Dryden stiffened. "Now wait just a minute—"

But he shut his mouth at another dagger look from his nephew. He could part with the papers. The vineyards, free of Cassandra Belle, were what he wanted.

"She mentions the curse in one of her letters to herself," he said. "That's how I found out the only way it could be lifted was for an Archer and a Liberty to fall in love at the vineyards—something the old bat never figured would happen."

"She actually articulates a curse and the conditions for its removal?" Cassandra asked, more the interested historian than the outraged great-great-niece.

"Not exactly, but it was clear to me."

Sam made a noise resembling a snarl and bounded back toward his uncle. "You're a lunatic, Dryden. There's no ghost and no curse. Cassandra will examine the papers from a professional standpoint. She's doing an article on Cassandra Belle, and now maybe she'll have enough material for a book."

Dryden shook his head. "You don't understand. That witch cursed us. She's been haunting Liberty Vineyards. That's why it's in disrepair. That's why no Archer's ever been able to make a go of it. I figured once the two of you fell for each other—"

"You'd swoop in and restore the vineyards and make yourself a nice profit," Sam said nastily.

"I need a place to retire."

Even Halliwell smiled at that one. Given his personal net worth, Dryden supposed it had been a bit of a stretch. But he wished he could convince his damned nephew that he'd meant well.

"All right," Dryden said. "The truth is, I intended to give

you and Cassandra the vineyards as a wedding gift. Now you've spoiled the surprise."

"My God, man, I don't believe you!" Sam threw up his hands in a mixture of rage and disgust. "You'd do anything to get yourself out of hot water."

"What," Dryden said, all innocence. "Aren't you and Cassandra getting married?"

Then he noticed that Cassandra Liberty was no longer in the room. He looked to Halliwell, who gave a slight shake of his head, which Dryden understood to mean he had no idea where she was—or wasn't saying if he did.

Sam had turned slightly pale.

And Dryden saw. His heart twisted, and he put out a hand toward his nephew. "Hell, Sam, I hope I haven't ruined everything for you."

"If anyone has," Sam said, squeezing his uncle's hand, "it's me."

Cassandra didn't breathe until she was on Dryden Archer's deck looking out at the Golden Gate Bridge. Blueprints; a box of Cassandra Belle's most private thoughts; arguing, contentious Archer men—it was awful. She'd had to get out.

"He's a meddling old man," Sam said softly behind her, joining her on the deck. "I apologize for his behavior. It was presumptuous of him to set us up, and even more presumptuous to assume his scheming had worked to his benefit and we were in love."

She managed a weak smile. "A heck of a blind date, huh?"

He skimmed her cheek with one knuckle. "Yeah. Cassandra—look, I don't know about ghosts and curses or what that old man in there had in mind when he got me to Liberty Vineyards. I only know that as presumptuous as Dryden was, he was also right. I love you."

She shut her eyes, wanting to believe him.

"There's no reason for you to believe me," he went on quietly. "I understand that. We were both manipulated, but Dryden's my uncle—we're both Archers, cut from the same cloth. Dryden's never settled down with one woman; my father never did. We're rogues and scoundrels and adventurers, just as you said. But—"

"But the curse is lifted," she said, turning to him, wanting nothing more than to feel his arms around her. She smoothed the back of her hand across his cheek, feeling the roughness of his night's growth of beard. No white-collar criminal would hire him today. He looked like a pirate. "Cassandra Belle's letter—I didn't want to tell you in there, but she clearly states she'll only stop hating Archers when a Liberty falls for one. I'm not sure it classifies as a true curse, but Dryden might think so. That's why it couldn't be the postman or the milkman. It could only be you."

He caught her hand in his, kissed her fingers.

"I was wrong about you, Sam, and about myself. I didn't trust myself to fall for the right man. I didn't trust you to *be* the right man."

His eyes, that clear, penetrating, mesmerizing blue, held hers. "I won't leave you, Cassandra. Not ever."

"I know." She smiled suddenly. "Now. Are you going to tell your uncle or shall I?"

"He's going to be as obnoxious as hell. He loves being right." Sam grimaced. "I suppose we should both tell him. You know, I intend to keep him to his word and get Liberty Vineyards for a wedding present. I'm up for a few changes in my life."

"I didn't mean about us. I think he already knows. I meant about him."

Sam looked mystified. "Him?"

Cassandra laughed, imagining the years ahead with this man. "Yes, him. Shall I tell your uncle or will you that you missed him when you thought he was dead?"

CARLA NEGGERS, an author known to and loved by many of you, is the newest star to be added to Pocket Books' romance list. She finished writing her first book and mailed it to an agent four months after her first child was born—when she was twenty-four years old and so broke she had to rent a typewriter. The agent took her on, the book sold, and since then she's become known for her wit, humor and fast-paced romantic stories, which appear regularly on romance bestseller lists and have been translated into more than two dozen languages.

Publishers Weekly has called her work "engaging" and "highly entertaining," and *Affaire de Coeur* has said: "One is never disappointed reading anything by Carla Neggers." She has received the *Romantic Times* Reviewers Choice award four times. Look for her first title from Pocket Books, *Finding You,* next year.

The daughter of a Dutch immigrant and a Southerner, Carla grew up in New England and lives in Vermont with her husband and their two children. She enjoys hearing from readers and you can write to her c/o Pocket Books, 1230 Avenue of the Americas, New York, NY 10020.

POCKET BOOKS
PROUDLY PRESENTS

SON OF THE MORNING

Linda Howard

Coming Soon
from
Pocket Books

The following is a preview of
Son of the Morning. . . .

THE STONE WALL OF THE DUNGEON WAS COLD AND damp against her back as Grace eased down the narrow, uneven steps. There was no railing, and she had to feel her way in the dark, for a candle would have alerted the guard to her presence.

The weight of the heavy iron candlestick pulled at her arm. Below she could see the single guard, sitting on a crude bench with his back resting against the wall, a rough skin of wine at his elbow. Good—if she was lucky, he had drunk himself into a stupor. Even if he had a hard Scottish head for spirits, at least the liquor would have slowed his reflexes. She hoped he was asleep, because given where he was sitting, she would have to approach him practically head-on. The light was poor and she could hide the candlestick against her leg, but if he stood up it would be much more difficult to hit him hard enough to knock him out. She was so sore and battered from the trip through time that she didn't trust her strength; better if she could simply lift the candlestick and swing downward, letting gravity aid her.

Ahead was the flicker of torchlight, but it didn't penetrate up the inky, curving stairs. Grace cautiously moved her foot forward, searching for the edge of each step while trying not to scrape her shoe against the stone. The air was cold, and fetid; the smell assaulted her nose, making it crinkle in disgust. The odor of human waste was unmistakable, but beneath that lay the sharper, more unpleasant odors of blood, and fear, and the sweat of pain. Men had been tortured, and died, in these foul depths that never saw the sun.

It was up to her to make certain Black Niall didn't join their ranks.

Huwe of Hay would sleep until morning, under the influence of whiskey and Seconal. Given how much he had drunk, she only hoped she hadn't overdosed him; as crude and disgusting as he was, she didn't want to kill him. The risks she'd run, back in Real Time, in getting the variety of drugs she carried had certainly been justified. Without the Seconal, she could never have escaped from Huwe at all, much less avoided being raped.

Her searching foot found no more steps. The floor was hard-packed dirt, uneven and treacherous. She stood still for a moment, taking deep, silent breaths as she tried to steady her nerves. The guard still sat slumped on the bench, his head nodded forward onto his chest. Was he truly asleep, drunk, or merely playing possum? As careful as she'd been, had he still heard some betraying rustle, and was he now trying to lure her closer?

It didn't matter; she had no choice. She couldn't leave Black Niall here, to be tortured and killed. He was the Guardian, the only person alive who knew both the secrets and the location of the hidden treasures of the Templars. She needed him, for only with his knowledge, his cooperation, could she keep Parrish from getting his hands on that treasure in Real Time. She wanted Parrish stopped, and she wanted Parrish dead; for that, she needed Black Niall.

If the guard was awake and merely being crafty, she would arouse less suspicion by approaching him directly, as if she had nothing to hide. Moreover, if he saw her, he wouldn't expect any threat from a woman. Her heart thumped wildly, and for a moment black spots swam before her eyes. Panic made her stomach lurch, and she thought she might throw up. Desperately she sucked in deep breaths, fighting back both nausea and weakness. She refused to let herself falter now, after all she'd been through.

Cold sweat broke out on her body, trickled down her spine. Grace forced her feet to move, to take easy, measured strides that carried her across the rough floor as if she had nothing at all to hide. The torchlight danced and swayed under the spell of some unheard music, casting huge, wavering shadows on the damp stone walls. The guard still didn't move.

Ten feet. Five. Then she stood directly in front of the guard, so close that she could smell the stench of his unwashed body, sharp and sour. Grace swallowed, and steeled herself for the blow she had to deliver. Sending up a quick prayer that she wouldn't cause him any lasting damage, she used both aching arms to raise the candlestick high.

Her clothing rustled with her movements. He stirred, opening bleary eyes and peering up at her. His mouth gaped open, revealing rotted teeth. Grace swung downward, and the massive iron candlestick crashed against the side of his head with a solid thunk that made her cringe. Anything he might have said, any alarm he might have yelled, dissolved into a grunt as he slid sideways, his eyes closing once more.

Blood trickled down the side of his head, matting in his filthy hair. Tears stung her eyes, but she turned sharply away, need shouldering aside regret.

There were two cells, and only one of them was barred. "Niall!" she whispered urgently as she grasped the massive bar. How was she best to communicate with him? Despite her study and preparation, she understood barely one word in thirty of the burred, rolling Gaelic the Highlanders spoke; reading it was one thing, pronouncing it something else. She felt more certain of herself in

Old English or Old French, both of which Niall also spoke, but Latin hadn't changed at all since his time, so that was the language she chose.

"I have come to free you," she said softly as she struggled with the bar. My God, it was heavy! It was like wrestling with a tree trunk, six feet long and a good ten inches thick. Her hands slipped on the wood, and a splinter dug deep into her little finger. Grace bit off a cry of pain as she jerked her hand back.

"Are you hurt?"

The question was in a deep, calm tone, and came very clear to her ears as if he was standing against the other side of the door. Hearing it, Grace froze, her eyes closing as she struggled once more with tears and an electrifying surge of emotion that threatened to overwhelm her. It was really Black Niall, and oh, *God,* he sounded just as he had in her dreams. The voice was like thunder and velvet, capable of a roar that would freeze his enemies, or a warm purr that would melt a woman into his arms.

"Only . . . only a little," she managed, struggling to remember the correct words. "A splinter . . . The bar is very heavy, and it slipped."

"Are you alone? The bar is too big for a mere woman."

Mere? *Mere?* "I can do it!" she said fiercely. What did he know? She had survived on the run for months, she had managed to get here, against all odds, and moreover, she was the one on the *free* side of the door. Anger mixed with exhilaration, surging through her veins, making her feel as if she would burst through her skin. Abandoning any attempt to lift the bar with her hands, she bent her knees and lodged her shoulder under it, driving upward with all the strength in her back and legs.

The weight of the bar bit into her shoulder. Gritting her teeth, Grace braced her legs and strained. She could feel the blood rush to her face, feel her heart and lungs labor. Her knees wobbled. Damn it, she *wouldn't* let this stupid piece of wood defeat her! A growl of refusal burst past her lips and she summoned every ounce of strength in her aching body, gathering it for one final effort. Her thigh muscles screamed, her back burned. Desperately she shoved upward, forcing her legs to straighten, and one end of the bar rose. It teetered for a moment, then began sliding down through the other bracket. The rough wood scraped her cheek, snagged her clothes. Using both hands, ignoring the need for quiet, she shoved the bar forward until it was free of one bracket.

Instead of continuing its slide through the other bracket, the bar slowed, then began tipping back toward her. Grace scrambled out of the way as one end hit the floor with a reverberating thud. The bar stood braced there, one end on the floor and the other balanced against the second bracket.

She stood back, breathing hard, trembling in

every muscle, but the triumph that roared through her was fierce and sweet. Heat radiated from her, banishing the cold as if she stood close to a fire, and she couldn't even feel the pain of her injured hand. She felt invigorated, invincible, and her breasts rose tight and aroused beneath her clothing.

"Open the door," she invited, the words coming out breathlessly despite her efforts to steady her voice, and she couldn't resist a taunt: "If you can."

A low laugh came to her ears, and slowly the massive door began to open, pushing the huge bar before it. Grace took another step back, peering hungrily into the black space yawning open between the door and the frame, waiting for her first glimpse of Black Niall in the flesh.

He came through the door as casually as if he were on vacation, but there was nothing casual in the black gaze that swept over the unconscious guard and then leapt to her, raking her from head to foot in a single suspicious, encompassing look. His vitality seared her like a blast, and almost palpable force, and she felt the blood drain from her face.

He could have stepped straight from her dreams.

He was there, just as he had been in the images that had plagued her for endless nights, as she had been when his essence had pulled her across seven centuries. Slowly, like a lover's hand drifting over the face of a beloved, barely touching as if too strong a contact would destroy the spell, her gaze traced his features. The broad, clear forehead; the eyes, as black as night, as old as sin; the thin, high-bridged Celtic nose; the chiseled cheekbones; the firm and unsmiling lips, the uncompromising chin and jaw. He was big. Mercy, she hadn't realized how big he was, but he was over a foot taller than she, at least six-four. His long black hair swung past his shoulders, shoulders that were two feet wide, and the hair at his temples was secured in a thin braid on each side of his face.

His shirt and kilt were dark with dried blood. He didn't have his plaid, but he didn't seem to feel the cold. He was wilder than she could have imagined, and yet he was exactly as she had dreamed. The reality of him was like a blow, and she swayed.

He looked around, his face hard and set, every muscle poised for action. "You are alone?" he asked again, evidently doubting that she had managed the bar by herself.

"Yes," she whispered.

No enemies rushed from the inky shadows, no alarm was raised. Slowly he returned his gaze to her, and even in the poor, unsteady light from the torch she knew he could see how violently she was trembling.

"Frail but valiant," he murmured, coming closer. Despite herself, she would have shrunk back, but he moved with the deceptive speed of an attacking tiger. One hard arm passed around her waist, both supporting and capturing her, drawing her against him. "Who are you? No relation of Huwe's, I'll wager, with such a pretty face—and a command of Latin."

"N-no," she stammered. The contact with him was going to her head, making her feel giddy. She lifted her right hand to brace against his chest; it was her injured hand, and she flinched.

Instantly he caught her hand, turning it toward the light. The long, jagged splinter had entered her finger lengthwise, and the end protruded just above the bend of the first knuckle. He made a softly sympathetic sound, almost a croon, and lifted her hand to his mouth. With delicate precision he caught the end of the splinter in his animal-white teeth, and steadily drew it out. Grace flinched again at the pain, rising on tiptoe against him, but he held her hand steady in his powerful grip. He spat the splinter out, then sucked hard at the sullenly bleeding wound. She could feel his tongue flicking against her skin, laving her hurt, and a moan that had nothing to do with pain slipped from her lips.

He lifted his mouth from her hand then, and the look he gave her was sharp and hot, startlingly aware. "I've no time for more, but I'll have the taste of ye," he murmured, this time in Scots English, and somehow she understood him.

He lifted her, turning to pin her against the wall. His big, iron-muscled body ground against her, from shoulder to knee, and her breath caught at the fullness of his arousal. Instantly he took advantage of her parted lips and set his mouth to hers. Her blood surged at the ravaging kiss; his taste was hot, tart, and uncivilized. He used his tongue with soul-searing skill, demanding her response, then deepening his advantage when she helplessly gave it. His hands moved over her body, cupping her breasts, her bottom, moving her against him.

He was panting when he lifted his head, his lips swollen and shiny, his eyes narrow with lust. "A pity I must go," he whispered, letting her slide to her feet. "Perhaps we'll meet again."

Shaking, Grace leaned against the wall, her mind a blank. He crossed swiftly to the unconscious guard and relieved him of his sword and dagger. He moved so fast that he had already reached the stairs before realization sank into Grace's mind. She struggled upright, her eyes wide. "No, wait!" she cried. "Take me with you!"

He didn't even pause, his powerful legs taking the stairs two at a time. "Another time, lass," he said, and disappeared upward into the darkness.

Oh, damn! She didn't dare call out again. She launched herself after him, but her legs were still shaking from the effort of lifting the bar, and from the effects of that kiss. She barely had the strength to climb the stairs, and there was no sign of him when she emerged from the dungeon.

She didn't dare sound an alarm, for after all, she didn't want him recaptured. But she didn't dare remain, either. Somehow she had to escape from this grimy hold and find Black Niall again. He wasn't a hero, damn him, no knight in shining armor. He was an arrogant brute, and he was her only hope.